THE GRANDM  *RS*
A Family P

D0978513

Glenway Wescott as a young man

THE
GRANDMOTHERS

A Family Portrait

GLENWAY WESCOTT

Introduction by Sargent Bush, Jr.

THE UNIVERSITY OF WISCONSIN PRESS

A North Coast Book

The University of Wisconsin Press
114 North Murray Street
Madison, Wisconsin 53715

3 Henrietta Street
London WC2E 8LU, England

2   4   5   3   1

Printed in the United States of America

The Grandmothers: A Family Portrait was first published
in 1927 by Harper & Brothers

The photograph of Glenway Wescott courtesy of the
State Historical Society of Wisconsin, WHi(X3)28206

Library of Congress Cataloging-in-Publication Data
Wescott, Glenway, 1901–
The grandmothers: a family portrait / Glenway Wescott.
412 pp.   cm.
Includes bibliographical references.
ISBN 0-299-15020-8 (cloth: alk. paper).
ISBN 0-299-15024-0 (pbk.: alk. paper)
1. Wisconsin—History—Civil War, 1861–1865—Fiction.
2. Americans—Travel—Europe—Fiction.
3. Young men— Wisconsin—Fiction.
4. Family—Wisconsin—Fiction. I. Title.
PS3545.E827G7   1996
813'.52—dc20   96-1902

To
My Mother

CONTENTS

INTRODUCTION

Sargent Bush, Jr.

The publication of Glenway Wescott's second novel in 1927 established him as one of the major American authors of his day. The reviews in the leading periodicals admired the achievement of this young Wisconsin writer who, even while living among the expatriates abroad, could write so discerningly, so eloquently, about the past in the upper Midwest. *The Grandmothers: A Family Portrait,* said the *New York Times* reviewer, "has a solidity and an integrity which assure it of more than transient consideration." Burton Rascoe, reviewing *The Grandmothers* along with the latest books by Conrad Aiken, H. G. Wells, and Ernest Hemingway, concluded that there was no contest: "Mr. Wescott's . . . completely overshadows the other books" (Rascoe, p. 87). "It is a novel," he declared, "that gives a new significance to American life." Others agreed. The book won the 1927 Harper Novel Prize Contest and the publisher's promotional ads puffed it as "Acclaimed from Coast to Coast." Four years later, a profile in *The Bookman* concluded that "the high distinction of his talent assures [Wescott's] place in the front rank of younger American writers" (Kohler, p. 142).

Those younger writers included the cluster of men and women who had emigrated to Europe in the twenties, where, in their collective disillusionment with modern life, they were identified by Gertrude Stein as "a lost generation." Hemingway, F. Scott Fitzgerald, and the somewhat older Stein were only the most famous of a large group of displaced American writers and artists who were "being geniuses together," in Robert McAlmon's phrase. Wescott had gone to Paris in 1925 after the successful reception of his first novel, *The Apple of the Eye* (1924), and had immediately been noticed, if not always favorably. Hemingway disliked him immediately and lampooned him in *The Sun also Rises* (1926) through a brief portrayal of Robert Prentiss (originally named Prescott until Hemingway's editor, Maxwell Perkins, convinced him to make Wescott's identity less obvious). Wescott's friends, however, included Ford Madox Ford, Somerset Maugham, Kay Boyle, Thornton Wilder, Isadora Duncan, Jean Cocteau, and Paul Robeson, to name only a few. Not long after his arrival in Paris, he and his intimate friend, Monroe Wheeler, moved to a little village named Villefranche-sur-Mer, just south of Nice on the Mediterranean coast, where Wescott wrote most of *The Grandmothers,* finishing it in November of 1926.

At a time when his peers were in the grip of the disillusionment of "Modernism," questioning the values of a world in disarray after a devastating war, Wescott was turning to the past, and to his own Wisconsin roots, to search for values. He imagined his way into the time of his pioneering forbears, tracing the lives of that generation and their descendants down into the era of his own childhood. He distanced the experience through his fictional center of consciousness, Alwyn Tower, who, like Wescott, writes as an expatriate in Europe. While the story has the potential for epic, the characters do not. The novel is, in fact, a series of accounts of disappointment, or, as one reviewer put it, "altogether a magnificent record of failure, a stately elegy on lives too fine for success" (Troy, p. 105).

In thus refusing to inflate the heroism of the ancestors, Wescott gave the book a special strength. Clifton Fadiman saw this: "Mr. Wescott's very beautiful and moving chronicle is possibly the first artistically satisfying rendition of the soul of an American pioneer community and its descendants" (Fadiman, p. 396). As one returns to *The Grandmothers* today, it is gratifying to find that, although more or less forgotten, it retains its evocative power even now. This strength is partly due to the author's mastery of a glistening and graceful prose style, a style described by various early readers as "lyrical." This quality sets him apart from his contemporary, Hemingway, whose trade mark was a very different, hard-edged, spare prose style, born of his early journalistic work, which proved well suited to the mood and message of Modernist thinking. Wescott's writing, by contrast, suggests more immediate comparison with the fine imagistic style of Fitzgerald's *Gatsby*. Wescott, after all, had begun his writing career as a poet. His two early volumes of poetry, *The Bitterns* (1920) and *Natives of Rock* (1925), were strongly influenced by the Imagists, especially H.D. and Ezra Pound, whose style Wescott had cultivated as a college student. After high school, he had enrolled at the University of Chicago, and soon became president of the campus Poetry Club, whose impressive membership at that time included such writers of future prominence as Elizabeth Madox Roberts, Yvor Winters, Janet Lewis, Sterling North, Vincent Sheean, and George Dillon. The Club invited various prominent writers to speak to them—figures such as Carl Sandburg, Robert Frost, Padraic Collum, Vachel Lindsay, Robert Herrick, and Alfred Kreymborg (Kahn, pp. 15-16). Though he ultimately settled on prose as his medium, his early immersion in this poetic milieu surely had a lasting influence on his distinctively nuanced style. Five years after the book's publication, Ruth Suckow, putting *The Grandmothers* in the same league with *Huckleberry Finn, My Ántonia, Main Street, Winesberg, Ohio,* and Carl Sandberg's *Chicago Poems,* identified the source of its unique force as "the poem, lyrical rather than epic" (Suckow, p. 177).

Yet, while his early literary friends had their influence on his work, a still more important factor for him was his Wisconsin background. Wescott was born in Kewaskum in Washington County, a small town some forty miles northwest of Milwaukee, about where Hope's Corner is located in *The Grandmothers.* His earliest years were spent on the family farm near Kewaskum, but when it became clear in his early teens that he would disappoint his father's hopes that he would help and succeed him there, Glenway was sent to live with a family friend one year and his maternal grandparents the next. He attended West Bend High School, and then moved on to live with his "Parson Uncle" in Waukesha, where he finished high school (Kahn, pp. 1-3). Thereafter, his moves took him progressively away from his roots, though he continued to revisit his family while they remained in Wisconsin. Charles K. Trueblood perceptively noted that Wescott bore out Henry James's admonition that "the art of fiction is an art of preparation; and perhaps not least among the excellences of Mr. Wescott's beautiful novel of early Wisconsin are the skill and scruple of his preparation" (p. 441). His retention of his youthful experience was an important part of that preparation.

In the company of his fellow American expatriates in Europe, Wescott achieved the distance he needed to write powerfully and evocatively of the Wisconsin he had left behind. Although his collection of short stories, *Good-bye, Wisconsin* (1928), most bluntly presents his critical distance from his regional past, it is *The Grandmothers* that most fully and masterfully expresses both the failures and the lasting values of Wisconsin's pioneer generation and their descendants.

For this reason, it is unfortunate that while some of Wescott's peers have continued to command an audience, *The Grandmothers* has been, if never quite lost to our awareness, at least repeatedly misplaced. It sold very well at first; Wescott himself said, by way of distinguishing it from most of his other books, "My semi-fictitious book, *The Grandmothers*, was a remunerative publication" (*Continual Lessons*, p. 79). It was republished three times during the writer's lifetime: by Harper's in 1950; by Atheneum in 1962; and by Arbor House, on the occasion of his eighty-fifth birthday in 1986. Now, some seventy years after its first publication, it remains a readable, sensitive, intricate account of earlier times and also an effective dramatization of the reconstructive power of the artist's imagination. In it, Wescott reconstitutes three generations of the history of the fictitious Tower family, following them from their migration from New York state to Wisconsin in the 1840s through the generation that fought the Civil War and into the lifetime of the central consciousness, Alwyn Tower. The similarities to Wescott's own family's history are clear, but this is not an autobiography. The book's genius is partly owing to Wescott's innovative use of the concept of a family's album of faded photographs and daguerreotypes as a model for his own verbal portraits, in successive chapters, of members of the family. In viewing such photos, Alwyn struggles to imagine the lives of those pictured, to recapture the essential features of the difficult, often disappointed lives of those whose stories, overheard and remembered, have made possible his own.

Wescott was probably not very concerned with—or perhaps even aware of—the fact that midwestern literature was finding a new literary respect in the twenties. Nevertheless, his novel participated in that movement. John T. Frederick had established *The Midland* magazine at the University of Iowa in 1915 and had published Ruth Suckow's first story in 1921. Willa Cather had come into her own with *O Pioneers!* in 1916 and *My Ántonia* in 1918. Sinclair Lewis was at the peak of his career in the twenties, while Fitzgerald wrote of the contrast between eastern and midwestern values. It was in 1927, the year of *The Grandmothers*, that

Wescott's publisher, Harper's, brought out in English translation O. E. Rölvaag's saga of hardship and deprivation on the Dakota plains, *Giants in the Earth.* Though the differences among the authors are important, perhaps it is not too much to suggest that in *The Grandmothers* Wescott achieved for Wisconsin what Rölvaag's *Giants in the Earth* did for the Dakotas, or what Cather's novels first did for Nebraska. For while writing the experience of three generations of the Tower family in a particular place, he transcends region to write of the experience of America itself. America, like Wisconsin, is a land of immigrants and migrants, a land of promise. In Wescott's view, that promise is unfulfilled.

Time and memory are primary themes for Wescott. Alwyn is like his admired Grandmother Tower in having "an extravagant love of the past" (p. 9). The stories of his grandparents and their children involve working through and interweaving complex temporal relationships. Returning to the Wisconsin setting in Wescott's 1930 short story, *The Babe's Bed*, the central character, again an expatriate writer, thinks, "Time is an unreliable thing . . .; it does not steadily pass but weaves back and forth" (p. 43). Memory helps to control that flux and to enable the rememberer to make sense of it while negotiating the way into an unseen but predictably different future. Dayton Kohler observed in 1931 that Wescott's "method is reminiscent of Proust" (Kohler, p. 144). This is a thoroughly appropriate connection, given the fascination with the power of memory in the book, but even more so when we know that while he was writing *The Grandmothers* Wescott was reading Marcel Proust's *In Remembrance of Things Past* (Kahn, p. 276), which he later described as "the supreme masterpiece of modern fiction" (*Images of Truth*, pp. 281–82).

The Grandmothers has no traditional heroes, for "a grievance was their birthright." The novel is full of believable, struggling individuals whose collective experience is wonderfully recognizable, yet it tells of the failure to fulfill potential. The primary grandmother, Rose Tower, tempers despair with stoicism to point her grandson to meanings that less perceptive individuals are incapable of seeing or understanding. He becomes a sure receptacle and mouthpiece for those memories. It is a book whose characters, symbolism, and style combine to reward its reader even now.

This book's title suggests the central importance of the matriarchal presences of Alwyn's two grandmothers. Alwyn's Grandmother Tower and his mother, Marianne, are set in sharp relief against the several women, including Grandmother Duff, whose darker lives of struggle end in defeat or at least compromised happiness. His great-aunt, Mary Harris, "the greatest of the pioneer women" (p. 71), according to Grandmother Tower, survived bad marriages to two men, having proposed to the second herself simply as a way to get transportation from the South back home to Wisconsin. Another great-aunt, Nancy Tower, is unable to endure a union with Jesse Davis, a crude if well-meaning man whom she deserts twice only to watch him return and to live in the shadow of her rejection until he, in his turn, flees. His Aunt Flora is much less stalwart than these women and fails to survive past age twenty-nine. But it is his father's mother, Rose Tower, and his own mother, Marianne, who provide the clearest positive examples of strength in the midst of loss and disappointment.

The men of the family seem, on the whole, less resourceful, less resilient than the women. Great Uncle Leander is a sensitive man whose younger brother Hilary has both a homosexual and an incestuous love for him. Their mutual recognition and fear of that love leads to Hilary's unexplained death during a night patrol in the Civil War. Leander cannot subsequently recover his pre-war life and disappoints his former sweetheart by rejecting her after the war. Consequently Rose marries the widower Henry Tower without any sense of deep feeling for him. Romance is disappointed; hard resolve triumphs. These memories of family history, all centered in the family seat at Hope's Corner, include pioneers, Civil War soldiers, women who find their own ways in a world dominated by male futility, military deserters and outcasts, all of whom know more defeat than victory, but who come to represent American experience itself. In the case of Alwyn's Uncle James, musical talent is squelched as he follows his father's wishes to become a minister, only to fall victim to a wife whose wealth proves emasculating. Neither romantic love nor artistic creativity fares well in the harsh natural and human conditions in which the Tower family story is played out. But the power of the narrative as an American story resides in this harshness. The fragments of family history, beautifully evoked through the memory of a youthful artist, make "a compelling narrative of American life" (Kohler, p. 144).

The reviewer for *The New Republic* oversimplified the work by calling it autobiography, but, in doing so, he praised it by suggesting it is "a not unworthy complement to *The Education of Henry Adams,*" a classic American autobiography (Troy, p. 105). The comparison offered more heady praise for a young writer still in his twenties. The expectation of future greatness proved in the long run to be a burden leading to frustration and disappointment to both the literary critical establishment and to Wescott himself. When he finally returned to America in 1933, he and Wheeler took up residence briefly in New York City and then later at Stone-blossom, a farmhouse in northern New Jersey given to him by his brother and sister-in-law, who provided much of his support throughout his career. Twenty years later, in 1957, the Wescotts moved to Haymeadows Farm, Glenway's home for the rest of his life. The world waited through the thirties for Wescott to produce another novel, but it was not forthcoming, despite his efforts. Only in 1940, with a superb novella, *The Pilgrim Hawk,* was he able to recover his literary productivity for a period that lasted through the publication of his fourth and, as it proved to be, final novel, *An Apartment in Athens,* in 1945. Despite the fact that this last novel was a best-seller, it did not compensate the author for his lack of a larger achievement. In 1947, ruminating on his recurrent long dry spells,

Wescott recalled Wheeler's remark to him some twenty-five years earlier that people would not make an issue of Wescott's homosexuality, "if you become a great writer." The older Wescott confessed to his journal that "The really grave fact of my life is that I have not been able to fulfill those expectations of me" (*Continual Lessons*, p. 178). Greatness, he well knew, had eluded him.

The Grandmothers engendered those expectations, but it also embodied achievement. In it, Wescott succeeded in exploring the experience of Wisconsin's earliest white settlers with imagination and a sense of personal identification. In doing so, he offered an eloquent statement on the enduring dreams of the people of "Hope's Corner," his microcosm of American experience. The final tone, however, is not one of despair, but of triumph in the survival of the power of art to shape the dense experience of a Wisconsin past. If Leander and James and Nancy and Mary and Evan and their relations are part of the story, the story itself is seen and understood by Alwyn, the author's alter ego. Through the combined powers of memory and art, Alwyn frames "a family portrait." Hope survives in art as well as in life, as Wescott eloquently demonstrates.

Works Cited

Fadiman, Clifton P. "Strangely American," *The Nation* 125 (1927), 396.

Kahn, Sy Myron. "Glenway Wescott: A Critical and Biographical Study," unpublished Ph.D. dissertation, University of Wisconsin, 1957.

Kohler, Dayton. "Glenway Wescott: Legend-Maker," *The Bookman* 73 (1931), 142–45.

Rascoe, Burton. "Four New Works of Fiction," *The Bookman* 66 (1927), 87–90.

Suckow, Ruth. "Middle Western Literature," *The English Journal* 21 (1932), 175–82.

Troy, William. "A Family Affair," *New Republic* 52 (1927), 105.

Trueblood, Charles K. "An Idyll of Pioneers," *The Dial* 83 (1927), 441–43.

Wescott, Glenway. *The Babe's Bed* (Paris: Harrison of Paris, 1930).

Wescott, Glenway. *Continual Lessons: The Journals of Glenway Wescott, 1937–1955,* ed. Robert Phelps with Jerry Rosco (New York: Farrar Straus Giroux, 1990).

Wescott, Glenway. *Images of Truth: Remembrances and Criticism* (New York: Harper & Row, 1962).

Henry Tower had four brothers and one sister: Harrison, John, Leander, Hilary, and Nancy.

Harrison Tower married Mary Harris, who had previously been married to a certain Dr. Brandon and to a man named Cleaver.

Leander Tower was a bachelor; and Hilary disappeared during the Civil War at the age of sixteen.

Nancy Tower married Jesse Davis, to whom she bore one son, Timothy, adopted after their death by her brother Leander.

Henry Tower married Serena Cannon; their only son, Oliver, died in infancy. After her death he married his brother Leander's former sweetheart, Rose Hamilton. They had six children: Polly and Ada, who did not live to maturity, James, Ralph, Evan, and Flora.

James married Caroline Fielding and had no children.

Evan, who changed his name to John Craig, married Susanne Orfeo, a woman of French and Italian parentage, by whom he had one son, Leander Orfeo Craig.

Flora was unmarried, and died at the age of twenty-nine.

Ralph married Marianne, the only daughter of Ira and Ursula Duff. Their eldest son was named Alwyn.

THE GRANDMOTHERS

1. INTRODUCTION: ALWYN TOWER AS A SMALL BOY. THE HOUSE. HIS GRANDMOTHER TOWER'S KEEPSAKES

UNTIL Alwyn Tower grew to manhood he never forgot that everyone was older than he. People remembered things not in existence now, and many of them had been born in houses which had vanished long ago.

A cabin which had stood in the melon patch had been his father's birthplace; and as a child, jumping over the heavy, downy vines, he tried in vain to find a trace of its foundations.

His uncle Jim, the minister, on the other hand, had not been born in the garden, but in a building which was now the woodshed. Alwyn asked himself how anyone could have slept in that poor shack, whose floor was the ground, trodden and scattered with chips, where the snow sifted in winter on the woodpiles. Of course when his grandmother had lain there with a baby in her arms, it must have been warm, safe, and pink, in the firelight. Now she was a strong old woman with sandy-gray hair; and only with difficulty, by calling to mind the family daguerreotypes, was he able to imagine a young mother in that vanished bed.

Alwyn's father and mother shared with his grandparents the third house on the farm which his grandfather had bought from the government when Wisconsin was a wilderness. In that house his young aunt Flora had been born, in what was now his mother's parlor, exactly below the spare bedroom papered with forget-me-nots where Alwyn himself had slept when he was a baby. The house had been rearranged frequently, and augmented by new rooms, porches, doors, and windows, as the family grew. Now the old people and Flora kept house by themselves in the south wing.

In their sitting room the sunlight burned brightly on stiff patterns of wallpaper, on the red garlands of the carpet, the ripples painted on the woodwork in imitation of quarter-sawed oak, and the false-Nottingham curtains looped up in the windows. A rack on the wall held a row of hand-painted plates, the work of his aunt and his great-aunt Nancy, decorated with birds, wild roses, and rosebuds.

Beneath the plate rack stood a couch, upholstered in rows of yellow tapestry biscuits, with a green button at each intersection of the crevices. It had the proportions of a lion's body—the legs carved in claws, the sloping back, the head uplifted under a mass of fringed pillows. In spite of its discomfort, Alwyn's grandfather took his nap there every afternoon, his spectacles in his hand, an open newspaper over his face.

In front of the couch in winter the woodstove crouched on a mat of zinc, with a rosy spot in the middle of each dead-black cheek. In summer it was kept in the woodshed, swathed in old carpets.

A bow-legged table spread with a lace tidy marked the center of the room; and on a square shelf just above the floor the great family Bible, studded with gilt nails, lay diagonally.

The corner between the windows was occupied by a secretary—a writing-desk which made, when it was let down, a noise like the winding of a large clock, and a pair of bookcases with glass doors, framed in jig-saw scrolls. The books on the shelves hid behind family photographs. A blue-and-white Wedgwood sugar bowl and a stuffed owl stood on one side; on the other a mandolin without strings, and three gray squirrels in a tree crotch; their eyes resembled beads, and in his tenth year Alwyn discovered that they were beads, in fact. Above the secretary hung a row of em-bossed portraits in one frame: Emerson, Longfellow, Oliver Wendell Holmes, Bryant, Lowell, and Whittier, equally complacent and almost equally muffled by untidy beards.

These great men, just beneath the ceiling, gazed across the room at a pair of enlarged pictures of Alwyn's grandparents in middle life: Rose Hamilton Tower's scarcely womanly head, the ash-blond hair combed back from her low forehead, her eyes un-usually small, pale, and close together, her mouth drooping stoically; Henry Tower's face, stubborn and melancholy, his teeth set so firmly that the cheeks protruded a little over the jawbone, the chin lifted in a knot between the two tufts of his faded beard. Though the heads within the identical frames were of the same size, one saw at a glance that this man was smaller than his wife.

There was a shell on the sideboard, a conch shell in the shape of a horn, which, when held to the ear, repeated the surge and collapse of breakers, infinitely faint, as if heard across the great width of America which separates Wisconsin from the sea. It seemed to the boy that in the same way every object in those rooms echoed the forces which had once been at play around it, very faintly, from a distance of years instead of miles. The pleated fabrics and sheets of old paper enfolded little, agitated ghosts; and the odor of unfamiliar clothes, beds, and pillows, the residue of spiritless perfumes and bouquets long since thrown away, suggested energies now exhausted and passions now forgotten: the energy which had chosen this farm in the wilderness, cut down the trees, uprooted the stumps, built and demolished the log cabins, and founded this home; the long series of passions which had in the end produced himself.

Sometimes he would ask his grandmother about one thing or another. Her eyes would grow vague with the intimate recollections which his question disturbed in her mind, so that he would expect a full and romantic account of them. But often she would merely say, "Oh, it is too long a story to begin now," or, "They are just old things which I've kept a good many years."

For the memory of another is like a ship which one sees coming down a bay—the hull and the sails separating from the distance and from the outlying islands and capes—charged with freight and cutting open the waves, addressing itself in increasingly clear outlines to the impatient eyes on the waterfront; which, before it reaches the shore, grows ghostly and sinks in the sea; and one has to wait for the tides to cast on the beach, fragment by fragment, the awaited cargo.

Alwyn's grandmother sat in the sitting room only when there were guests, or when, by the south window, she held the *Milwaukee Sentinel* or the *Christian Herald* on a level with the ridge of her old-fashioned corset, discovering what went on in the world through her unsuitably small spectacles. Her life, like that of primitive women, revolved about the place where food was prepared. Her thought and even her recollections were accessory to whatever she was doing at the moment; they resembled her habit of whispering to herself, often with vehemence, while she worked. So it was in the kitchen, her broad lap full of pea pods or stockings to be darned, with one eye on a simmering kettle or the bread rising in pans, that she was most likely to satisfy her grandson's curiosity. Sometimes she replied to questions which he was too young to ask with obscure allusions or partial avowals, which, like the rays of a magic lantern, illuminated with disconnected pictures the darkness of many lives—in fact, the darkness of life itself.

Her large kitchen looked as cool and solid as a room built of stone. There were things in it which, though they had been made in the old days, were still useful: a copper kettle, dented and discolored here and there by verdigris, which served as a foot-bath; a great, green flour barrel into which a hen who had wandered through the open door fell one day, beating up the flour with her wings; a sugar barrel with a handle; and two hand-hewn chests, one of which had been brought by the Towers from York State, part of their baggage on stagecoach and canal boat.

In one corner a short pump brought up rain water into a sink from the cistern under the floor. When the pump was out of order a trapdoor was lifted, and a pail attached to a pole was lowered into the abyss. Alwyn shrank against the wall, not only because he might fall in—it represented all the abysses with which his elders dealt so carelessly and capably; and out of it there breathed a strange odor associated in his mind with the body of a rat, white and swollen, which in his sixth or seventh year had had to be removed from the water.

There he observed his grandmother's meals in preparation—all the food characterized by his mother as unwholesome: potatoes in a black spider, frying in a quantity of bacon fat until they were brown; headcheese and the crackling of rendered lard; platters of leathery eggs; saturated pies; and baking-powder doughnuts so rich that they stained one's fingers. She would give him a doughnut, saying, brusquely, "Ask your ma before you eat it, or she'll fly up in the air!" Upon which he would remember his mother's remark, that all the men of that family were dyspeptic.

In the kitchen alone, of all the rooms in the house, Alwyn could imagine his grandmother as a girl, standing up very straight against that green plaster wall; her cheeks not quite rosy (for whoever had colored the familiar daguerreotype had mixed violet with the red); each gold earring swinging in the shadow of a curl; the black lace mitts and the watch fob; the bonnet of straw and ribbon, the great skirt wired and ruffled and hung with bows. Her sober eyes gave no sign of imagination and no sign of surprise at whatever they saw. Over the itinerant photographer's head they

must have seen miles of tough bushes and grass; strong
men chopping down the forest in a high wind; pigeons
dropping heavily from branch to branch; pasturing
deer continually alarmed. . . . And like the wild
morning of that world, the eyes in the daguerreotype
were cold and clear, and were not anxious about the
afternoon or the evening.

"Whew! the heat!" the grandmother would say to
the dreamy boy, wiping her flushed face on her apron.
"Your pa will want some cold water in the field. Take
the pail and run down to the well and bring up a little
to the house, and then you'd better take a fresh jug
to the men."

Alwyn would pause on the doorstep. There lay the
countryside which, sixty years before, had been her
wilderness—changed no less than she. Many gravel
roads running parallel through the distance, as white
as marble; chickens dusting their feathers in them,
frightened away by automobiles. Thousands of tele-
phone poles making the sound of a tuning fork. Reap-
ers, cultivators, sowers, hayrakes, tedders, and racks,
creeping like mechanical spiders over the slopes. Cattle
of all colors under the hickories. Sunshine flashing on
the tines of pitchforks, on idle plowshares, shovel
blades, and the sides of tin pails full of lunch. Sunshine streaming in the orchards over large apples which
seemed to revolve in the leaves. Clouds which looked
like pieces of pleated linen. Far away, harnessed
horses in miniature, and men wearing blue shirts, their
arms bare to the biceps; and over their heads the sky
full of heat waves gliding and curling. . . .

Alwyn never thought of the wilderness as hot, and did not know the origin of his clear sense of what it had been: cool and solid, forest beyond forest; no mountains, but instead, at an incomparable altitude, thunderhead on thunderhead the color of granite. Exactly in the center of the high, gray light had balanced an eagle. Catamount, bear, badger, deer, foxes, passenger pigeons, and birds of prey, had been so scattered among the trees and ravines that one never could have seen two at a time. The world had seemed empty; the great hollows had echoed and re-echoed. . . . Then, into the Mississippi Valley the pioneers had crept, with chests and sickles, axes, flails, and oxen in docile pairs. They had hesitated; and their figures had been dwarfed by that space, and at first their voices in that silence could not even have been heard.

That wilderness of history and hearsay, that distorted landscape of a dream which had come true before it had been dreamed, was there where it had been —but buried, buried under the plowed land, the feet of modern men, and the ripening crops. Probably Alwyn would never see its like. The pioneers were dead or unrecognizably old. The doorstep on which he stood happened to be a marble gravestone—discarded when a finer monument had been erected in its place or when a body had been moved to another cemetery. The chiseled side was turned toward the ground, and it occurred to Alwyn that among the letters of a name, a date, and an inscription, silvery beetles lay side by side, and against the urn or the clasped hands or the weeping willow, the earth as well was cut by the worms with illegible curlicues.

A great bowlder by the hitching post looked like the Ark of the Covenant at the back of his grandmother's illustrated Bible—he would sit on it when he got back from the field and crack hickory nuts. Cherry and plum trees stood in perfect order along the garden fence, the leaves of the one glossy and stiff, the leaves of the other curled back on the stem. The lawn was cut in two by a path which ran down to the road, and on his grandmother's half of it her roses grew. They were all cinnamon roses, a thicket of stunted bushes, the stems covered with short thorns, the blossoms spicy and disheveled. She would say, "That was the kind we had when I was a girl." For her, like pressed flowers in a book, or a bit of wedding bouquet folded in paper and fastened with a pin, they were a keepsake, a pretext for reminiscences.

Her extravagant love of the past was a way of continuing to be a mother, now that she was only a grandmother. If the men and women she had brought into the world had still been dependent upon her as they had been in their childhood, or if she could have usurped her daughter-in-law's control over Alwyn and his little brother and sisters, she would not have been so tireless in her efforts to remember and communicate what she remembered. She did not trouble to tell Flora or her grown sons about the old days—she never had; they heard her stories at second hand from the children, or overheard what was not intended for them. But the adventures she could relate, the judgments she could make with authority upon matters of which her daughter-in-law knew nothing, gave her an opportunity to impress upon these children—whom she could not instruct, or punish, or reward—the moral lessons of a period which had come to an end almost everywhere except in herself.

To this end she treasured all the heirlooms, including in her custody certain souvenirs of her husband's young manhood: such as the certificate of his first marriage—a large sheet of paper on which, under a black and white nosegay, one could still read his name and the bride's name, Serena Cannon; and a curl from the head of their son Oliver who had lived only seven years.

Serena Cannon had made the hair album which was the show piece of the collection, a copy book bound in vermilion paper with two or three tiny garlands of hair on each foxed but substantial page. In all there were fifty-six names, badly faded, in a script full of old-fashioned flourishes, and fifty-six garlands, having a great variety of designs: braided hoops, medallions like bits of Spanish lace, and spider webs, combinations of loops and zigzags and coils and shadowy scallops, executed in every quality and shade of hair—gray of tin and gray of iron, sandy and chestnut and dead black, one maroon and one almost orange; fine, coarse, wiry, or subtle; long threads spread out in spirals, and threads not long enough to encircle a space as big as the end of one's thumb, and stiff locks in which the form of a curl still pulled at the knots which held them. Most of the names were unknown to Alwyn:

Letitia, Judith, Clara-Belle, and Sophonisba; Enoch, Luther, Cyrus, and Phineas; Cannons and Standishes and Crosbys and Valentines—families which had died out or gone West. But he found, under a blond oval, the name of his mother's father, *Mr. Ira Duff;* under some dark plaited threads, *My husband Henry O. Tower;* and a lifeless wisp, marked in a woman's hand-writing, *My little son Oliver,* and beneath it, in another script, in ink of another color, *Deceased Dec. 4th, 1867.* Alwyn was bewildered when his grandmother explained that this book took the place, in those days, of a photograph album. He was unable to deduce a face or a life from a lock of hair; but an incongruous refinement rose like a ghost or a perfume from between its pages, and was added to his conception of the early days—a refinement which was the fancywork of a woman with an unimaginable face, a woman without history, whose only son was dead.

Serena Cannon was famous for her hair work and had left to her husband's family another masterpiece, a wreath as large as a funeral wreath: more than one head of hair wound and tied on a skeleton of wire; padded flowers in the form of Turk's-cap lilies, frayed leaves and swollen buds all bristling with the ends of individual hairs; and the wreath as a whole—when the old hat box was opened and the tissue paper lifted—quivering like a venomous spider.

Alwyn saw in his mind's eye a pallid woman, the veins on her hands very blue, the hands themselves moving in a mass of hair piled on her lap. Once, when he was ten years old, his grandfather muttered to his grandmother, "You'll let that child spoil Serena's things! She was a saint. . . ." Alwyn ran out of the house and climbed into the maple tree, wondering what made her a saint and why he was afraid.

There was a box of arrowheads which had been picked up on the farm over a period of seventy years: triangles of delicately chipped flint, some like alabaster, some flesh-pink, some black—and these looked more cruel than the others; so many that the boy imagined them falling like a hailstorm over the whole land before his grandparents came. There were two strings of wampum traded by the Indians for some hens and a worn-out hoe.

There was a watch chain of braided leather, and his great-grandfather John Tower's silver watch, wound with a key, three-quarters of an inch thick, the lid over the face decorated with birds and cat-tails. There was a picture frame, not Serena Cannon's work, but his great-aunt Nancy's: leather daisies and bunches of grapes and tendrils, varnished and tacked on strips of wood.

There was a glass basket, of oblong panes bound together by tape; it stood on the highest shelf of the kitchen cupboard, and inside it one could see a litter of old papers—letters, newspaper clippings, announcements of births, and obituaries.

There were the patchwork bedspreads, the thinnest and oldest also made by his grandfather's first wife: the pattern, a basket of cubic fruit as high and as wide as the spread, of uniform blocks of muslin yellow with age and Turkey-red cloth now scarcely pink; upon

which was imposed the almost invisible pattern of
the quilting itself—meticulous stitches in even, over-
lapping circles.

There were the crazy quilts: scraps of every sort
of dress goods, bordered by zigzag or log-fence stitch-
ing: watered black silk, flowered foulard, plaids,
changeable taffeta, red and yellow poplin, green challie
and cashmere in Paisley patterns, blister crêpe and pon-
gee—cut in diamonds and horseshoes and fans and
meaningless shapes, embroidered here and there with
bees, hearts, and leaves.

Alwyn's grandmother could identify piece after
piece: "My sister Abigail's best dress when she was a
girl. The dress I had made when your grandpa and
I visited the relations in Iowa. Your aunt Flora's
first party dress. A sacque that a woman named Minerva Foote gave me to cut up into a jacket for one
of my children. The goods your mother's aunt Melissa
Duff went on a lumber wagon to Milwaukee to get
a whole bolt of, so nobody should have anything like
it—she was the meanest woman ever lived! My
cousin Matie Share's basque. The dresses of my two
little girls who died—their names were Polly and Ada.
The dress your mother was married in." She intended
to make a crazy quilt for each of her grandchildren.

There were the daguerreotypes in leather cases,
one in a case of tortoise shell on which there was an
inlaid lily, brought back by his grandfather from the
South. Unknown men and women in a north light
that was eternal; good, bad, and indifferent people.
. . . The adolescent boy, cross-questioning his grand-

mother as to their identity, wanted to ask them questions as well—with no hope of being answered, since
they were dead; curious and proud, he wanted to be
able to explain to himself their failures, to love and
hate them as they had loved and hated one another.

In the afternoon he often went by himself to her
south bedroom, at the opposite end of the house from
his parents, brother, and sisters, where the noise of
everyday life sounded very softly or not at all. There
he climbed on a clothes barrel covered with wall paper,
from the barrel to a chest of drawers, placing a newspaper under his feet in order not to scratch the surface, and then into a recess on top of a built-in wardrobe, warm from the kitchen stove on the other side of
the wall, which was called the chimney cupboard.

All around him, as he sat dangling his feet over
the edge, lay the magazines which his cousins sent from
Milwaukee, full of editorials, love stories, advertisements of steamships and hotels, portraits of diplomats
and actresses—the materials of every imaginable future. Between the chimney cupboard and his future,
there were to be so many transitions; causes and effects which one was not even expected to understand;
alarms, changes of heart, and hesitations; everything
to be endured, and nothing prepared for. . . .
Nothing prepared for, since no one knew what had
begotten what; sons did not understand their parents'
lives; no one thought about tragedies which had come
to an end. The past covered one's footsteps all too
promptly; present moments were always in the act of
vanishing; how then could the future be anything but

a riddle? Years of misconstrued events, and unreasonable aversions, and useless ambitions, and nightmares. . . .

The boy turned the pages of the magazines listlessly.

Side by side above the chest of drawers, on a level with his knees, hung a pair of portraits of his grandmother's two little girls who died, enlarged from tintypes: two sober faces like boys' faces, wearing round white collars; one looking straight ahead, good-natured and unabashed, the other resting her chin in the palm of her hand with a sick child's thoughtfulness.

Across the room, also on a level with his knees, there was a large religious chromo, "The Rock of Ages": a girl dressed in what looked like a muslin nightgown, a young girl with streaming hair tossed against a rock in the sea, and clinging to a cross. There was no sky line; there were neither birds nor ships. What did it mean? Useless to ask—he knew as much as he would be told: it was not a real sea or any particular person or an actual darkness, but the night of the soul. The catastrophe, the black sky around it like the wall of a great well, the leaden breakers, and the soapsuds foam—all stood for something else. The dull crests kept on tirelessly booming in the picture; the girl could not have heard a comforting voice if there had been one. Deprivation and disappointment; loneliness without a horizon, without birds. . . .

All the secrets of all the lives must be like that— they could not tell. All they could do was to hang such a picture on the wall, or merely in their hearts. Would anyone ever tell?

That day he and his little sister had been looking at the daguerreotypes, at one in particular—a handsome, bearded young man in a uniform with two rows of brass buttons. His grandmother had looked over their shoulders, and she had said, "Do you know who that is?"

They had been surprised, for she always expected them to recognize the members of their own family. Of course they knew; even his little sister knew.

Sitting in the chimney cupboard, Alwyn puzzled over her question and her answer. Perhaps she had felt an impulse to mystify them, or the tediousness of having too many secrets to keep. She had said, "That was my soldier sweetheart."

They had not been able to understand. It was not her husband, their grandfather, but his younger brother—their great-uncle Leander, who was dead.

Alone in the chimney cupboard Alwyn determined, one day, sooner or later, to know that story, and as many others as he could. . . .

"Why didn't you marry him then, grandma?" his little sister had asked.

She had answered in a low tone which implied that there were things which could not be explained, even things which passed her understanding. "Well . . . He didn't want me. I don't blame him."

2. ALWYN'S KNOWLEDGE OF AMERICA AND HIS FAMILY

YEARS after, when all his grandparents were dead, Alwyn sat in a watering place in the Austrian Alps, where there was a cluster of iron tables around a café, where nineteenth-century waltzes were played and the cakes were good.

A boy, on whose cheeks the round flush of illness darkened, was insisting wearily in French: "You Americans lack the sense of sin. You have discovered the fountain of youth; it has made you cruel. . . ."

A great psychoanalyst who looked like an old Protestant minister wavered along the path; and a middle-aged princess brought biscuits in a paper bag.

Lifting two heavy rings in the air with his blue-white hand, a hunchbacked critic could be heard saying, "The psychology of love undergoes a complete revolution every twenty-five years. In America, I am told, every fifteen years; but they have no fine arts, so their passions are lacking in interest."

The grave, well-modulated voices rose against the steady crying of a river, somewhere below. Far below, a plain lay, patched with cottages and tidy crops; far above, a number of soft mountains were brocaded by ice; and over the valley walls seven cataracts fell, shivering on the stone in mourning—seven vines the color of pewter.

Alwyn was glad to be in Austria; but because of the odor and the bells of two or three cattle which were driven past, perhaps because of the poor fat princess who, it seemed, regretted civilization, he began to think of the early days of America, particularly the early days of Wisconsin and his family. And the river beat in the small valley as ardently and roughly as the heart of a Middle Western forest.

Wisconsin, his grandmother's wilderness. . . . He remembered one of its little hills; fancied that he sat, not in Gastein, but on one of its hills, dreaming of its history. Slain trees, and timber wolves slinking in search of young pigs, and weather-beaten children stationed in poor crops to scare off the deer. . . . He tried to picture to himself his ancestors: ignorant men with delicate bodies, hoping for wealth as a reward for virtue; boys with chapped mouths hunting by the light of lanterns; fearless girls becoming sickly mothers. A company of dead or distant relatives, on a continent without much elegance, without palaces, without rest. . . . There sprang up in his mind a great number of stories and fragments of stories, in which they were gesticulating and embracing and working.

Alwyn daydreaming in Austria, a little self-consciously a poet. . . . And for a moment the well-bred voices, the philosophies, the orchestras, were swept away. For a moment all Europe seemed less significant than the vicissitudes of pioneers, men who were anonymous unless they were somebody's relatives. He did not quite like their suffering, their illiterate mysticism, their air of failure; but he understood them, or fancied that he did. It did not matter whether he liked them or not—he was their son.

Among them, of their marriages and love affairs,

there had also been born a composite character, the soul of the race that was not actually a race; something so vague that one recognized it only as an atmosphere, a special brightness, or a peculiar quality of the temperaments and customs and fortunes of Americans; as if it were the god of the place—half invisible, and so large that one could see at a given moment only the great arch of its foot, or the dim luxury of its flesh, or the electricity of its eyes, or the jewels on its giant hands and head. It had been born in the stables, the cabins, and the schoolhouses where music, religion, and the three R's had been taught in turn. Who could describe the mask that was its face, or estimate its strength, or define its character? Whatever it was, it was the hero of the stories that he knew, the tales of his grandmothers. By comparison with its dwelling-place, Europe seemed only the scene of a classic play continually repeated; for a moment only. . . . But there was that moment in every day of Alwyn's life.

On another night he was dining with friends at La Turbie. Around the hotel arid meadows ran down to the cliffs, meadows where sooner or later the moonlight would come, gently cropping the stone like a flock of sheep. They sat on a terrace, looking over the balustrade and the cactus upon Monte Carlo —the casino, the harbor, the large rock covered with palaces.

One friend said, "Madame R—— is ill."

Another, "I hate myself for gossiping, but after all . . ."

And the first: "The less said about it the better. But I think as you do; the name of her illness is—hate. The young man . . ."

One asked, "So she hates him now?"

And another answered, "Having loved him long enough."

The little city below was anxious to please, sparkling on the seashore; the electric light writhed as if it were foliage on fire. As a child Alwyn had imagined that heaven would be like that; as an adolescent, the whole of Europe; and it woke other recollections of childhood.

Ostensibly as a comment on Madame R——'s affairs, he began, "My grandmother Tower . . ." He talked of her soldier sweetheart as if it were someone they all knew; how when he came back from the Civil War, he did not want her; how she had married instead his elder brother who was a widower; how she had said, "I don't blame him."

His friends listened quietly because they were old friends, familiar with his passion for relatives who were dead, relatives who had been very poor, off there in the States. But one asked, "How do you know all this?"

Alwyn said, "She lived with us when I was a child. I watched them all closely then, much too closely. . . ."

As he remembered his childhood, it seemed that much of it had been spent in the center of a carpeted floor; and all about in a circle of rocking-chairs there had been women and men—grandparents, and their

friends, and old cousins, and great-aunts, and uncles;
and behind each one a life had extended into the past
like a corridor—poorly lighted, long corridors winding away in every direction, through reticence and
forgetfulness, to their youth; and in the ring of rocking-chairs, the child for whose existence all the corridors had come together, had shivered in the gusts of
emotion which blew vaguely down them, and tried to
understand the strange syllables which echoed from
one life to another.

Alwyn's friend looked at him sharply over the
grapes and figs on the table. "A good woman. . . .
But I don't understand how you found out her secrets.
You know them as well as if you had been her lover.
But it all took place before your father was born. She
didn't tell you that story as you tell it, did she?"

"Not in so many words. . . ."

"Of course you knew them all—your grandfather
and grandmother, your—great-uncle, wouldn't he be?
But they were old then, very old, I should think; and
old people don't tell that sort of thing. Don't be
cross," he added. "You know that we prefer you even
to your grandmother. But what do you know about
her and what have you invented? Perhaps imperceptibly invented . . ."

Someone else went on, "Tell us, tell us, please,
exactly which elements of that story you know to be
unquestionably true?"

When Alwyn smiled and murmured, "But I don't
know," they smiled and spoke of other things.

But he was troubled by their questions. His knowledge of himself, of his native land, began with stories like that. After all, were they true? How true?

A child in a ring of rocking-chairs, shut in by secrets. . . . He had wanted to understand as other children want to be understood. A phrase of his grandmother's, certain glances exchanged over a letter, funeral sermons among greenhouse flowers, a caress which he had surprised, an antipathy still evident though worn out by the passage of time—each had had its peculiar spirit with an enigmatic face. They seemed to have bent over him even in the cradle, like amorous women, veiled, strangely bedecked, in old-fashioned dresses. Mysteries, some alive and some dead; and the dead had clung as close as the living. One had taken his wrist in its dry hand; one had slipped its arm without weight over his shoulder; and another had placed on his forehead its long fingers like a wreath.

He had been excited and frightened. No one else had seemed to notice them; his parents had looked away, toward things that were actually happening or going to happen. His grandmother, like an official representative of the past, had told stories without motivity, without a moral, and had replied to his timid questions literally, perhaps timidly.

But he had ignored nothing and forgotten nothing. In so far as he could he had learned the bare outline of everyone's life. Then his grandmother had said, for example, "Your great-aunt Mary Harris laughed like that woman," or, "Don't let a little dirt drive you mad, the way poor Nancy Tower did." He had noted every word of sentences he was not expected to understand, and added each detail, in his memory, to its proper nucleus. Little by little he had uncovered the life of his elders; little by little he had grown up. . . .

His mother, to explain her differences with his grandmother, his grandfather's harsh temper, his father's melancholy, had touched upon secrets which, deliberately, she would not have betrayed to a child. In New Mexico his uncle John Craig, who had lived away from the family since he was a boy, who had been more or less an outsider then, had told him things the others had forgotten or were ashamed of. Alwyn had given dead people the faces of daguerreotypes and tintypes, old people the young faces of fading photographs, or invented their appearance according to vague indications of traits peculiar to this or that branch of the family; and placed all their quarrels, infatuations, and disappointments, in a setting of childhood's exaggerated landscapes.

After he had left home, when most of his older relatives were dead, certain things of which he had remained in ignorance had continued to trouble him. For the personages in rocking-chairs, the questionable spirits leaning over his cradle, had embodied not only the past, but the future—his own wishes and fears; and he was not to be content until an everyday light had unveiled all their faces. To bring an end to his childhood, to drive its ignorance out of his heart, to conduct or try to conduct his own life in its alarming motion, he had been obliged to lead in imagination many lives already at an end. Now and again the riddle of his own experience had resembled one of the past's riddles; his personal solutions had solved them as well. Spell after spell had been lifted. He had been possessed by a family of spirits—now at last they were exorcised; and in their place there was this family of stories which he could not have remembered, but seemed nevertheless to remember.

In his nineteenth year he had written a historical essay, based upon what he had found out about his relatives: a summary of all these unwritten biographies; as it were, a short biography of America. A professor had praised it; his mother had said that she could not understand it; he himself had been proud of his work. One night, in a hotel on the French Riviera, he found these pages and reread them:

At first there broke against European sea walls, the edge of a uniform world of water; somewhere upon it America lay, a phantom putting an end to its uniformity. Down to the seaports came disappointed men—no one who was happy would have set sail for a phantom. Some were hopelessly poor: they had dreamed of states in which all the poor would be rich, and their revolutions had been crushed. Some were sickly: they had invented moralities to curb the appetites of others, who in turn had abolished their laws. Some were bondsmen, sold for a time. Some were failures and the sons of men who had failed: success being impossible on this earth, perhaps it would be possible on a continent which a few years before had not been on the earth. Some were criminals or adven-

*turers, whose regret wore masks of bravado. Some
wanted to rule, whose fathers had not been kings.
Some received in hallucinations a knowledge of pure
ceremonies, by which they were not permitted to worship. All were disappointed—minorities going out to
form a majority against the world.*

*In dangerous boats which tottered up and down the
water, when they were not seasick, they sang. Some
believed that America was like a goblet lying in the
ocean, and when one drank from it one would become
so happy that one would dare to remember one's
grief. Some tried to believe that it was an earthly
heaven or heavenly earth, where saintliness which
other men would worship would be easy, where wealth
would be apportioned according to saintliness. Those
who died were never disillusioned; and the waves
among which they were laid seemed to sing feebly
with those who were left on the boats.*

*Not one ship sank; and they landed on a long coast
of bushes and stone, of stagnant water and sand.
The redskins were dangerous but pitiable, in their animal hiding places; and as the whites proceeded to ex-
terminate them they could never bear to think what
they were doing. Their own number was reduced
by diseases; those who did not die were strengthened
by the thought of the early Christians.*

*They shot red squirrels flickering in the trees, and
turkeys (great, enameled birds); and planted the Indian corn. They gave thanks when there was enough
to eat, and repented of their insignificant sins when
there was not; in the beginning the crops were always*

*meagre. The evidently poor land kept its wealth se-
cret, like a young mother who thinks herself a virgin.*

*It was the land which God had given them, and it
was poor. So God was poverty, but He was poverty
which would become wealth. He was a precept by
which poverty would be changed into wealth; He was
a law. There were songs and talk about sin, but few
transgressions. Preachers of genius painted evil in
such perfect colors that men vomited and women
fainted in the churches; they made the agony of some
seem sweeter than love. Dangerous witches appeared
among them and were condemned; and on the chest
of a man accused of commerce with spirits, heavy
stones were laid one by one until he died.*

*They went further west. Over the Northwest Ter-
ritory mouth organs quavered between embarrassed
kisses, and cabinet organs quavered between prayers.
From the half-ashamed love-making sprang a great
population, and from the prayers muttered in new log
cabins, the certainty that the God of poverty had
blessed this people with His uplifted, enigmatic finger.*

*They came to the Far West, and found valleys as
large as kingdoms, without kings; red mountains and
others the color of pearls; deserts below sea level in
which no fire was visible, but the earth was ashes;
and extremes of temperature as in hell, and heavenly
climates. They wasted great forests and unearthed a
plunder of oil, coal, and metals.*

*The whole continent came to resemble the childbed
of a virgin; amid cries of axes and moaning sawmills
and finally a groan of factories which rose overnight*

*in fields of refuse (in smokelike folds of stained linen)
wealth was born. There was rejoicing as extravagant
as the singing of angels. In the celebration which took
place skyscrapers were built, so tall that they swayed
continually, so strong that they never fell. Pride
wounded too many times turned into energy. Whoever faltered closed his eyes and summoned up a fierce
idealism. Men, women, and children worked side by
side, making of delicate nerves a machine. In the noon
of their holidays guns were fired and great schemes
invented.*

*They did forget grief in the efforts they made to
annihilate it, and became the laughing race of the
earth. Unhappiness was treason; no tragic arts
flourished. The slaves which had been shipped from
Africa and outcast Jews who took refuge among them
brought tragic songs—to which the Americans danced.*

*Men grew rich in a day or overnight; they could
always grow richer; the future was illimitably generous. Nevertheless, millions remained poor. Before their eyes lay the feast—they could not eat; and
though there were millions of them, each felt alone
in his poverty. They grieved, but stifled their grief,
being ashamed of it; for if they worked harder, if
they had led purer lives, if they still worked harder.
. . . Those who did not give up hated life secretly;
those who did, despised themselves.*

*The New World was troubled; even the rich were
troubled; they did not have an excuse for rest. They
knew that God was poverty; was He not then an end-
less struggle? He seemed to have vanished when the*

*struggle was over, leaving some lonely. Like a beg-
gar, homeless as they once had been, He haunted others, who did not know which to be ashamed of—
their wealth or God. He was also the precept which
turned poverty into wealth; the poor in their envy
would not let the rich neglect Him when He had served
His purpose; and the rich tried to force upon the poor
virtue and the rewards of virtue, for they were lonely
in the midst of rewards. There was also a puritanism
which was genuine remorse for the sins of others. So
a series of sad persecutions took place.*

*It became the land of extreme youth. Middle age
was merely a struggle; old age was a time when failure
could not be disguised, or a time of success which did
not satisfy. Men envied young men, and put them at
their sides in positions of great responsibility, so that
from eyes which glittered with reflections of the future,
their eyes might catch fire for a moment. The whole
country had one symbol: a very young man, always at
the beginning of a career, always beside his mother.
For she taught him to revere success and taught him its
maxims. He would never forget that when she had
been at his side, the mirage had seemed real and not
far away; he would never again be so happy as he had
been, under her spell. So young wives imitated the
mothers of the men they loved. America became a
matriarchate.*

*Meanwhile the colonists had moved and moved
again, from east to west, into every corner of the
continent; and each migration repeated, with a little
less religion and a little more weariness, the pilgrim-*

*age which had brought them there: disappointed men
going further, hoping still . . .*

*At last there was no corner where wealth and joy
might be thought to dwell, no riverbed without a city,
no empty valley, no more coasts. At last those pilgrims who had failed to discover their hearts' desire
had to look for it in heaven, as it had been in Europe,
as it has always been. Disillusioned but imaginative,
these went through the motions of hope, still pioneers.
They will be seen while America lasts, proud and poor
(like pretenders to royal blood, the site of whose
throne has long been forgotten) among mechanics,
surgeons, singers with androgynous voices, reporters,
professional players of games, orators, gamblers in
food, hooded vigilants, gold diggers, salesmen of
salves, film stars, architects, trance mediums. . . .*

It was too well, that is, too badly written, in the
style (Alwyn thought) of a public speech. He regretted
its impiety, was ashamed of its anxious, artificial
elegance. But he had not changed his mind; it was
all true, true of America—he was sure that he could
prove every assertion by an account of somebody's
life.

But underneath his balcony a crowd of American
sailors from a warship in the harbor quarreled around
a French girl who had fainted away. Their presence
reminded him how ambitious, indeed pretentious, his
essay was; how much its subject was a family affair.
Once he had believed that all Americans, because they
were Americans, had embarked upon the same ad-

venture; now he realized, very humbly, that there were many adventures. That of the sailors, for example, who were snarling at one another and shaking hands. . . . Idly, he drew rows of hearts along the margins of the typewritten pages, and read them again, half aloud, because the careful sentences suited his voice. The noisy sailors were quite as American as he, but he could hardly understand a word they said. As for his essay, he felt a certain pleasure at having displayed his intelligence, as having been intelligent at all when young; beyond that, it did not satisfy him. An honest generalization of one family's intimate history, true, perhaps, of America as a whole. . . . And the sailors made it ridiculous. Suddenly he felt that he had no native land—he had a family instead.

Disillusioned but imaginative, going through the motions of hope. Pretenders to royal blood, the site of whose kingdom has long been forgotten. Perpetual pioneers—the Towers were men of that sort. "Well, he's a Tower," his grandmother had often said, as if in explanation of her husband's behavior or that of one of her sons. What had she meant? Alwyn decided to write a character sketch, enumerating the traits of his relatives. Turning over the pretentious essay, he took a fountain pen out of his pocket and wrote on the back of its pages:

A curl of dark or ash-blond hair on the forehead; a smile as strained as a frown; obstinate blue eyes which seemed to see visions, and mouths which doubted them. Proud men with fine bodies, frequently ill.

Slight men who had a talent for music and an aptitude for every sort of culture, of which they were suspicious as forms of weakness; men who were slightly ashamed both of their gifts and their neglect of them. They did not love cities, but loved the country as those who take refuge in it from cities do. Thoughtful without shrewdness—not one had ever got on in the world. Ill-advised by their imagination, they never forgave themselves for the mistakes they made; and, in secret, employed that same imagination to perfect their melancholy, as a saint perfects his sanctity.

They were sober, religious, and conscious of not being appreciated. In the wars which were fought they never achieved the rank which was due them; their painstaking bravery went unrewarded. They believed in democracy, hoping that it would reinvest with power those who deserved it. They marched at the head of processions, but the processions always turned down a side street, leaving them alone.

Generation after generation of coarser men—their inferiors in probity, in talent, in dignity—took the good things of this world away from them. Immigrants who began life as their hired men, ended as landowners and holders of mortgages on their land. The Towers worked harder and harder, always beyond their strength; and the harder they worked, the more their resentment grew.

For somewhere in England, in the sixteenth or seventeenth century, they had lived on the land as gentlemen. Two younger sons had been obliged to

*come to America in search of fortune. They had
failed to find it; their descendants were still seeking,
seeking among fools and brutes. Superior men,
cheated of their inheritance, disguised as inferiors and
unable to reveal themselves. . . . They said little,
but this conviction took possession of all their minds:
they were not born to be beasts of burden; they should
not have to work as these others worked; they were
not menials, but deserved a sweeter fate; life was
unjust. This conviction was inherited by every Tower,
from father to son; and in that inheritance younger
son shared equally with elder. A grievance was their
birthright. . . .*

Alwyn knew this grievance in himself in so far as
he resembled his father, his little old grandfather,
Leander and Hilary his great-uncles, his great-aunt
Nancy. He was glad that he understood them; it
might save him, in a measure, from the family pride
and brooding, the family resentment and doubt.

Every five seconds the lighthouse in the harbor
threw a flake of light over his head on the ceiling of his
room. Most of the sailors had made peace and
vanished into bars and improvised brothels along the
quay. One of them, at least forty years old, unman-
ageably drunk, was being taken back to the ship by the
guards; he lay down on the pavement and sobbed:
"I want my mother! I want my mother!"

Resting his elbows on the iron railing of his balcony, Alwyn fluttered the pages of his work. Two
records of his opinions, one about America as a whole,

one about his family—that is, the paternal branch of his family: they were of little value. Staring into the dusky Mediterranean, he thought of the Tower stories, the lives of his mother's parents, Ira and Ursula Duff, of pitiful, red-headed Flora, his uncles, the minister and the deserter, his great-aunt Mary, the adventuress, and all the others.

There in his hands, uselessly, were two statements of their significance; but the best way to explain what they meant would be, quite simply, to tell the stories themselves. Less impossible but more difficult than what he had attempted. . . . Stories like a series of question marks; questions which did not require an answer, questions at peace. He was content with their ambiguities, so he knew that they were the end of understanding, or at any rate, the end of trying to understand.

Trying to understand, for his own sake, shadowy men, women, and children. . . . And as he thought of their lives, he was surprised by regret (their regret) which weakened and then strengthened his will: regret that the time for laughter and ease, even for him, seemed never to come, while work never came to an end.

3. His Grandfather Tower's Character. A Fragment of Autobiography. The Rest of His Life

DURING his grandfather's lifetime, the alpaca jacket which he put on when he came in for supper swung from a hook on the door of the chimney-cupboard room. It held the shape of his body and soul: the sharp angle of the sleeves at the elbow meant irascible vitality; the empty pockets, poverty and indifference; the imprint of the stooped shoulders, fatigue; and the contradictory flare of the collar at the back, pride.

He died when his grandson was twelve years old; so that Alwyn as a man could recall only the mysteriously impressive pictures which a child remembers. The clearest had a background of roses, his grandmother's cinnamon-rose bushes. Large bees staggered up and down in the scent of the old, bright thicket whose blossoms were all imperfect, hanging in great numbers on the tough stems, as if they had fallen there by chance. The bent old man came down the path from the woodshed with a look of great exasperation fixed on nothing in particular. His beard was parted in the middle, and fell on each side of a large bone button in his shirt collar; his rheumatic hands were clenched; and wherever he went, he seemed to be elbowing aside invisible people in his way.

There was little of importance left for him to do. He got up at daybreak to feed the hens which fluttered uncalled at his heels, flinging the grain behind him and taking no notice of them; so that there were sudden cries amid the drumming of their bills, and agitated flights away from his unsteady feet. His clear, wide-open eyes were often indifferently unfocused, as if the eyes of his mind were downcast. But he examined the sky at dawn with infinite care, to prophesy the weather; for he knew the meaning of sun dogs in winter (two pale blotches crouching on the horizon at the right and left hand of the east) and understood the color of clouds, and the various kinds of wind.

During the day he chopped kindling in the woodshed; cured the hams in salt and brown sugar, and smoked them with hickory chips; killed chickens for the table; and brought vegetables to both kitchens (his wife's and his daughter-in-law's), husking and silking the sweet corn, and breaking winter squashes with an ax. Above all, he worked in the garden, digging, planting, hoeing, transplanting, and weeding even patches of turnips, corn, parsley, and carrots, melons, peas, oyster plant, beets, parsnips, and early and late cabbage.

He offered his grandson (then seven) one cent for every five cabbage moths that he could catch. Some were pallid, some deep yellow; Alwyn caught many of both colors with a butterfly net. But the old man said that a boy of his age ought to know that only the females laid eggs from which cabbage worms hatched, and harshly refused to pay for the others. Alwyn could not forgive him.

The children were not allowed in the garden, unless their grandfather sent them to throw clods at one or two old hens who continually found holes in the fence. Sometimes Alwyn would ask timidly to go with him to look at the melons. The old man, only a little taller than the boy, stooped over the cantaloupe vines, and fingered the stems to see if they had begun to pull away from the ripening fruit. He thumped the watermelons, but was too deaf to hear the sound they made, like the beat of a small drum under the earth; and finally took from his pocket a horn-handled knife, cut a triangle in the rind, lifted it out, and peered down into the flesh: if it was pink, the plug was replaced; if it was blood-red, that melon was placed in a tub of water in the cellar. Alwyn knew as well as his grandfather how to test melons, but felt that something ambiguous was also being accomplished, that he was in the presence of an old, powerful magician, engaged in ceremonies among the vines.

Alwyn's father often said, "Your grandfather was no good at farming, but he is the best gardener in Wisconsin."

The striped beauty of the garden, its geometrical outlay of faultless plants on clean soil, suited his refined spirit better than large, weather-beaten fields. It was dear to him also because it took the place of the farm he had cleared in the wilderness, now beyond his control; for he was no longer strong enough to work on the land, and his son would no longer take orders from him. So he referred to the secrets of the soil in this or that field with the arrogance of one

who does not expect to be listened to, and angrily made
fun of Alwyn's father if a crop failed.   Injurious
things were said in anxious voices, things hardly meant
to be heard; and there were, from time to time, bitter
quarrels.

Once when Alwyn was nine he came round the corner of the house suddenly.   His aunt Flora and his
grandfather were going to the village; the horse and
buggy stood by the porch.   But the old man strode up
and down, trampling the wild violets which were
planted there, and muttering.   Flora wrung her hands
and absent-mindedly tore the veil which hung from her
hat.   His father was there, sobbing—Alwyn had not
known that grown men ever wept.   In the doorway
his grandmother stood with her arms folded, a look
of resignation that was half scorn on her face.

The trouble had something to do with the horse
and buggy.   Suddenly the old man sat down on the
porch and stared straight ahead with his farsighted
eyes.   Alwyn's father stammered then that he was tired
of being bullied, and the girl defended him and reproached their father—both speaking loudly because
he was deaf.   They were telling him that his life was
over and he must not interfere any more—things were
hard enough for them without that.

Then the grandmother saw the child, and said:
"Run behind the house, Alwyn!   Run behind the
house!"

Stumbling with tragic excitement, he obeyed.

That evening he saw that they had all grown gentle,
as if it were the responsibility of each to make the other

forget what had happened; and his father and grand-father sat quietly side by side on the porch.

During the last six or seven years of the old man's life he was never in good health. As a small child Alwyn thought this resulted from chewing tobacco, a habit condemned in the family. Even his grandfather himself had said, "Look here, boy. Don't ever take tobacco. I learned when I was a boy—those were bad times." Meanwhile he had put as much as he could hold between finger and thumb into his mouth, as if to demonstrate the fatal power of the old days.

Alwyn's grandmother gave this explanation of his illness: "Your grandpa has never been a well man since he went to the war. It spoiled his stomach."

He feared and despised doctors, and read all the patent-medicine advertisements in the newspapers, be-lieving for a moment each flowery promise of an end of pain. He received many pamphlets by mail—testi-monies of miraculous healing, illustrated by photo-graphs of ugly men and women who had been suf-ferers—and wrote for salves, powders, and tonics. His wife sighed and shook her head whenever an agent drove into the yard with a valise full of samples; but the old man invariably described his symptoms, the ambitious salesman invariably expressed his sympathy, gave advice, and received a large order. Every drug-gist in the neighboring towns also prepared for him personal recipes.

All these medicines accumulated in the tall kitchen cabinet: vials and pill boxes and squat bottles, bear-ing the formidable names of diseases in lists like incantations, decorated with portraits of heretic doctors, Mothers this and that in lace bonnets, and benign priests. He tried them all, and they failed. At last he found relief only in Duffy's whisky, which he drank from a teaspoon because he was a total abstainer. He was able to eat less and less, and sat by himself after each meal—his fingers interlaced, on his mouth the shape of a cry for pity that was never heard.

Though in the midst of his family, gardening faithfully in rain or shine, his isolation grew more extreme than that of any sick room. The children feared him, or feared his pain. In the woodshed he gnashed his teeth because the cats got underfoot; if the price of grain or pork fell, or La Follette made a speech, he gnashed his teeth as he read his newspaper. His grandchildren learned that they might be the objects of the same irritation. Furthermore, he was deaf; they did not know how to pitch their voices so he could understand, and were not tall enough to speak in his ear, though he was a small man. So they never asked questions, and he scarcely ever told them stories.

There was one, however, which he told on various occasions, and Alwyn could not understand why he remembered it or what it meant: "Early one morning, when I was a young fellow and going to the barnyard to milk, I saw a man leaving the strawstack and running down the road. After a time I saw him coming back again. The day was foggy—you couldn't tell about a man more'n six rods away. He turned round and got out of sight. I wondered what was wanted, so I watched through the horse-stable window. Pretty soon, there he was, stopping once in a while and going toward the stack. I ran out and shouted, 'Look here, stranger! What in creation are you after?' He was as white as a sheet and shook from head to foot. 'Excuse me, partner,' said he. 'I slept in your stack. I left a pair of shoes there.' 'My stars, man! Go and get them!' I told him. 'I don't want any man's shoes but my own.' "

He told this mysterious anecdote and one or two others like it, with an air of great satisfaction. But of his more important experiences, never a word. . . . Indifferent to the future, set aside in the present, he must have been brooding all the time on his plans which had failed to materialize, his dreams which had given him no rest. But he said nothing, being too ill to idealize and too proud to regret anything.

His wife had kept a few relics of this youth which he seemed to be concealing. Hating war, he had burned his uniform and thrown away the badges; but there was a dog's-eared Testament which he had carried in his breast pocket; a screw-topped inkwell of dark wood into which he had dipped his pen (all the letters were lost); a splinter of a tree under which two generals had signed a truce, the soldiers in a frenzy having cut down and divided it; a silver ring shaped like a wedding ring which had belonged to his sixteen-year-old brother Hilary, who had been taken by the Rebels and had never been heard of. He made no comments upon them; his wife explained what they were; and when she taught the children Civil War songs, he went out of the house.

He had been a musician in the war. There were a pair of drumsticks, blackened where sweating hands had held them, and a trumpet without a mouthpiece. There were the fife and the flutes; the fife like an ebony wand, the flutes wrapped in red flannel, their German-silver keys interlaced around the one of cocoa-wood and the other of a wood called grenadilla.

Sometimes the old man took out the fife, paying no attention to the fascinated children who gathered about. One shoe tapping a nervous beat on the floor, he played the hysterical tunes of the 'sixties. There was something unearthly in the melody made by his hard lips, pressed on the little black rod as if in a kiss; and the children shrank, ravished by a kind of fright. Alwyn dreamed of the Civil War—a war of little old men, deaf and sad, tapping their feet on the hot rock in the South, a war of piercing music off the key.

He seemed scarcely human to his grandson—an old ghost of another epoch, a ghost which, even in its youth, could not have been very young. All that Alwyn ever knew of this inconceivable boyhood and young manhood was based upon the vague accounts of others, except what his grandfather himself wrote about it the year before his death.

Everyone was surprised by his consent to write the history of his life; his children spoke of the important contribution he could make to pioneer history, hoping, perhaps, that, in a sentence here and a paragraph there, he would break his long silence about himself, as it were by accident. He was to be seen at the double secretary, covering sheets of foolscap with his crabbed script, muttering complaints of the stiffness of his fingers. . . .

Being urgently requested by the members of my family to write a brief history of my life, together with some incidents connected with the early settlement of this part of Wisconsin, I have very reluctantly consented to do so.

I was born in the State of New York, Onondaga County, town of Lafayette, village of Cardiff, February 15th, 1830. My father's family consisted of five sons and one daughter, all of whom excepting two have passed to the Silent Land. In the vicinity where we lived, a gentleman by the name of Farrar, owned and operated an ax manufactory, but the stream on which his plant was located was too small to furnish sufficient power to meet the demand, so he conceived the idea of going West in pursuit of a location suitable for his business. Arriving at Milwaukee and securing the services of (what was then called) a Land Looker, they continued their march Northward when unawares they came to the banks of Stony Creek in Washington County. This, said Mr. Farrar, is the identical place I have been looking for.

Upon his return home language failed him to fully describe the beauty of the new country and the bright prospects of its development in the near future. At that early period the West was beckoning to the overcrowded East to come and help to organize what has proven to be one of the grandest and best States of the Union. Such was the force of his argument and persuasion, that my Father concluded to accompany him and seek a home in the far-away West.

They both soon disposed of their belongings and on the 8th day of September, 1846, they secured passage in the city of Syracuse on a canal boat for Buffalo. The voyage lasted one week. Arriving in Buffalo, we found the "Propeller

Princeton" about ready to leave her Dock for Milwaukee and as soon as our goods could be transferred we commenced our long and tedious journey around the great chain of lakes, toward the setting sun. On entering Lake Michigan through the Straits Mackinaw, a terrible storm awaited us, the wind and waves carrying away the smokestacks of the vessel and making it necessary to chain the cabins to keep them from being blown overboard. After being tossed to and fro for a whole week we were finally put on Terra Firma in the city of Milwaukee. The entire voyage occupying two weeks, which is now being made in less than twenty-four hours. We soon found that our lot was cast in a strange land and among strangers.

Fortunately, Mr. Farrar had a brother-in-law by the name of Wilcox living about three miles up the lake and one of the very early settlers of Wisconsin. To his home we wended our way, as it seemed to be necessary to provide a place for the families to live while the men were absent building their houses on their land. In the meantime Father had bought a yoke of oxen and wagon and proceeded to lay in a store of provisions, consisting of one barrel of salt pork, one barrel of flour, half bushel of beans, five bushels of potatoes, tea, coffee, sugar, etc., and a stove. Thus equipped, one bright Thursday morning in the first part of the month of October, we started on our journey to Washington County. Late Friday evening found us at what was called the Aaron settlement and three miles from our destination. At daylight Saturday morning we started for our new home in the forest, consuming the entire day in making the three miles. There were logs to be chopped and drawn out of the way, swamps and marshes to be avoided, trees to be marked in order to find the road again. Arriving at our destination, Father returned to the Aaron home to spend the night, leaving us boys in the woods to guard the team and provisions. We went to a little marsh near by and cut each an armful of marsh grass which we spread under the wagon, on which we placed a blanket, making a bed fit for royalty to occupy. After retiring to our novel sleeping room, we were soon lulled to sleep by the mournful voice of the hoot owl and the sweet, silvery song of the whippoorwill.

On Monday morning Father returned and we began cutting logs of small size, to build a cabin, in which to live during the time occupied in building the log house. In two days a shelter 10 x 12 ft. was erected. We brought moss from a little spruce swamp near by and stuffed it in the crevices, which answered admirably in keeping out the wind and storm. For a door we hung up a blanket.

I was unanimously chosen cook, while our bill of fare consisted of pork, potatoes, bread, beans, and an occasional extra of wild game with which the forest abounded. The streams and lakes were also swarming with fish of the finest quality. I may say however that my education in the culinary art as well as in many others had been sadly neglected. But my observation of my mother's kitchen had impressed me, that it required no sleight of hand to boil potatoes, fry meat, and bake beans. When it came to the bakery division that was another problem and one over which I stumbled and was obliged to take our flour to a neighbor's three miles away and persuade the lady of the house to do our baking, twice each week. I went for the bread, carrying it on my back in a flour sack.

We were three days in raising the building, the neighbors being so widely separated, coming a distance from four to six miles. I may add without boasting, that I did the cooking for the crowd those three days, and the compliments I received, added not a little to the opinion I held of myself as an A No. 1 cook.

I must refer briefly to the construction of the house. All

the sawed lumber in the building was in the two doors. That which was necessary for floors, partitions and casings was split from poplar and basswood logs, and hewed one side which was called puncheon. The material of the roof was split from oak two or three feet long, which were called Shakes. The crevices in the side of the building were filled with clay. After making a fireplace in one end of the house we declared it perfect, and ready for occupancy.

Having completed our labors, we were ready to go to Milwaukee and bring the family to their new home. On Saturday morning, Father and I started on our long, tedious march of forty-five miles on foot and long before the rays of the morning sun began to dance among the tree tops of the forest, we were well on our way. We made no halt on our entire journey. Sundown found us a long way from our destination. The night was dark as ebony; neither moon nor stars came to our relief, and often we were obliged to feel for the wagon tracks with our hands, for fear of straying off into the bush, but constant plodding finally brought us to our temporary home. The clock struck twelve at midnight, as we opened the door of the dwelling, fatigued and mud-covered, from head to foot.

The next day (Monday) Father went to the city and engaged two teams, one horse team with spring wagon, the other an oxen team and lumber wagon. The former to take the family, the latter the household goods. My younger brother and I were left to accompany the man with the ox team and the goods. The roads were in a most horrible condition and the next thing to bottomless. Night found us in the vicinity of Germantown. We halted and engaged lodging with a good-souled German who was the proprietor of what was then called a Tavern. But what was our surprise, on going out the next morning, to find our goods dumped on the ground in the yard and our teamster (I suppose) well on his way back to Milwaukee. While my eyes are not a fountain of tears, I must admit that they were a little moist with anger and wrath at the man who had left us in such a plight. But after a good hearty breakfast and the advice of our genial host, we went on our way toward Stony Creek in hope but not much rejoicing, and reached home that evening. The family was safely sheltered, but the implements for housekeeping were still dumped on the ground in Germantown. The following day Father started afoot to find the goods and some one to bring them. On his way he met Mr. Rix driving two yoke of Mulley oxen, hitched to a lumber wagon. This was his opportunity. After some preliminaries he promised to go and bring the goods, which he faithfully kept, occupying two days' time in making the trip.

We spent the winter in cutting down the trees near the house, and farther away, with a view of getting the land in shape for producing something on which to subsist. The spring and autumn of 1847 witnessed a high tide of Emigration to this section of Wisconsin. Families coming from Ohio, Pennsylvania, New York and many from Europe, especially from Germany and Ireland.

Just at this time a serious question confronted the pioneer mothers in this section of the township. They said how, when, and where are we going to educate our children to prepare them for the duties and responsibilities of life and good citizenship. There was but one answer to their questions: *viz.*, the school. A school we must and will have. It is a well-known fact, when the women of a neighborhood are united in carrying forward an enterprise of this nature, they are terrible as an army with banners, and failure is an unknown quantity. A meeting was called to which most of the settlers responded. The question of securing a site and building a schoolhouse was taken into consideration. It was decided to locate the building as near the center of the settlement as might be. The place was finally agreed upon, but unfortunately the land was owned by a man in Milwaukee by the name of Wait, who had bought it from the government the previous year for speculative purposes. The next question was to get into communication with him. It being late in the season, what was to be done must be done without delay and some one must go to the city and confer with Mr. Wait personally.

No one volunteering, I was delegated to foot it to Milwaukee and transact the necessary business, and to start the next day. Mother put up a liberal lunch consisting of corn bread and honey, with a good large piece of cold roast venison. As soon as I could see my way I started on my long wearisome journey of forty-five miles. I made no halt until I walked into the city, just as the sun was hiding behind the western hills. I had no difficulty in finding Mr. Wait, for Milwaukee at that early period did not resemble the Milwaukee of the present day. I made known to Mr. Wait my errand and he seemed highly pleased with the proposition, knowing that improvements of that nature would help to increase the value of his land. He most kindly invited me to take supper with him, and I could not find it in my heart to refuse him, for I was short at that particular time of hotel fare. After supper I informed him that I would like him to execute the lease that evening. In a very brief time I had the Document safely pinned in my pocket. Whether the gentleman mistrusted the leanness of my wallet, or whether from a true Christian spirit, he cordially invited me to remain with him overnight. I accepted with thanks from down deep in my heart. I also informed Mrs. Wait not to disturb herself by getting me an early breakfast. After thanking them again for their kindness, I was glad of an opportunity for resting my weary limbs.

The following morning, long before the sun's rays sparkled on the waters of Lake Michigan, I was a long distance from the city, and in the dark forest. As daylight approached I noticed a little clearing in the woods a short distance ahead of me. On approaching nearer I saw a small log house and about an acre of cleared land. About this time I began to feel unmistakable evidences that I had not been to breakfast. No smoke was rising from the chimney of the house and a poor prospect of getting anything to eat. On peering into the garden, I discovered a fine patch of flat turnips. I skipped over the fence, filled my pockets and hands, and went on my way rejoicing and eating turnips. They tasted (to me) like Paradise Apples. At noon I came to what was then called Manor's Tavern, I think in the vicinity of Richfield, knowing I had just the amount of change, (*viz.*, 12½ cents) to pay for my dinner. I stepped into the hotel and ordered the dinner with just as much confidence in myself and assurance as a guest of the Hotel Pfister or Plankington in Milwaukee.

After satisfying my hunger, I resumed my journey, and a little after dark I arrived at the end of my long walk.

The men of the district soon rallied and commenced cutting logs for the building. In an incredibly short time the school-house was completed. Benches or seats were made from split logs and hewed on one side, with legs fastened in. A huge fireplace adorned one end of the room and a large box stove the other. The architecture (in style) was the same as that which prevailed in the surrounding country.

The first school was taught by Mr. Allan Frisby. He boarded at our home. I did not attend school as my services were demanded in the woods, cutting down the forest. Mr. Frisby was my own age and withal an expert on the violin, while I made no little pretension to being an adept with the flute. So we whiled away many a long winter evening in front of the big fireplace, giving free concerts and furnishing our own audience.

At this time, the inconveniences of a new country began

to weigh heavily upon us, the greatest of which was the lack of funds. We were obliged to have supplies brought from Milwaukee with an ox team. These consisted of corn meal, a scanty supply of wheat flour, beans, a few groceries, etc. For our meat we depended entirely upon the wild game of the forest, which also abounded with wild bees, with abundance of honey. For coffee, we obtained a root which grew in the bed of the creek called Evans Root which dried and scorched in the oven made a very palatable drink. Sometimes Mother used to run short of saleratus. She would burn a few corn cobs and use the ashes instead. This was called Cob Ash, and answered a very good purpose. In a word we lived the simple life, up to the utmost limit.

The year 1847 was one of great hardships and privation, having no team or cows, consequently no milk or butter. During the winter we had cleared the timber and brush from three or four acres of land. We were told before leaving the East that all that was necessary to raise a crop in Wisconsin was to chop a little hole in the ground with an old ax, drop in the corn, place your foot on it, and go on your way rejoicing. While this system might have been all right in theory, it proved an utter failure in practice. We worked all summer on that little clearing, hoeing the ground all over with hoes, but did not get an ear of corn for our labors.

If the pioneer Fathers suffered the hardships and inconveniences incident to the settlement of a new country, likewise the pioneer Mothers. To them was committed the care and training of the family. She was expected to look after their wardrobe, to keep them decently and comfortably clothed against the rigors of the long, cold winters. I well remember my own dear Mother who used to sit the long winter evenings through, and by the dim light of a tallow dip, with needle and thread, darn, patch, make, and cut down the worn garments of the older to fit the younger, and was often at her wits' end to adjust matters in a satisfactory manner. Were any of the members of the family sick, she was both physician and trained nurse. No hand like Mother's could soothe the aching brow; no voice like hers could give comfort to the troubled spirit. Dear to us is the memory of our pioneer Mothers.

In 1848 my brother Harrison, who was a millwright, came on from the East and erected a sawmill on Stony Creek, which was a great convenience to the settlers. Immigration was very brisk. The sound of the woodman's ax and the crash of falling timber were heard in all directions, indicating that the Herculean task of making Wisconsin what it is to-day was fully inaugurated.

In the fall of this year the State authorized a State Road to be laid from Port Washington to Fond du Lac. The road was surveyed directly in front of our house. The commissioners made our home their headquarters as long as they were able to reach it nights. They were a jolly big-hearted Trio, and their stay with us made an Oasis in the Desert of Our Loneliness. We passed the evenings in front of the big fireplace, singing songs, spinning yarns, etc. In thinking of those bygone days I often think of these lines, "Oh, for the days that never will come back." During this time my imagination was not idle, but pictured to me the old stage-coach with its four-horse team loaded with passengers and the driver blowing his bugle announcing his entry into the village. A scene to which I used to be a daily witness in our Eastern home; but like most other visions of my early years, with the lapse of time it vanished. The road never materialized.

The pen slipped from his hand, that fine, pointed hand twice deformed—by hard work and rheumatism. How should he go on? A pioneer youth; that much was done, the beginning. . . . How had the promise of boyhood been kept? What had come after?

He might have written of his first bride, Serena Cannon. Trembling, in ruffles of muslin, by the pear tree he had planted the day they were married. When she loosened the net from her hair it fell down slowly in folds as black as a crow. While he cleared more land, plowed with the oxen, and planted corn, she did needlework and made wreaths and hats of braided straw. In the dusk they talked of the future. The birth of a son; her fear and her cries; the little body pressing against her suddenly grown-up breast, white, almost blue-white. He was an old man now and the father of six more children; but the part of himself which had been Serena's lover had not lived to maturity—it lay in the past, still interlaced with her body.

He might have written of the Civil War. Farewell. Glad to be going as a musician so that he could hold himself a little apart from the rest, remembering her with his flute at the head of the regiment. The officers—he had known them at home—loafers and bullies; some were drunk, and one of them smiled all the time and found excuses to flog his orderlies with his bare hands. Dysentery, quarrels, and obscenities. Stupor in a blare of music, his lips pursed, his fingers dancing automatically on the flute stops, among men in badly tied bandages. He was often too ill to play in the band. When the fifer was sick, he played the fife. The drummer died; and the army could get along without a flute (Serena's flute); so he took the dead man's drum. Then came the news that his little brother Hilary had disappeared after a skirmish between Union and Rebel troops in Tennessee; and he dreaded the sight of his poor mother when, if ever, he should get home.

Peace was declared. He could not sleep, and felt like a sick animal hurrying home to die. But he knew that he would not die, not there beside Serena; he would grow strong, prosperous, and happy. She had written that their boy Oliver had learned to talk.

Home-coming. Serena lay in a fever. She was not delirious, but too weak to say anything. He never slept, and marched around the bed, and scarcely dared to speak; for he knew that he himself was delirious, in secret. All night her eyes were fixed on him, larger than other human eyes. She died. He wanted to lift the cheap, stiff sheet to look at her body—he had not touched it since the war began; but he thought it would be sacrilege, and did not dare.

A widower. Rose Hamilton, his brother Leander's sweetheart, had lived with Serena and helped her. When Leander returned, he did not marry her as she expected, but went West instead. Henry blamed him, and felt responsible as the elder brother. And how was he going to take care of little Oliver? The child loved Rose. So he asked her to marry him.

It was part of his duty not to let his young wife know his despair; she could not comfort him. His old mother lived a few miles away with his brother John, mourning for Hilary; Henry visited her two or three times a week. They sat side by side, and her roughened fingers often smoothed his forehead. Finally she died; and he resolved to let death have its dead, and to be gentler to Rose. Then his boy Oliver died, and a week later Rose's first child was born, a little girl named Polly.

The rest of his life seemed unimportant. Children were born; Rose always seemed young and coarse; he tried to be kind. There were other deaths, but none so unpardonable as those which had already taken place. The laughter of his sons—he wanted to enjoy it, but could not; their troubles—he left them to his wife; they were her children. There was another war, and his son Evan, who had been so hard to bring up, deserted from the army; he knew that he ought to forgive him for what he himself might have done, but he never forgave anything.

Meanwhile the West, that point of the compass which had glittered with hope like a star, came to resemble the East—the light went out of it. Many years of life had been allotted him, and with them had also been allotted hard work and poverty. Every hope had a rendezvous with disappointment.

The old man sat at the double secretary under the embossed portraits of Longfellow, Whittier, and the rest, and stared at what he had written. What more could he write? What were the picturesque details which had filled the margin of his life, once life had begun in earnest? How could he describe the oxen and the yoke hewn from a single block, the flail joined by a strip of horsehide, the breech-loading gun and the powderhorn—when his mind's eye, only his mind's eye, kept filling with tears? It was too late to shed them now; it had always been too late. He folded the sheets of foolscap and put them in the family Bible. He was seen from the porch, and the expression on his face was so terrible that no one asked any questions.

After his eighty-second birthday he had to stay in bed. One day, as the doctor strode away across the lawn, Alwyn asked his grandmother the name of his illness. "Shrinking of the stomach," she said. He was starving to death.

A few days before the end his grandchildren were taken in to see him. They stood in a row at the foot of the black-walnut bed. On two pillows lay his brown face, thinner but no older than it had been for years, the energetic, indifferent, blue eyes staring over their heads.

This was no magician, Alwyn thought; he was old, but not powerful. Alwyn's little sister sighed. He held his breath, and heard his own heart like a drum slowly beaten with one finger. The old man lifted his head impatiently, letting it fall back on the pillows, and the children were hurried from the room.

The small boy knew even at the time that his grandfather had not died with that convulsive motion; but he would always feel that he had been present at a deathbed. What did death mean to him then? It meant that an old man who was too deaf to hear what was said to him would not complain of the noise they made any more; it meant that they could go into the garden whenever they liked; it meant also that they would have to work in the garden.   These unimportant things—and something more: it was as if the world, in one moment, forgot much that it knew and had never been willing to tell.

4. His Grandmother Tower's Girlhood. Her Soldier Sweetheart. Her Marriage

ALWYN'S grandmother came to Wisconsin in 1847 as a child of three.

She grew up among bearded men, hunters and trappers. George Hamilton, her eldest brother, could not read or write; Enoch had lost one arm in a sawmill; a cousin named Tom Gore also made his home with them. The ironwoods around the large cabin smelled of skunk, whose black-and-white pelts, with skins of mink and beaver, turned inside out on boards, swung from the lower limbs. The three men shot squirrels, rabbits, young coon, and deer for food, and hunted foxes and timber wolves for sport. They went by night to the trees where the passenger pigeons roosted, picked them off the boughs, wrung their necks, and tied them in bunches with string. They said: "Pretty soon, smart fellows like those Towers'll spoil this country. Make a woman's country out of it, just like Kentucky. We're goin' to git out then, west."

Firearms and pouches hung upon pegs, wet boots stood by the fire, and venison smoked inside the fireplace. Their grandmother, whom they called "the old woman," fingered her corn-cob pipe in one corner; she was stone deaf and hated the men. Their mother grumbled, but indulged them as if they were sickly children. She said, "The world is a man's world; women might as well make up their minds to it."

Rose and her sister Adelaide walked four miles

through the woods to attend school, stoning the bushes into which a fox or a badger had vanished, terrified of stags. The schoolhouse occupied a clearing on one of the Indian trails, and two or three times a year the pupils were allowed to stand outdoors to watch a tribe of Pottawottamies pass. The ponies were unshod; their hoofs were broken and spread apart, their hocks deformed by spavins; and their ears, full of burrs, flapped with each stumbling step. Kettles in pairs, rude implements, and tent poles, lay across the withers. The round-headed babies like dolls of copper, borne by the squat women on foot, gave no sign of life though horseflies crawled round their nostrils. A pack of dogs followed, one gray bitch whining and running back and forth in the leaves. The men had formidable mouths, and many of their hard eyes were veiled by cataracts. They rode without saddles, on folded blankets, the muscles of their bent knees lying flat on the bone like thongs of leather.

Rose remembered how her grandfather had been killed in Kentucky. He had been in the sugar bush, stirring the maple sap which boiled over the iron rim of the kettle. When he looked up he had seen two savages who sat in a tall tree, watching him; he had shot them, one after the other; their half-naked bodies had fallen in the underbrush. After that other Indians had waited their chance, and one day had scalped him. Indians like these. . . . But these were harmless. Why didn't they fight? Rose wanted to fight for them or against them, because they were male and emaciated, and looked neither to the right nor the left.

Down the corridor of light branches and stiff trunks they vanished, leaving behind an odor of wild humanity, dogs, and dried meat.

Often Rose walked up and down the trail, hoping to meet them by herself. One afternoon men galloped from village to village with word that the Indians in Minnesota were on the warpath, burning and killing and coming south. She went to stay with a neighbor, Mrs. Aaron Smith, who had six children and whose husband was absent. They watched for two nights with shotguns laid across their knees, the little ones tossing in two beds, the eldest wide awake with excitement. The mother trembled continually, but whispered to Rose the news of the community. They listened, clutching the oily guns, but could hear nothing but the struggle of the branches with the wind. Rose was frightened when a child began to cry, or when dogs whined round a carcass in the forest, but she would not show it; for she felt like a man, defending the weak woman and her babies. Meanwhile, in the far north, tuberculous tribes were howling to keep up their courage; then all the ponies, spotted with sores, faltered, and they rode no farther; it was the last raid in that part of the West. Rose liked Mrs. Aaron Smith and was sorry to go home.

She and Adelaide played truant from school, creeping over the hill, careless of punishment, but eager to enjoy a holiday before they were caught. Their cousin Tom Gore was hoeing in the potato patch; he shouted: "Get back to school, young hussies! Get back there!" and chased them and pelted them with clods. They fled all the way back, not stopping when they left him behind, panting with pleasant excitement.

When she was thirteen years old Rose had a mature woman's breasts and a boy's awkward elbows. Tom Gore tried to kiss her one day when they were alone, and ran after her. She climbed up an apple tree. He caught her ankle and threatened to tear her skirt, but she whipped him with a small branch until he went away. She complained to her brother George, and Tom Gore received a thrashing. After that he called her a tattletale whenever he dared, but seemed to bear no grudge.

During August and September the girls picked wild berries for the market. One morning Rose caught yellow-and-pink spiders to put in Tom Gore's bed, keeping them in her hat. Then the two girls heard laughing voices and went in the direction from which they came—boys' voices at the swimming hole. . . . They crept into a bunch of elderberry bushes. Adelaide whispered, "It's wicked, it's wicked," and Rose covered her mouth with one hand so she could not betray their presence. Adelaide hid her face and would not look.

Sumach dangled its leaves like parrot feathers in a round, black pool. Shirts, trousers, and shoes lay on a mound of butternut roots and sod. A naked boy stood there, white and gaunt; he splashed in among the others. Rose wanted to be swimming with them; the sight of male bodies did not trouble a girl reared in a cabin of careless men; she was comparing their grace and their energy. There were seven: one

sat cross-legged on a log which lay over a bed of cress;
on the round chest of one, older than the others, red
hair glistened in the spotted light. One was lean, one
was short and clumsy, one weak; and the strength of
the strongest was common. Six climbed up on the bank
and put on their clothes; under cover of their shouts,
Adelaide, whose modesty had grown tedious, slipped
away in the woods.

When Rose looked at the one who was left, she
did not want to be swimming there, feeling instead a
surprising, sweet embarrassment; it was the fourth
of the Towers, Leander. Hilary, the youngest, lay
in the grass, also watching his brother, with sad,
bright eyes. The others did not wait. Leander
floated on his back, the color of amber in the water.
He was two years older than Rose, and she preferred
him to all the rest. His blond curls washed in his
eyes, and he laughed with a sound of little splashes
of water lifted and let fall. Resting on one elbow,
Hilary waited uneasily. Rose envied him because,
by the accident of birth, he was Leander's playmate;
they worked side by side in the fields, and slept in one
bed. At last they too dressed and ran down an aisle
of poplars, leaving Rose alone in the elderberry bush.

As she walked slowly back to the berry patch, hanging her head, a fox crossed her path; it looked like
a dog whose pelt was on fire—she did not even throw
stones at it. She found the basket of berries and her
hat; the gold-and-rose spiders had returned to their
webs, but she had forgotten them.

She grew tired of the life at home. She wanted to

look like a lady, like Arabella and Ursula Raeburn, like young Mrs. Henry Tower; and it was difficult to bathe and dress amid the gibes of her brothers, under Tom Gore's agitated eyes. She thought that short skirts made her resemble a boy who is too fat; so a yellow taffeta dress was made for her, with a hoop and seven rows of ruffles. She forced Adelaide to pierce her ears with a darning-needle, and her grandmother gave her a pair of gold earrings she had brought from Kentucky. She put up her hair in a chignon and trained a damp curl over each ear. Her cheeks were as rough and pink as a cinnamon rose.

Then she took a school three miles from home. She was slow at books; the schools she herself had attended had been unruly; so each night she studied the exercise in the speller and the arithmetic problems which she would have to teach next day. She was not afraid of half-grown men, and understood tomboys; the school board congratulated her upon her discipline. The large girl in a grown woman's dress who returned to Hope's Corner at the end of each week had reason to be proud.

On Saturday nights Henry Tower held a singing school in the Corner schoolhouse. He struck the key with a tuning fork and taught them to sing by the scale, *Do re mi fa so la ti do.* All that family were singers; Henry led the men with a pure voice which sounded lonely among the rest, and his lovely wife Serena led the trebles. Hilary still sang with the women—his voice, very sweet and shrill, less like a voice than an instrument—sitting beside Serena, seeming to sing only for her and Leander. Rose also sang for them. She wanted nothing in the world, neither in the wilderness she knew nor in the countries she would never know, but to be acceptable to that family, loved by Leander.

At the end of an evening she said to him: "Will you take me home? I'm frightened to-night."

He only blushed; but Henry had heard, and he whispered, "Leander, behave like a gentleman."

Serena pressed her hand and said, "I hear you're doing finely with your school."

Hilary followed them as if it were a matter of course. But in the dark she could touch Leander's arm, stumbling more than she would have done if she had been alone, and the tips of her fingers tingled.

Soon the neighbors said they were sweethearts, and they were together wherever they went. Miraculously, Leander did not seem to see that she was less beautiful than Serena. He never touched her, but she had read no books and did not expect caresses. Love meant gentleness and courtesy; it meant having many opportunities to enjoy his tireless grace, and being proud as if it belonged to her, and forgetting that she herself was too heavy and too tall. Her failure to understand him moved her as nothing else could. And when that which passed her understanding was kind, she did not require kisses to feel a tumult like that of wild bees over their hidden honey.

They stood under a mountain ash in the autumn. He wore a corduroy jacket the color of his hair and skin. He had grown a beard which did not hide the blush and the smile which took turns in his face. She knew that Hilary was watching them, perched on a log fence; she wondered why, but she did not care. The young tree drooped with its clusters of mature berries, like drops of something suspended over their upturned faces, drops bright as blood, not human blood—the blood of angels. "It's a beauty," Leander said. Rose forgot that Hilary existed and that she existed; there were only two things in the world—the tree and Leander.

If she had been imaginative, if she had ever feared anything which was not physical danger, she would have feared Hilary. Staring at her, his eyes grew large, as if they were a great pair of tears about to fall; and he bit his lips until they bled. One evening she thought it was love; another evening, when he muttered, "Girls who pretend to be afraid of the dark—" she knew it was hate. When Leander was not with them, he was friendly and timid. They met by accident in the woods and gathered mushrooms all one afternoon, and she taught him to recognize a rare variety, almost indistinguishable from others which are poisonous.

Then the Civil War began. Her brothers went quickly, well pleased with the adventure. John, Harrison, and Henry Tower enlisted.

One night she stood with Leander by a gate. Dreamily he said—but with a tone which was like that of decision in a dream—"I suppose I'd better go."

Rose turned sick; she had not thought of that. She clenched her fists in hatred; he was too young, and

he was hers. . . . Then there followed this realiza-
tion, novel for the primitive girl: that was the sort
of thing Towers did; there were ideas and ideals,
quite separate from themselves, quite unimportant,
which they cared about, so much. . . . She would
learn to care, she who wanted to be a Tower—it was
time now. So she laid her fingers against his chest
and felt, through the coarse flannel, his breath going
in and out in a miniature tide; and one word was
almost impossible to pronounce. "Maybe," she said.

So he enlisted. Hilary refused to be left at home;
his mother wept, and he wept with her, but they could
not change his mind. And the farewell night came
upon them all, more suddenly, it seemed, than any
night had ever come upon its own day. The spring
stirred all about Rose and Leander when they said
good-by—beckoning sprays of wet leaves, flowers he
would not find in the South; Rose had no eyes to see.
She was thinking that if he died down there, it would
mean that death was more living than life and more
rich, with a blond boy in its arms. . . . Then she
felt the awkward softness of his kiss—the first kiss;
she smiled, because that was a woman's duty, and because his lips were sweet; and he turned away to go to
war, with his little brother.

When Rose's school closed, Serena Tower asked
her to live with her. She had been received into the
family; she was proud. There was little money,
though Henry, who had enlisted as a musician, sent
home his pay. Rose grew fond of Oliver, the slight
child with languorous eyes, and came to love Serena

more than anyone else in the world but Leander.
Serena was never in good health. Rose did all the
work, trying to make the men they hired care for
Henry's farm as well as he would have done, a difficult task for the daughter of shiftless farmers. She
took a man's responsibilities, and learned the cost of a
man's gentleness.

It was a long war, long as an illness during which
one knows that at its end the time will have passed
like an hour of sleep. There were letters, brief, monotonous, and precious. The draft began; Serena and
Rose were glad that the inevitable had not come to
them as an officer of the law. The widowed mother
of five soldiers sat with them on the porch, thinking
chiefly of the fifth, who had already broken her heart.
They knitted socks, sewed military garments, and
scraped linen to make gauze for wounds, praying that
it would be placed on the wounds of strangers. Lists
of casualties were published. Then Leander wrote that
Hilary had disappeared. His mother fell to the floor,
and refused to eat for many days. After that it was
their duty to express hope tirelessly, without any hope.
Serena fell desperately ill. Suddenly peace was declared. Rose had not time to feel impatience for the
home-coming, caring for the sick woman, the child,
and the old mother for whom alone there was to be
no home-coming.

Leander was the first to return. Rose drove to the
station. He stood before her, heedless and gaunt.
He kissed her. They could not speak. He got into
the carriage; she took up the reins. She told him that

Serena was ill; they said nothing of Hilary; the sound of water had gone out of his voice. They drove to his mother's house. Never again in her life was there to be a moment as cruel as that in which he stumbled forward, fell on his knees, and hid his face under the old woman's hands. Rose closed her eyes; it was not enough—she could hear their sobs; and she herself was all but a stranger. So she got into the carriage and drove away, quite unnoticed.

That afternoon he came to his brother's house. Serena, who had been lying in an apathy which no voice could penetrate, wept when she heard his voice, and cried out, "No, it is not Henry!"

They left Adelaide in the sick room and walked toward the hills. Finally Rose paused and said (for the first time to him and the only time in her life): "I love you. Are we going to get married?"

The pupils of his eyes, large and dark, were shaking. In that voice of some other man, a man who was still in the South, he answered: "I don't. . . . In the war. . . . You don't know— Try to understand. . . ."

But Rose did know and did not need to understand. That knowledge and lack of knowledge could not be endured quietly, standing up, and not alone. She gathered up her heavy skirts and ran, like the wild Hamilton girl who had ceased to exist.

She was crouching on a porch. A man was driving into the yard and getting out of a buggy. She had pressed her head between her hands so long that the gold earrings had left marks on her cheeks like scars.

In that moment she knew what life was made up of; she would never forget again. As if from a great distance, by transference from someone else's thought, she knew that Serena was delirious—it was the doctor who was walking up the path—there was work to be done.

Two days later Henry came. He was too late; Serena could not speak. After the funeral Rose went home, thinking that the rude cabin would never give her up again.

At the end of the month Leander went to California. Henry Tower was living alone with his little son, and one day asked Rose to marry him. She felt as if she had been dead, in an apparent eternity of lazy hunters, their gibes and their quarrels; and suddenly, in the widower's melancholy voice, permission to return to the earth she loved was granted. Leander had not wanted her, but she was acceptable to the Towers.

It was her duty not to let her husband see how she grieved for his brother; he could not comfort her. She did not hope to be loved, and she realized once more how rough and homely she must appear beside the memory of Serena. She continued to grow heavier; the coarse roses did not disappear from her cheeks, but came to resemble dead rose leaves, covered with a network of tiny veins.

Life was not sad, though Henry was obstinate and sad. She never understood him. Would she have understood Leander? She often found him unreasonable; but after argument and protest, when his eyes grew abstract as if they were staring at things which did not exist, or when a rare, bitter word escaped from his tight lips, she folded her arms and gave in.

Her mother-in-law died, saying at the end, "Now I know that Hilary is dead; he will meet me on the other side."

Little Oliver died, and a week later Polly was born. Four more children were born; their names were Ada, James Arthur, Ralph, and Evan. There were deaths in the family, but her children were spared; she gave thanks to God.

Then an epidemic of scarlet fever broke out in the community. Henry and five-year-old Ralph fell sick. An old woman named Minerva Foote came to help her. Henry was delirious and called her Serena. He and Ralph got better. The little girls fell sick. Rose cried by the hot kitchen stove, the hot sunlight pressing through the shutters.

Old Min Foote said: "Now you stay away from them. Who's going to cook for the hungry mouths if you come down with it? I'm childless; I've nothing to fear. They're not yours, anyway—they're God's now, till the fever is past."

Polly and Ada died. Life was teaching her methodically; this was the second lesson; she was a strong woman and could learn. On the day of the funeral the heat was broken by a thunderstorm. The cheap little coffins were of the same length. Rose attended two other funerals that week, children's funerals, saying, "It shall never be said that my sorrow has hardened me toward others."

In the spring of 1884 she received a letter from Leander, which read:

DEAR SISTER ROSE,

I want to come back to the old country. If you'd rather I didn't, please tell me so. I've made some money and would like to buy a little house near you and Henry. After these long years, I love my own people more than ever before. Love to Henry and your children.

Henry said nothing. Rose was glad he was coming back to Wisconsin. It was his home. He would be forty years old and greatly changed, as they all were. He would be her brother now, yet not like a brother, for she understood her brothers; and the Towers were men she could never understand, men she could only love, quite humbly.

Leander's return marked the middle of her life. Thereafter, absorbed in maternal duties and matriarchal reminiscences, she took every disappointment for granted and wanted nothing for herself. In fact, she was more like the strong, serene grandmother, perfectly willing to be old, whom Alwyn knew, than like the girl who had loved Leander.

5. HIS GREAT-AUNT MARY HARRIS.
HER LIFE AND TRAVELS

WHEN Alwyn was ten years old there was a solemn excitement at the farmhouse. His great-aunt Mary, the most romantic member of the family, was dead, and her daughter, a woman in black veils whom no one had seen before, brought her body to be buried at Hope's Corner, as she had requested. His grandparents and his father and mother went to the station to meet her, and they proceeded directly to the cemetery.

There Alwyn and his little sister waited on a stone pile, and stared over the fence, over the shrubs and the monuments, at the nearly soundless funeral. The tall stranger and the great blue-gray box had come a thousand miles from a place called Oklahoma City; and Alwyn breathed heavily as the coffin, covered with bouquets, disappeared in the new grave, because the heroine of an old story had come back to the place where her travels had begun.

This one of his great-aunts had undertaken many journeys in her lifetime. Later in the day her daughter, sitting on the porch between Alwyn's grandparents, told how her house was cluttered with souvenirs of the last journey, a trip to Europe, which appeared to have hastened the old woman's death: water in tiny bottles—water of the Rhine, the Jordan, the Nile; chips of stone from the Alps, and Vesuvian lava; shells from the Channel and the Ægean Sea, all carefully labeled; pressed flowers, a box of sand from the

Sahara, and a picture frame of Italian mosaic like petrified confetti, in which she had placed a tintype of herself and her sister Eliza when they were girls. The care of these relics was a problem; no one had any use for them; they would have to be thrown away. Alwyn wanted them, but his mother said it would be too expensive to have them sent from the Far West.

Mary Tower, born Harris, had been brave, energetic, and virtuous; and Alwyn's grandmother, who had not seen her for half a century, loved her still, and said she was "the greatest of the pioneer women." This adventurous life embodied not all the womanly qualities of the period, but all that his grandmother admired and meant to praise. So she told the story of it whenever she was asked, and in her very old age, on important occasions such as family reunions or Thanksgiving dinners, she began it without invitation.

Thus the life of this woman was fixed in Alwyn's memory like the plot of the first book he ever read. A life in profile, an almost incredible history, a boy's adventure story with a single female musketeer for heroine. . . . Her death added nothing to the adventure, and subtracted nothing from it; Alwyn's grandmother went on repeating the story—the same words appearing in the same order—as if she had been dead a long time, or had never actually lived, or could never die.

So, quite naturally, as Alwyn grew up, the October afternoon on which she was buried, among her relatives and his own, mingled in his memory with the afternoons of her girlhood, at the very beginning of the story. Autumn stood that day like a scarecrow at the crossroads, and the blackbirds, pigeons, and plovers fluttered overhead. Autumn had stood there before, its great sleeves flapping in the wind; and birds in October never know which way they are going. Across the road, like a large dry-goods box, stood the district school which he attended, where, before the Civil War, the dead woman's sister Eliza had taught.

In Eliza Harris's day it was a hard school. The pupils had to stand around the stove in winter, three or four at a time, to keep their ears from freezing. Girls with full breasts and wild boys in their teens founded friendships and flirtations on plans to shame her and make her cry before the class.

One evening, when her work was done, Eliza turned the key in the lock and started home. She shivered at the clumps of bushes so close to the road that they seemed to stagger to meet her. As she passed a willow thicket two or three girls ran out, howling, with switches; half paralyzed by fear, she stumbled away, but received a dozen cuts under her long skirts. Speechless with sobbing and incessant fits of coughing, she pushed open the door of her mother's cabin.

Her failure as a teacher was a tragic misfortune, for her mother and sister lived on her salary. After Samuel Harris's death his widow had sold the small farm he had cleared in the 'forties, rearing the children on the proceeds; now they were penniless.

The widow Harris resembled Eliza. All that evening she shuffled up and down the one room in which they lived—Eliza crying in one corner, sixteen-year-old Mary giggling irrepressibly in another—now raging against the young hussies of the school, now scolding her daughters in turn.

Having been too frightened to see which ones had attacked her, Eliza said nothing to her pupils next day, and left the schoolroom unswept; and the following afternoon Mary came at four to help do the work and to take her home.

Mary was small and plump; she had an olive skin and ash-blond hair; and her way of speaking quickly in a low voice reminded one of a bird. Together they put the room in order and went down the road, Eliza peering into thickets and hanging back.

"It was there they set on me before," she said, but they passed the place unmolested. Suddenly there was a war whoop, and two girls jumped out of another bush, brandishing willow switches. Screaming feebly, Eliza left Mary to face them.

"Devils! You devils!" Mary cried. "I know you, Allie Jones! I know you, Mary Ann Murphy! You'll catch it for this! You'll catch it!" Eliza stumbled forward and backward, wringing her hands; Mary stood her ground. "Run! Run or I'll stone you," she shouted, throwing handfuls of gravel at the girls in flight.

Mary made her sister visit the parents, as a result of which one girl was thrashed, another was taken out of school, and Eliza's authority was strengthened. Mary and the widow gave her advice, but her misfortunes excited her beyond all thought of policy; ineffectual tantrums made her ridiculous, and many parents thought her a tyrant. Matters went from bad to worse, and she coughed incessantly.

There was a harelipped boy who tormented her; he was too big to punish (she dared to whip only the little ones) and it was useless to speak to his father; both father and son were proud of being hated by her. One day in January, when the small children could not get through the drifts, this boy tipped up the bench on which he sat, so that a fat girl rolled on the floor. "Order!" shouted Eliza. The girl and the harelipped boy sat down again. "Ezra, stand in the corner," said Eliza. Smiling, he rose; the fat girl tumbled off the end of the bench again, and the school rocked with laughter.

Eliza overturned her chair and took up a heavy ruler. The boy with the harelip lifted his elbow in front of his eyes. There was a dead silence which frightened her. She set her teeth, broke the ruler in her large hands, and threw the pieces in his face.

A growl rose from the back of the room. "It wan't his fault," one shouted; another, "Do what we said we would." One ran to the door, one opened a window, and the two oldest boys jumped over the benches, lifted her roughly, and threw her out into a snowdrift.

Eliza lay in the snow, choking with anger. Then she waded around the building, went into the entry, and pushed at the door. "You shan't get in here for a while," the one who was holding it muttered. So she shook the snow out of her sleeves, put on a coat, and went home.

During the night, in a paroxysm of weeping, a small quantity of blood escaped from her lungs, and the next day she had a fever. The school was closed for ten days, and then a substitute was hired. "How Eliza Harris had been put out" was common talk, and the subject of two or three quarrels. The widow and her daughters were dependent on charity. All winter the neighbors brought stove wood, sacks of potatoes, and hams, tallow dips and corn meal, and eggs in hand-woven baskets. On the bed, Eliza closed her eyes while her mother complained of unruly girls and what they deserved. Mary did all the work cheerfully.

The widow Harris talked of her relatives in Missouri as if distance had cheated her of a resource to which she had a right. Some one suggested that they be sent south; ambitious men and women who begrudged the provisions, those with large families to support, and those who pitied them, welcomed the solution with equal relief. Two box parties were given in the spring, to which the girls brought supper for two in decorated boxes which were sold at auction to their sweethearts; and a purse of money was given to the helpless women.

Mrs. Harris wrote to her brother, and when he replied, preparations were made for their departure. She dreaded the trip down the great, savage valley; perhaps dreaded no less the welcome of a brother she had not seen in years and a sister-in-law whom she had never seen. Eliza was eager to escape from a

State peopled in her imagination with wild girls bearing switches. Mary was glad to go, welcoming all the years of the rest of her life as if they were people about to become friends.

They went down the Mississippi on a river boat. There were whisperings of the water and a sound of kisses around the prow as it advanced through regular ripples which were like a wedding veil. Negroes on invisible boats sang in the dark, burdening it with their hearts' burden. Spring quickened its pace, and the deck was drenched with unfamiliar odors and unusually sweet rain. Three women going south. . . . The tanned captain followed Mary with his warm eyes as she moved excitedly among the hampers and sacks and bales.

They disembarked and drove overland through poor cotton fields where slaves were at work; and at last they found their relatives, a gaunt, booted man and a plaintive woman. The blond South dozed by the river—it would never wake up; and over the incessant lapping of the water there was a lapping of dry wind, like the river caressing the earth scantily clad with bushes, and like the river yellow with dust.

Mrs. Harris complained, and her health failed. A sallow young man with red eyelids who had come from her home in Vermont began to feel a dolorous excitement in Mary's presence, and finally proposed marriage. When she said No, he trembled with either anger or sadness, and turned his attentions to Eliza, dwelling on the disappointments of the West and wooing her with praise of the East. Mournfully but enthusiastically she agreed. So Eliza and he were married. The preacher had to raise his voice above the sobs which the widow muffled in her sleeve; a few boxes and carry-alls were packed, and they said good-by.

Then the widow Harris died, leaving Mary alone. She was unhappy with her relatives. Her presence reminded them that they had no children; her dependence reminded them of their poverty; all the coming and going, and the widow's death, increased their longing to return to the East—they dreaded death in Missouri. They had nothing to say to Mary; their silence at meals made what she ate seem like the bread given to a tramp on the doorstep, to whom one never knows what to say. So she sat sadly on the porch when her work was done, watching the birds go north; there must have been one in all their number as lonely as she—but luckier, having its wings. She scarcely ever sang now; but when the tunes rose round the dusky shanties they seemed to be sung for her, more heartless tunes than any she could sing.

Her aunt was always ailing, and the doctor, a widower of fifty-nine, lean and cheerful, came to the house every three or four days. Mary knew that he liked her. One day he found her alone, drawing water from the well, and said: "You're not happy. You ought to be happy. Before I leave, go down the road a ways. Meet me. I have something to say to you."

When she got into his buggy he said: "I am lonely. And you've no home. If you will marry me, I will give you a good home."

Mary considered it as a vague necessity—like another journey down another river; there was no likelihood of music on that stream, only years without danger or liberty. Six months later her uncle and aunt returned to the town in the East where Eliza was living; and Mary was the last of her family on that frontier.

Dr. Brandon had a small plantation, six darkies, and innumerable patients. Mary was lonely. She played with the pickaninnies, washing them in the creek and spreading them out on the grass to dry, and with the doctor's help nursed all the sick slaves in the county. On some days she tried to learn their songs; on others she tried not to hear them. The Missouri women gossiped about the way she behaved.

There was a young mulatto named Tartar, the doctor's most valuable slave, who had cooked for him and slept in the house while he was a widower. Mary was always aware of his presence, and never forgot that he was as young as she; and once or twice, as she lay by her husband, this boy's ugly face rose out of her sleep; she confused him with the night because they were the same color, and feared both.

Then in far towns whose names people heard for the first time, the Civil War broke out. After a few days the State was divided, neighbor against neighbor. Private hatreds paraded in uniforms of opinions hastily put together. State rights and the souls of the negroes were taken as a pretext for murderous appetites, and many slept with shotguns at the head of the bed.

The doctor said to Mary, "Better not be seen from

the road with the blacks. All the old women will
talk."

He was a Unionist. "Slavery doesn't matter," he
said. "There'll always be slaves, whether we buy 'em
or pay 'em wages. But a pack of desperadoes can
rule round a post office; they don't get so far as Washington. So if the Union breaks up, we go to wrack and
ruin."

He expressed these opinions recklessly beside the
sick beds of both factions. The fanatical Unionists
could not defend him because he was a complacent
slaveholder, so that of all those whom the Rebels
hated, he was the weakest as well as the least discreet.
An old man, thinking only of politics and the battles
in the East, he paid no attention to the echoes of war
in Missouri, the drunkenness of war increasing around
his house.

Tired by the anger of sick Rebels whom he continued to visit, the doctor went to bed early one night.
In the same room Mary tried to read *Pilgrim's Progress* by the light of two candles, but her attention wandered. She was a married woman now, and her
marriage was like a return from childhood of the
father she could scarcely remember. He too had been
kind. But she was tired of Missouri, tired and terrified. She had heard of a man named Cleaver who was
starting north in a few days with a team and overland
wagon; if only the doctor had loved Wisconsin as she
did. . . . But he had never been there. So she would
have to stay always on the frontier between the North
and the South, with a war breaking out between the

two. She dreamed of the war, the lifting of row on row of mournful trumpets, far away. . . . Would it stay far away?

The stove stood in one corner of the room, her table in another, the door in another, and in the fourth, the bed where presently she would lie, and perhaps fail to sleep, beside the husband who was like a father. She knew by his breathing that he slept, and thought of the sighs which revealed, in the daytime, how troubled he was.

A knock at the door. There were two men, strangers, on the threshold. "We want to see the doctor." Their mouths were so drawn—evidently someone was ill.

"My husband has gone to bed. I will wake him. Won't you come in?"

The two men shouldered her aside and strode across the room, one of them fumbling in his pocket. Then a shot was fired. Mary fainted away.

She lay in the center of the dark, broad floor. The room was empty—frightful and empty. She stumbled to her chair under the candles; she did not need to look at the bed. She was all alone now. Why didn't the darkies come? They must have heard; they were afraid. She could not stay there alone.

The young negro slept in a shack by the door, and she whispered into it: "Tartar. Tartar."

More faintly still he whispered back: "What, missie?"

"Come. They've killed your master."

He slipped in, looking infinitely young, younger than

she now (for she was a widow). His eyes sought the bed, but he turned so they could not reach it.

The two flames fattened while the two candles decreased in stature. Silence lay in the corner with its arms outstretched on a wet pillow. Mary and the boy sat face to face, the distance between them the length of the bed; it was as if they were keeping watch at the head and foot of a bed. Mary was not thinking of the future, not even of to-morrow, nor of anything. Strange how white Tartar's mouth was. . . . And why did the dark plantations betray now and then the anxiety of a dog? No feet and no wheels on the road, the road running north and south down which the war had come, without any trumpets.

A moth staggered in out of the dark and around the candles, narrowly avoiding the flame, and fell at her feet. Blunt wings, white and tan; from the middle of each wing a spot like an eye looked at them. Mary covered it with her handkerchief and let it out through the window; it was so dark that she could not see it fly away, and she began to shudder. More deaths were hiding there, deaths which had not yet happened, and perhaps crowds of nameless men waiting their turn, two by two, to knock at her door. She could scarcely find her chair in the unconsciousness which rolled up under her feet; but she did find it, or she would have fainted again.

There, sitting in the chair which faced her chair, was the black boy. She felt like a fugitive who finds the trace which he has left a moment before, which will betray him a moment after. How swiftly and quietly they would work if they came back and found her and a negro at the head and the foot of the bed, sitting quietly together. How soon they would finish and go! It was madness to stay there. She began to stand up, began to speak. . . .

But she saw Tartar's eyes. So piteous—and they seemed to take the blame for what had happened, for what might happen still; his black face took the blame. The blood ran out of his cheeks as if he were ashamed. By the look on his face, he was begging her not to speak, not to notice him, not to say that the doctor was dead, because he was a slave, that she was in danger because he was her slave now. He had known the old man longer than she; he had as much right to stay there as she had; she could not ask him to go, and she was afraid to go herself. In the trees by the window, the dark sighed as if content with its perfidy.

The negro was as quiet as the body on the pillows; and the charm of their stillness took the place, for Mary, of courage and safety. Far away, a cockerel warned them, by a hoarse note, that day was about to break. Mary tried to get ready for its coming. A pair of fresh candles flickered less. They sat face to face. . . . Creeping up under the sky at last, the morning, with its little gusts, shook the oleanders by the door.

"I can go now," Mary said.

"Where?"

"To the Sanfords'. They're the nearest Union people."

She took her husband's purse out of his coat hanging on a chair, and a roll of bills from a cream pitcher on the shelf, and covered her head with a shawl. Tartar went over to the bed and stood looking down at the stained sheets, his teeth chattering, his tears falling. She left him there.

Rebel houses slept by the road like watchdogs, harmless in sleep; one little black dog sniffed and whined as she passed, and rawboned cattle came down the lanes. The first rays of the sun were as pale as if they also had watched through the night. Three miles of difficult gravel and sand. . . .

She began to call when she drew near the Sanford house. Women in nightcaps came to the door; she told her story; one of them cried and expected her to cry. The men put cartridges in their shotguns, stood them behind the door because she looked frightened, and watched from the windows.

In the middle of the morning a boy came running down the road with the news that a gang of Rebels had buried her husband, burned her house, and were driving her slaves off south.

In fact, a wisp of smoke could be seen over a hill. Behind Mary's back there was the rustling of the women around the stove, their muttering and whispering. She could scarcely ask herself the simple questions: Where shall I go? What can I do? She spoke of the river boats going north, though she did not have money enough for the passage, and learned that the service had ceased on the declaration of war; only a few darkened barges went up and down still, laden with guns, gunpowder, and drunken men—fugitives.

All morning she looked out of the window without seeing anything. About noon the muttering ceased behind her; the family withdrew, and later she saw them gathered around the stable door and knew what they were talking about: the danger of giving her a refuge, the expense of giving her a home. It did not matter what they said. Her husband lay somewhere in a pile of damp gravel, and men were driving her slaves away, crying in the sunshine.

Mary thought: there is that man; there is that man who is going north. A man in an overland wagon, horses, horses galloping north—nobody else could help her. She did not listen to the women of the house when they came in; she touched her body now and then as one touches a purse in one's pocket to be sure it is there. She turned toward Mrs. Sanford. "I'm going to see some friends." The mother and her daughters bit their lips; perhaps they knew that she had no friends.

She walked to a village called Maladee, six miles away, stumbling and trying to make a plan. His name was Cleaver. Was that his name? How could she find him? Her husband had said that the postmistress was for the Union. Among kegs of molasses and sacks of flour, salt, and coffee in the bean, this little woman stared at her with one eye—the other eye was blind.

"Where can I find Mr. Cleaver who's driving north?"

"Ask at the inn. Like as not he's there. I hear he's stabling in their sheds."

Four men spitting tobacco juice from the veranda;

they dropped their feet off the railing. A fat young woman with no upper teeth appeared on the threshold. Mary paused in embarrassment. The young woman dropped her eyes; the men's lids flickered in a row. They knew, even they knew. To them she was already a lonely widow, a young and pretty widow, and they were wondering what she would do about it.

Mary was humiliated but encouraged. "Is Mr. Cleaver here?"

"If you want to see him, you'll find him in the back yard with the horses."

A walk led around the new, dilapidated building. She stopped at the top of three steps which descended to the yard. There was a man on his knees by a great wagon. Her courage failed, and she steadied herself against the trunk of a cottonwood. He was greasing the wheels. She saw the neglected curls running down the back of his neck under the coat collar.

Then he stood up; from the top step Mary realized how tall he was, and caught a glimpse of his face: the soft forehead, the rough sideburns, the moist, bad-tempered mouth. Then she unbuttoned her high collar and folded it back on her shoulders. Lifting her head, she descended; very softly the crinoline brushed the trunk of the cottonwood.

"You are Mr. Cleaver?"

He breathed heavily through his mouth and nodded.

"You are going north?"

"In the morning."

The most important question was the hardest to ask: "Are you going alone? Are you married?"

"All alone. No, not married." The moisture in her eyes, her nervous mouth, her immodest throat, had an appearance of passion. So he forgot that they were strangers and did not notice that she scarcely looked at him.

"Will you take me with you?"

He flushed and drew himself up to his full height. She had won. They walked behind the stable along a little path. She told him her name and her story, making the story less tragic, lest he cease to be flattered. He said nothing about the war; apparently he had intended to leave before it broke out. They made plans; they might have been lovers. He kissed her. Mary had never been kissed by a young man, but his breath was musty with drink.

He let her walk back alone in the dusk. There was a moist place on both her sleeves above the elbow— the axle grease from his hands. Without wanting to die, she wished that she were dead; but even the journey north would come to an end.

She said to the women who were making up a bed for her (the first of many): "I am going north. I have money." They pitied her less, and anger was added to their anxiety. She said, "I will pay you," and they were ashamed. She fell asleep, finding it very strange to sleep alone.

The next morning she went back to Maladee and talked to an old preacher, letting him think she had known Cleaver while her husband lived. He seemed afraid of her, and stammered: "It is a time of war.

God will forgive you. I will perform the ceremony at once."

She stood up before him with Cleaver at noon, and at three o'clock they drove out of town, Mary in her impatience wanting to whip the horses.

Twelve miles were covered before dusk, and all the way Cleaver smiled sleepily to himself, sliding the oily reins through his fingers. They put up for the night in one of seven shacks on a sandy hill above the Mississippi. At twilight the girl looked down into the tangle of currents and great, mechanical whirlpools, and thought of putting an end to her fatigue, already intolerable—of joining, like a lonely vagrant, that caravan of waters. If the Mississippi had flown north. . . . But her home was in the North, if she had one; so she turned back. The bed in that village was wide, but there seemed to be no room for her in it, shrinking from the giant she had married.

They drove north, keeping near the river where towns were not too far apart. Tracks in the sand, new highways of gravel, lanes overgrown with grass. . . . They came to impassable routes, were lost upon détours, and filled quicksands with brush; the horses limped and had to be reshod. He drove while she tried to ease the pain in her back; she drove while he slept with his mouth open. The summer followed them north. The team sucked up water from muddy springs. Cleaver scooped it up in his hands; they lost the tin cup, and Mary drank from his hat. In large, empty valleys the hoofs and the rattling spokes made a sound of delirium.

In some cabins along the road they received a grudging hospitality which they were not allowed to pay for. People were curious. A number of men called them spies; a number of women suspected that they were not married. Innkeepers cheated them; Cleaver was not willing to pay double for a night's lodging, out of bravado; liquor was expensive, and Mary knew that their funds would not last to the end of the journey.

He made friends with women in rowdy taverns, and once or twice Mary had to hunt for him from room to room before dawn. It was always hard to keep him sober enough at night to go on in the morning. Once, as they drove out of a village, he shouted that she was a loose woman who had fooled him into marriage. She covered his mouth with her hands; still, drunk, he mistook her gesture, and began to make love in the wagon, dropping the reins.

They stayed outdoors when the weather was good, to save money. Over their heads the stars glistened like tinsel. Mary thought of her slaves, their kinky heads done up in bandanas, their mouths all wet with watermelon juice. Where were they now? As she lay half asleep she imagined they were near; the night was so dark, their faces so dark—she would not be able to see them if they were near. Slaves marching and singing—and the branches of the trees swung down like whips; but one whose face she remembered did not march with the rest, did not sing (Tartar, the doctor's boy), but stood by himself, every night, looking down at the dead man. Often she wished she had stayed and gone further south with him, for they were both slaves. Would his bondage come to an end before hers did? She wondered which side was winning the war.

She was gaunt and weather-beaten. There were sore cracks in her skin, and one bruised finger did not heal. Her clothes were in rags; she wore a man's coat and a hat of braided straw unraveled at the brim. Cleaver beat her on the slightest provocation.

One night, when it was raining, he started a quarrel in a saloon; a man in high boots cursed her on his account; and they had to leave town at once. The world was full of men like that—booted men; and as she drove through the stormy darkness she thought of them all, without anger, now at last without fear— they had done their worst; and the one she had married, fast asleep in the back of the wagon, made sounds which were almost words but meant nothing.

They crossed the Mississippi near St. Louis, avoiding the city, for they had been told the sheriffs there would demand explanations. They had no more money. In Illinois one of the horses broke out of the stable into a field of wet corn, had colic, and died; they sold the overland wagon, bought an old cart, and went on.

When they came to a town, Mary went from house to house, begging for work to pay for their board; she mended clothes, helped with butcherings, scrubbed floors, and did heavy washings. They moved more slowly, stopping two or three days at a time. Cleaver would make friends in a saloon and want to stay where they were, making fun of her homesickness; but his

friendships were brief, he feared the draft, and remembered, perhaps, that among friends she could earn
more. And sooner or later he would give offense in
the house where she worked; they would have to hitch
up the horse and go on. She was sick, but did not think
again of taking her own life, for beyond Illinois lay
Wisconsin. The road seemed to have no end.

South of Chicago, Cleaver lost the horse and cart
at a game of chance. Mary tried to find the man
who had won, to plead with him; but he was a stranger
and had driven out of town. So she worked for a
month in a general store; an old woman gave her ten
dollars; she denied herself food and hid her savings.
One afternoon they went with the mail wagon to Chicago, took passage on a lake boat to Milwaukee, went
on to Aaronsville, hired a buggy from a livery stable,
and drove to Hope's Corner.

There was no festivity for the home-coming. The
Hamiltons took them in; her old neighbors came to see
her; Cleaver sulked in the barn. Mary could not
talk; Adelaide Hamilton told her story all day long.
Sitting with downcast eyes in the center of the room,
made ugly by deprivation and pain, made stupid by
happiness too long delayed, she did not weep; but
everyone she had known wept at the sight of her.

They moved into a small house which was vacant
while a young man was in the army. Cleaver drank
less, hired out as a farm hand, and registered for the
draft. More than a month passed. Mary watched
the blackbirds and bobolinks, larks, water birds, and
warblers, go south, through the trees of her child-

hood, as the spotted leaves fell; and resolved never to follow them again.

But one day in November Rose Hamilton came running to the house. "I hear your husband's been talking down at the store. They think he's a Rebel. They've given him a day to leave town."

Mary trembled and sank to her knees. The girl helped her to a chair, repeating what she knew. There were footsteps in the yard. Cleaver came in; he clung to the door knob. Rose hurried out by the other door.

"Well, Mary, we're going south again." The clock struck twice, and he sighed, his large body seeming to droop in his clothes. "They say I've got to. I mean those fools down yonder."

Mary said: "Well, Cleaver, I guess you're going. But I'm not."

It was the quick low voice, low like a pigeon's— many times it had roused his anger! He shouted, "And you're coming with me!"

"No. I reckon not. I've had enough of the South. Anyway, I've got to stay here and have your baby."

He threatened; he could not strike her, for he was afraid of her now, afraid of her condition; and he shed a few tears.

A serious man named Will Davis, who gnashed his teeth slowly as he spoke, came to the door to tell him that it was true, what had been said at the store. The men of the country were roused; it was a time of war; Cleaver would have to go. Mary was in the room, but seemed to pay no attention, and said nothing.

She began to put a few clothes in a bag for him. He

kept asking her if she would join him after the child had been born. She would not promise. At noon the next day he set out, and Mary closed her eyes in order not to see him look back.

The child was born dead. Mary grew stronger. She received a post card from Springfield and a letter from Bowling Green: Cleaver had registered for the draft again; he was steady; he had found work; he told her to come. She did not answer. Then a lawyer in Tennessee notified her that he had divorced her to marry again.

The war was over. The men were returning. Mary was teaching school where Rose Hamilton had taught before. Harrison Tower, a millwright, brought her back from her school to Hope's Corner every Friday night, and she loved him almost as if she had been a girl. They were married, and after several years moved to Oklahoma, where they led a quiet and prosperous life. A son and daughter were born, whom she named Brandon and Elizabeth. She was famous in a large circle of friends for her stories of the old days, regarded Wisconsin as her home, and always said that she wanted to be buried there.

On the Tower lawn, after her funeral, her daughter Elizabeth told her aunt Rose about her mother's later life and death; and Alwyn sat in the grass, pretending to read, but near enough to listen.

In her sixty-sixth year, after she had grown accustomed to widowhood, when her son-in-law was in good health and her little grandson had gone away to school and there was nothing to keep her, she decided that she had not seen enough of the world. So she went to visit Eliza; and they sailed for Liverpool in the spring. Together they stayed in Brighton, Monte Carlo, and Homburg, as well as the capital cities, and joined a conducted tour of Egypt, Palestine, and the Near East. Eliza, who had changed little, complained, grew tired, and was ill at the wrong moments; Mary bullied her affectionately. She herself was intrepid in visiting monuments, in subduing officials and porters, in pronouncing the names of foreign foods.

But she grew tired of a continent whose youth had not been identical with hers; she said that the Egyptians and even the Italians were too much like the slaves in the South. She grew timid in trains and hotels, thinking, perhaps, of the men who had hurt her long ago, though she would not admit it to her sister; and she said, "I miss the birds I am used to," the birds of the Mississippi Valley. So they came home.

Eliza, who hated the West still, would not go to Oklahoma with her; so the two sisters parted after a long embrace, and Mary went on alone, a little old lady, brown and plump, in a cloud of veils. When she arrived at her daughter's home, she took to her bed, saying: "No doctors, if you please. I'm very well. But I've earned a good rest."

On the day of her death she said, "I've taken a good many trips in my time," and raised her eyes to the mosaic picture frame in which, arm in arm with her thin, timid sister, she herself as a girl looked down undismayed at her deathbed. They heard her whisper, "Still far to go."

6. His Great-Aunt Nancy Tower's Unhappiness

AFTER the Civil War, Alwyn's great-aunt Nancy Tower married a man named Jesse Davis, and went to Iowa to live.

Two years later a hired carriage drove into her brother Henry's yard. Rose opened the door. Nancy stood on the porch with her child in her arms. Her long fingers were spread in a star against the child's body, sustaining it anxiously. Quite at ease, as if her arms were a chair, the baby boy gazed at his unknown relative.

"Rose, I've come home for a little while. I've brought my child Timothy."

Rose rang the dinner bell—clang upon clang breaking in the solid sky—and presently Henry came in from the fields. When he kissed his sister she burst into tears, gave the child to Rose, and hurried out of doors.

Henry said: "Nancy is overwrought. She was always delicate. Say nothing about it to her."

When she returned she glanced at her sister-in-law timidly and murmured in explanation, "I was lonesome in Iowa."

She had married for love. Jesse Davis's father was a live-stock dealer in Iowa, and he had spent two summers with an uncle who was the Towers' nearest neighbor. Red-haired and heavy, he had worked and shouted in the harvest, while Nancy watched him from a log fence wound with wild vines, her chin in the palm of one hand. At a lake picnic he had come out of the water in a torn blue shirt knotted between his legs, unharnessed a young workhorse and galloped along the shore, beating it with his heels. Nancy had clung to a tree trunk, faint with admiration and terror. Then he had leaped back into the water, and as the light of a half moon filtered into the daylight had floated and swum among the sticky reeds; and he had forced Nancy to wear on her head water lilies in a wet crown.

Young men had never paid attention to her, because she was timid and not unusually pretty. Jesse Davis had forced his love upon her. On Sunday mornings, having searched the marshes, he had brought her bunches of swamp orchids, and on the back of the hand which had thrust them into hers the hair had glistened in a fringe. The girl had shivered and wept; but that hand, brown as the orchids and soiled by the muck of their roots, had seemed to close upon her heart.

But now she did not appear to think of going back to him. Day after day she helped Rose as if it were her own home. When letters came from Jesse, she slipped them hastily into her bodice as a young girl would hide love letters. Henry was surprised that she did not read them aloud.

Both families were troubled. At the end of a month William Davis, Jesse's uncle, a strong, stupid man, complained to Henry: "Nancy does wrong to stay up here so long. Hard on Jesse. I can't guess what ails the girl."

A week later Henry received this letter from his brother-in-law:

I guess you don't realize that Nancy went away from home without notifying me for how long or why. You are her blood and if you comprehend her whims please write. I have been a good husband to her and it is her duty to come back but she doesn't answer my letters. Please write,

Your friend and brother-in-law,

Jesse.

Henry asked Nancy, "When do you plan to go back to Iowa?"

She smiled half-heartedly, as if to distract his attention from her miserable eyes. "Why, don't you want me to stay any longer?"

"It's not that, sister. I wish you'd never had to leave home. But we can't do what we like in this life. There's your duty to Jesse. Have you anything to complain of in his behavior?"

"Oh, Jesse . . ." she cried with apparent relief. "He's a born bachelor. I guess he's a lot happier without a woman there to nag him."

Henry said to Rose: "Nancy must be prevailed on to go back home. We'll ask brother John and Will Davis and his wife to Sunday dinner."

"It'll do no good to force her," Rose replied. "She seems to have fancies. Maybe she's not quite right in her mind since she married."

His face darkened. "Don't say such a thing, Rose."

They came from church: Mrs. Will Davis in black silk, happy and determined; her husband and John

Tower in broadcloth, celluloid collars, and black ties sewed into bows. As they ate the large dinner which Rose had prepared, their eyes blamed Nancy for the blame which they felt called upon to express. She kept the child on her knees. A thick sunbeam fell at her side, in which specks of dust climbed and descended like aimless, miniature people on a staircase; she passed her fingers back and forth in it; the motes took flight, and Timothy clutched at the lean shadow of her hand.

Rose wanted no responsibility for what they were going to say—it was for the Towers and Davises to settle between them; so she cleared the table and remained in the kitchen.

"My nephew writes . . ." Mrs. Davis began, her fine eyes sparkling. "You do wrong, that's my opinion, not to be a good wife to him."

Nancy turned pale. A woman in a dress which glistened darkly, and three men—their glances hard and tired—sitting in a circle. Why had she not thought of an explanation to offer them? She tried to think of one, and suddenly she herself could not remember why she could not go back to her husband.

Her brother John said, gently: "Nancy is a good wife. She has had a long visit with her folks, and now she will go home."

The child laid his little red hand on his mother's trembling mouth and began to whimper. Rose came in from the kitchen and took him out on the lawn where her own children were playing.

Nancy stood up. "Make no mistake," she said in a loud voice. "This is my home. I haven't any other.

But I'm helpless. I'll have to go where you send me." She stood rigidly in the center of the room; her lips continued to move, as if she were giving them a complete explanation, voicelessly.

Mrs. Will Davis snapped her fingers. "Niece, there is no cause to take on so!"

Nancy stopped, and took Henry's hand, "Forgive me, brother. You don't understand, but—you know best." She ignored the other woman. "Uncle Will, write Jesse that I'm coming. Now we'll say no more about it." Then she sat down. "Aunt Permelia, is your brother getting on well in California? I wonder if he ever sees Leander."

To their amazement, she made them talk of other things. So they had their way; and she returned to Iowa.

In January Jesse wrote once more:

Dear Friends:

Nancy can't seem to settle down and be happy. She is expecting another baby. Can't you pay us a visit and I think it would reconcile her. It would do you both good to have a rest and see this great state. My business is fine and I would be willing to send you the fare thinking it would do Nancy good.

Rose left her little children with her sister Adelaide. They arrived in Beacon, Iowa, early in February. Jesse met them in the village, and they drove through the snowdrifts, the jangle of the sleigh bells keeping them from talking.

Nancy, flushed with pleasure and embarrassment, led them to the spare room, and showed them her house proudly. A cot for Timothy stood beside her narrow bed, and she did not open one door at the back of the house. "That is Jesse's room. It was meant for a hired man, but he likes it best."

The soft-maple floors gleamed as if they were marble. She lifted the grass-green shades in the parlor windows. There were armchairs drawn up around a table shining with wax, a crocheted tidy on the back of each; and in a cupboard a dinner set decorated with brown bamboo and birds stood in faultless array amid the paper-lace borders. Rose said, "You keep house as if it were a religion."

A blush colored Nancy's pale cheeks whenever Jesse came into the house. He was a coarse man, boots to his knees, with filth in the creases; his finger nails were black, and his red mustache stained by chewing tobacco; there was an odor of the stable wherever he went. He had a look of shame and anger, and Rose understood him—he was like her brothers.

Boisterously, proud of a sharp deal in horses or cattle, he would stoop for the laughing child; but his wife would cry, sharply, "Don't touch him"; then hesitate, smile half-heartedly, and murmur at last: "You haven't washed. You'll spoil his clothes."

Rose found an opportunity to say to him, "Maybe, Jesse, if you kept yourself up better, Nancy would be more satisfied. You know she's overdelicate."

He hung his head. "I can't be governed by her notions. She married me as I am. I can't change my ways."

Their visit had failed. It was as if there were to be, sooner or later, a trial of Nancy's character, and she considered them only as eye witnesses. She talked inconsequently of her housekeeping, Jesse's habits, and the heat of the Iowa summers—though it was then midwinter. Henry seemed to know what she was talking about, and gnawed the tip of his mustache.

The cutter in which they drove to the station held three, so Nancy did not go with them. Rose said: "Bear up, Nancy. Don't take it so hard. Jesse is kind and a good provider. You'll get used to his ways."

Henry kissed her, clenched his teeth, and walked away without looking back; he could not blame his brother-in-law, nor forgive him.

The cutter slid away in a trough of discolored snow. Nancy began to weep, not because the relatives had gone—she needed to be alone. The house was quiet and sweet, hidden in a snow bank; if she could have it all to herself, with Timothy asleep . . . A sinful thought—for a woman has to have a husband, and a child a father. She fingered her wet cheeks—ah! she had touched the horse blanket, had folded it round their feet; and she hurried to wash her hands. Then she sat in the immaculate parlor and tried to be happy for one moment. But her nostrils quivered; there was an odor of Jesse's stables, faint, floating around her head; and she shrank in the chair, as if it were an invisible hand lifted to strike her.

Spring. The snow and ice went away in thick floods. The sun, rather red and heavy, mounting in the sky, made her think of Jesse in the first summer of their acquaintance. It was lifting itself up to caress every bit of refuse and impregnate every furrow. From the kitchen window she could see wet pyramids of dung being scattered over the fields. In foul nests little chickens which resembled yellow roses broke open the buds of shell; and the garden began to bloom, though she was not strong enough to work in it.

Summer. July burning again, and the air smoky with flies. Nancy could not breathe and could not stop breathing. It was their wedding anniversary; three years ago this same heat had been love. Jesse was to blame. She loved him; love and repugnance were one. She thought, I am a wicked and lost woman.

The evening star peered from a tree; it was like the eye of a bird, a sick bird. She tried to be more religious, in order to forgive the world its uncleanness. With a gross gesture life began; it could end only by decay; if Timothy died, his body . . . Filth fed the roots of the clean plants; Jesse's stables provided her child with food; it was God's plan. Love married to disgust, everlastingly married; it was a sacrament; it was sinful to want to divorce them. She could not repent, but she could be humble; and in her humility she remembered that her own body was not pure; no earthly water could wash it. An impure cradle. . . . Nancy threw herself on the floor, and knew that the pain of her second childbirth had begun, too soon.

Jesse wrote to the relatives in Wisconsin:

Our little girl was born too soon and died. Nancy did not see fit to shed a tear. There is no sense to her misery and it has made her inhuman. She was very sick, but is now doing well.

Later:

This is to inform you of very bad news. My poor wife seems to be failing in her mind. She won't let little Tim drink milk and she washes him until he gets so tired he cries. She is so set against me I don't know what I am going to do.

In November they received a letter from Nancy herself:

DEAR BROTHER AND SISTER,

I want to tell you that they're taking me away. They call it a hospital, it is an asylum. I'm writing so you won't blame Jesse, he's had more than he can bear. They say I'm losing my mind and I suppose they're right. I always thought it would end this way.

Before his wife's eyes Henry's emotion shook his whole body. It was not pity; he had endured his disaster; everyone had to bear his own, at least everyone of that family. It was not pity—it was fear. His own sister broken by insignificant things, in a despicable combination. . . . Could he himself be broken as well and whining madness be uncovered? Her breakdown betrayed their common weakness, hidden by dignity until now. She would not be able to forgive herself; he, too, was humiliated—brotherly love taking the form of shame.

Seven months later Jesse wrote:

They say that Nancy is all right again and she came home. I find her much the same, but she is more clear in her ideas and more patient with me. God is my witness that I didn't want her to stay there any longer than needful but she's far from a well woman. Knowing what her trouble is now, I try to overlook more.

The next letter was from Nancy:

It is wicked to say so but if they had let me have my child I'd have been willing to stay in the Asylum. I dread the summer. I guess you'll say something is wrong with my head still. Don't blame me.

In September Jesse wrote once more:

My poor wife is getting more flighty again. I can't say what to do. If she has to go again I'll have to give up the little boy, for I can't take the care of him that ought to be taken.

In October, without warning as before, Nancy arrived in Wisconsin with Timothy. She threw herself on her knees at Henry's feet, striking the floor with her hands. Rose did not know what to do with herself, so she took Timothy away.

"Don't send me back," Nancy cried. "I'm all right. Don't shut me up again. I'm not crazy. I'll be good and work. I'll do what you tell me. But don't send me back."

Far off under the trees her child could be heard crying, cries muffled in Rose's apron. Henry knelt and prayed. When he stood up his mouth was as firm as if he had not been praying abjectly, but had merely risen from his chair at a family council.

"My mind is made up," he said. "Stop crying. You shan't go back. I'll write Jesse. You ought never to have married. Don't cry. You'd better pray." Then he left her and went to find Rose.

She lived with them until spring, when he found a little home for her in Aaronsville. A miracle took place: as soon as she became accustomed to her new way of life, she gave no sign even of eccentricity. Rose said: "You can't follow the ways of God. Nancy is as sound of mind and body as I am."

She had only one whim, a desire not to be called Mrs. Davis, but Nancy Tower, as if she had never been married. Soon she was earning a good living as a dressmaker and a weaver of rugs. She became proficient quickly in all the feminine accomplishments of the period, and gave lessons in china painting, embroidery, and leather work. She was a noted housekeeper, whose recipes for cakes and jellies were as celebrated as those of any cookbook.

Timothy grew to be a tall boy of great beauty. He resembled Jesse in many respects, but it was not necessary for Nancy even to forgive him for what had been unendurable in his father.

During his twelfth year they were spending a day at Henry's, and she went up on the hills alone to gather elderberries. Here and there in the pastures lay a stone pile, like an altar, on which mullein stood in the windless atmosphere—stalk beside stalk of pale yellow fire; and there was a clucking of invisible quail. Nancy stripped the berries from the bushes in drooping, maroon clusters.

Then she saw Rose's little Jimmie hurrying up the slope. "Aunt Nancy!" he cried; but at first she could not understand the rest, because he was out of breath. He drew near. "Aunt Nancy! Uncle Jesse is down at the farm."

She dropped the basket, the elderberries tumbling out on the short grass. She remembered her husband's letters asking to have the boy at least part of each year; he had come for Timothy.

Her nephew started down the hill again, picking up little stones to throw at gophers. "Come back here, Jimmie," she called. "Where is he now?"

"He 'n' Tim started for a walk toward the Old Well."

He and Timothy. . . . She lifted her skirts and began to run. The little boy stared after her, threw down his pebbles, and hurried home. She was running like a wild animal. Halfway down the hill her hair came down. She frightened a gray cat that was out hunting; it took flight up a tree. She slipped through a barbed-wire fence, tearing her dress. She stumbled in the furrow of a plowed field and fell. Down a lane where there was a spring, leaping from bog to bog; down an aisle of willows. . . .

They were leaning against the railing of the Old Well. Jesse looked prosperous and unhealthy; he was fingering a gold watch fob and his new suit was spotted with grease. He stared at her disheveled hair, her dirty, bruised arms, as if he thought that she had gone mad again.

The boy said in his embarrassment: "I'm glad to see father. Aren't you?"

"Well, Jesse, you've come. . . ."

There was a long pause. A young bull bellowed along the fence not far away, stamping the sod; and a bobolink rose through the sunshine and came down in the parachute of its music.

"You can't have Timothy," Nancy said. "He's

my boy. I've brought him up. I've worked hard to support him for years. You mustn't take him away."

"Well, Nancy, I thought I could give him opportunities."

The boy hung his head, ashamed to have spoiled their reunion, and walked away.

"All right, Nancy, since you take it like that. I don't want you to have another attack."

"I won't have an attack," she said, fiercely. "I've made my way alone now for a long time. I'm strong, Jesse. But Timothy is all I've got."

He stammered: "Say—say no more about it. I'll go away again. But, Nancy, I'm getting on in years. I'm lonesome."

She pitied him. "You can come and live with us if you want to. You weren't to blame. I'll make a home for you."

"I wouldn't do that. No. You'd get worse again. I'd be to blame." He was husky. "Good-by, wife." He kissed her and started back to the farmhouse.

She could see Timothy on the crest of a hill, swinging a stick and cutting off the tops of blueweeds; she called to him, but he did not hear. She started to run after Jesse—but what could she say to him? So she sat down on the cow trough and wept. From a slender elm a leaf fluttered through the air like a bird, and lit on the ground.

Three months later she said to Henry: "Jesse has written. He wants to come and live with me. I've written him to come. It's right he should. He's Tim's father. I'll be glad to make a home for him. He's not in good health, and he wasn't to blame."

Henry stared at the sky and shook his head obstinately.

"You can't believe I'm all right, can you?" she murmured. He had nothing to say.

Jesse arrived. There was a room for him with a door of its own into the back yard. He found work by the day, and later began to drive for the livery stable.

Henry said: "You oughtn't to allow Jesse to work in a stable. You know it'll make you nervous again."

She smiled quietly. "He's always been with horses; he'll be more content. I'm glad he's doing what he likes. I shan't mind. I want to show that I don't mind."

Henry was anxious. Rose said: "Nancy is a changed woman. She has a wonderful character."

Jesse had changed more than she. He was a heavy, worried man, not boisterous any more; his constant anxiety was grotesque. Nancy, busy with her dressmaking and living for her son, seemed only half aware of his existence. Her good-natured admonitions were more terrible than tragic reproaches. He was never at ease in the house; exchanged his shoes for carpet slippers when he came in; was afraid to sit down in the clean chairs; and ate with downcast eyes for fear his wife or son would look at him with disapproval.

Henry refused to hear his complaints, so he complained to Rose: "I'm not a man in my own house.

She can nag at me without saying a word. Tim takes her side. She treats me as if I were a boarder."

When he was working away from home he was more like his old self, coarse and happy-go-lucky. But he grew strange in his ways, arguing with himself as if in his second childhood, and giving the horses in the livery stable strange names: Lavina, Jesse, and Jubilee, instead of Topsy, Dobbin, and Baldy. He was a man who had provoked madness—it might happen again; and he felt the angry loneliness of those who are dangerous to others.

He wrote to his brother in Iowa to dispose of his house and his share in their father's live-stock business —yards, pastures, horses, and wagons. He drew all the money out of the bank when it came.

Nancy remarked: "I don't know what has become of Jesse's money. Goodness knows I don't want it, or need it either. But I hope he hasn't made some outlandish investment."

One Sunday afternoon the Towers had a visitor: a stout woman of middle age in untidy billows of brown percale. Her hat tipped forward under an ostrich plume like a horse's mane. She advanced over the lawn in a stately fashion.

"I don't know as you remember me. I am Mrs. Jervis, a widow, and live over by the sawmill. I went to school to you, Mrs. Tower; I was Lavina Trump. Your brother-in-law, Mr. Davis, stayed with me the time he was working on the State Road. I want to ask your advice about something."

She was embarrassed without being distressed.

"Well, you see, it's this way. Jesse was quite nice to me. It seems he's not so happy at home."

She cleared her throat. "Now the other day he came for a visit. I noticed how he had something in a handkerchief. He told how he had sold his property in Iowa. Now what I want to ask is, is there any trouble between him and your sister, that is, his wife, and is he planning on leaving her? Because I've always had the greatest respect for your family, and don't want to cause any trouble. Because all of a sudden he gave me the handkerchief and said he wanted me to have it and would like to marry me. It was full of bills—really a lot of money. I thought I ought to tell you."

Henry sprang to his feet. "The man is mad!"

"It was his wife, I thought," the widow murmured. "I heard she was out of her mind once."

Rose clapped her hands together. "The Lord help us!" she cried. "This beats all!"

"He's been acting queer," Henry continued, pacing about the room, "and now he doesn't know what he's doing. I'll have him taken in custody. I tell you, he's mad."

Mrs. Jervis sniffed and wiped her eyes. "I'll tell him. I'll stop seeing him. To mislead a widow—it was hard." She took her leave, trying to be majestic and complacent in a way that suited this turn of events.

Henry said to his wife, "Don't breathe a word to Nancy about this widow."

Jesse announced a few days later that he would have

to go back to Iowa to look after his affairs. "You must understand, Rose," he said, "that I'm a miserable man. My only friend, a woman you don't know, has showed me the door. There's no place for me anywhere."

He never returned, and did not answer Nancy's letters. She wrote to his brother, who replied that he was doing chores for a well-to-do farmer who was bedridden, and was in poor health himself.

Nancy did not understand why he had gone; in one way or another, it must have been her fault. His breakdown was a mocking repetition of her own—her own reversed. She asked herself if she ought to have led a different life, and could not answer. Confused and disappointed, she mourned for the fat, unreasonable man she had loved, for the marriage from which she had fled. Timothy was impatient with her melancholy, as his father would have been; and in fact, no one could understand her.

Then Leander came home; he had always been her favorite brother. He had been away during the entire period of her troubles, and wanted to know what had happened; so she talked to him by the hour.

It was a trial of her life and character. His thin face never frowned, never smiled; the tired woman, tired of her own courage, hoped that God's face would be as indifferent and gentle. He understood. Not any one person had forgiven her—not Henry or Jesse or even Timothy, not Leander whom she had not wronged; but somehow, she had been forgiven. As

she told the long, redundant story she reexperienced
the terror of being loved, the shame and loneliness of
having lost her mind, the pity of being a widow without the intervention of death; reëxperienced all these
things, and did not mind them any more.

7. His Great-Uncle Leander Tower's Return. The Adoption of Timothy Davis

THERE was a small house which appeared to have stolen out of Aaronsville as a heartbroken man withdraws from a crowd which he has joined for distraction. Upon his return to Wisconsin, Leander Tower bought it, with all the furniture its owners were willing to leave behind them. His cottage in California was occupied by tenants; but he knew very well that the surrounding fields, on which they hoped to make a living as gardeners, were less fertile than ashes, and doubted whether the rent would ever be paid. So he decided to become a rural postman, and in due time was given an appointment.

Every morning before dawn he harnessed a little sleepy mare, called at the post office for the mail bag, and drove from house to house over a fixed route. He placed under the visors of mail boxes letters from distant sons, post cards covered with kisses, testimonials of drugs which cured all pain, mental and physical, and seed catalogues; and sold stamps and envelopes to housewives or to haggard little girls in pigtails. No one dared to say that he read the post cards, but everyone was embarrassed by his look of understanding.

The correspondence in his custody, none of it addressed to him, represented life and his relation to life: hastily written outcries, half-articulate avowals, and merely practical questions and answers, passing impersonally through his hands. The syncopation of the horse's hoofs, the faint thunder inside its body when it ran, the drifting fields and branches, soothed him; his mouth relaxed and his eyes grew drowsy. . . .

Winter was a hard season for the postman. The pure sky hung down like a bridal veil. Moist snowflakes pressed with a cruel sensuality here, there, and everywhere. Blizzards reached inside the closed wagon and inside his coonskin coat, to embrace him. High drifts had to be opened with shovels. There were bad days in January when he did not dare leave the village, and the routine which relieved his melancholy was interrupted. But the Wisconsin spring, so remote in January that one forgets what it is, returned at last automatically, its damp mouth half open, full of music—never looking at Leander with its abstract eyes.

He began to surround his house with a garden. One could not see it over the mock-orange hedge; but intermingled with the odor of dust, of sweating horses, of a sweetheart's cheap scent, the passer-by was likely to detect the odor of Leander's herbs: sweet basil and carroway, fennel and coriander, dill, sage, summer thyme, true lavender, and wormwood. The whole garden, without the usual showy borders, without the usual golden-glow and peonies, resembled that bed of herbs. The voluble earth, fond of assertions and repetitions, had been forced to whisper a nervous poetry.

He separated the plants, each one perfect of its kind, by artificially arid spaces, and covered the roots of an Ophelia rose with a pavement of pebbles. Two moss roses appeared to bleed from their own thorns. There was mourning-bride thrust full of stamens, one or two flame-flowers, and moonwort, and rock arabis. In the autumn, on the brown dusk, a day-lily with its pale face of a frightened boy, went to sleep.

Leander placed a stool on the path and crouched there, hiding his mouth in his lean hands. A dwarf chrysanthemum sprinkled the air with acrimony. The walls of the sky, like those of a church where nothing has ever been consumed by burning, smelled of a dead fire. An atmosphere of fatigued passion, where passion had never been free. As if he were a man so old that no night is of interest in itself, his thoughts always began: On such a night . . .

The Civil War. A village turned into a barracks, a fence turned into a stable. A mule broke loose and kicked a dog, which rolled howling in the bushes. Candlelight pointed by tents. The odor of oleanders and diseases. An accordion out of breath on a soldier's lap, roughly embraced and crying out. Here and there on the ground camp fires lay like red roses. Seeming to inhale the perfume of one of the fires, there stood Hilary all alone.

Leander could not recall clearly the days when his sister-in-law Rose had been his sweetheart, but he could remember remembering them during the war. Military sorrow mixed with sweetness—Rose's former sweetness: the cinnamon rose muffled in thorns, the rose all burning cheeks and awkwardness. Then the bright mornings had been so bright that love had thrown shadows in every direction, so bright that he had paid no attention to the shadows. . . .

Shadowy Hilary following them over the hilltops, watching them from a rock or a log fence; a very calm attention, without curiosity—the boy understood everything about love but its cause; watching with the fright of one who sees something unnatural happen every day. One night, one of the boy's hands extended toward Leander (in silhouette against the window over the bed they shared), the other hand taking it by the wrist and drawing it back. A good-night kiss, abrupt and as it were disdainful. Strange behavior. . . . On which of these occasions had Hilary been asleep? Day after day, night after night, intermingled with Rose's wide-awake passion, these obstinacies of sleep. . . .

Then Leander had thought it sufficient to be fond of his brother; years too late he tried to understand him. Hilary's enthusiasm for the war should have reminded him that it would be fatal: delight in being a frail child in the army, because Leander had to defend him night and day against bullies; delight in the fact that relatives and friends were far away; displeasure when letters arrived. His excitement was a sort of joy, a sort of joy which broke his heart because he knew it could not last forever.

For Leander the war and his own life were divided in two parts by the hour of Hilary's disappearance. Nine o'clock of an evening in 1864: singing interrupted, the jokes of great fear, half-starved horses whinnying, the enemy close in the dark. Just after the boy left him, staring back over the camp fire with one of those cold expressions which cover inexpressible feeling, Leander understood what it all meant, and whispered one word to himself: "Love . . ."

He knew now, in his fortieth year, that if he had been able to believe what he had whispered then, he would have felt an impossible yearning; that if it had been peace time, if he had been at home, he would have been afraid. But the war that night had been altogether fear. One despair more or less, one word spoken or unspoken, changed nothing—the war went on. About half past nine the guerilla fighting, which lasted all night, had begun with loud curses in two dialects; a gun discharged, and a dog screaming here and there, having been shot. And no one had realized until midnight that Hilary was not in the camp.

Over Wisconsin the moon rose, and it looked like a silver pitcher, and a little stream from its mouth splashed on Leander's temples. He thought of sleep: "If you sleep with the moon in your face, you'll go mad," his old mother had said. He went indoors, gathered up the remains of supper—folding cheese in paper, laying aside cobs of sweet corn for the pig, pouring out milk for the cat when she came in from hunting—and blew out the lamps.

But there was no rest in the wide, second-hand, walnut bed. Coming to him over the pastures, the music of a barn dance throbbed as if it were a blood vessel in his own body. He was healthily tired, but could not sleep; he had to go on thinking all night about that hour which had divided his life in two parts.

His regiment was established in a deserted village called Belle, in the Tennessee hills, a little way from the army itself (exhausted along that part of the line by dysentery), to distract the Rebels. A swamp at the foot of the hill was always full of their sharpshooters. A little road was the boundary line; it was called the Bad Road—nobody walked on it. The best shots in the regiment, lying on their stomachs under trees, waited for a Southern face to show in the leaves. If one's foot slipped on the edge of a gully, one was never heard of again.

There were three brave sisters from Michigan who traveled about, giving concerts for the men; they sang at Belle that night. In a creaking cart drawn by a mule and escorted by dirty, bearded boys, they drove into the village and climbed up on the church veranda. Three women of middle age—the firelight shook on their slightly red faces. They opened their chapped mouths, and three tired, half-male voices—now in unison, now separated in simple harmonies—sounded loudly among the broken porches and the tents. One or two bats hurried in and out of the window without panes over their heads. They sang, *Break the news to mother, Tell her I love no other; O my Darling Nellie Gray, They have taken you away; The Battle Cry of Freedom* (in which many of the men joined); *Tenting To-night;* and *In the Gloaming.* Hilary and Leander sat on the cot at the door of their tent.

No one understood what happened then. Perhaps the pickets along the road had drawn away from their posts toward the singing. Or a Rebel came up out of the swamp and slipped between them. A shot was fired; canvas was ripped by a bullet. The singing stopped on a high note; one sister clasped her head, another pressed her fist against her mouth; a hoop skirt caught on the balustrade and tore. Another shot was fired, and something crashed heavily in the brush. The sisters climbed into the cart; somebody whipped the mule; soldiers ran ahead, holding their guns in both hands; the cart rattled out of sight up the hill toward the army. There was a long silence.

A tired lieutenant limped into the firelight to give an order: the pickets were to keep as close to the Bad Road as they could; the rest were to stay where they were, inside the camp, but nobody was to go to bed. He stumbled over a sleepy little negro who was the soldiers' pet. The child vanished, whimpering; the officer sighed.

Leander lit a candle in the tent. Hilary looked as if the singing had made him drunk. Leander took a purse from his pocket and unwrapped a tintype of Rose: the earrings in the shadow of ringlets, the black lace mitts and great ruffles, the face waiting its turn, waiting for peace to be declared. "I go out to the Bad Road at midnight," he muttered.

"What are you moping about? What is the matter?" his little brother muttered.

Leander was taken by surprise. "Oh, we've had enough of this. I want to go home."

"Home to Rose . . ." the boy whispered. "You're not my brother any more." He put his lean hand on

Leander's wrist, and the fingers opened and closed. "I wish . . ."

"What?"

"I wish—the war would keep on always."

Leander stared at the tintype, and below it the young excited fingers, and between them the short yellow hairs on his own wrist catching the candlelight; and he saw Hilary's other hand creep up among the wool blankets. Suddenly Hilary snatched at the picture. Leander thrust it into his pocket, and he was holding the boy by one shoulder. "Don't be a fool," he said huskily.

The boy stood up. Something which had given off sparks for many days, for years, had caught fire in the dangerous night, in the singing and the homesickness—it burned by itself; and the boy's thin body seemed to sway inside the tent. "I wish," he said with great difficulty, "that I'd never been born—your brother. I'd rather—be dead. I don't—count. The war won't—last. You'll go back—to her. What'll I do? I want, I can't—"

He stooped, and was outside the tent, and stared back over the dying camp fire.

Leander resented the understanding which followed; he was too tired to think, and too lonesome; that night was too dangerous to think in. But he could not help whispering to himself, "Love . . ." He wondered where Hilary was, and thought of hunting for him among the soldiers. There was a noise of running and two or three reports near the swamp. He cleaned his gun. At midnight he crawled on his stomach to the Bad Road; the tired man who was there crept back toward the tents, and Leander whispered to him: "Tell somebody to find my brother. I don't know where he is." He killed a Rebel. After that everything was quiet. The man who relieved him toward dawn said that Hilary could not be found.

Leander as a man of forty, sleepless in his empty house, repeated that night in his imagination. The dawn when it appeared was greenish and sluggish— so had that other dawn been. They had not been able to find Hilary among the bodies which lay in the bushes. Leander felt sick at dawn, but he was a strong man; so he would get up, harness the mare, go on his mail route, and work in the garden; he could do what had to be done. Nevertheless, he realized that he ought not to go on much longer living alone.

He was universally respected, but had no intimate friends among his neighbors. The farmers were embarrassed by his flower garden and his sad politeness, and country women regard bachelors with timidity. It was clear that he did not mean to marry, and those who had maiden sisters growing old in the family resented his peculiar way of living.

Because of their love of flowers, he and Mrs. Ira Duff, a woman who was not generally liked, came to be friends. They exchanged seeds, bulbs, and cuttings, and read each other's half-dozen books; she put gifts of cookies and preserves in the mail box; he grafted her young fruit trees and prescribed remedies for worms and blight; and every week or two they spent an hour together in rather formal talk. He was not a churchgoer, and Mrs. Duff would say: "Leander, a man of your refinement would do well to attend church. It looks as if you didn't think yourself as good as those that do."

"Ursula," he answered invariably, "I do not understand God's will. I can't pray for what would come too late anyway, and I can't see fit to say Amen to the life I've had to live. I'm too sad a sort of man to be a hypocrite."

The proud woman, whose husband was notoriously insincere and pious, smoothed the pleats of her dress. At the end of their conversations they were always separated by two sets of secrets, to which neither referred directly.

Leander often thought of going to church with his family, in order to teach a Sunday-school class. He was drawn toward boys of his little brother's age and tried to gain their affection, making kites as large as barrels, setting the broken legs of dogs in splints, and distributing puzzles whittled out of basswood with which they might mystify one another. On the Fourth of July expensive fireworks were set off in the garden, and he did not complain when his lilies were trampled underfoot. Hilary would always be young, since he was dead; so Leander was unwilling to be old. He watched their rude, flushed faces, and listened to their laughter; he also flushed, with eagerness and anxiety, and tried to understand the remarks which they shouted to one another in his presence.

Sometimes he imagined that Rose's boys resembled Hilary; but they were rough youngsters, and suspicious

of him, like all the rest.   For he could not tolerate
their hunting, the amorous cruelty with which they
killed things and carried in their pockets rabbits' feet
and birds' tails.   He was strict in other ways—angry
if they spoke immodestly of women; and all their mothers approved his good influence.   So it became a mark
of prudery and effeminacy to be his friend, and at last
the good postman began to seem ridiculous as well as
sad.

His relations with his family were warm, without
spontaneity.   Rose offered him the same love, pretending to nothing and understanding nothing, which she
gave Henry; it embarrassed him, seeming to be less
than a husband would want and more than a brother-in-
law had a right to.   He himself could do no more than
remember that he had loved her.   Love had been his
way of being happy when he was young; he had grown
old overnight, and unhappiness had become a habit.
A seventeen-year-old habit . . .

Seventeen wild summers and winters in California
—there was neither fall nor spring out there.   The
uneasy peace which he enjoyed in his brother's house
aroused a host of images of the West, otherwise un-
recalled.   A lofty place full of fat foliage and pro-
voking flowers, where the sun crawled away to sleep.
A grunting sort of laughter, loose women, and spilled
liquor.   Gold like a drug in newspaper bundles or
dirty pockets; one shouted when one heard of it, and
got drunk because somebody else had it.   Tedious danger day after day, as if the war had never come to an
end.   There Leander had made fun of all the spells

which had been laid uselessly on his youth, even Hilary's spell. In the lamplight, with one of Rose's children on his knees, the ascetic man often shook his head incomprehensibly, having heard in his own mind a venal whimper, or a curse, or a mouthful of obscene song. Only the fact that after Hilary's death his heart never could be warm again had saved him from dissolution.

He received from Henry a limited affection. The little man was anxious to show that family ties among the Towers had endured the trials of life. But he believed that he had a right to have a brother whom he could admire, and regarded Leander as a weakling, a man with a sick will.

Leander asked himself many questions as the three sat in silence: Had Henry married Rose because he had run away? If he had become Rose's husband, would she have loved him no more than she loved Henry? Was she capable of other love than this deferential devotion? How much had she understood? Sometimes he was hurt by her lack of interest. Whom did she blame: him, or Hilary—or God? She seemed to blame nobody.

When in 1885 she was pregnant once more, Leander learned that she had forgiven the boy his share in their tragedy, if she had ever known that he had a share; for she announced that she meant to name the child Hilary. The day after its birth Leander stood by her bedroom door. Rose was amazed to have given birth to a female child. Her other little girls had died; she had three rough, strong boys;

the world seemed to be a man's world. . . . "I was going to name it Hilary, as you know, Leander," she said. "What shall we call the little thing? You give her a name."

Between the lace curtains Leander's eyes seemed to hunt an aisle through the trees, a dip in the sky line, where he might catch a glimpse of his garden. "Call her Flora," he said.

Then he touched with one finger the tiny hands, red and still wrinkled, and the reddish-yellow down on the tiny head. He too wanted a child. He envied the domestic affections of that house, and contrasted it with the quiet, empty cottage among the snow-in-summer and the lilies (now beginning to dry up) where he slept with recollections and was childless.

His sister Nancy was nearest his heart. They two had disgraced the family; level-headed people had thought them nearly mad; and they experienced an intimacy of regret. But it was a one-sided intimacy: she told the history of her heart; he dared not tell his history, so he held his peace. His excesses in California had been brought to an end by satiety, not by remorse; no repentance and no expiation—there was not enough energy left, he supposed. If he had talked about that, to Nancy, for example, he would have been a sort of outcast at once. More or less an outcast as it was, though no one else knew it; for that story set him apart from the rest without being told.

He said to himself quietly (not pitying himself) that he was the more pitiable of the two. His tragedy had come to an end; Nancy's had not. His brother was dead; her husband was alive, and when everything else failed, she could hope for a miracle. He had nothing to hope for; miracles were not performed on the hearts of the dead. There was Lazarus . . . But Lazarus had been dead only a little while—twenty years had gone by since the war; and if Lazarus had been a boy like Hilary, he would have refused to come to life.

As Nancy talked to him, he talked to himself, without moving his lips, repeating, contradicting himself. No, Nancy's troubles were always at an end; because she was a woman and less thoughtful than he, she had the gift of letting each moment vanish immediately into the past; day by day she outlived yesterday's sorrow. In Leander's mind every moment left an indestructible remnant, as each dying coral plant in the sea leaves a bit of stone where it lived, pink with its blood which does not fade. All the moments of his life lasted; that nine o'clock during the war, for example, when he had felt Hilary's yearning and his reproach, resembling hate so closely . . .

He smiled as he saw Nancy's eyes brighten, and realized that from the mask of his affectionate face, while she had talked and he had failed to listen, she had received a sort of blessing or absolution. Then she went down the path toward the road, where over the hedge he could see a horse's mane and its withers, and her son Timothy's face. Leander smiled severely; certainly he was the more pitiable of the two, for she had Timothy.

Timothy Davis was a boy of great stature and almost perfect beauty. He was indebted to his mother's family for his eyes blue as a plum, his pointed lips and small nostrils; he inherited from Jesse Davis the burned pink of his skin, his very large hands with round nails, and a certain rudeness of bone and ripeness of muscle, even in childhood. He was the sort of boy who would be mild in ruthlessness, who would reject more gently than other men accept what they have longed for, who would long for little or nothing, and who would never have to learn, or hesitate, or pity.

When he was sixteen, his mother, lying in bed with an influenza which no one feared, was startled by a premonition, and sent him for his uncle. When Leander entered his sister's bedroom, her eyes hesitantly uttered the word death, but she said merely: "You must be lonesome there by yourself. Tim can help in the garden. I've spoiled him but—but he's a good boy."

Leander understood only with the final sentence what her eyes were saying.

A few days after her death in December, 1885, Leander received a letter from her husband's brother in Iowa, saying that Jesse had gone west with a railroad construction gang as a teamster, and his whereabouts were uncertain. He showed the letter to his nephew, and said anxiously, "You might as well stay with me, don't you think?"

Timothy said, "I could shift for myself, I guess . . . But I s'pose I'd be lonesome. Thank you."

Leander ceased at once to consider his life as a homogeneously bitter thing, with a familiar logic and cruelty of its own. He was not afraid of the incon-

gruity of his happiness. He no longer dreaded the
mail route, but welcomed the cold, the obliterated
roads, and the blizzards; for at home by the fire was
Timothy, waiting for him and dreaming over a book.
Leander knew that he did not actually wait, being incapable of impatience; but he mingled his emotion with
the boy's unconcern, deliberately; every day he himself
waited in imagination for his own return; so great was
his joy. It was poignant joy, because he thought its
days were numbered—Jesse would send for his son.

But in March Timothy received a letter from his
uncle in Iowa: "Brother Jesse is dead;" the name of a
town in Texas, the date of a month in midwinter; "if
you are a strong, steady boy, would be willing to give
you a job in my business." Timothy raised his eyebrows as if death were a stranger who had entered the
room rudely, without warning.

Leander asked: "Would you be willing for me to
take out papers to adopt you? I shall leave some
property out West which may be worth a lot of money
if people don't get as sick of California as I did."

"All right," the boy answered.

Spring came down along the full watercourses, and
its eyes seemed to single out Leander. For twenty
years he had seen the yellow and gray bills of the birds
move, without hearing what they sang; now he could
not believe his ears.

There followed three years of happiness, very difficult happiness which prevented him from remembering the war. Instead, night after night, he was kept
awake by a troubled gratitude for the yesterday and

to-morrow between which that night lay. California came into his dreams as if it were a hope; there was a tune which he could not hear but saw lying out straight in the air, a mountain broken open and turning into a rose—but never a dream which disturbed the next morning. His desires did not hurt; they were a secret which enriched him with its embarrassment, and he loved his nephew more because he could keep it from him. He told himself that Timothy gave him the place in his affections which his father had not filled.

The boy was magnificently idle. Sunshine was his energy—he lay in it; the fire in the stove was industrious for him—he nestled close to it. Every morning he tried to make coffee before Leander went out with the mail, and every morning Leander actually made it. He shivered sleepily by the hearth, his wide throat unbuttoning the flannel nightshirt, his legs crossed inside an old fur coat, and often fell asleep again before Leander left the house. He pretended to work in the garden, but was afraid that his awkward hands would hurt a plant. He knew *Gulliver's Travels* by heart, and would read no other book, gazing at his hands and imagining himself a giant in a race of dwarfs, gazing at the hills or the great clouds and imagining himself a pygmy in a race of giants. Leander wanted to teach him Spanish, but he learned only one song, which he shouted beautifully and incorrectly. Leander tried to rouse in him some ambition and wanted him to go to college; but the boy could not remember from day to day, of what he was failing to be persuaded.

Rose understood him. "He is what my brothers ought to have been," she said.

Henry muttered, "That boy won't amount to much."

Leander was content. So many anxious hopes of their family given up at last; one pair of Tower eyes which refused to look into the future; one flower not fertilized by hopeless ambition; one less regret to wither on the family tree. No embarrassment, no vanity, no resentment or covetousness or haste. . . . Timothy reversed the family formula, which was to be proud in anticipation, ashamed in retrospect. His hopes were humble; therefore, Leander thought, he might be happy to the end of his life.

Leander's wages from the government were small, and it was often difficult to make ends meet. But in 1887 his tenants in the West suddenly paid the overdue rent. It was a good omen; and he thought, incidentally, that for some reason his property must have increased in value, that the renters had hastened to fulfill their obligations lest they be ejected. He gave Timothy as much spending money as he dared, in view of the family disapproval. Every six months thereafter a payment came, and they had everything they wanted.

For three years Leander's felicity did not seem to diminish, but prepared its own end as a summer does. He had certain principles, rooted in emotion, which could not be set aside, even to please Timothy. There was his horror of hunting. "If men weren't so used to killing animals," he said, "they'd not kill each other." He told again and again how he and his brothers and their like had exterminated a race of large pigeons, feeling for their feet among the branches at night, strangling them, and carrying them home in baskets, more than any family could eat. He made the whole world seem for the moment nothing but a dreary woods where birds had been slaughtered, and as he spoke a dark disapproval of his sensibility increased in Timothy's eyes; it was like the twilight in a tree which favors the designs of hunters.

Furthermore, the fine young men in the country, including Timothy's cousins, worked all day and were usually exhausted at night. Those with as much time on their hands as he had—younger sons of retired farmers, village merchants and barkeepers' boys, and livery-stable drivers—were on the whole passively vicious and drunken. Leander thought that drunkenness was appropriate only to sorrow, and wanted his boy to have as little to do with one as with the other. So, courteously but severely, he prevented him from forming close friendships in the village.

There were moments when Timothy's impatience was evident. This impatience seemed to say that he did not want one man's affection to displace the good-natured approval of the whole world; that he did not want to have to say yes or no to anything, and did not want to love or be loved. Then Leander would realize, for a moment, that only some sort of slavery could hold two men so unlike together: the slavery of common memories, or duty, or poverty, or passionate love. Timothy was free. Leander would gaze at the young giant sitting with his face in the sun or curled up by the stove; the hair on his head like a military cap of fur, his magnificent hands seeming to promise to break whatever they touched. And Leander would feel as weak as he had once been strong—very suddenly he would remember Hilary's young worn-out face over the camp fire the night he had been strongest, and fear a further punishment; regret was not enough. . . .

He decided, nevertheless, to behave as if he trusted the future—the Towers had hastened too many disasters by looking forward; and he hoped that now at last God would want to prove that He was good.

But the best of life is over when satisfactions begin to age one as disappointments have done. Joy proved its reality by leaving scars on his face, smaller but deeper than those of sorrow. He began to look haggard and sad even when he smiled.

Rose and Henry were anxious. "Leander is by nature a bachelor," they said, "and ought not to have a son on his hands—it is too much for him."

During the summer of 1887 he was ill for a week. "I don't know why," the old doctor said, "but you seem to need a rest."

He let his substitute go on delivering the mail two or three days after the doctor had pronounced him a well man, and he and Timothy went to Port Oliver on the lake. They boarded with the storekeeper's wife. Rose had made a pair of bathing trunks from some red-flannel underwear, and Timothy swam by the side of the fishing dory they rented. When he stood up his chest rose in a great V out of his lean waist, and his thighs arched forward a little from his lean hips. Leander shouted when he sprang overboard and the water splashed in his face. Timothy rowed, grimacing in the sunshine; and Leander, in the stern, watched the gulls hesitate and let themselves be blown by the wind, and the boy's hands coming rhythmically forward, pulling down his knotted shoulders. After supper they walked along the dunes, and Timothy sang and threw stones into the waves. Leander said, "Some day you must see the Pacific."

The following winter Timothy discovered a sweetheart—a girl named Iris Lodge, nicknamed Irish. Henry was displeased: "You let that boy of yours take up with a wild no-'count girl, and a Catholic, besides. Poor Nancy was a God-fearing woman. Your ideas are too loose, Leander."

Leander could imagine Timothy's emotion (imagining, perhaps, more than the boy felt) because the girl had almost colorless eyes, so sensitive that they continually took refuge under her slant eyelids, and because her mouth was red, pointed, and not gentle. He bought a third horse, so that there should always be a fresh one in the stable to take them to and from husking bees, dances, box parties, and picnics. The boy thanked him by going out night after night, leaving him alone. Sometimes Leander had a certain irritation to hide. One day in the village store he heard the lovely girl call him "Tim's father and mother"; but she was almost servile in her smiling politeness whenever they met.

In the early autumn of 1888 an astonishing thing happened. A solitary woodcock made its home in the underbrush of a butternut grove above the house.

Several times at dusk Leander saw it in one of a row of scrub oaks which grew along a stone fence down to his garden. He was amazed, for the woodcock is more shy than any other game bird, and asked his nephew to keep its presence there a secret. Every night he watched among the bushes, dividing the week into days of its retirement and days of its appearance; and at last began to scatter crumbs and small grain under the trees it had visited. He never saw it eat, and supposed that small, ordinary birds consumed his offering; but little by little it grew bold, and from one stunted tree to another, from the dusk inside a tree to an exposed branch, approached the house.

One day after sunset Timothy called him to the kitchen window, and there it was in the garden among the chrysanthemums, looking like an infinitely old bronze ornament, walking and leaping slowly. They whispered behind the windowpane, complaining of the clouds which their breath made upon it, for the twilight was cold. Something about the bird's appearance seemed to indicate its unlikeness to others of its kind— its unusual courage, and the intuition by which it knew itself safe and loved. When it stood on a patch of soil, touching a clod now and then with its bill, Leander half expected it to pass from the visible to the invisible without another motion; but it rose at last and fluttered away heavily in the dark.

It came again. Leander waited for it, daydreaming of angels, thinking they must resemble Timothy in certain respects and the bird in others. It made him feel lonely, because no one he had ever known would be so moved by the sight of it as he was—no one but his little dead brother.

It came often. Timothy brought his sweetheart to see it one evening. The strange fowl came punctually, as if by appointment. They went through the cellar and stood in a row on the steps of the outside entrance, resting their elbows on one leaf of the folding door. Iris was more excited by it than Timothy had ever been, her breath coming and going over her lips, her eyes revealing some sort of intimacy with it—that of jealousy, or worship, or desire. Leander's gaze met Timothy's across her narrow forehead, and he realized that neither of them was paying attention to their bird; it was as if another wild, casual guest had joined the woodcock in the garden. Suddenly it struck the air once or twice with its wings, and flew away more swiftly than usual.

The next morning Timothy said, limbering his arms inside his blue nightshirt, "Iris wants that woodcock."

Leander's heart skipped a beat.

"To make a hat of it," the boy continued. "Some other girl has one—a Milwaukee girl."

Leander remarked timidly, "A young savage, your sweetheart," searching the boy's face for some sign of disapproval; but its beauty was pure, and closed, and idle. He could not swallow his coffee. Then Timothy smiled affectionately; it was enough—as good as a promise.

But for five succeeding nights it did not appear—not in the scrub oaks, not in the garden. Leander was made miserable by a fear that some sportsman had discovered it, and by what his nephew had said—not by distrust of him; but there must be other girls who would like feather toques, other boys who would be proud of it when it was dead.

On the sixth night Timothy had gone to the village to buy meat and bread for their supper. Leander sat by the window until he gave up hope of the bird's coming, then lay down on the couch for a nap. He did not fall asleep. He heard the cart clatter into the yard and Timothy throw down his bundles on the table. He did not open his eyes when Timothy tiptoed through the parlor and began to get supper with a great noise of pans and spoons. Leander enjoyed his invisible awkwardness, and wondered what he thought of when sleep seemed to be between them—but of course there was something equally impenetrable between them all the time. He was beginning to fall asleep. . . .

A gun was fired in the garden. Leander sprang to his feet—he had let the boy keep that gun because it had been his father's. He stumbled into the kitchen. Timothy's shadow hurried past the house with something in its hand—why hurry now? Timothy came in by the back door. He lit a lamp. "Been asleep?" he said.

Without knowing it, Leander had been facing a blank wall as if it were a window; he turned around. "Well, I see your girl's going to have her . . ." His voice failed. "Hat," he whispered.

Curiously, there was amazement on both faces. Leander caught a glimpse of his own in a mirror

framed in leather flowers (Nancy's handiwork); it
had a dry appearance, a gray color. The boy was
staring at him—at him—with a sort of horror; he
could not understand that. "Why did you do it?
Why did you do it?"

"She dared me," the boy muttered.

Leander sat down. Timothy sat down, and when
he moved, his elbows thumped on the table. At last
he said, "There's something I've got to—I've got to
tell you something."

"What? I don't blame you."

Silence.

"I can't stand it," the boy began.

Silence, and barely loud enough to be heard,
"Stand what?"

"I can't stand having you—feel so bad."

"Doesn't matter. Don't you mind."

Silence. The boy said patiently: "I've been thinking . . . I can't stand it here. I want to go away."

The silence kept asking why; Leander did not want
to know. But the boy continued: "I'm a man now.
You take things too hard. You love me too much.
I'm too young." He spoke very gently. "I feel like
a brute. I don't feel easy here. Things like this'll
keep happening. I want to do what I feel like and
like other fellows do. I can't stand it."

"All right," Leander said. Each time there was a
silence of the same size as the words which had been
spoken. "I'm going to bed now. Get some supper
for yourself. I'm not hungry."

He came back to the door. Timothy had not

moved. "What do you want to do? Where do you want to go?"

"I don't know."

"All right. We'll think of something."

The next afternoon Leander went to Rose's for the noonday meal, and sat all afternoon in her kitchen. Little Flora sat on his lap; he showed her his watch and placed Hilary's silver ring (like a wedding ring) over two of her fingers. He scarcely spoke to Rose. She said: "You have a sickly color, Leander. You must take care of yourself."

That night he took from the cupboard where he kept his papers a letter which had come two or three weeks before and which he had not known how to answer: a letter from a land agency in California offering him a large sum of money for his property, so large a sum, in fact, that he supposed it was worth more. He showed it to Timothy. "Would you like to go out there? I'll go to town to-morrow and have a deed made out to you. I always meant you to have it; you may as well have it now. It's not much good to me."

Timothy could not speak for joy. He put his arms around his uncle and kissed him. Leander shrank from his strength, as very old men shrink from their sons.

"We've got enough money in the house for your fare. Better go soon. You don't need to be miserable here any more." He added, as if he were ashamed; "Don't tell your uncle Henry or the others that I'm giving you the land. They know how I've always been a failure at everything. Please don't say that you don't want to live here any more. We'll tell them that I'm sending you out there to look after things. I guess California's not so bad as it used to be, when I went west. Be a good boy out there."

The night before he left Timothy was in the far bedroom, hunting in a chest for a picture of his father. Leander sat by the kitchen stove, not moving, scarcely breathing, not yet able to think. His cold fingers shrank from one another.

Then in heavy, lovely tones, a little off the key, the one Spanish song sounded from the other end of the house. Timothy could sing only at the top of his voice. Then the song broke off. Leander thought, he does not want to hurt me. A little later the boy began again thoughtlessly, and ceased at the end of the second phrase. Leander thought, he would be singing if I were not here. He could not endure the silence in which that music had been stifled on his account.

So he went outdoors. There lay the garden, severe and fragrant: the chrysanthemums talking to themselves, and the sky mottled a little like a lemon peel. Most of the flowers were gone—the lilies, the day-lily, the little weak ones, the great rose. Most of the vivid leaves, half destroyed by the frost, fainted from their stems. Most of the birds were gathering to go south, gathering, he thought, like the companies of young soldiers before the war; now that Timothy had stopped singing, their din in the marshes was the only sound to be heard. . . .

The garden seemed finer that evening than ever before. Autumn had perfected it as he had planned—autumn with its rags and tatters, its hard, clean hands. It was perfect now and his heart was broken. He fell on his knees in the path.

He was too old to wait for Timothy to come back. He thought, there could be no more surprises. How could even death surprise him now? And life had little left to reveal; he had played both parts; he had been the one who rejected and the one who asked.

Mechanically his hands began to pluck away a dead leaf here and there, to crumble little clods about the roots, as they had always done; but they found a place where the soil was pitted, where something dark and wet had fallen in drops; and there lay a small gray feather. Then he began to break and tear the chrysanthemums; the tough stalks hurt his hands, and the leaves and blossoms gave up their last perfume. No tears came to his eyes, and the violent motion of his chest was regular, as if he had suddenly learned a new way to breathe all the rest of his life.

But he was afraid that Timothy would discover him there: so as soon as he could, he rose and went into the house.

8. THE DEAD. HIS GRANDMOTHER'S FINAL GRIEF. THE PHOTOGRAPH ALBUMS

LEANDER TOWER did not live to be an old man. In fact, Alwyn's grandmother survived most of the friends of her youth. In 1912 her husband passed away; Mary, Nancy, her sister Adelaide, and two of her brothers, were dead; Leander and the two little girls had left her behind long ago. They had forgotten everything, she supposed, leaving her behind to remember for them: how they had lived, what they had wanted, and what the early days had been like. She had always done her duty; and now there was nothing more to do but honor the dead in her old age and go, in God's good time, where they were.

She was an active woman without much imagination; but she took pride in one or two poetic phrases which referred to the hard mystery of her experience, the mystery still intact when she had told all she could tell. As primitive people said, My love is like a rose, or, The sea is our mother, she would often say, "Life is like a great county fair"; and fall silent, resting her strong index finger against her cheek bone.

During that silence her grandson, gazing in admiration at her solid hand and drooping throat, her resolute, shortsighted eyes, would complete the comparison, detail by detail, and prove its justice to himself. Then he would wonder if there were many people in America who did not know what a county fair was; how well he knew!

Life is a great county fair . . . A village of rickety buildings inclosed by a fence too high to climb; a narrow entrance, a narrow exit. A multitude of laughing or irritable people dragging awe-stricken children by one hand. Many spoiling their appetites with the unwholesome refreshments that are for sale—some of these hiding afterward because they are sick. Some stingy, some extravagant; nearly everyone wanting to be more prosperously dressed; everyone tired to death. Women indignant at the neglect of their men; little ones whimpering because their mothers are out of sight. Long separations being brought to an end; good-bys beginning new separations. Love-making on the sly. Games of chance—the players always losing, the proprietors always poor. Eager or scandalized blushes in the tents where there is nakedness to be seen and music to be heard. Shouting around the pits in which human anomalies and sick wild animals are exhibited. Sleek horses charging around the race track in the dust. On a high platform the jugglers, inexpensively gorgeous in spangles and skullcaps, in the red, yellow, or blue nudity of tights, automatically running great risks and making patterns in the air, and seeming to find the loud applause inadequate. . . .

All gathered together for a competition which involves every sphere of activity. In the inclosures and drafty halls are exhibited bread, pies, cakes, conserves, and honey; exercise books and drawings of children, and every sort of fancywork; fruit, flowers, and vegetables, on shelves—a vertical, withering garden; cages of fowls and pigeons; and swine, cattle,

sheep, and horses, of all ages and breeds. Innumerable onlookers, cynical or enthusiastic according to
temperament; the judges, though no better than the
rest, granting or withholding honor and small money
prizes; the exhibitors anxious at first, proud or humiliated at last.

Three days, four days, or a week—and it is over.
Stalls and shelves emptied, tents bundled up and tied
with rope; crates, baskets, cages, lumber wagons, carriages, and racing carts, lovers, enemies, and little
worn-out boys beside their irritable, sometimes intoxi-
cated fathers, going through the narrow exit, with
crying geese and bulls and lovely mares and rams
whose curls are full of sawdust—on their way now to
sweet autumn pastures and matings with whole flocks
of ewes after the first frost—each decorated or not
with ribbons, varying in color according to their
strength, their beauty, their conformity to the standards of their kind; the procession separating at crossroads, one losing sight of another in the dust and the
gathering darkness as the great countryside absorbs
them once more into itself, and seeming to have disappeared.

So his grandmother's family and friends had been
scattered. The living were in California, New York,
Montana, New Mexico; the dead lay in many places—
perhaps no single burial ground could have held them
all.

For Alwyn the cemetery at Hope's Corner took
the place of a city child's park. In certain evergreens
there were sparrows' nests which resembled untidy

blond wigs; butcher birds lived in a cedar, and once or twice he found a dead mouse which they had hung on the thorn of a honey locust or a hawthorn. Old-fashioned roses, lying smothered in the grass, pricked his ankles. Lilies of the valley spread in a light green blanket, so that the graves on which they had been planted seemed to grow larger year by year. The headstone of a girl with a lovely name, Drusilla John, had fallen down; the coffin had collapsed, hollowing the sod above it; and Alwyn sat there by the hour, his legs under the marble slab as if it were a table, reading his favorite books, writing letters to his only friend.

The lots of his relatives were well kept, in proportion to the degree of kinship. The original families, with the single exception of his own, having left the community, the rest of the graveyard was a thicket of weeds, lilies, bushes, roses, and birds' nests; the conquered wilderness had reasserted itself, in miniature, over the conquerors' bodies.

Alwyn's grandmother said, "The neglect of the graveyard is a shame to the present generation," and held herself responsible for its general upkeep. So in the autumn she drove about the country in search of a man not too busy with the harvest to mow it, offering to pay him well, even willing to have the work done on the Sabbath. As the community filled up with German Catholic immigrants who bought the farms of the old settlers, she made it her business to see that the latter were not forgotten; as one of a proud, subjugated race would try to teach the history of the land and the names of its heroes to ignorant invaders. Eleven

Civil War veterans, including her husband, were buried at Hope's Corner; and every year she persuaded the teacher of the school across the road to arrange a Decoration Day program of recitations and old songs. She took bands of children to the woods to make wreaths and bouquets, and attended the exercises, shepherding the scholars from grave to grave, speaking to those who showed a little reverence, often laughed at by those who had been badly brought up.

These were the dead of a great period of the nation's history, eleven heroes; she honored their graves as a lesson to the living. Her own departed ones—she scarcely knew where some of them were buried, and it did not matter. She never thought of them as asleep under blocks of marble and granite and drooping bunches of trilliums, mandrake blossoms, and anemones. They were awake somewhere, doing their duty, whatever it was, nobly, invisibly. . . . Probably they had forgotten her—life was remembrance, so death must be forgetfulness; but she could not forget them for a minute. Left alone at last amid the scenes of their youth, she clasped her souvenirs to her breast, and yearned for all the dead as a mother yearns for children who are living, but no longer children.

She scarcely differentiated between absence and death. She was not likely to see again with living eyes those who were the breadth of America away—each year one or more was added to their number. The others, the dead, were separated from her only by the fact that she herself was still alive. At her age all good-bys were alike.

But according to her faith the phases of the moon took place above their heads, the absent and the dead alike. When the new moon appeared, other old men and women prophesied the weather according to an Indian tradition: a warm, dry spell if the two horns pointed to the sky, rain if the crescent, like a dipper, seemed to spill water on the earth. But she was indifferent to the weather; for her that slight heavenly body swung like a lantern above the house, above the old farm, high enough to be seen from every State in the Union and every foreign land, high enough to be visible even to those who had crossed the boundaries of the world.

So once a month she walked under the cherry trees in the dusk, startling the white pullets and cockerels which burdened the branches. She lifted her eyes to the lovely sickle, sharpened almost out of sight by the luster which continued to rise over the hills from the sun; and wiped away her unwelcome tears with a corner of her apron.

Then she would say to her grandson, who, believing that she was lonely, followed her: "You know, I always think of those who are dear to me when there is a new moon. It is my custom. The same moon shines on them all, the same new moon." In spite of her tears she spoke firmly, indeed contentedly.

But when her daughter Flora died in 1914, this fortitude came to an end, and serenity gave way to despair. Death was acceptable twice during life: before it began in earnest, and after it was over. Little children died—death deprived them of nothing; their mothers were strong and could bear it. Those who were old belonged to death, as if by contract; she was willing that nature should take its course. But the death of a lovely, unmarried girl was intolerable and against nature. She herself should have been allowed to go instead; life had had its way with her for more than half a century; she could have said Amen.

Hitherto, time had been given her in which to recover, to develop new habits and enjoy new hopes. Now it was too late; she would not live to see the end of this anguish; she could never begin again. She had always accepted things as they were; having protested, she had folded her arms and given in; but her will would never be at peace with the Will which had determined Flora's death. There was nothing to do but leave the world, unreconciled, and, because of the insubordination of her heart, half ashamed.

She had been proud of her life, the masterpiece of the divine Hand which had guided her hand, a vast and somber picture. The gesture which had drawn certain lines had hurt her; certain colors had been her life's blood; but looking back she had been able to view the result without much pain and with approbation. Now the giant Hand, with a final stroke, with the stain of a final wound, had spoiled their work.

In the past it had seemed natural for those who had the same sorrows to weep together. Now she could not bear to be seen weeping, apparently ashamed; it was not her fault—but those who have been strong, when they are crippled, want to hide their deformities. She would say to the children, "I can't have you here now; run off and play," and sit alone by the window, weeping without covering her face, her cheeks red and shining with the continual tears, her worn-out eyelids fluttering, her lips moving as she repeated to herself the fact that her last-born child was dead.

When she had been happy she had been able to endure the thought of all her former griefs. Now these wounds, suffered and healed long ago, burned with sympathetic pain; and the story of her life, the whole history of the family, seemed unmentionably sad. If young people realized how life ended, they would not want to live; so she would hide her despair and say nothing. Therefore, during the last years, she said very little about Leander, or her husband, or their close relatives, or her sons. Instead she drew near to those who had never been near her heart, and preferred to talk about them.

Accompanied by her grandson, she made a round of afternoon visits to old men and women whom she had known indifferently for years, who had never been more than neighbors. Before them she could pose as a wise woman, strong enough to endure the afflictions which God in His violence had imposed. Distracted by their weaknesses, she could ignore for a few hours her own weakness and dismay. She defended herself from their questions with a hard good nature—the humor of her rude ancestors, hunters and soldiers and vagabonds, masking her heart and hiding the wreckage which death had left in it at last.

She talked to her grandson with a startling sardonic gayety about these people and others like them who were dead: relatives whom she had happened not to love, his grandfather's friends, the friends of her friends. The disastrous comedies of their lives diverted her from the grief which was all that was left of hers; she could be as brave about their troubles as she had once been about her own. She dwelt without pity on their paradoxical characters, their avowals and frauds, their astonishing whims and failures; and at Alwyn's request identified among her photographs many of their faces.

There were two albums of embossed leather studded with buttons which resembled shoe buttons, and one with celluloid roses glued upon a velvet binding. There were daguerreotypes in cases closed by a metal clasp or a loop of worn cord, which Alwyn opened and tried to read as if they were a library of miniature books. At the left a leaf of red satin, at the right in a mat of beaded gilt the portraits: heads and busts and family groups, pygmy men and women as if seen through a telescope—the men in a daydream, the women anxious about their children, their lovers, their clothes. Mouths like bits of carved wax, nostrils of an insatiable arrogance; eyes long closed in death—or the young, suspicious eyes of men and women who were now old and patted Alywn's head and peered at him dimly and beneficently—staring out of the picture frames as if he were an enemy in disguise. . . . The lifeless light (in which innumerable photographers had covered their heads with large, black handkerchiefs and imitated a bird with their hands) half hid and half revealed all the possible combinations of all the motives there were—greed and sensuality and courage and compassion and cruelty and nostalgia; all the destinies there were—manias, consolations, regrets.

The same motives and similar destinies existed still; but these people whose playground they had been were gone. Nothing came back from the oblivion into which they had vanished (for old age and death were equally oblivion) not a sound came back but a little slightly exultant, unhappy laughter—Alwyn's grandmother laughing for them.

He listened to her comments—old-fashioned maxims, scraps of tragi-comic narrative, implicitly mocking, explicitly compassionate—and what she told revealed little more than the photograph albums themselves: another set of pictures, photographs of actions and opinions, also noncommittal and badly focused. But he knew what she knew and tried to forget: that each picture was a tomb where a dead heart (or merely the youth and freshness of a heart which was now old) lay buried—buried with its affections, its apathy, its fury. He knew that on each insignificant grave there stood (though he could only guess what it was) a secret like hers, wild and perfect as a wild flower, nodding in its everlasting leaves, or dangling from a broken stem. . . .

Laura-Belle Barry

Mrs. Barry, born Laura-Belle Allen and married in her youth to her cousin Will Allen, had once been plump, melancholy, and ravishing—to which the portrait that Alwyn's grandmother kept because both her brothers had been in love with the lady, bore witness. Her father was the merchant in Aaronsville in the days when stores were few and far apart, and any price could be asked for the necessities of life; he was prosperous, but by nature pessimistic.

Laura-Belle wept over all the boys who loved her. Even her young husband's passion did not wake her from a resentful daydream. She gave birth to two perfect children; they died of scarlet fever. Her father was believed to be guilty of fraud and died mysteriously. Finally Will Allen was killed; a magnificent spotted bull gored him and trod him underfoot. After his body had been rescued, Laura-Belle stood staring over the fence at the beast until she had to be taken away by force.

When she came to her senses she was a new woman. She never shed a tear for the dead man, but grew more and more emaciated. She began to take an interest in everything and everybody, and then began to be noted for her sense of humor. She dressed in red, and since this color was supposed to enrage bulls, no one dared to ask her why. Eventually she married Barry, a drunkard, and merely laughed at his excesses. Between them they wasted her small fortune, and at last were penniless.

In her old age she wore a ragged, red, one-piece garment or an old dress covered with black braid and jet buttons. If anyone noticed her clothes, she would tear another hole in them, smiling pleasantly, and say, "Blessed be nothing." She was a saint, though something of a busybody, sparing no one when she spoke. It was reported that even on her deathbed what was left of her once lovely and heavy body—burning eyes, blue-veined hands, long braids of silvery hair, skin and bone—was shaken again and again by her crackling laughter.

Apparently unconscious of the sound of her own laughter, Alwyn's grandmother said, "Nobody could make a sound like that when she laughed if a hard life hadn't been too much for her. But it was enough to put the fear of God into your heart, and gave a bad impression."

Mr. Sam Peters and wife, born Melissa Duff

A little man as vague as the wisp of yellow beard between his mouth and his Adam's apple. An unkind, vigorous, and well-dressed woman. She was Alwyn's great-aunt on his mother's side of the house.

His grandmother Tower would say, in his mother's presence: "That was the most miserable woman that ever lived. I never knew anybody else too mean to give a slice of bread to a tramp that asked for it. Your ma is a wonderful woman; my only complaint is that your pa married into the same family as Melissa Peters."

Alwyn's great-aunt Melissa ruled and humiliated her small husband. On one occasion he rose in revolt. She made up her mind to visit her relatives in Canada, spent so much money for new dresses that he could not afford to hire a housekeeper in her absence, and made no mention in her letters of returning. At last he sent a telegram, signed with her brother's name: "SAM VERY SICK IF YOU DESIRE SEE HUSBAND ALIVE COME HOME AT ONCE IRA." He met her at the station, smiling foolishly, and seemed quite willing to endure, until the end of his life, her heartbreaking tirades.

Cousin Matie Share

His grandmother's cousin who took care of them in 1854 while her mother visited in Kentucky. Her brothers sat around the house, teasing Matie; they pinched her and dared each other to strip her of her new calico dress and hang it on a tree; and she threw sticks of stove wood at them.

No one did any work: either the cows were not milked, or the cream got too sour to churn; so there was no butter to put on the children's bread when they went to school. Matie told Rose to milk a cow herself and take the milk in a bottle for their lunch. Rose and Adelaide were afraid that the scholars would laugh at them; so they hid the bottle in a hollow stump and stole away by themselves at noon to drink it.

Captain Ed Hawks

This boy was the perfect soldier. Fifteen years old when the Civil War broke out, he ran away to a town in Dodge County where a company was preparing to go south. Every day or two he sent someone to find out if his family would let him enlist. At last his father consented: "He might as well go. He'll never be good for anything else."

The child took three prisoners, and was made a captain before peace was declared.

Laughing sturdily, Alwyn's grandmother said: "I guess old John Hawks wouldn't have been much put out if something had happened to Ed down South. He was a shame to them, being the only lazy man in the family. He'd work harder to keep from working than anybody else ever had to."

Josh Arbuckle

This was the hired man who ate skunk.

Alwyn's grandmother said, "In my day, if you had a sore throat, you tied your stocking, warm from your foot, around your neck; and if that didn't cure you, skunk oil was considered the best remedy. We rendered their fat ourselves, and put it up in bottles."

One day, when Alwyn's father and his uncle Jim were boys, they brought to the house the flesh of a skunk, carefully stripped from the pelt in order not to break the sac which contains the stinking secretion. Their mother put it in a spider on the stove to try out the fat. A little later Josh, the hired man, came in, ravenously hungry after his morning's work in the cold, saw the meat frying, and thought the boys had shot a squirrel for dinner. He took a fork off the table, removed a bit from the pan, and ate it. Alwyn's grandmother laughed heartily at the face he made when she told him what he had eaten, and laughed still, after thirty years, whenever she remembered it.

Baltus Valentine

A portly face full of blood, with ruffled whiskers. This was the man who suffered from violent tooth-ache. When it afflicted him he ran outdoors, bellowing so that he could be heard half a mile away. A heavy man clutching his head with both hands, elbows in the air, galloping round and round the strawstack in the blazing sunshine. . . .

Mr. Peter Greeley

This man was a notorious miser, but the daguerreotype showed him as he had looked at the age of twenty-three. An anxious, effeminate face; his moistened hair combed low on his forehead, resembling the parallel strokes of a pen; a wing collar standing well apart from his throat, and a black ribbon fastidiously knotted.

He played a fiddle in his youth. His father had left him one hundred and fifty acres of rich land. He was disdainful of many girls who would have been glad to marry him; but as each girl gave up hope, one delicacy or another vanished from his person; spots of grease multiplied on his clothes; the high collar was forgotten; he ceased to wash, and his hands were covered with red cracks. He sold the violin, and told the woman who kept house for him that he could take care of himself.

Then he lived like a saint who has no god, filthy and miserable, imagining that beastly sins were being committed in the community, and denouncing whoever dared to speak to him. In middle life he sold his property for a large sum of money, keeping only the house and the lot on which it stood. One day he was found dead in the kitchen, holding a battered saucepan in his hand. He had neither relatives nor friends, and the neighbors never discovered what became of the money.

Listless boys with their hands full of stones took the windows for targets, and the rooms were never dismantled, except when someone looked in who was poor enough to want a tin pail, a cup without a handle, a three-legged chair, or a piece of a rusty iron bed.

Alwyn's grandmother enjoyed exciting the children with talk of the undiscovered gold. From time to time they visited the tumble-down house, and found nickel spoons in a drawer, mismated shoes inhabited by mice, and a curious collection of nails all bent in the same way. Alwyn was not tall enough to look into the chimney cupboard; so he climbed on a box and explored it with one hand, which came away empty but for spots of dust in the form of pennies on the tip of each finger.

Mr. Homer O'Sullivan

This well-educated, unsuccessful man looked ill at ease in the photograph; it had paralyzed a singular restlessness of mind and body. But his mouth continued to say yes with a downward, and no with an upward, inflection.

He read Tom Paine and was almost an atheist, hating Christ for His effeminacy and loving Him for His virtue. He defended the Mormons, and at one time advocated Free Silver ardently. As a Good Templar he induced many people to sign the pledge. For him life was a thicket of ideas, and he fluttered from twig to twig like a hungry bird.

His wife was a paralytic; he fed her with a spoon, dressed her, lifted her out of bed in the morning and put her back in the evening; she was his child for forty years.

Mr. Eli Williamson

His grandfather's friend who had gone mad at the sight of a lynching. He had still been sane when this likeness was made, but his hollowed eyes were full of wonder and the violence of a child's fear of violence.

A hired man named Carty had been lynched. He worked in a German family consisting of an old farmer, his wife, and an orphan grandson named Chris. The old man sold a wagonload of hogs and brought home the money. He went down into the cellar through a trapdoor to fetch some cider, and when he came up Carty hit him on the head with a hammer. The little boy ran out the back door and hid in a cornfield. Carty struck the old woman and forgot the money.

The neighbors heard the old woman scream. The

murderer was found before midnight, shuddering and moaning in a haystack.

The next morning a neighbor's wife, a strong, sick woman, went around from house to house with the child Chris; she shouted and rolled her eyes, and the little boy whimpered all the time. Women stood on front porches wringing their hands; men in barns leaped for their axes and pitchforks, not knowing what to do with them; and a crowd collected around the post office.

About four o'clock the mob took Carty, who turned pale and prayed or pretended to pray, out of jail. Someone's fast trotting horses were hitched to a cart. The murderer was roped to the axle; the horses raced up and down the road; his body dragged in the dust. Someone set his pet hound on the man, and all the dogs of the town followed—mongrels, hunting hounds, shepherds, and terriers alert as birds—all barking and some tearing the victim with their teeth. Then the mob hanged Carty from the limb of a tree.

Mr. Eli Williamson, looking down from his house which stood on a rise of ground, went mad.

Mr. and Mrs. Ebenezer Bolt

The wedding picture of a widow and a widower. Each loved the other's money, and life was not long enough to adjust their differences.

Alwyn knew them as a very old couple when they lived in Aaronsville. They took a pint of milk for their breakfast, and in order to avoid the shock of a large expenditure at the end of the month, paid for it in turn every morning. The milkman stood on one leg near the door while it was determined by a long dispute which had paid the preceding day.

Mrs. Bolt wore a rusty black dress which closed at the back with a long row of hooks and eyes. Sometimes, after the insults of the milk, her husband refused to fasten it, or she refused his assistance. On these mornings, she appeared wearing it wrong side before—the frills of the bodice drooping over her shoulder blades, her bosom cruelly pressed by the hooks and eyes.

Except in this matter of money, it was a happy marriage.

Mrs. Bolt had a twin sister named Linda, who, having lost her mind, lived in an asylum. Knowing that Linda was dangerously ill, she would not open the door to the superintendent who called to announce her death, fearing that she would be asked to bear the costs of burial.

Mr. Jim Hallow, Mr. Solomon Royce, Mr. Peters, Mr. John James, etc.

There were many portraits of men of approximately the same age who had fought shoulder to shoulder with Alwyn's grandfather during the war. Their faces, even the youngest, reminded one of death, as if, having escaped it in battle, they had begun at once to look forward to the time when they would be too hard of hearing, too nearsighted, or too feeble, to escape.

Alwyn had seen a number of them, soon after his grandfather's death, at an old soldier's reunion in Aaronsville. These veterans, scarcely able (on account of rheumatism, heart trouble, strokes of paralysis, dyspepsia, or hardening of the arteries) to enjoy their glory, told heroic, interminable anecdotes, hoping to make the young jealous of it. Their nervous wives pitied them, remembering that their prestige was based on the mere fact of survival and could not last much longer. Some soldiers' widows who were present, as if to keep a chair vacant for an invisible guest, tried rather timidly to take part in the reminiscences. Only Alywn's grandmother was at ease with the men, dignified and sadly contented, rather like an old soldier herself.

Breathlessly, their white beards tossing here and there, awkwardly, and with an air of bravado, two grandfathers danced a jig; they were like a pair of condemned men dancing in their chains.

Mrs. Sam Goodwin

This was the fiercely bright face, amid wisps of gray hair, of a woman who had adopted three children in turn, all of whom had died.

Uncle Peter Barlow

Alwyn had seen this man in the eighty-fifth year of his age; and between his eyes and the unrecognizably young face in the oval daguerreotype which lay in his hand, the image of the old story teller appeared, seeming to represent all story tellers. Gripping his cane with a hawk or an eagle's hand, he had sat all one afternoon beside a well-traveled road, common butterflies fluttering about his head, hens and guinea hens going upon obscure errands about his feet. From time to time there had been a flickering between his eyelids, as in a bed of ashes the falling ash of a twig will seem to be fire itself. And he had told Alwyn a story which has been told in a hundred versions in every tongue, declaring that he had known all the characters in his youth:

"It happened to a boy named Thomas—Jim Thomas. He was a sickly little fellow, scared of 'most everything. That night he was fetching home the cattle, his father told me. The cows came home by themselves, but Jim was nowhere to be seen. His father hallooed and hunted down the road and found the little fellow in the grass, crying as if his heart would break. He told his pa that a night hawk flew down by the cattle for flies and scared him.

"Now in my time families not well-to-do, when they had a death, just put up a board and drove a nail in it and hung up some flowers. There were some of these boards in the graveyard—this was in York State.

"It appears that that afternoon some tough boys at the school had called Jim a coward and dared him. Like as not he was turning that over in his head when he got so scared of the bird. They dared him to go after it got dark to the grave of a woman named Mrs.

Gore, one of those wooden monuments, and pound on it with a stone so as they could hear and know he actually was there. Now Mrs. Gore was a woman whose life was a burden, and the hired girl that worked for her husband made out she saw her ghost, and there'd been a lot of talk about that. It appears that little Jim figured he'd best do it and not be a laughing-stock.

"So the boys came whistling round his house after dark and he sneaked out unknown to his pa and went along to do it. He took a rock by the side of the road and went into the cemetery. It was pitch dark in there under a lot of trees. The boys were waiting by the side of the road and they heard him pound on the monument, and then he gave a terrible shout. Some got scared and ran home, and two or three of them came sniffling to get his father.

"His father took a lantern and went down and found the little fellow with his coat hooked over one of those nails that were intended to hang posies on. He must have thought the ghost had taken hold of him. The father carried him home and sent for the doctor. The doctor thought it was heart failure. However that may be, he was dead."

The old man had smiled as if the story pleased him, as if he had ceased to see any difference between tragedy and comedy in what had happened so long ago.

Another day he had told another story:

"In York State in the early days there was a man named Lucas who had a son who was a terror. Old

Lucas was a godless kind of man himself and a widower, and he'd not given his boy a very strict bringing-up, I reckon; but he turned religious and got baptized. The boy was wilder than ever—drank and swore and got girls into trouble and wouldn't work for more'n a few days at anything.

"One winter the boy was hard up and came home to live and stole some money which his pa kept in a coffeepot. His pa found it out and commenced to give him a beating. But the young fellow was beside himself, and he got hold of a shotgun and took his pa by the coat collar and dragged him out of doors.

"Now old Lucas had a fine orchard full of every kind of apple tree, and greengages and berry bushes. So the boy pulled him along into this orchard. And when they came to a little seedling, he said, 'Pa, bend that!' And Lucas did. Then they came to a big tree and the boy said, 'Bend that, you old devil, or I'll shoot you!' Old Lucas hollered and got down on his knees and took hold of the tree and held on to young Lucas's knees. A neighbor's little boy, there in the currant bushes, saw the whole performance, but he was too scared to go for help. So young Lucas shot his father. Of course they put him in jail, and he was never heard of again.

"I had a son myself, but he died when he was a young fellow, and I don't even know where they buried him."

During Alwyn's twelfth year, this old man appeared in his dreams, and in a youthful, melodious voice told stories too senseless and too cruel even to be remembered in the daytime. But he died, and at last Alwyn remembered him only when he looked at the photograph albums.

Mr. and Mrs. A. Rollo

A bridal pair before a vista painted on canvas, beside a taboret like a dancer with iron legs crossed at the knee.

The bride's coarse veil droops like a lace curtain against the groom's broadcloth. They are as shy as if they were young; but he is a little bald, and yesterday she was a spinster. Their eyes are looking, not for what they desire, but for the body of desire itself, lost and perhaps dead. Their mouths are the sort which will never tell whether they find it or not.

This couple was childless.

A boy whose name had been forgotten.

He wore a flowered vest. A pointed curl lay on each of his temples like an arrowhead.

This boy was so beautiful that Alwyn wished he could say to himself: This is the way my father looked when he was a boy. In fact, as he well knew, Ralph Tower had been a rough, homely youngster.

9. His Uncle Jim, the Minister, as a Young Man

RALPH TOWER, Alwyn's father, was not an educated man. Because of their poverty his parents could not hope to send more than one son away to school. They wanted a preacher in the family, for no calling was so honorable as the ministry. Jim, their eldest, was more studious than the other two boys, spoke fluently, and took pains with his appearance. So, while still almost a child, he was chosen to receive an education, and it was useless for Ralph and Evan to have ambitions; they would have to stay on the farm in any case.

The three grew up together happily and roughly. Their mother disciplined them with a worn army belt which hung behind the door; their father ignored them unless there was work to be done. They spent all their spare time in the woods, hunting coons by lantern light, trapping muskrats and skunks, which they drowned and washed in a deserted well. One evening a cow who had dropped her calf alone in the marshes, charged them, and Ralph, the last of the three to take flight, broke his leg. Later Evan fell from a beam in the barn without being seriously hurt, and when he was eleven a furious ram kept him in a tree for several hours. Their clothes and their bodies exhaled a faint animal odor, which, according to their father, made the house smell like a wigwam. They were afraid of girls, and preferred each other to their friends. Undernourished but energetic, half savage but hopeful, a poor farmer's ordinary sons, dressed in overalls or grown men's clothes hastily cut down, with copper toes on their boots and rabbits' feet in their pockets for good luck—until their late adolescence they were as much alike as young dogs of the same litter.

Then mature character developed out of the characterlessness of boyhood, and they drew apart, at first imperceptibly, then with decision, as if, while roving like aimless wild animals over the countryside, they had come upon roads leading in three directions; and Jim, suddenly sober and self-conscious, began to look toward the future which the piety of his parents had chosen for him.

Those were hard times in Wisconsin. They heard their father say to their mother that the farm would have to be mortgaged before long; and for some time the younger boys thought they were as well off as Jim, for apparently, in that family, no one could have a start in life.

But in 1894 Timothy Davis began to send their uncle Leander money from the West every month. Leander was in poor health, and one day he proposed to his brother and sister-in-law that an "old bachelor's wing" be added to their house; the money Timothy sent should pay for it, keep them from running into debt, and enable them to send Jim to college as well. Henry and Rose promised to care for him as long as he lived; so he gave up the mail route, sold his house and garden, and as soon as the new rooms were completed made his home in one of them, where he sat by himself all day, paying no attention to the farm-work, rarely taking part in family discussions, and watching his nephews with the timid solicitude which is an old bachelor's way of loving another man's sons.

The youngest, Evan, was a wistful, freckled stripling with a quick temper. The path of an unlucky life seemed to have been blazed ahead of this boy by his peculiar spirit which no one understood, and people began to say that he would come to a bad end. He loved no one but his uncle, and it was certain that he and his father would never be at peace. He kept threatening to run away from home, and Ralph at least knew that sooner or later he would.

Ralph wanted to go to a school in Milwaukee and become a veterinary surgeon, having a passion for animals, dreaming of race horses, and prize bulls, and dogs worth as much as a whole farm. But he was obviously the one who would never go anywhere, who would have to make sacrifices, and learn to be patient with their father as he grew old and arbitrary. His brothers were going to leave the country, but he would have to turn back among the still only half-cultivated hills, to go on being what they had all been as ignorant children, what their forefathers had been: a child of nature. He was strong, obedient, and moody, resenting what the future might do, as if, mysteriously, at the age of eighteen, the past had already done its worst.

In the autumn of 1895 Jim, the lucky one, went off alone to a little college town to learn how to preach virtue and pious progress and the fear of God: a rudely handsome young man, anxious, awkward, and eager to please. The allowance which he received from home was inadequate, though it looked so generous to his puritan father, so magical to his brothers; but his pleasant face made it easy to find employment in the afternoons and evenings; he was used to harder work, and study was child's play.

He had many talents, and for four years he was pleasantly occupied by small, gratifying successes. There were boating parties, Sunday night suppers, and picnics; embarrassed, idealistic friendships; and a series of best girls with rigid waists, pompous hats, and exciting flounces. He took part in the brutal wedge-football of the period, winning as a trophy a turtle-necked sweater adorned with a great scarlet A. His hair parted in the middle and falling over each ear in a loose, blond wave, he won an oratorical contest with a speech called "Macbeth and Iago, or Intellect and Ambition." He developed a fine bass voice, and traveled all over the Middle West with a male quartet. He was photographed again and again, usually in profile, and clippings from small-town newspapers were sent back to the farm, where they were read aloud with astonishment.

Though none of his friends were irreligious, culture seemed to be more highly regarded than mere religion. He experienced some things and thought about many others of which his father at least would have disapproved. He was being prepared for life, not precisely, he felt, for the ministry; for a glorious destiny, perhaps, but perhaps it would seem inglorious to his loving, narrow-minded family; and he began to think uneasily of the hard-working men on the farm and their expectations.

The Spanish-American War broke out, and one day his mother wrote that Evan, having nothing to look forward to at home, had joined the army. America had been at peace since before Jim was born, and he thought of war as if it were death itself, and pictured the island in the south as a military graveyard, full of soldiers and flowers. At any rate, reckless Evan would be the sort of soldier who has no future; he might as well be dead. The family had grown smaller by one. Ralph would do what their father had done before him—work the land and care for the old people; there was no one but Jim left to do what their father had wanted to do. Their father's life had been a long, impatient prophecy, a prophecy of success at last for one of the Towers, which Jim alone bore the burden of having to fulfill. So he felt many tired, fanatic eyes upon him—not only his father's, but those of the other aging pioneers who had conquered an empire in which no one had yet become famous, and his envious brothers' eyes, especially Ralph's. Dreaming of family councils around his bed during which it was decided that he had wasted his opportunities, Jim began to feel that, like an heir apparent, he had no right to dream, nor to make plans or friends, nor even to marry, except as it furthered the ambitions which his family had, and which he was obliged to represent.

There was a girl named Irene Geiger who, among others, wanted to marry him. She also had a beautiful singing voice, and intended to prepare herself for grand opera. They sang together. Her father, a wealthy brewer of German birth, said with great feeling: "Young fellow, you certainly sing fine. You must get your voice trained."

Jim dreamed of changing the direction of his life, knowing that if he married this cheerful, ambitious girl, her father would give him every opportunity, sparing no expense. He told himself that his family expected of him fame, having passed their lives in obscurity, and prosperity which they might share, having for generations lived and died in poverty; that he stood on the brilliant threshold of an unexpected life, of a career more brilliant than the ministry; and finally that music as well was a divine persuasion, like argument and prayer. He pictured himself in a satin suit and the blaze of footlights, singing as easily as a meadow lark, while the large bouquets of admirers who had forgotten all their troubles fell on the stage around him. He was at once listener and singer, and a flood that was both light and sound troubled him and then made him forget his trouble. A sort of excitement poured also from that imaginary stage into his mind, even into his body, so that when he held Irene's hand he fancied that he loved her as the heroes of music loved their heroines; for a moment he forgot not only the imaginary audience, but the actual audience of father, mother, and brother, anxiously watching his life.

Would not his father and brother be ill at ease in that future audience, with their Sunday coats glossy at the elbows, their celluloid collars slipping up around their strong, red throats, their hands hardened by hammers and shovels and harnesses? At the thought of them, Jim felt lonesome and cold, though he stood with his sweetheart under the chestnuts on the campus, and though those chestnuts were in bloom; and he remembered how, when he was a six-year-old boy, walking home alone in a winter twilight through the woods, having found a handmade whistle in his pocket, he had blown on it as loudly as he could, in order to forget that he might get lost and freeze to death; perhaps that was what music was for. . . .

Irene was very much in love, and often embarrassed him by forcing her way into his heart, as a woman might throw open a door and rustle into a room where a young man—his heavy head in his hands, his forehead wrinkled, his eyes half closed—broods upon his limited resources, and his ambitions, and the opposition to them which may arise. But his new ambitions were hers as well, and she held in her generous hands resources which seemed to him scarcely limited at all. So at last he made up his mind to marry her.

At the end of May, chaperoned by her cousin, a sturdy German spinster, he took her to Hope's Corner to be seen by his parents, taking with him as well for their approval his new plans for the future, about which he had not dared to write a letter. As they drew near the farm he thought of the old-fashioned morality of which it was an unbroken stronghold, and began to study the bright, overdressed girl beside him with anxiety, almost with disapprobation; and he wished that Evan were there, so that by contrast he might seem to his father an obedient son—that his uncle Leander were there to defend him, as he always defended the young against the old.

After Evan had gone away to war, Leander had fallen ill, and upon his recovery had announced that he was going to California. "A sick spell at my time of life shows the way the wind is blowing. I want to see Tim again before I die." Knowing that he overestimated his strength, and hoping that he still had a long time to live, the family had discouraged him; but a little before Jim's visit he had set out alone.

So Jim would have to speak for himself; and in imagination, he heard himself stuttering, or saw himself unable to say anything at all.

In the evening, after the preliminary greetings had been accomplished by his parents with a noncommittal, awkward, but faultless courtesy, the German girl, eager and unabashed, sat down on the organ stool, and sang, *"I dreamt I dwelt in marble halls."* Jim sang, and joined her in one or two duets. Then she played the prelude of a passionate aria; the old cabinet organ rattled as her vigorous tread filled the bellows with air, as her capable hands pulled out stop after stop; and when she pressed open the swell-box, her skirt spread out over her knees like a great satin bagpipe. But Jim whispered that this piece would not please the family, and they sang instead a two-part anthem. Irene looked appealingly, as it were over the series of strong, high notes, toward his parents, and gazed at Ralph as a woman in love does gaze at a young man who may become her brother-in-law—gazed, in fact, a moment longer than she ought to have done.

The stern father, though proud of Jim's talent and his own understanding of music, listened suspiciously. Little Flora wept with pleasure. Their mother said, "Now that—that is singing I can appreciate. I wish Evan and Leander were here to enjoy it."

Then Flora was sent to bed. Ralph took a lamp, escorted the two ladies, who pretended to be tired, to their room, and returned. Jim was standing dramatically in front of the organ, as if he were going to sing again—without accompaniment this time.

"Pa—ma—" he said, "I want to marry Irene."

Ralph blushed. Jim looked at his mother, and she looked at her husband for permission to congratulate her son, but his face was inexpressive; his twisted hands, one on each knee, did not move.

The silence was miserable. Jim ran his forefinger around his collar. "I want to be a singer. I guess I'll give concerts, with her. I can do that better, better than be a minister."

At last the father answered. "No. It's not right. I won't have it. We've spent too much on your schooling—"

"It won't cost you a cent," Jim pleaded. "Irene's father is well off. I'll be trained with her."

"How did he make all this money?" his father inquired scornfully.

"He's a . . . He was a—brewer," the young man admitted.

"There you are. A brewer!" his father snapped. "I tell you, it's enough to make a man lose heart!"

Jim's mother said, "Now, Henry, if he's set his mind on it—"

"No, sir. I didn't bring up my son to be a good-for-nothing singer."

There followed another sharp silence.

Jim bit his lips, cried, "I'm a grown man," and strode out of the room.

Presently Ralph said, "Good night, pa and ma," and followed his brother.

The mother rose. "Well, Henry, they'll have to get married sooner or later. And live their own lives. We can't stop them."

"Say no more about it," he replied.

She went into the kitchen, set the batter for the breakfast pancakes on the stove to rise, and began to prepare for the night.

Henry Tower noticed that he had been left alone. After a time he pulled open the top drawer of a bureau, took out his flutes and his fife, unwrapped their flannel coverings, and lifted them one by one to his lips. He gazed into the finger holes, which had looked up at him all during the last war like a row of small, expressionless eyes. His favorite son a good-for-nothing singer. . . . He was glad that Evan, the least obedient, was a soldier; war was bad, but better than disgraceful behavior. He blew very softly into the flutes, not only so that no one in the house should know what he was doing—that part of him which loved music playing so softly that the part of him which hated it could not hear; as, of two people lying side by side, the one who is sleepless whistles a little in the night. He knew what no one else had discovered, that he was growing deaf. His rheumatic hands closed on the flutes as if he meant to break them, and he walked across to the window as if he meant to throw them away.

His wife opened the bedroom door. She saw him put away the instruments and wished that she had not, knowing that when his weakness had been exposed he never gave in to it. She sighed, for her husband, for her son—whichever would have to give up in the end. The Towers would have to settle their differences between them; she could not take sides.

Meanwhile, in the room over their heads, the boys were undressing slowly. Jim sat in his nightshirt, staring angrily at an eagle woven in the rag rug with its wings outspread; it was clear from his expression that he meant to go against his father's will.

Ralph threw his shirt and trousers on a chair, and removed them at once, lest the odor of the stables be transferred to his brother's college clothes. "You can't do it," he said without any introduction. "Can't marry her, Jim."

Jim looked up hopelessly. He expected sympathy and encouragement from everyone as young or younger than he, but they were all against him; Ralph on his father's side. . . . "Pa's too old-fashioned," he muttered. "Unreasonable. Things are changing."

"I'm not talking about pa. Getting married doesn't change much."

"What do you mean, then?"

In the silent room both brothers breathed heavily, and the lamp gulped on the table as the kerosene went up the wick, and they could hear the blows of a horse's hoofs in the stall, like those of a fist on a great wooden opponent.

"Well . . ." Ralph began gloomily—"Well, when I took her to her room, that old maid went ahead. Your girl held my hand. She kissed me." Knowing his own passions, he expected to see an angry movement or a change of color, but Jim only prodded the rag eagle with one foot.

"You know," Ralph went on, "I'm going to get married pretty soon. Marianne Duff. Her engagement to that bishop's boy turned out to be nothing. We love each other. She wouldn't do what your girl did. I couldn't have such a thing happen."

Jim stared in astonishment at his brother, his brother's excited eyes, his large earth-colored hands working to turn back the cuffs of the nightshirt. Jealousy, the jealousy that a man ought to feel, that he ought to feel and did not. . . . He asked himself if he really loved Irene.

"Besides," Ralph insisted, "you hadn't ought to be a singer. Pa's made sacrifices. Only one of us boys could have a chance. I gave up wanting to be a veterinary so you could be a minister—we all want you to. You sing well enough already. Singing doesn't count—it's not much of a man's job."

Jim's dream of a career changed. Everyone left the great hall in which he had wanted to sing, that is, everyone he loved; just a few supercilious strangers would be there, to make fun of the country boy—no one who loved him. Suddenly he felt that it was a lonesome business to have his good luck and be educated. Apparently, in a measure, it would satisfy Ralph to have his lucky brother preaching the gospel. Apparently music was a private, even a selfish pleasure, whereas religion comforted everyone. It was a lonesome business to be selfish.

Ralph had nothing to add. He knelt on his side of the bed to say his prayers, forcing Jim to his knees, though there was not a whisper of thanksgiving in his heart and he did not know what to ask for. Looking strangely weary and deaf, Ralph said his prayers proudly, with his eyes only half shut, as at the end of a serious council the head of a family prays for them all. Jim felt like a boy who has heard the last words of a father or grandfather, and is afraid to try to get along without a blessing. Ralph was younger than himself, but it takes youth and strength to represent an authority as immortally old as that seemed to be. Over the patchwork quilt—of serviceable materials that had worn well, in dull colors that did not fade—Ralph's dark head, as he whispered almost perfunctorily to himself and God, nodded slightly as if he were giving his consent to something and refusing something else. Refusing Jim's new ambitions; refusing, incidentally, the girl who was not worthy of being his sister-in-law. . . .

Then Jim thought that only a man who is nobody's son and brother can do what he likes—he had been a son and brother before he knew what music was. He had seemed for a few months to be an exception to the family rule of disappointment; there were to be no exceptions. His dream of a career, the career of the dream itself, was over. Whether he liked it or not, it would be a lifework in itself to recompense them for the opportunities they had given him; whatever he wanted to represent, from now on he would have to represent their ideals. Perhaps, he thought, that is all it means to be a servant of God.

As a servant of God he felt exceedingly humble, so humble in fact that he did not feel ashamed—not of having disappointed them, nor of being about to disappoint Irene, nor of the likelihood of disappointing himself all the rest of his life. Ralph, though younger, was more of a man than he; as he stood up, Jim saw how his body was one hard, thick knot from head to foot, which would never be untied. Love in Ralph's heart was the passion which he had pretended to feel, which he might pretend to feel again, and perhaps never would. Ralph, at the end of a hard day's work, said his prayers with a sober passion, as he ought to be able to do and was not. Ralph, as if by inheritance or by instinct, had in his heart love, and religion, and obedience.

He himself, James Arthur Tower, had only his talents. A mouthpiece, to sing only when the joy of others required song, which was not often; to pray, whether he had anything to pray for or not, out loud, for others, because he had a gift of speech. . . . Just as Ralph rose from his knees, Jim thought of his prayer, the prayer of all such men as he: that he might make use of other people's passion, in his life—he would have need of it; and that those who loved him should have no reason to be ashamed of him; and that he might never be found out. His will had been broken, and he felt as if he did not have a heart of his own to break. Ralph blew out the lamp, and the two brothers slipped into bed.

Next morning the postman, Leander's successor, brought the news of Leander's death. He had had a stroke of paralysis on his journey west, had been taken from the train to a hospital in Oklahoma, and after lying unconscious for three days, had passed away. The letter came from the Catholic priest who had buried him.

In the sorrow and confusion of that morning Jim's trouble was almost forgotten. He could not wait for it to be remembered, having to return to college with his guests. His father took leave of him with these words: "Well, Jim, we know best. You'll get over it."

Jim gazed at Ralph; Ralph stared impassively at him.

"You've got a duty in this world," their father added. "You've got to bear witness for the Lord. Remember that."

Irene overheard, and did not altogether misinterpret their glances, in which there was evidence of mourning for something beside the old bachelor's death—mourning in which she, though a stranger, had a part.

As they went back in the little slow train, the German aunt who believed that a prompt marriage must have been arranged, peering into their gloomy faces, congratulated herself aloud on the fact that she was an old maid.

Jim never told Irene that the visit had failed, that his father and brother were stronger than he; she did not need to be told. A flood of tears seemed to run into her heart whenever she thought of it, whenever she sang; but all her friends and even she herself observed that it gave her voice a new beauty, which encouraged her to go on with her career alone.

Jim worked all summer as the college president's secretary, entered a theological seminary in the autumn, and at the end of September went home to be the best man at his brother's marriage to Marianne Duff.

10. His Mother's Girlhood and Marriage

IRA and Ursula Duff, Alwyn's maternal grandparents, were unhappily married; moral fanaticism and the extraordinary strength of both their characters had made of this common situation a bizarre tragedy. He was despotic and malicious, but she had succeeded, by intelligent malice and courage, in living in harmony with him, if not in peace. He was consistently insincere; she was too haughty to hide her resentment or explain it, and in general bore all the blame. Even their two sons, when as adolescents they ran away from home, muttered that it was their mother who was a demon.

She was a woman of singular beauty; her regular features wore a scarcely perceptible grimace of disdain; her protuberant eyes were piercing and sad. As she uttered the most cruel opinions very audibly, very mildly, there was never a trace of emotion in her melodious voice. All those who had anything to hide, even from themselves, had reason to fear or detest her; and her husband made friends with them on that basis. Accused by resentful neighbors and relatives of being unworthy of affection, she was too candid in her own defense; which not only offended the few admirers of her virtue and intelligence who accused her of nothing, but exposed her anew to her husband's skillful vindictiveness.

So it was in an atmosphere of anger and idealism that Alwyn's mother grew up, devoutly sheltered from immorality and irreligion, cruelly exposed to still more cruel passions: a lonely little girl singing old hymns and memorizing long rhymed prayers in the shadow of a woman's disaster, watching intently with large, gray-green eyes, but asking no questions.

As a child of eight Marianne saw that her mother had no friends, clung to her as if to hide the fact that no one else had the courage to love her, and began to receive in consequence all the tenderness of which that supposedly hard heart was capable.

At the age of twelve she had to admit that her mother was in fact proud and mercilessly outspoken, and had to learn not to try to defend her, even against schoolmates who had heard that she was a sort of witch.

When her brothers left home, Marianne would have hated them for their injustice and lack of respect, had not the Gospels which her mother read aloud to her every afternoon expressly forbidden hate. Before she was fourteen she realized that her father had fostered their resentment; that her mother's unpopularity as a whole was his work; that he was a sort of sorcerer, unctuous and loquacious, who had shut her up behind an impenetrable wall of his deceit, his pathos, his private unkindness and public saintliness, where she was growing old angrily, like an innocent prisoner in a mysterious jail.

Then, as ignorant people fear death and happy people, pain, Marianne feared the further effects of his malice. What was to protect her when her turn to be its victim came? At fifteen she prayed every night and morning that he might grow gentle by a sudden disenchantment; but later she imagined that there were pure spirits who may not change, and thereafter pitied him, more or less as the devil has always been pitied by devout women.

His hypocrisy put her on her guard against life's prevailing hypocrisy. Her mother's utter loneliness suggested the solitude of the soul which only living for others could alleviate. Continually on trial before those whom she knew, her mother was like all men and women before God sitting in judgment. It was easy to conceive a half-divine Spirit, all malice, in the image of her father; and to love so cold and enigmatic a mother confidently was in itself a sort of mysticism. It was but a short step to that of the Protestant faith: the lonely effort to distinguish every false appearance from its hidden reality and the entire world of this world from the immortal universe; the hopeless effort to discover how to be free of the one and serve only the other.

In the month of June of her sixteenth year, in the presence of everyone she knew, she was baptized by immersion in the Anne River during a Free Will Baptist revival.

Her father offered a long, vain prayer at the water's edge. The people of the congregation, otherwise merely those who detested her mother, drew closer like a crowd of saints—hard, loving faces all scarred with shadows under the willows, in the summer sunshine. She took three steps forward on the spongy bank. Then the first touch of the cold current seemed to burn her bare feet, and the minister's arms hurt her a little as they bent her backward. For a moment she believed that she was drowning, infinitely far beneath the suffocating, bitter, heavy, noisy water, though the Anne River was shallow.

Later she cried uncontrollably in her mother's arms; but when she recovered from the shock of the ceremony, she found that she was happy and felt that she needed her mother less than before. By the river water, by the pure shame and excitement, an ignorant girl had been made responsible to God—lonesomely so, without an intermediary—for a grown woman's life. She was as jealous of that responsibility as if it were pure love; not even her mother should share it. This was formally the end of childhood. But she believed that she could keep its happiness as long as she kept its purity. Happiness was a duty as well as a miracle. . . .

Meanwhile her mother's melancholy increased, and after her baptism Marianne regarded it with a new, anxious independence. Her mother was as pure as a child. But did not virtue lead to happiness? What was it, then, which ruled her, and took away her illusions, and led her on from one defiance to another, the days of her life leading nowhere? If she imitated her mother, where would she be led? She was afraid to follow further, even in imagination.

In her nineteenth year she had a strange dream. There was a tall hedge of exceedingly dark foliage, and suddenly the thick leaves were drawn apart like a curtain. Her mother entered between them, very

quick and stately, as if upon a stage or into a circus
(though Marianne had never been to the theater and
had seen only the outside of a circus tent). The dream
went on; she grew more and more frightened. Her
mother rode an iron-gray horse, seated upon a woman's
saddle, her full skirts folded and wrinkled in a great
heap behind her, wearing a small hat with a red veil,
holding in her hands a bow and arrow. She rode out
of the woods and down along the river in which Marianne had been baptized, and splashed into the water;
and wherever she went, all those who were not pure of
heart fell down and disappeared—not because she
wished them harm, but because neither their joy nor
their sadness could be compared with her sadness. And
although she came out of the forest as a sort of Diana
—Diana dressed as women did dress in Marianne's
girlhood—Marianne understood that she had been
driven there like a hunted animal, and had merely disguised herself as a huntress in order to escape.

That dream so minutely painted, that hour of sleep
drawn tight like a piece of canvas, hung for months,
a bright, heavy picture, over the bed in which she slept.
It drifted out of itself into other dreams, mingling with
their lack of meaning, and troubled her for days at
a time.

Thereafter she loved her mother without trying
to draw any conclusions. Virtue did lead to happiness. . . . In her mother's life, childlike purity had
led only to an old woman's despair (for she was already growing old); but that life was exceptional and
not for her to try to understand. Such an extremity

of sadness was a wild thing, dangerous even to see. It was as if God had permitted a heathen disaster to take place, perhaps merely to show His mystery, perhaps to teach His angels a lesson; there was nothing in it for human beings, at least for Marianne, to learn. . . .

And thereafter she would no sooner have thought of going to her mother for advice than of kneeling in the woods before an Indian mound, or whispering her troubles to a spring of cold water, like a savage. Thus, uneasily, her thought ran ahead of her from day to day toward the future, very softly, very fatally, coming between her and her mother, until her twentieth year, when she met with the accident of love.

One evening in the spring of that year, outside the Hope's Corner schoolhouse, Ralph Tower, without warning, lifted both her hands and took her lips between his lips—for one second that was long. They were standing in the dark on the trodden ground under a honey locust in bloom which poured its fragrance down upon their heads. Marianne felt a painful astonishment—a strange emotion, because the astonishment was recognition and the pain seemed to be a privilege.

"I'm sorry," Ralph muttered, and ran and stumbled back to the bright schoolhouse, where a party was in progress.

He had left her all alone. Luxuriously the locust shook out its flowers in dead-white clusters. There was no warmth in the blood which ran up and down her veins. She stood there, trembling, and did not cry.

Then she realized that even as a little girl she had been pleased by this boy who was now a man, and that suddenly she had been made a woman. Her modesty had prevented her from counting the number of recollections which had linked her to him with that prolonged attentiveness which is the innocent heart's way of hoping. If she had counted them, she would have been afraid to come out alone with him in the dark. Now it was too late, but she could not keep from doing so, nevertheless.

The people in the schoolhouse (her mother, her father, perhaps even Ralph—all that family sang) began an old song, *Farmer in the Dell*. As automatically as an echo, her mind repeated the words after them, though she could hear only the tune. But instead of going inside, she crept into her father's carriage in the shed until her mother came out to find her and they went home.

No one had ever touched her before. Her mother had taught her that she should never be kissed except by the man who loved her, whom she loved, and whom she would be permitted by marriage to love as long as she lived; to her sober spirit this had seemed very natural. For another month she was confident in the future—that is, in their eventual love, betrothal, and marriage; but her confidence steadily diminished.

But Ralph said nothing about it, indeed avoided every opportunity to see her alone; and whenever they happened to meet, some sort of fear was evident from his expression. She read its meaning: fear of what she had been led to expect, fear of consequences. . . .

She tried to believe that she misunderstood it; she tried to endure her final conviction that she had not. She did not complain to her mother; she tried not to do so even in whispers to herself.

She could make no effort, neither ask for an explanation nor undertake even the humblest tentative of intimacy. This was a woman's weakness; but by protecting her from further humiliation, it counted as strength, and she resented it as strength; for she thought that she would like to pay her humiliation the compliment of illness or even death.

She had nothing to look forward to, so she looked back at her lost innocence, the reverse of a promised land, exaggerating its perfection and its peace. So swiftly, so gently, so thoroughly, her happiness had been undone. . . . As a flying seed will debauch a whole meadow with flowers, one kiss, one caress not even wished for, had spoiled her peace of mind, even her good health. For there were rhythms in her body to which she stumbled impatiently when she went out to walk alone. There was fever in her forehead, and an abnormal snowy freshness on her lips and tongue. Her pillow was full of faces which were terribly alike, and when finally she fell asleep, her own hands touched her and woke her up, seeming to be the young farmer's hand which had taken them that night against her will, and locked them both easily in its palm, and let them go again too soon, also against her will. Her will was weak and wasted itself upon opposite wishes. . . .

When she had explained why she had hid in the

carriage outside the schoolhouse, her mother had said, "Now you must forget all about it."

She envied the simplicity of this attitude, ready now to pay its price in sorrow, since there was sorrow in any case. But if the episode had actually been repeated, as it was in several misty dreams during the summer, she would have kept her own counsel. She was no longer a young girl over whom a mother may watch, but more a woman than her mother, who had left a part of womanhood behind her when she lost her confidence in others, her readiness to weep, her hope. Marianne had hope, though nothing to hope for; and tears often refreshed her as her mother was never refreshed by anything.

Meanwhile, the midsummer peonies broke into bloom, and their stems broke down under the weight upon the shabby lawns. Her mother's little peacock opened its feathers and fanned itself nervously, and before it rained fluttered upon the gables, whimpering in a clear, disagreeable voice. The sun rose in what had been the dead of night, wearing upon the horizon a bright humidity like a mask of hot iron and pearls. . . .

And perpetually she saw in imagination the strong, homely young farmer's face, visibly, invisibly, beside everything which her small world contained, as if it were a tear in the corner of her eye.

What had she done to deserve this misery—sickness and magic mixed? Had she ever wished for love? Never—not in a single daydream, not for one lonely moment of unwilling aloofness among other girls in love. Ralph alone was to blame.

She thought that it was her Christian training which enabled her to forgive him, but found forgiveness all too easy, being merely a disguise of love. Until she stopped forgiving him—that is, stopped loving him— he would continue to hurt her; there would be continually more for which he would have to be forgiven. So, because she loved him, she ought to do penance for the wrong he had done, by hating him. . . . She could not even keep clear in her mind these duties of disappointed love, much less accomplish any of them.

There were other sources of bewilderment. For one whose eyelids droop and whose eyes ache, the world itself seems to be shrunken and inflamed; so the atmosphere of her home grew even more sinister than it had been when, but for its unhappiness, she would have been happy. It would not be difficult, now that she knew the sickness love produced, to keep her virtue perfect; but with her heart so stripped of its indifference, so stimulated as if by a drug, she began to fear for her faith, dreading the influence upon it of her mother's loveless irony, her father's piety and lies.

So she resolved to leave home as soon as possible. In the autumn she went away to a teachers' college, and soon after Christmas accepted a vacant position in a Sheboygan school. She should have been happy there. Her slight beauty ripened with a delicate solemnity; she had inherited her mother's good taste in dress and gestures and ways of speech, which emphasized her gentle virtues; and she was loved by everyone. Loneliness had been a child's palace and stronghold, but since it had been broken into by the young farmer, the image of whose briefly passionate face she could not put out, she was afraid to stay in it. So she made friends with Evangeline Gay, a woman ten years older than she who had a small independent income and lived with a brother and his wife; and later accepted the attentions of a suitor named Paul Fairchild, the son of the Episcopalian bishop of Sheboygan.

Having prepared himself for the law and then lived in England with his mother's relatives, Paul Fairchild had come back to Wisconsin to rest after an illness. He was idle, romantic, and not quite candid; the sort of young man who seems to be a bachelor as soon as boyhood is over, very likely to be passionately in love, but unlikely to attach much importance to the fact.

Marianne took pleasure in his politeness and his culture. Hoping it was true, she wrote to her mother that if he continued to deserve her respect, she might learn to love him and be willing to consider becoming his wife.

Her father got up in the night, took the letter from the pocket inside her mother's skirt as he often did, read it, replaced it, and the next morning began to announce to his friends and his enemies, "My daughter is engaged to the Episcopalian bishop's son."

Bishop Fairchild was a famous man; his son, who had lived in his father's diocese only a few months at a time, had aroused everyone's curiosity. Emphasized by Ira Duff's extravagant way of speech, the news traveled quickly and widely.

Late one afternoon Paul Fairchild came into Marianne's schoolroom and said, "Your father says that we're engaged. So much the better. I love you."

Shocked and confused, ashamed of having written anything to her mother before he had spoken, Marianne did not deny it, did not protest, and was scarcely aware of his discourtesy. But, pressing her hands against his shoulders, she did avoid his kiss.

"Please go now. I have work to do. I must—" She lost her voice. She sat down at the desk. Her cold fingers fluttered the sheets of paper on which her pupils had written themes; on the first page she read, in a small boy's determined hand, "The Stars." She saw, far off at the left, the winter sun going down, divided into squares by the window.

"Please go. I must work," she repeated; and then her body sagged against the table—she had fainted away. Her head fell forward and lay on the pile of themes as if it were a pillow.

The young man caught her shoulders so that she did not slip out of the chair, and stood there in stupid astonishment, unable for a moment to rouse himself from his emotions of a lover. Out of a great white jug marked *Water* drops fell in threes to the pail below with the rhythm of a waltz. But he could not move to put water on her face without letting her fall. . . .

In the school yard several pupils drew near; one

of them was crying; one spoke loudly in a sneering voice. The young man was embarrassed; if they should come in. . . . He judged by the sound of their voices that they were old enough to understand, to misunderstand.

He lifted Marianne in his arms and put her down on a bench. Then he took one of her hands to kiss it, but at that moment her heavy, weak eyelids opened. "The Stars," she said. "Oh, what is it? What has happened?"

The young man smiled and looked ashamed.

"I am all right now." She drank a glass of water eagerly, as if it were from thirst that she was suffering. "Please go."

But he did not move. Then she saw his troubled eyes running to the windows and the door, and understood him better; so she added: "You must. I asked Evangeline Gay to come here for me."

He left her alone, seeming glad of an excuse.

It was a poor excuse, for she had asked no one to come. She dragged herself back through the snow to the house where she lived, and with ice-cold hands laid herself in her bed as if she were a dead body.

She felt little resentment toward her father or either of her lovers. What had happened was more odious than human conduct could be; it was like an illness, like the progress of an illness from the forefinger to the ring finger, from the arm to the breast, and so on. . . . An illness which would not even kill her; but her self-respect was dead—worn out, suffocated, filthily bandaged, and still sore, though it was dead.

If life was like this, was she duty bound to live? If her soul was immortal and could be so compromised, would it do any good to die? Marriage sprung like a trap beneath her driven feet; God the father as dishonest as her father, tricking her with accidents. . . .

For a moment, in her sorrow, she destroyed her God. Horrified by the involuntary evil of her thought, she beat her forehead with her fists, closed her eyes, and wished that she might never have to open the latter again as long as she should be obliged to live. For a moment she had destroyed God; but because she loved Him, she created Him again.

So she determined to accept it all: the consequences of her mother's betrayal, her father's lying, Ralph's neglect, and Paul Fairchild's love. Crumpled up on the bed, stone-cold in the cold, red light of the sunset which poured through the window, she fought intelligently to keep her soul from falling down to hell. For if she rejected what God permitted, she believed, it would fall and change as it fell, as certain angels had done, into a dead-alive thing whose eternity was all one such afternoon. . . .

But could she, with courage and intelligence, hold herself at a certain altitude above all evil, including death—as the wings of a bird hold it for a moment in the air after a bullet has lodged in its heart, opened its heart? Could such a moment last as long as her life? She spread out in imagination her youth and her bravery as if they were wings. Suddenly she felt that she was ready—that is, ready to marry Paul

Fairchild. And he should not discover what was in her heart; Ralph should not either, nor, perhaps, should God. . . . She would lie to them faithfully by the way she would live; she would love them all three equally.

Something like a soothing drug was running in her veins where the blood had seemed to cease to run. Her landlady knocked at the door and called her to supper; she did not answer.

She lay there without answering until she heard a familiar whistling. Then she rose and slipped carefully along the wall toward the window until she could see into the street where Paul Fairchild was gazing up over the hedge with a bunch of yellow roses in his hand. Hiding behind a half-closed shutter, Marianne tried to like his vague, intelligent face and at this distance, unknown to him, to enjoy the roses. He whistled again; she did not show herself at the window. To-morrow she would be ready for him. . . . She studied his anxiety and discontent, and watched him go away.

That night she wrote a letter to her mother to announce her engagement definitely, phrasing it in such a way as to put her father in the right without asking what had happened to betray her.

The night was as long as a lifetime. In effect, so strong was her imagination, it was a lifetime—that of Paul Fairchild's wife. She was by nature and training too just to think that the future would be uniformly unhappy; but a definite distaste was occasioned by her anticipation of certain pleasures and rewards which ought to fulfill, but would surely fail to fulfill, her dearest hopes. . . .

Nevertheless, she was content with her decision—above all, proud of it. Her loneliness, if she did not marry, would be a perpetual reproach to Ralph for the wrong he had done her; and altogether womanly in her passion, she believed that she did not want him to have to give it a moment's thought. Now that she had given him up, she could say proudly to herself as often as she liked that she loved him, which helped her endure the humiliating fact that he had never loved her. And when, just before the dawn, she said her prayers, bowing before God's pride, she gave thanks as well for her own, saying that it was the spirit of God in her heart. Her mother, under different circumstances, had said as much.

Marianne's engagement to Paul Fairchild lasted all that summer. She became the governess of a banker's children in order not to have to return to Hope's Corner. Her mother believed that she wanted to be with her future husband, and referred to her happiness in every letter with an unhappy woman's skepticism and envy.

But by autumn Marianne had given up hope of every sort of happiness. Her thought was all anger, and it trembled upon her lips in sentences already formed; so she began to have to look forward shamefully to the time when she would be saying things as spiteful as those for which her mother was famous. All her life she had seen what marriage could be at its worst—hers would be as bad; even her good qualities would play an evil rôle, as her mother's had done. Her life, more and more like her mother's, more and more thoroughly spoiled. . . . An unkind fate having set to work to spoil it, she herself had added the finishing touch by promising to marry.

Every day she told herself that she ought formally to break her promise. But Paul loved her; he would be crafty as he had been in the beginning; she was tired—increasingly tired since that night in the spring when with such difficulty she had made up her mind to do what was still undone. So tired that the events of the past and finally those of the present merely haunted her, as life haunts one upon a sick bed who may be alive and may be dead, who cannot tell. . . . Day by day the future tiptoed carefully across the present into the past without waking her from this nightmare of being about to marry a man whom she did not love in the least.

Often she did not think of him as her future husband, and he did not always try to usurp a husband's privileges. Then she found him an agreeable companion, distracting her attention even from their relationship, consoling her even for distress which he alone had caused.

But by the autumn she was entirely disillusioned as to his character. He was weak, indolent, naturally irreligious, naturally libertine. He gave her no opportunity to know his father, the bishop, never spoke of his mother, and expressed no desire to visit her parents. He seemed unwilling to wait for God's blessing upon their union, and meanwhile did not help her to fix a date for the marriage.

Patiently, tactfully, with that deliberate pretense of innocence which is the youngest and purest form of cynicism, she avoided his caresses. Often she tried to persuade herself of an emotion which even then it was her duty to feel, or tried to believe that she would love him in time, in due time. On these occasions she realized that she would never marry him, and was bitterly ashamed of herself for not telling him so.

During the summer he found two gaited horses which he could rent, and taught Marianne to ride. On a gray horse, in a broadcloth dress turned into a riding habit, she looked exactly as her mother had looked in the dream two years before, and often thought of the resemblance. One afternoon late in October they rode out along the bluffs over Lake Michigan, and came to a wooded hill surrounded by a fence, and could not find a gate. So they dismounted, tied the horses, and made their way up through the woods toward a little cliff which they had seen from the road, in order to look down from it upon the lake.

The ironwoods made a pallid, artificial evening, in which Marianne observed an ugly expression on Paul's face: a repeated look sideways, a crude, unspoken syllable in one corner of his mouth, a stiff wrinkle from one temple to the other across his forehead. . . . He walked a step or two behind, stared hard at her, and stumbled. Glancing back over her shoulder, Marianne watched this expression with eager, unsympathetic interest, seeing suddenly that his love, if it were provoked, might provoke her hate, and so set her free. They came out under the harder stare of the whole sky in the clearing on top of the hill.

Among the rocks they found a grassy hollow shaped like a large armchair. They were above the horizon like a thin-lipped shell and above a dripping cloud which lay in it; above the lake covered with tight indentations and ribbons of foam which were continually being tied and torn; above a fish hawk which continually went down and made mistakes at the surface of the water.

But suddenly Paul cried, "This is nonsense!" and began to pleat her skirt with his nervous hands.

She frowned and shrank away from him. "Don't. I don't understand—"

"I love you," he stammered. "I want you to love me. Of course you don't." He was panting between his words. "You sit there like an old woman. Sit and admire nature!"

The fish hawk dropped again, plunging into one of the indentations and breaking a great cord of foam. Paul's hands were fighting with her left hand. "Paul," she said, "you do not wish to offend me. You don't know what you are doing. I am afraid of you. Get up. We must go back. If you love me, you don't want to hurt me. Wait—"

"Wait. . . . No. If you love me—now. Don't talk religion to me. I've heard nothing else all my life and it hasn't made me any happier or better. Now. We are engaged. It is enough."

Marianne knew then that she had a right to hate

him. "We were engaged. We were, until today. I break my engagement now. Let me go. I tell you, I will not marry you." She hated him because he smiled.

"You'd better not," he said. "You'd better not. Listen. Two girls promised to marry me before. They weren't so good as you are. Everybody knew; nobody has paid any attention to them since. I hated them. If you don't marry me, people will think— they always do, anyway. You can't always do what you like—I love you too much." He was smiling, but his eyes were full of tears.

The sweat sprang in the palms of Marianne's hands. He had come closer and closer to her. She tried to say to herself that he was out of his mind and not to blame. She struck him full in the face. At that moment she was glad, for she knew that they were done with each other at last; having had to defend herself, she would not even be able to pity him again.

He sprang to his feet and stumbled a little way off under the trees. He was pacing up and down and beating the ground with a stick like a desperate child.

Then Marianne got up and ran down through the woods. He did not see her in time, and she reached the fence before he did. When she untied her horse, its panic told her what to do: she struck it across its nose with the reins; it galloped away. Then she mounted Paul's horse fearlessly, shamelessly as well—having to sit astride because of the saddle, her skirts pulled up almost to her knee. He tried to follow her a little way on foot; she left him behind.

At the edge of the town she tied the horse to another fence. No one who knew her saw her come home.

She lay across the bed with her feet and one hand hanging toward the floor; a sort of sick paralysis held her there. When Paul Fairchild had tried to hold her on the hilltop, she had said to herself, "This kiss will not hurt me as much as the other did." She had been mistaken; she was going to be ill.

Her landlady came up to her room. "I am not well," she explained. "I felt bad; I fainted away."

"Shall I send for the doctor?"

"No. I feel better. I got too tired riding. It will be over in a few minutes. Ask Evangeline Gay to come."

Evangeline Gay stood at the foot of the bed. The girl's eyes and mouth were empty of emotion—they told her anxious friend nothing; but her nervous hands, along the ruffle of the pillow and up and down the pleats of her riding habit, like those of a deaf mute, spelled out an extreme distress. She had a slight fever and a greatly accelerated pulse.

"You poor child," Evangeline said, "whatever is the matter, it has gone on long enough. You're going to give up your school. I'm going to take you home. If you're not strong enough to talk me out of it, you're weak enough to do as I think best."

Marianne obeyed orders in order not to have to talk. Furthermore, she was ill and would not dare to get well in Sheboygan, for Paul Fairchild would be there at the foot of the bed as soon as she could be seen. He came the next morning, but Evangeline had instructed the people of the house to send him away. At noon they set out together for Marianne's home.

Mrs. Duff met them with a horse and buggy at the Aaronsville station. As they passed the Hope's Corner schoolhouse, Marianne slipped out of the seat and hid her drawn face in Evangeline's lap. The mother, who was driving, scarcely glanced at her, but stared fiercely over the playground, among the monuments and trees of the cemetery, and across the withered cornfields, as if to discover there who or what it was that had made her daughter ill.

It was a false illness, a mere excuse for her distress of which she could give no other explanation. So except for that moment under the honey locusts which leaned out from the school grounds, Marianne was able to control it until they reached home. But when at last she lay in her own bed, a fever declared itself with great force. It seemed to be a breathing, solid body like that of a human being; it curled up beside her on the same pillow, and slipped over and rested on her breast. She slept under its weight, and there, weeping softly even in her sleep, she was as happy as she expected ever to be again.

Evangeline was introduced to the father, a handsome man with curls in his beard and large eyes that resembled lumps of some kind of blue stone. "I hope our girl hasn't been led into temptation off there away from her folks and home influences," he said. "People's tongues will be wagging—"

"You would do well," his wife interrupted, "not to speak evil of her yourself."

The two women waited for him to leave them alone. Then the mother cried, "What ever has happened?"

"I don't know."

"Is it the fault of that man she means to marry?"

"She said nothing against him." There was a pause, neither knowing what the other expected of her. "I must go back to Sheboygan in the morning," Evangeline added. "She will be all right. She needed rest."

The proud woman begged her to stay. "Marianne enjoys perfect health—it is one of the few things I am proud of. There is some mystery about this. And I am afraid that she will never tell me what the matter is. She had grounds for believing that I would disapprove of any man she meant to marry. You see, my own marriage, though my husband and I are God-fearing and resigned, is not all that it should be." She made this confession without a sign of embarrassment. "But Marianne will not be afraid to tell you her romantic notions, because you have never been married."

Ira Duff came into the room. "You understand," he said mournfully, "my wife is fittingly upset, for it was she who encouraged Marianne to leave home against my will, and hid from me this engagement to the bishop's son as long as she could."

His wife laughed softly. "As long as I could wasn't very long, for you're as good as any pickpocket to ferret out my letters, and better than a town crier to make our secrets the talk of the whole country."

Evangeline was afraid to leave her friend alone in such a house.

The village doctor came, failed to identify an actual illness or to find a satisfactory explanation of the symptoms there were, and prescribed rest and one or two innocuous remedies, glancing meanwhile with dull suspicion at Mrs. Duff, as if she were the cause of it all.

Evangeline established herself in the bedroom to watch. Marianne slept and pretended to sleep. Often her face was languid and haughty—the face of a middle-aged woman strong enough to die of an exceptional weakness, without explanations, mutely. Evangeline said to Mrs. Duff: "It is a sickness. I am not a doctor. She has nothing to tell. I had better go back to Sheboygan and ask no questions."

But Marianne smiled half-heartedly one morning, and asked to have some flowers and one of her mother's potted plants brought up to her room. She said that she was hungry, though she scarcely touched the tray when it came.

The next day was the Sabbath. The Free Will Baptists of Hope's Corner had united with the Presbyterians of Aaronsville, and the minister had another congregation to preach to in the morning; so services were held at three o'clock. Marianne's cousin, Clara Peters, a grim woman who had married beneath her, came to spend the afternoon, and Evangeline went to church with Mr. and Mrs. Duff. They got home just before supper and found Marianne alone. "Poor

Clara discouraged me," she explained, "and I sent her off to her mean husband."

After the evening meal she asked for the Bible with the largest print, and held it up resolutely toward the lamp until her mother left the room. Then she said to her friend, "You were late coming back from church. Whom did you see? Where did you go?"

"We went home with the Towers. Your mother wanted to visit that old bachelor who has been sick, Mr. Leander. He was all wrapped up in crazy quilts. He said—"

But Marianne had turned pale; it was as if a heavy white net had been thrown suddenly over her face, in which her bright eyes seemed to have been caught and lay burning, lay very still; in which her mouth struggled and finally lay still.

And her friend remembered how, in the uncomfortable pew, Mrs. Duff had lifted the cape of her coat and whispered behind it: "Do you see the young man sitting with his folks in the first row by the window? They are the Towers, the finest people in the country. I thought a few years back that Marianne had lost her heart to that young Ralph, the one of their sons who is here. Nothing came of it, of course, and anyway I guess the Towers wouldn't care to be connected by marriage with my husband. . . ."

Now, at the mention of them, Marianne's face turned white and lay still as if it had been caught in a net. A net of misery, excitement, and hopelessness and hope interwoven. . . . The spinster put out her hand quickly as if to catch hold of a thread by which it might be undone, and said at once, conscious of her cruelty: "Marianne, I must go back home. And you know, I shall have to see Paul Fairchild. What shall I tell him?"

The girl lifted her head from the pillow. "I have nothing to say to him. I shall not see him again."

"What did he do to you?"

"It doesn't matter. I don't care what he does. I never cared what he did. I'm sorry," the girl whispered.

The older woman whispered as well: "Then there is another—some other—then that other one is . . . The one you do love."

Marianne turned scarlet. "No, I—haven't any right. . . . How do you. . . . He—"

Then for a few minutes there was nothing for her friend to do but watch a pitiful spectacle: the girl tossing on the bed in a sort of infant agony, and stuffing the bedclothes in her mouth, and beating the pillows.

Evangeline heard Mrs. Duff come swiftly up the staircase. But she stopped in the corridor, where she must have been able to hear the girl's stifled weeping. She stood still outside the door, and then tiptoed down-stairs again, intelligently obliging Evangeline to be a mother to her child—because she was a spinster and did not know too much about marriage.

The girl grew quiet. Evangeline bathed her flushed face and said: "You'd better talk to me. Now, before you stop crying. Before you get mysterious and des-perate again."

Then she stopped crying. Suddenly she sat up in bed, and in a monotonous tone of voice, slowly but without faltering, as if she were remembering not the facts, but words and phrases with which she had often told it before—to herself alone—recited, painstakingly recited, the story of her disappointment. The sentences began with "Even when I was a child, when we were in school together, though I didn't know," or "Mother brought me up so innocently, I thought," or "I was ashamed," or "It broke my heart. . . ." They ended with "It was too late," or "He didn't care and I had no right to think he did," or "He didn't mean anything by it—it was all in my imagination."

Evangeline muttered to herself: "It wasn't. It won't be. Not if—" She was astonished; for suddenly there had come together in her mind all Ralph Tower's gestures, phrases, and expressions, that afternoon. She examined them and compared them with what she was being told; at last she had no doubt about their meaning. Inquiries about her happiness, her health, her marriage; a resentful silence for several minutes after every answer; the sound, when he did speak, of a lump in his throat; embarrassed glances at his parents to be sure they were not listening; his eyebrows contracted, half hiding his small eyes. Anxiety, wounded vanity, jealousy. . . .

Meanwhile, as if she were merely telling a story, a story which had to be told to the end, its bitter end, Marianne went on from her brief, humiliating encounter with one lover to her humiliating relations with the other. "I wrote my mother about Paul Fairchild, and she let my father think I had promised to marry him, and he told everybody."

"She didn't, by the way," Evangeline said. "Your father got the letter out of her pocket—she told me."

"Oh," the girl cried, and was silent for a moment, and seemed to be staring back at her girlhood compromised, her broken heart rebroken, her strength worn out—six miserable months which might have been avoided. Then, less with the patience of a desperate girl than with that of a story teller, she tried to go on where she had been interrupted. "You see, Paul Fairchild—"

"Don't tell me about Paul Fairchild," Evangeline interrupted again. "He doesn't matter—you said so yourself."

The girl said no more and lay staring humbly at nothing.

Her friend went over to the window. It was late at night. There were some cattle moving in the dark in the orchard. A great, aged moon was coming up over the country with a great quantity of amber. The turkeys in the apple trees were awake.

Evangeline made up her mind what ought to be done for Marianne, what she could do. Perhaps she was merely going to make a fool of herself, not even for herself, and accomplish no more. She shed a few tears and wiped them away.

Then she sat down again, and told Marianne exactly what Ralph Tower had said, and how he had looked when he said it, and what she thought about it. At last she used the word love.

Marianne, shivering, held her breath.

"You two need a go-between. Your mother will be of no use. After I'm gone there won't be anybody to manage things for you but God, and whether He will or not is a question. You don't know what this young man's intentions are. So I'm going to see him and find out. Your mother ought to have done so. According to her, it was your father's fault that she couldn't, because her own marriage is unhappy. I am an old maid," she added dryly, "and I believe in love. So to-morrow, bright and early, I'm going to have another word or two with this young man."

Marianne clung to her like a child and begged her not to. Evangeline paid little attention, thinking of the task she had set herself, and how she had better go about it. At last Marianne whispered, "Don't tell mother, if you are going."

Evangeline slipped out of the house the next morning soon after sunrise, and an hour and a half later came back, tired, grim, and satisfied. Mrs. Duff was waiting in the garden. "Where have you been?" she asked. "I saw you start out, but I thought best not to bother you."

"I've been to the Towers'," Evangeline said. "It is all right. Will you drive me to the station this afternoon? For I'm not needed here any more."

"So that is it. The Lord preserve us," the mother said solemnly. "There is not a human being on this earth I have ever loved but my daughter. And I have no faith—miserable woman that I am."

Then Evangeline wept, and turned aside among the

currant bushes. Mrs. Duff hurried indoors, calling, "I-ra! I-ra!"

A little later, going through the hall to the staircase, Evangeline heard Ira Duff's resonant, false voice rising and falling in a heavy rhythm, and saw them, the sharp-tongued wife and her hated husband, kneeling side by side in front of the sitting-room sofa, their backs very straight, their eyes closed, like a bride and groom before an invisible pastor.

"You've been crying," Marianne said, and tears which, according to what her friend had to say, would be those of joy or of sorrow, came to her eyes.

"You cry yourself, to your heart's content," Evangeline replied. "You might as well cry now, for if God is good you'll have no cause to for many a day." She spoke with a blunt, mechanical joyousness. "I waited by the side of the road until he came along on his way to the cheese factory, and then I waited for him under a tree until he got back and came there."

Marianne's tears ran down across her face, without expression, still patient; she did not succeed in speaking.

Evangeline went on hurriedly but with difficulty, trying not to emphasize her words: "I have one question to ask you. Tell me. In so many words. That man—I mean Paul Fairchild—he never took, he didn't take—I don't want to know, it's the man you're going to marry. Nothing wrong happened? That's not why you're so miserable, is it? That's not why you're sick—"

"Stop," the girl cried huskily. She had lifted herself in the bed upon her elbows. Her eyes were fixed; her voice was hard, hurt, and full of joy. "I am a good girl. He kissed me once. They, they both— did, once."

Evangeline was ashamed of herself, of Ralph Tower, of men; so she went on with the cruel monologue which had begun as a question. "Men always ask that—good men, Christians. They are hard, hard. I guess it's their right and duty. Don't blame him. I'll have to see him again and tell him, before he asks—"

"Stop, Evangeline," the girl repeated. "I don't blame him. I deserve it, because. . . . Don't ever speak of it again." She closed her eyes and whispered, "But why didn't he tell me—all this time? Oh, why, then . . ."

Therefore, dutifully, Evangeline gave a circumstantial account of the meeting. "You know," she had begun by saying, "you have broken that girl's heart." Because she was a spinster, she had tried to put him in the wrong. She had failed, because he had always been in love, and because of Marianne's engagement to the bishop's son who had a bad reputation, and the suspicions it had aroused.

The slight, strong man had spoken laboriously, like a giant for whom human speech is petty and difficult. He had made up his mind when a little boy to marry Marianne. He had been ashamed of having kissed her. They had been too young to marry then. He had been afraid of himself, of his own nature; self-control had always been hard for him. So he had avoided her, until the time when, safely and honorably, he could ask her to be his wife. Then she had gone away; he had believed that she had forgotten or had never cared. Then she had become engaged.

In his small hazel eyes there had been a look of instinctive suspicion, the suspicion of ultimate unhappiness which was natural to him. He had torn up leaves by the handful with his calloused hands, and at last had blushed under his dull sunburn. Then he had spoken soberly of his other suspicion and had asked the question which Evangeline had not dared to answer on her own responsibility. Then he had stood up, turned his back on her, swung round, asked her pardon, and muttered: "Good-by. I must get back to work."

Evangeline, having nothing more to tell, smoothed Marianne's forehead with her finger tips. "You had better stop crying now," she concluded. "God is good. You will be happy."

The girl leaped out of bed and fell to her knees. Evangeline left her alone. When she returned with the mother they found her half dressed, and with great difficulty persuaded her to go back to bed. After the noonday meal Evangeline said good-by.

Marianne was glad that her friend was going away. She herself had to go on to a rendezvous which no friend could keep with her, in a gleaming, uniform solitude, a sort of wilderness—that of being loved. Innocent and not ignorant, she trembled a little at the prospect. Not knowing why, she kept remembering that Ralph was the best hunter in that part of Wisconsin. She felt a jealousy of no one and a nostalgia for no particular place. She kept remembering the kiss which had now been justified. These things embarrassed her in Evangeline's presence; it was a blessing, she thought, that her mother did not believe in love and therefore would not pay any unusual attention to her. She scarcely paid attention to Evangeline saying good-by.

Mrs. Duff took Evangeline to the station by the road which went past the Tower farm, and when they saw Ralph plowing in the stubble field, the spinster got out and trudged across the furrows until she met him. "I'm going home," she said. "Go to see her. She is waiting. It is all right. She is as pure as the snow. What fools we were . . . Good-by."

The young man's body, like that of a giant, though small, sagged against the plow handles. He hid his great hands behind his back as if he ought to be ashamed of them. He said: "Thank you. Good-by."

"Glory be to God, that's all right!" Evangeline said as she climbed back into the buggy.

"The glory of God is made of our troubles," the older woman answered resolutely.

Late that afternoon Ralph came to see Marianne. He sat by the bed and could say nothing; his dark mouth covered with dust quivered instead. He kissed her hands and hurried away.

There was no courtship. Another man had wooed her for him. God had wooed her with His errors, His intoxicating tenderness, His intrigue. Evangeline, who would never have a chance to speak for herself, had spoken for her; the spirit of God, Marianne thought, in the person of an old maid. . . .

She grew strong quickly, realizing that she had not actually been ill. She saw Ralph every day or two, and made friends with his father, who, to his mother's astonishment, was pleasant and communicative in her company. With genuine enthusiasm Mrs. Tower accepted Marianne as her son's future wife and the mother of her grandchildren to be born; but they never knew how to be intimate friends. Marianne's own mother, in her pride in the alliance, was happier than she had been for years. When the tragic news of Leander's death in Oklahoma came, she said regretfully, "Now he will never know about the marriage. . . ."

Marianne herself was not impatient for it to take place. Having tasted the bitterness of man's passion (its contagious unrest, its deliberate neglect, its suspicion) before the sweet, she was glad to wait until she stopped fearing vaguely that it might be altogether bitter. The passage of time would obliterate the humiliation of her other engagement and hush the gossip about it. Meanwhile a separate home was being prepared for them at one end of the Tower house, where Leander had lived. So the wedding was postponed until the following September.

Evangeline Gay and James Tower were their witnesses. Ralph's face—brilliant with intelligence of an unintelligible emotion, tragic to his elders who were present, humble and sunburned—was like that of a young wild animal being baptized. They stood up in one corner of the parlor before a mass of asters and autumn leaves. In the midst of the ceremony Marianne remembered her baptism in the Anne River, thinking that the arms of the man who was at that moment becoming her husband, those arms close beside her, very tight in the broadcloth sleeves, were even stronger than the minister's had been; that the flood in which she was to be submerged this time was not cold, and would be scented with straw of the stacks outside the window, with sheepfolds, linen, and candle wax.

Unlike that of Cana, water was not changed into wine for this marriage. There was but a frugal supper and little festivity. And swiftly the wine of passion itself changed for her into the pure water of Christian married life.

11. His Father. His Uncle Jim's Later Life. The Religious Faith of the Family

ALWYN'S father always loved to hunt. When he could afford it and the farm work was not too pressing, he went north in the autumn during the deer season. Then his brother Jim, the minister, came from Chicago with a little armory of guns and cases of expensive fishing tackle; and the two went off together, to forget, in a tent under the hemlocks, that one had sacrificed his future to the other, that one was happy and the other unhappy (though they might not have agreed which was which), and that an abyss of prosperity and college education lay between them.

After they came back, the farmhouse smelled of hides, and for months little meat was eaten but venison, which made Alwyn sick. His uncle Jim's handsome face glowed with the conventional poetry of recaptured boyhood, with delight in the photographs which he tinted artistically with transparent water colors, with pride in the analogies which had been suggested to him in the north and which would serve him in many private conversations if not in sermons.

Alwyn's father, on the other hand, talked by the hour of exaggerated dangers and mystifying sensations of danger where there was none; of men who lost their compasses and strayed in circles and were found half dead; of timber wolves baying up and down the darkness; of stags marching slowly into clearings to keep a rendezvous with him; and he spoke very shyly of killing things, as if to kill were a love gesture. Then there was upon his face a shining expression of tenderness without pity and violence without fault, which was the equivalent of beauty—though he was what is called a homely man, with his very long nose, his low forehead, his delicate, outstanding ears, and small eyes.

When he was first married fox hunts were still held in the county—cutters and teams of young horses racing around the snowy fields and marshes, and waiting here and there for the hounds to bring the fox across the road. Now most of the hunters he knew went to the woods merely to get drunk together away from their wives. And the immigrants who were steadily buying up the land were not sportsmen; they hunted out of season, only for food, and exterminated the game fish with nets. One year he held the office of game warden, was menaced and even stoned by loafers along the mill races in little saloon towns, and arrested many lawbreakers. It was good sport, but very lonely; indeed, all the sport which was left in that part of the world was lonely.

So he took his little son with him along woodland paths where partridges walked, moving their fine throats and crowned heads, uttering a sort of girlish, insane cry. Or before dawn they drove many miles— the boy wrapped up in strong-smelling blankets, the horse's hoofs ringing under the mist—to small, hidden lakes not yet emptied of bass and pickerel. Alwyn held his breath as in wet boats they ventured out from the piers as if on a pane of glass, and shuddered automatically when a gun was fired or a bleeding bird or animal was found in the bushes. But the company of the timorous, overwatchful boy did not satisfy his father, then (as he grew up and his character crystallized) embarrassed, and finally displeased him. Alwyn was disappointed when he ceased to be taken along; for the heartbreaking landscapes, the blue herons like dwarf angels, the stateliness of other birds and animals just before they were disfigured by their own blood, his father's silent, primitive enjoyment, even his own distaste and fright, had enchanted him.

During the winter months his father earned money as a taxidermist, having taken lessons from a man who had spent a vacation at Hope's Corner when he was a boy, and later having studied it from a book. He was remarkably skillful, and many sportsmen brought him their dead trophies to mount, so they might hang permanently in the lodges of secret societies, in dining rooms and dens. Alwyn invariably felt sick when he went into the room at one end of the house which was his workshop. Bodies of birds and small animals bleeding slowly on newspapers, while his father imitated them with wire, tow, string, and wet clay; the pelts drying on wooden forms and the bird skins turned inside out, and dusted with cornmeal and arsenic; scraping-knives in the skulls of deer; the odor of stale meat and green bone; the rank odor of water birds' flesh, almost black with oil. . . .

There one winter he built a life-sized stallion on a frame of slats and heavy wire, modeling every tendon and vein from photographs of a dead race horse. It was so large that an opening had to be cut in the wall to take it out. He said, "I often wonder if what they call sculpture isn't a lot like my work." With the light of the desire to be proud of himself in his eyes, he reminded one more sharply than most mature men are able to do, of the waste, wreckage, or abandonment of gifts amid which youth is turned into maturity.

When at last the birds balanced on curious crotches which he sought in the woods, he put in black-headed pins, bound their feathers into place with thread, and painted their beaks, eye sockets, and feet; and when the raccoons, squirrels, foxes, or lynxes stood on varnished pedestals which a cabinet maker prepared for him, he caressed and bent their limbs, to give them back, falsely, what he and his like had taken away— life, its grace and its agitated peace. He worked as patiently as if he were bringing them to birth or at least bringing about a resurrection (though he was only making their death resemble life a little) ; and he tried to make Alwyn see the charm of what he was doing.

He tried in vain; the boy stared at him unhappily. There are things which require not sensibility but the lack of it to be felt, and he was still too imaginative to understand them. Not until he grew to manhood was he to be able to bear the thought of his father's intimacy with so much agony and death.

Even then he was to remember with dismay a large snow owl caught in a trap and brought uninjured to his father, who poured chloroform on a handkerchief and placed it in between the bars of the cage. The immense bird's plumage, oyster-white and sand-white, was like velvet embroidered with a sort of alphabet. It snapped its brutal beak and stretched its wings as if they were lame with fatigue. It grew drowsy, straightened its sagging neck with a royal movement, and nodded again. At last Alwyn's father dared to reach inside and cover its nostrils with the cloth; and in the shadow of his large brown hand the milky eyelids fell finally. For months thereafter Alwyn woke panic-stricken in the middle of the night, having felt that hand passing gently over his own face.

His father loved the lives of animals as well as their death; and in his movements and the tone of his voice there was a charm to which, like strong slaves, they responded humbly. Old sows let him handle their litters, and he could make nervous ewes—who will not usually give suck even to one of twin lambs if, having fallen unnoticed in a corner of the fold, it does not smell like the other—accept the lambs he offered them as their own. When the neighbors' heifers were brought to the barn door, his great bulls walked forth mildly as if to play their parts in a ceremony which he had arranged.

The farmers within a radius of fifteen or twenty miles paid him to break vicious colts. He could tell which ones had been abused; he petted these and fed them apples and turnips; he whipped others who had no fear. Then he would hitch one of them to a low, light cart from which he could fall without risk, and attach to its legs a complicated set of ropes. It would begin to kick; he would bring it to its knees, or even throw it deftly on the ground, muttering phrases which seemed to be hypnotic; for its ears would shiver, its wild, bloodshot eyes roll, and convulsive sighs go in and out of its nostrils. He would repeat these exercises with infinite patience, with obvious delight; and at last one bad young horse would be broken and ready for work, and another would take its place.

For minor animal diseases and in cases of emergency, he was often called upon to serve his neighbors as a veterinary surgeon. He could puncture the bellies of horses and cattle swollen by colic, and knew how to make delirious stallions take bitter drenches from a bottle. With his sleeves rolled up over his heavy upper arms, he would go into the dark stable to deliver a young heifer's calf by force. Alwyn wanted to follow him on these occasions; but his father recognizing his excessive sensibility by the fact that he felt as modest or even ashamed in his presence as in a woman's, he was never allowed to watch either birth or breeding. On the other hand, he was allowed to hold the legs of young boars and bull calves while his father castrated them, working so deftly that they did not even scream before the last stroke.

Alwyn's father himself believed that this was his principal talent. "If I could have gone away to a veterinary college—" he said again and again; the sentence never had an end. "It was fate," he would add, "and my father had no patience with me." Fate personified by a small, dyspeptic man (Alwyn's grandfather) who had never forgiven anything, never seemed to remember anything, and who had never changed his mind. . . . Alwyn's father would go on talking about it in a muffled and dreamy tone of voice, but never blamed his brother. "Jim had his chance; it was right that he should. But there was only one chance in our family. . . ." Then, seeking his wife's eyes and gazing around at his mysterious children, he would conclude, "Jim has had good luck—but I guess I wouldn't change places with him."

Three or four times every year Alwyn's uncle, the Rev. James A. Tower, came lonesomely, complacently, back to his birthplace; and at first Alwyn could not decide whether even he was satisfied with his lot. He seemed to return from another world, with his suits of English material, his thick ties made of scarcely worn ball dresses, his golf hose, cameras, and watch fobs, his strong sentiment for nature, his loneliness and optimism; and at first glance seemed to resemble his poor relatives only by accident, without actual kinship. . . .

His mother, half forgetting that he was her son, never bullied him or forced him to take her into his confidence, and, in spite of his cultivated imagination, never tried to explain to him her conception of life as a great county fair, or her cult of the new moon. His little nieces adored him because he looked happy and could afford to be generous. Because he still loved hunting, fishing, and country food, his brother defended him from the accusation of having changed. His sister-in-law, Marianne, was genuinely fond of him, but, for reasons which were obscure at first, did not approve of the life he led.

The minister brooded lovingly upon their lives, the labor, the poverty, the narrowness of outlook, which were still established where he had been born, comparing these things with the conditions of his later life and calling the contrast progress. There he still saw himself as young and marked by good fortune for the future, as in a certain mirror of all those in the world, and in it alone, one catches a glimpse of a face one can be proud of. There he would have denied the least of his disappointments, and there he counted his blessings, thinking that he saw life in proportion.

One afternoon Alwyn sat beside his uncle on a hill-top. Spread out below them lay the farm: the poor house with its wooden coronet around the chimney, the desperately weeded crops, the faded washing floating between the trees, the dung heaps steaming with ammonia, the pigpens and rusty farm machinery. The elder of its two eldest sons (Alwyn born in the house, his uncle in what was now the woodshed) gazed down upon it and shook his head. "I am a fortunate man," Alwyn heard him whisper to himself.

Three years after the marriage of Alwyn's parents he had been ordained, and thereafter had occupied the pulpit of a fashionable church outside Chicago. He had preached a cheerful, modern faith, and had been remarkably successful with young people. His resonant voice, his fine presence, his warm but discreet social relations, had made the deacons of his church proud, those of other churches envious. Bishops and devout philanthropists having begun to speak of him, his ambition had been excited anew by the ministry as a career, and he had forgotten music and the hopes he had once founded on it.

But meanwhile he had also forgotten Irene Geiger, and had married a wealthy girl named Caroline Fielding. Her mother and her two sisters did not relinquish their claims upon her, especially when one of them was ill; and she herself had always suffered from periodical nervous pain. So the large house in Chicago and a sick room, otherwise their nuptial chamber, in which she would crouch alone day after day and night after night, began at once to divide her time exactly between them. The young minister might as well have been a bachelor. At last it seemed wise for him to retire from the active ministry for the present, in order to live in Chicago with his delicate wife, who was also so conscientious a sister and daughter.

His family scarcely saw her for years. At last the summer came when she felt strong enough to be taken to the farm. There, in spite of her sober elegance, she looked like a young actress in the common daylight: her beauty already hardened by anxiety and authority, her youth hampered by a quantity of parasols, smoked glasses, gloves, flowered hats, and dark blue veils to protect her skin from the dust. With a certain timid arrogance she seemed to welcome her new relatives on the threshold of their own home.

She brought a quantity of missionary magazines containing pictures of laughing, muscular savages; and the country people might have felt that they had no place in her world, being neither prominent representatives of Christian wealth and culture like those among whom it was her privilege to live, nor heathens to whom it might have been her privilege to have been sent. Alwyn and even his father wanted to talk to her about their ambitions, but she listened with disapproval to any expression of discontent. Her mother-in-law wanted to tell her about the old days, but she believed that the important history of the West was that of the development of churches, seminaries, and wealthy families in Chicago. Everyone waited on her while she stayed. She took pains not to reveal by too much gratitude how uncomfortable she was in the farmhouse, and ignored its poverty, feeling that they were duty bound to be satisfied with their station in life, as she was with hers, and not wanting to remind them of the difference between the two.

She never remodeled her rich, draped, braided frocks no matter how the fashions of inferior women changed; and later, when Alwyn visited her home, he saw the kinship between them and its upholstery, its alcoves of taffeta and plush, and the rigid brocade with which its windows were symmetrically draped to keep out the light.

That house was a veritable museum of Middle Western luxuries. In the bathrooms the mahogany closets, wash-bowls, and tubs were lined with flowered porcelain; and the faucets were the heads of a number of dogs—dead family pets, copied from the life—out of whose bronze mouths the water trickled. Rug lay upon rug; brass lamps stood beside music boxes, under decrepit chandeliers. A tall, stringless harp was wrapped up like a mummy in the music room, and there was a bust of Music with Chicago soot on its nose. The ceilings had been decorated by an Italian professor with a mass of birds, curlicues, butterflies, and flower beds upside down. Tiers of paintings and steel engravings portrayed snow scenes, kittens playing with balls of yarn, missionary dispensaries in foreign lands, and bouquets the color of moss and dried blood. From a life-sized portrait in oils of the father of the family, the late merchant prince Cromwell Fielding, one hard, idealistic eye, over the wavy beard which fell to the middle of his chest, appeared to govern the ranks of tasseled armchairs and sofas. In the dining room great services of French china waited to be used; but in these degenerate days there were not many people worthy of an invitation: a few doctors of divinity, a few heroic missionaries upon furlough, a family of cousins in the East, one of whom had been first lady of the land, a poor cousin who had lost his money by foolish investments and worked in a clothing store. . . .

There, surrounded by her mother, her sisters, and these infrequent guests, the retired minister studied, and in general failed to understand, his wife's extraordinary character. In it, as in the house itself, an elaborate worldliness served as a setting for puritan austerities; and her vanity merely emphasized her virtue. Her opinions, varying in expression no more than if they had been memorized speeches, her deli-

cately self-conscious observance of the proprieties, her
chaste beauty, her air of playing a noble rôle before
a chosen public, inspired him with the awe of a child
ushered for the first time into a theater and told that
the great actress is a member of his family.

Alwyn Tower, another country boy, equally sensitive to the theater and whatever resembled it—though
without the bias of his uncle's early ambitions and
romance—was equally impressed by his aunt's character; but he felt an obscure fear of it as well.

Having no children of their own, they extended their
hospitality to Alwyn and thought that they were ready
to make all the necessary sacrifices for his future. His
aunt's sisters watched over him excitably; her mother
was suspicious, but found no dignified way of expressing her displeasure at his presence; his aunt loved him
sternly, his uncle with a childless man's embarrassment.
Then from the streets of the great city, criminally
alive, draped with dirt and gas, full of bleached and
bitten faces, scented with slaughter houses, he came and
went over the threshold of the ugly palace (one of
those in which progress and millionaire civilization had
been born) and watched the events which took place
inside it.

They were like the episodes of a long symbolic play
at which part of the audience may laugh, while the
rest shudders at the secret meaning. On Friday afternoon the ladies went with their own carriage and
coachman to the symphony concert, occupying the same
seats as long as they lived. A pet dog sometimes ate
one of the new kid gloves which were laid on each of

their beds every Friday before lunch. On one occasion it caught one of the canaries during its bath; one of the sisters fainted away, and an old sewing woman sprinkled her face with lavender water, dropped the bottle, and bandaged the bird with cotton batting and thread. Finally this dog escaped from the house, was run over, died, and was buried beside seven others; and the old mother, pitifully frightened, denounced automobiles. Every Sunday morning she sought an excuse not to go to church, usually found it, and usually obliged one of her daughters to stay at home, lest she be lonely. She was but superficially devout; the church was a great mansion like her own, and she would have undertaken the menial tasks of God's house, as of her own, only if there had been no one to do them for her. Fortunately her daughters felt their sacred obligation to make her happy, by comparison with which even divine service was a sort of self-indulgence.

Caroline Tower genuinely loved her husband, and love often produced a vague tumult in her emotions; but logically conservative in spite of it, she dealt with her duties in the order of time—her mother came before her husband. She wanted him to be a clergyman: God's house and work came before everything in the world—except her mother's house, which was a sacred establishment as well, a sort of sumptuous private chapel to the glory of motherhood, which is the source of the glory of God.

So her husband was ignored whenever his desires conflicted with the rulings of her conscience as a daughter. He still hoped vaguely to bring about a change in their way of life, to rouse in her heart, even by accident, a passion which would set aside her other obligations, or to profit by some interference of Providence, as for example the death, in God's good time, of his mother-in-law, to whom he was devoted, nevertheless. Meanwhile he believed that his family on the farm must be satisfied with him, now that he was not merely working for God's kingdom of virtue, prosperity, and enlightenment, but was a part of it himself; and though scarcely a minister of the gospel and almost a bachelor, he was content with the exceptional dignity of his deprivations, in a world of poorly dressed, impious, uneducated men.

Then suddenly Caroline died. Dying was just like one of her headaches; therefore she did not realize what was happening until it was too late to do more than think of her soul and its metamorphosis. She gazed at her mother, her sisters, and the opulent room, as if in truth she were leaving them behind forever and were willing to do so; but gazed at her husband with the still sharper anguish of a mere separation. Then her face assumed the first look of humility which he or even her sisters had seen upon it; it became the childish face of one maddened by regret—regret for everything believed, everything done, everything left undone. And before the end she whispered, "In my Father's house are many mansions, many . . ."

The family sorrow produced such a pandemonium in the house that the horror and momentary despair of James Tower, in fact not quite a member of the family, were scarcely observed. He hid in corners of the drawing-rooms and the long, dim corridors when he was not needed; he went up to Hope's Corner and tried to hide among the flocks, trees, and furrows of his boyhood—hiding from the storm of sorrow and waiting for it to pass, determined to go then and take up his ministry where he had put it down.

For a time sorrow added a certain sensuality to the abstract, liberal doctrines which he had been taught in the seminary and sent forth to teach; and he felt his vocation more strongly than at any other period in his life, either before or after. He would idealize his bereavement and make it public; it would be a consolation to others. He would direct their eyes upward to the ideal place where—trailing restlessly up and down, cloud folded about her distinguished head like one of her veils—she intimidated him by her dead perfection, by the distance between them, scarcely greater now than it had always been, and by the gaze upon which her eyes had finally closed. Every day for almost a year he told himself that presently he would look for a vacant parish in which to begin the great work which everyone had expected of him—even she, though she had previously had other things for him to do.

He had been her humble servant from the first. On her deathbed she had rewarded him with a look which meant, he believed, that no one would ever love him as she had loved him then, and that she regretted leaving nothing and no one but himself. This gave him a sort of pride for which his good fortune in other respects had not prepared him; looking back upon that moment, making the most of that pride, he was to be even less impatient than before with abnegation, home life, and servility. And as the sheer pain of his loss came to an end, her presence in the vague paradise of his memory grew less and less sufficient. He began to remember her qualities as if he were in danger of forgetting them, and therefore drew nearer to her mother and sisters, in whom, even during her lifetime, her character had been reflected, shadowy aspect by aspect.

The younger of the surviving Misses Fielding, Anne, was physically the image of her dead sister; but her beauty had somehow vanished, though she was still a young woman. Her strength of character, mournful and reserved—as it were a throbbing of the atmosphere wherever she was—resembled Caroline's as much as one note of a great bell resembles the next.

Miss Ada Fielding was uncannily successful with flowers, birds, and animals, charmed little children, cheered and influenced missionaries, invalids, and servants. But there her power ended; for the rest of the world (in ignorance and compassion, in fear and trembling) she could only pray. She and Caroline had saintliness in common.

For the ghostly presence of his wife's loveliness, Jim was dependent upon her mother, in whom—less ephemeral than the old woman's youth and the young woman's very life—much of it had survived. Mrs. Cromwell Fielding was a delicate personage in watered silk, satin, and kid, feathers and chains, baroque pearls

and enamel. Like beauty itself, she feared nothing but
death, and would not permit a funeral or a will to be
mentioned in her presence. She loved her possessions,
especially those that she could see and touch, as a
naturalist loves his dead butterflies, an alchemist the
liquids in which immortality may be in solution; and
spent her time in self-sacrificing labor among them—
seeming to her son-in-law the personification of beauty,
which picks up and puts down, loses and finds, counts,
multiplies, and mixes, the base materials without which
it is never seen.

Naturally these three women were opposed to his
leaving them to occupy a pulpit. For Ada he was a
surviving part of her dead sister's life, and she wept
at the mere thought of his being taken away as well,
by God. Anne suggested briefly that it was mere human vanity which made him impatient to resume the
vocation, for which, furthermore, others were better
fitted than he. Mrs. Fielding maintained that charity
and idealism began at home, which therefore was the
proper place to exercise them and serve God; it ought
to be service enough for him to serve her; and when
she spoke of it, her flashing old eyes, like those of a
young temptress, made him look the other way.

There was also wealth. It was an aspect of Caroline's character—not merely something she had
possessed—because she had always possessed it and because she had never forgotten it for a moment without ever having to give it a moment's thought. In
Jim's imagination it adorned her departed spirit as a
saint's image in a reliquary is adorned. It hung

heavily; it sparkled; it doubled and faded—bewildering to a poor farmer's son—in every room of the house where, like a ghost, she seemed to stay because it was. So if he had had to leave its sacred precincts, he would have lost her a second time; her ghost would have died, in the great deathbed of his memory.

There was also a theological dilemma. By temperament and training he was inclined to a very liberal interpretation of Protestantism. Only the most arbitrary orthodoxy was suited to the strong souls of his relatives by marriage. But if he applied that orthodoxy to their lives as frankly and earnestly as in other quarters he was accustomed, indeed was expected, to apply the laws of a looser belief, he would be obliged to condemn them altogether. In his heart he could not blame them; but he did not know how, theologically, to justify them. How, for example, would he go about it to preach a funeral oration for one of them? At one moment, thinking of their doctrines and listening to their criticism of others, he would accuse them, in spite of himself, of hypocrisy, vanity, selfishness, materialism; a moment later, he would be idealizing them with all the force of his imagination. At last, to his great relief, the gentleness of his nature triumphed thoroughly over his unkind judgments.

So for this family's sake he abandoned his ordained ambitions, as for his own he had abandoned others. Having a talent for obedience, naturally endowed with the patience and politeness which family life requires, he then bent all his efforts to being a perfect son-in-law and a widower.

When he first arrived in Hope's Corner for one of his visits to his brother's family, his face would be as handsome as ever; but the contented smile would give way slowly to a look of pleading. He was afraid that one of those on the farm would accuse him of having given up the ministry for mere love of luxury and idleness; he was afraid of discovering by accident what they thought. . . . Knowing that his nephew Alwyn had as little taste as he for the life of poor farmers, he would talk to him by the hour about his melancholy as a widower, about his problems which were insoluble though already solved; and would be depressed by the boy's avid, noncommittal interest, unable to judge from it what account of his avowals would be given Ralph and Marianne. Then he would go back gladly to Chicago, to his family by marriage, his family by death, among whom at any rate he was not blamed, if not highly appreciated.

In the rich house he passed the rest of his life quietly. He sometimes thought of himself as a commoner with secret liberal views in the villa of an old queen, having been married to one of the ladies-in-waiting. Still in awe of its sluggish and sumptuous power, and wistfully eager to be admired by the younger generation, such as Alwyn, he thought of dedicating it to worthy, modern causes; but he was not certain what they were, and had no authority in any case. For example, he would rouse his nephew's interest in the large library: red leather editions, as large as dictionaries, of the Victorian poets and Shakespeare, uncut sets of George Eliot, Dr. van Dyke,

and John Burroughs, and bound volumes of the best
monthly magazines; but Mrs. Fielding would hide the
keys of the bookcases lest a volume be "mislaid."

As time passed he rarely spoke of anything but the
Fieldings, rationalizing their prejudices, uneasily explaining and defending them, defending without explaining himself. . . . Alwyn saw him give up every
least ambition save to go on being a good man and a
gentleman, and saw a series of senseless duties invented by the ladies to discipline him, as Alwyn himself, the other farmer boy in the house, was being disciplined.

The most serious family problem during Mrs. Fielding's later life was that of servants. The overfur-
nished mansion and its mistress both needed the attention of maids, seamstresses, coachmen, and janitors.
As she grew older, she could not endure the presence
of those whom her daughters could find to employ.
Spying upon the face of a new cook, her fine, three-
cornered eyes would discover a sort of modern in-
solence; the man who came to wax the floors would
anger her by a radical smile. Present-day help had
no respect for her, at least no reverence; worst of all,
they regarded her requirements as the whims of an
old lady who would soon be out of the way. It was
as if she saw death making use of their eyes to intimi-
date her; and she, having death's eyes, glared back at
them, at their youth and strength which would not last
even as long as hers had. Miss Anne and Miss Ada
spent hours in interviewing applicants, whom she discharged in the twinkling of an eye; and finally, with

great satisfaction, she reduced the members of her family to the duties of domestics.

One day a janitor, after helping himself to raspberry cordial, addressed her by the name of his former employer. Her son-in-law took his place, temporarily; but he gave satisfaction, and no other janitor was ever hired. He fed the hens, beat carpets, mowed the lawn, kept the flower beds clean and gaudy, stoked the furnaces, carried out ashes, and shoveled snow from the walks, saying that only a farmer's son could do these things so well.

He did not seem to grow old. Organic weaknesses made their presence known by the vague melancholy of indigestion and the irritability of fatigue, but they did not insist; they were merely waiting until there should be need of them to complete his discipline. He thought, when he thought of it at all, that life with a firm, exquisite hand like that of a loving helpmate (his own) had put him in his place. He was not happy, but he was content; and when he visited the old farm, he looked back indulgently upon his ambitions: love, music, and the ministry—unwise wishes of a selfish boy.

He would have been less at ease in the farmhouse if he had remembered more clearly the morality and religion of his parents, or if he had understood his sister-in-law Marianne's even sterner beliefs which now ruled where he had been a boy, and there prepared her children to condemn him—though she expected them to be too courteous ever to show it.

The religious atmosphere in which Alwyn grew up

was inherited in large part from his grandmother Duff, though fundamentally her piety had been no more than a public attitude, assumed out of loneliness and defiance. The few people she admired were Christians, and it could never have been said that she was not as worthy of the name as they. But without any respect for the father of her children, her sorrows had grown too bitter to come under the jurisdiction of God the Father, a God of resignation and forgiveness. The steadfast refusal to surrender to either of them had given her spirit, as she had grown old, an infidel grandeur, a fortitude more stoic than Christian. Young or old, all that she had had by way of a personal religion had been a sort of poetry; its arbitrarily fixed rules happened to be Christian doctrine, but it was not at all the poetry of God—rather that of worldly dignity, disappointment, and vanity of the spirit, that of conducting herself properly and proudly.

Under the influence of this unhappy poetry, Marianne Tower's strong, happy beliefs had been formulated: the same pattern of belief, but with peace in place of resentment, confidence instead of desperation, white where black had been—her mother's disillusionment reversed. The very principles on which America was founded were the result; and like certain of the Pilgrims, she represented them with the competence and heedless ardor of a woman under an enchantment.

There was also about her religion, as there had been about her mother's irreligion, a royal assurance and a slight suggestion of vainglory. She would have been willing to spread it by force, particularly in view of its importance to the nation as a whole, meanwhile coercing the doubtful with contempt and the lukewarm with enthusiasm, for lack of other sorts of authority. Like a state religion, it could not have existed without hypocrisy—plaster to hold the edifice together, many hypocrites around the few men and women of pure rock; a tribute to its power when faith—the tribute to its charm—was not forthcoming. But she did not complain of hypocrisy, preferring that people should pretend to be better than they are (which pretension is a sort of humility) than that they should acknowledge their failings and cease to be ashamed of them; and remembering that the only one of her father's lies which her mother had never challenged was his prayer when they had knelt together on the kitchen or sitting-room floor.

Like Catholicism, her religion required adherence and obedience before faith—mere willingness to believe and reform before the unerring comprehension of God in detail. She thought that faith was a private, indeed a selfish experience which took place after a sort of sickness of curiosity about God, in a lonely bedroom, for example, with sighs and stammered prayers and many vague tears. She could imagine very well how it happened, that intellectual prodigy, there in secret. But secrecy was dangerous; in it temptations as well as God invested themselves with magic and dazzled the excited soul, the soul as vague as tears, and in it dangerous sensibilities came out as stars do in the darkness—which she had learned, indeed, to her sorrow.

So she did not overrate this or any other mystic experience, and was comparatively indifferent to the puzzles of what to believe and their theological answers. Giving herself to God meant merely being responsible for her life, her virtue, her usefulness to others and to the world as a whole—individually responsible to Him, not to the schoolmasters of faith, pastors or priests. Therefore she had to consider and believe only those doctrines which could help her to recognize her duties and overcome the discouragement which was almost the only temptation she ever encountered. It was sacrilegious to worry about the rest; only a bad scholar would turn to the back of the book to hunt for answers, or to play with problems which he could not yet profitably solve. Kept busy by divine forces—conjugal passion, poverty, good health and illness, motherhood—engaged not in fathoming God's opinions but in the illustration of those she knew instinctively, she did not find much time to gaze in the direction of His face, or to wonder what human face it resembled.

Thus, though Protestantism is a branch of Christianity founded upon faith, Marianne Tower, like most American Protestants in this respect, was entirely concerned with works: with severities, kindnesses, abstinences, successes, which all the world could see; with prayers and testimonies which all the world could hear and understand; with sin instead of heresy, reform instead of repentance; with serving more than with loving God.

Her love of God was principally a sort of grateful admiration, and admiration for reasons which would have entitled other gods to a share in it. Doubting as little as poets and children do, she believed every miracle of virtue she heard about, no matter by what religious principles, with what sort of divine guidance, it had come to pass. Therefore she would have honored any god who, to her knowledge, was arrayed in the esteem of entire races, upon whom as on a corner stone families were founded, and by whom public morals were regulated. But her knowledge was limited by church magazines and tracts which libeled the religions of the countries to which missionaries were sent (the executives and propagandists of American Christianity having realized, perhaps, that it harbored the germs of polytheism); and she knew no other god but God, in whose veins there was Jewish blood—God of clean and respectable living, innocent thought, and industry.

One day when Alwyn had come back from school, full of what he had learned about heathen religions from other sources of information than hers, and was sitting on top of the flour barrel in the pantry where she was at work, he said that he did not believe in missionaries going to foreign lands to lead races away from their own deities and undermine the culture and customs which suited them.

She asked, "Tell me, Alwyn, are you beginning to lose your faith? Don't you believe in God?" In the beginning she had hoped that he would become a minister.

"I do, mother," he said, with a vague sense of being courageous. "But I don't want Him to— I don't know, I'm not sure—that He isn't the same as the others."

Gazing into his eyes, she did not need to be told that he spoke of another god than God. She shed tears, wiped them away, and threw back her head. "Well, my son," she said, "we shall see if your God can do for you what mine has done for me."

Touched and troubled, Alwyn asked himself if in reality he had a god of his own, what help he needed, what help she had received; and in his confusion, he preferred to think of her beliefs. . . .

Her religion—perhaps, Alwyn thought, American Christianity as a whole—was a religion of ideal prose; all the beauty it had was the elegance of a perfect law, a Napoleonic code. It deified Jesus, but deified Him as a social leader and teacher martyred for His virtue, a compassionate attorney at the right hand of God the judge, and a fulfillment of the half-political prophecies of the Old Testament—whose jurisprudence of hygiene, family relations, patriotism, and commerce, its morality resembled.

Even Alwyn's mother was confused, in teaching her children, about the meaning of Christ's strange parables. Perhaps He had not been a success as a teacher, not having laid down one precept which did not require interpretation before it could serve as a basis for conduct, or given one example whose significance could not be mistaken. But His ravishing voice was still more persuasive, not only to children but to herself, than the voices of those indecent, vindictive, but comprehensible men of genius, the Jews who had come before Him. So when she closed the Bible and continued in her own words, it was to repeat the Old Testament moral lesson (subtly modified by more civilized feeling, by changing customs, by a pure woman's refinement, and by her nearly superstitious respect for education), but as if it had originated upon His lips.

In spite of its complex origins, her morality was not at all ambiguous. She believed that money was the result of ability, and was in itself an ability or talent (the money which in Christ's parable the master had given his servants to multiply had actually been called talents). It was power for good; to waste even the smallest piece of it meant wasting potential charity, educational opportunities, and at its source, the dignity by which God's kingdom on earth ought to be supported, made known, even advertised. More of it than could be spent painstakingly, painfully, she regarded with suspicion. An ardent desire for success proved the sincerity of one's efforts, whatever they were—but Christ had failed; therefore, once any sort of success had been achieved, she regarded it suspiciously as well, and judged it by its fruits, which ought to be very nearly those of failure: humility, self-denial, pity for others.

She believed the human body to be sacred. Therefore all those things which disagree with it, or change its reactions and way of functioning—deforming shoes and clothes, alcohol, excess of other sorts of food and drink, idleness—were sacrilegious. Good health was the body's virtue; and it also was a talent of the capital lent by the Master.

According to her, love, often as automatic in its influence as a drug, often wasteful of time, health, and money, existed only to bring men and women together in marriage. Trees and plants, because they had no responsible souls, had the right to put forth more flowers than fruit; but for men and women even one kiss given in vain laid waste the heart and blighted the fruit of the fruit-bearing kiss of marriage. Marriage existed to people the continent with witnesses for the Lord, who gave it—no, who lent it.

When she spoke of the continent of America to her children, it was as another talent, like the ability to sing or speak fluently, to tame animals or govern men or children. Alwyn saw it then in his imagination, a fantastic bird's-eye view: lying by a miracle between the disastrous North and the sickening tropics; a vast mass of wood, fur, grains, metals, flesh, fish, fruit, electricity, and inspiration; flooded with milk and syrup; smelling of unemployed fertility; stained with rivers and refuse and the blood of the early settlers; rising into the sky in the West in young, red, weatherbeaten wrinkles and wounds (and when the first missionaries saw the Rockies they named them the Blood of Christ Mountains). . . . A talent that a whole race had, just as an individual might have a talent for mathematics; and whatever the others were, it would always be the principal talent of Americans, as long as it lasted. Lent, not given; to be guarded and risked and multiplied and used to the glory of God, the owner.

Alwyn, thinking of what he had learned about history and its classifications, said to himself that his mother, though only a poor farmer's wife, might be called an aristocrat. The lowest classes serving the whole of society (that is, the state) out of hunger and servility—but these did not count in America, where almost no one was hungry. The upper classes also serving it, to amuse themselves and to gain their ends of vanity and glory, usually bound up with the destiny of the state; prodigal enough to give away their sons, therefore making soldiers, priests, men of letters, orators, figureheads of them. The middle classes serving only themselves, bringing up sons in the interest of the family fortunes, seducing the sons of others if they had none of their own—the Fieldings were people of that sort. He thought of his uncle Jim among them, as timid as the last heir of a branch of deposed royalty —ashamed of its poverty and fanaticism, himself without either heirs or pretensions—in their grudgingly hospitable, merchant prince's palace. . . .

Then Alwyn thought (and it may have been the vanity he had inherited from his grandmother Duff which suggested it to him) that perhaps America's only aristocracy existed—not among millionaires, trying to earn money and get the most out of money as if they were still poor—but in poor homes in the country, in the strong, ignorant imaginations of such women as his mother and grandmothers, who had a sense of responsibility to God before the nation, to the nation (though they had little to gain by its glory, little to lose by its ignominy) before the family, and to the family only before themselves; aristocratic because of a vague sense of having had actually aristocratic grandparents, many times removed, and because their religion happened to be public rather than private, putting good behavior above the joys and pains of faith, judging private virtue by the public good. . . . Thus Alwyn began to make his peace with the tormenting sense of having come down in the world, which was his birthright as a Tower.

It was true in any case that his grandmother Tower had been proud to give to the world her most gifted son, Jim, all that she could afford to give, and that his mother wanted to give all her children. The latter would say, "I sometimes think that I am like a stalk bearing a great many flowers, almost more than it can bear; when they get ready to open, perhaps it will break—I shall be willing. All your father and I will need in our old age will be a place to lie down to rest forever. I am giving my life for you children in order that you may give your lives to others. . . ." She spoke as if she herself and her children had royal obligations to some sort of kingdom, and did so not merely out of maternal vanity, but because of her religion.

Perhaps, properly speaking, it was not a religion at all, but the jurisprudence of a moral commonwealth. She had no need for anything else after her marriage.

Intimate emotions which seemed to her sacred, took the place of specifically religious exercises. Thanks to the former, she was not spiritually impoverished or chilled by a faith which was all ethics (as those whose lives were more placid, more prosperous, and less rich, might have been); so she was the perfect Protestant.

Alwyn's uncle, the minister, felt this. During one of his visits Alwyn heard him say to his father: "Ralph, your wife is a saint on earth. We have been peculiarly blessed. Caroline was, too, while she lived." Hearing his dead aunt called a saint as well, Alwyn was jealous for his mother.

It was in regard to him that her judgment upon spiritual matters showed itself as most evidently superior to that of her mother-in-law, who had no patience with hair-splitting, resented disapproval of Jim, and pronounced him perfect, though his way of life did pass her understanding. Alwyn's mother was the more thoughtful of the two, and her beliefs had crystallized while teaching them to her children; whereas in the hard early days his grandmother had had little time to think, and had been able to teach her children only by means of the old belt without a buckle behind the kitchen door. Their differences of opinion were more important than profound, being merely those between taking for granted and knowing logically one and the same thing, between roughness and refinement in its expression, between one generation and that which followed it. They were particularly important to Alwyn, because it was his mother's reasonable version of the faith of his fathers—more suitable to his nature because he was above all his mother's son— which determined in large part the beliefs for which eventually he was to desert that faith altogether.

He enjoyed even her injustice toward his uncle Jim, for example, because at a time in his life when all that was inarticulate seemed merely stupid, and when opinions had more charm than they were ever to have again, a certain intolerance proved how fault-less her opinions were. So he soon found himself obliged to agree with her about the minister, whom, because he was courteous, handsome, wealthy, and well educated, he instinctively preferred to his other relatives.

In fact, she blamed her brother-in-law less than she pitied him, blaming him only to point a moral for the children whom she was going to send out in the world as he had been sent. For their sake she in-sisted on the fact that he had wasted his opportunities, and exchanged the family birthright of anxiety, am-bition, and loneliness, for the comfortable approval of a family that was not even his own. If music was his true calling, the sort of divine persuasion for which he was better fitted than for argument and prayer, he should not have given in to his father's and brother's disapproval. Having undertaken to be a preacher, he should not have ceased for the sake of domestic con-venience. Coming from a poor family as its gift to the world and having retired from the ministry, he should have found something better to do than to indulge a rich family's vanity and serve its petty needs.

In general she preferred the appearance of perfection and unity in the least distinguished lives to noble qualities—such as the self-control and self-sacrifice, devotion to the dead, and generosity, which Jim displayed—haphazardly thrown together in a life which seemed to have developed along the line of least resistance; and had no doubt that her husband, without great intelligence or any pretensions, was the greater man of the two. Furthermore, it was a Christian's duty to give, not merely a good example, but one which could not be misinterpreted, which did not require explanations to be made by those who loved him, allowances by those who did not. Simple integrity was a duty as well as a source of happiness. . . .

Alwyn himself, as scrupulous at least as his mother, did not want any religious faith compromised by devious individual behavior, and did not want to consent to one himself which he was likely to have to compromise. Immoderate like other Americans, other adolescents, he already believed in extreme positions and deliberate apostasy—not in accidental reaction, nor in vague decadence of the old toward the new. He was quite ready to reject, for himself, his family's beliefs, but not on the basis of any less perfect embodiment than his mother's life; it would indeed have been unfair to judge his uncle's ideals by his representation of them.

Then the problem of formulating a set of beliefs which would be in harmony with as many of his instincts as were ineradicable (as his mother's beliefs seemed to be with all her instincts) troubled him and gave him pleasure; and during his adolescence, many religions seemed to burst vaguely into bloom at once in his imagination.

He had learned that God was one and uniform; he felt that He was legion. "Thou shalt have no other gods before me. . . ." He believed that he had seen the others already, under ordinary circumstances, very slightly disguised by the lives of ordinary men and women such as his relatives—thorough and shameless, as deaf to interruption, as busy as death. . . . They came to his attention also by way of pictures and books: the splendor of devout savages as he had heard about it, the bitter-sweet nobility of extinct races, the Greeks, for example, as it had been written about. "Thou shalt have no other gods. . . ." And he fancied himself in love with them all.

He had learned that God, who created man, was the lesson man was to learn long after by his painful experiments, mistakes, misery, and contentment; the body of knowledge of what for most people in ordinary walks of life is likely to result from this or that course of action; God handed down from father to son, mother to son; God the law. Alwyn felt that He was also the breaking of the law. At any rate he had already formed a vague resolution to break it; could he break it as well as his mother had kept it?

Naturally timid, he realized that even to be an outlaw, a more or less effective exception, would require more strength than, by himself, he would have. "We shall see, my son, if your God can help you. . . ." And if his God were gods? Would not his life, if he committed himself to them all, be a sort of Tower of Babel in which the divine workmen would merely dispute among themselves in all their tongues, and accomplish nothing? Each had power; had they any power in common? Could they, together, do what one of them could do—what, for his mother, one of them had done?

For her religion had indeed brought about a miracle of energy and peace; it was also true that marriage had made her religion what it was then. As mere doctrine it had been a birthright and a dowry; her husband, who had no talent for thought, had added nothing to it. But the evenly passionate years had changed its bearing upon experience, and as a method of living, it had been a sort of marriage settlement.

She not only believed, but felt, as by a physical instinct, that the curtain of death would not go down upon her drama of love; a drama of two characters with their children and their children's children—by virtue of heredity and immortality the cast would never be changed. And when she compared it—its dignity of citizenship, its perfect and tender monotony, the brightness somehow continually shed upon its humble scene—with her girlhood, the latter seemed to have been a melodrama of insubstantial puppets, agitated by a hand which had trembled for many reasons, and for no reason at all.

The motives of that melodrama had been dread of the future (and now that she was a mother, each moment was very naturally the child of the one before); servile dependence upon others, her angry

parents, for example (and now the entire world outside the four walls of her home might have been destroyed without leaving her in despair); loneliness
(and she had given birth to children enough to begin
a new race, companions for her on earth and in
heaven); and the obscure need of emotions, caresses,
pride, pain (and now, day for day, she was scarcely
equal to the feast of feeling which was her daily
bread). . . . So contented was she that, in retrospect,
she regarded the thoughts of her girlhood as other
women regard the dolls whose mothers they have pretended to be.

And marriage had swept away, with the mist of
sadness, her springtime mysticism, which had been an
imaginary communication (as it were by messages,
signals, and amorous glances) with what was beyond
understanding. Now, in the person of her husband,
what was beyond understanding lived in her simple
house; she slept within reach of its strong, however
tired arms. Mystery was in God the equivalent of
passion; from time to time it had taken (and would
take) possession of her. But she would no more
have thought of trying to rouse or control it—even
by curiosity, speculation, or yearning—than if it had
been a man's passion; she did not even ask of the
moody lover whom she had married the right to say
yes or no. Thus all that was enigmatic in religion—
the bitter effort to fathom God's apparent indifference,
to accept the evil which He permitted, the amorous
effort to have the truth naked of its disguises, to reach
the point where mortal desire leaves off and serene,

immortal satiety begins—gradually wrapped itself in
the same pure shame and darkness which hid away
her marriage bed. Those riddles were for the sor-
rowful—the disappointed and disabled and victimized;
as such at least she, when merely the Duffs' daughter
and Paul Fairchild's fiancée, had been faced with
them.

Paul Fairchild might never have existed; Ralph's
great hand, at its first touch, had obliterated the
traces of him in her mind. Until she came to tell that
story as a lesson to her grown children, she did not
try to explain even to herself the evil rôle he had
played in her youth; then, disdainfully overlooking his
failings, she concluded that her own subservience had
been at fault. Nor did her father, the diabolic, pitiful
old man to whom she was as devoted as she could
be, trouble her otherwise than practically. Thus it
happened that out of her theory of life, as out of a
picture (warm white on white against white) the devil,
like a black shadow, had faded.

This was love's negative work. Positively, it gave
her strength and kept her young. (Indeed, it kept
them both, and their love-making, young; for twenty
years the farmhouse was electric with it; and even
the youngest of their children grew up in the fragrant,
restless atmosphere of a new marriage, as if in the
heart of the lightning which cools a midsummer night
in Wisconsin.) Repeatedly with child, a number of
illnesses obviously in abeyance, thin and no taller than
her children when they were adolescents, able to afford hired help only when actually ill—no one under-

stood her vitality. On certain days, without warning, it would be exhausted; then, her face for the moment the color of old age, her voice dreamy, her quickened breathing scarcely to be divided into words, she would find herself unable to work, and would creep away to rest. Perhaps lying with her eyes closed all afternoon in the empty bed, she would draw strength there from her companion, who would be far off in the woods or fields among his little wild beasts and great domestic animals. . . .

Ralph, a child even in manhood, and a child of nature, drew strength from those animals, from the land, from heat and cold, from physical experiences— but drew his spiritual strength from her. If obliged to think of any complex problem, he suffered from pains in his forehead; she thought for him. He was timid and conservative; all his abilities would have been handicapped by a deaf pessimism, but for her thoughtful speech which charmed him into action— that of being a good father, farmer, and citizen— charmed him like a sort of cheerful music. His passions were entangled in and blinded by melancholy; at the end of a few months of an unhappy marriage, one or the other—desire or discouragement—would have left him no better than a heavy, broken-hearted animal. A Christian as it was, without her help he would have been unable to conceive God except as a father's tyranny, or as violent pleasure, or death. The light, steady wave of her character breaking constantly upon his temperament had worn away its roughness, given it brightness and another sort of distinction than its own: that of the wrath and force of instincts mixed with intellectual gentleness, that of animality the heart of which has been touched and not broken.

Incompatibility of the sort which puts an end to fugitive affections was the basis of their permanent and essentially religious devotion to each other. Each, like a portion of a circle, found in the other what was needed to balance and perfect himself. Trait for trait, each was strong where the other was weak; each was the opposite of the other—an opposite as symmetrical as that between man and woman physically. The good-tempered years, as they passed, brought about an interweaving not only of their interests and affections, but their characteristics. Death, to take one of them, would have had to leave a part of that one behind, or mutilate the other to carry off its momentary share of the two, inextricably married.

This process, this mystery, constituted at last the family's one enduring mysticism. Schooled by the discipline which in Marianne's hands Christianity had become, her children were to inherit, as if it were a religion, a theory of love, which would probably be interpreted by them in terms of various religions, various kinds of good and bad behavior, and which, changing its form but keeping its vitality—as in transmigration a vast, vague soul, typically American— would probably be heard of for some time to come.

During one of Alwyn's summer holidays he went with his parents to a Methodist camp meeting on the other side of the county. He and his mother drove

a single horse, his father following in a carriage with
the little girls; and they stopped for the noonday meal
with a family of friends. There was a newborn baby
in the house, and his mother shed tears as she held it
in her arms.

When they were alone again, moving swiftly
through the dust between the cloudy fields of timothy and waves of turning grain, he asked, "Why did
you cry?"

"Because I want another baby." At that time she
knew that for accidental physical reasons she would
not be a mother again. "I shall be glad when I am
a grandmother, with your little ones at my knees.
Before very long, you know. . . ."

It was the first time she had noticed that he was
almost a grown man, and he knew that he should be
proud, but was embarrassed. "The people I pity
most on earth," she added, "are your uncle Jim and
old Mrs. Fielding and her daughters. I don't see
how a woman can be religious without children."

They reached their destination. The annual revival
took place in a grove, along the edge of a deep ravine
where, it was said, there had been rattlesnakes. On
the camp grounds there were dormitories for men
and for women, hidden from each other by a thicket;
the auditorium, a sort of vast wooden tent; a dingy
hall in which meals were served; and a number of
cottages rented by particularly devout and prosperous
families. There were quoits played with horseshoes
by the old men, and exercises of physical prowess for
the young in sweaty shirt sleeves and cloth caps too

small for their heads. Between meetings the speakers, among whom were several bishops, balanced in rocking chairs beside their wives on the various porches. Certain rough but quite unexceptionable young couples played in the mossy gorge, the male faces red with the summer and with excitement, the girls disheveled and gay. A number of dry, gentle women tried to occupy everyone with Bible classes and games. This was one of the fountainheads of western Protestantism, and epitomized its mean amenities, its lack of mystery, its vast, somewhat emasculate, but primitive power.

Alwyn sat on a bench between his parents during the afternoon service. His uncle, the minister, had been expected to join them there; he had not come, presumably for family reasons. The hymns were miserable; he had heard one of the tunes in Chicago in a cheap theater.

Then a little man limped forward on the platform draped with flags. He was the founder and director of a school for lumberjacks in the north woods near Lake Superior, where Alwyn's father had gone to hunt. In the simplest words he talked of his students, great brutes of all races, few of whom could read or write; how they worked by night in the basement of the little building making cement blocks, both to pay their individual expenses and to support the school; how their hard hearts were touched by love of the Lord; how, for lack of room, equipment, and funds, many had to be turned away. Then, tears shining on his sharp, lonely, cripple's face, he recited: "The desert shall rejoice, and blossom as a rose. . . . Then the eyes of the blind shall be opened, and the ears of the deaf unstopped. Then shall the lame man leap as an hart; for in the wilderness shall streams break out. . . . And an highway shall be there, and it shall be called the way of holiness—wayfaring men, though fools, shall not err therein. . . . No lion shall be there, nor any ravenous beast. . . . Sorrow and sighing shall flee away."

Alwyn had never seen nor heard so moving a man. He compared him with the family minister, his uncle Jim; but almost in shame, he wished that he were beside the latter in the great, odious city mansion, rather than where he was; and suddenly thought of him not only with a certain lack of respect but with profound gratitude—he scarcely knew why. . . .

There followed a testimony meeting. Most of the statements of faith were made by women and by men of the clergy, men poorly paid to do so, speaking for others or for others' sake; most of them had evidently been made before, the very old, intoxicating, weak words falling into place as one expected, with a sound of satisfaction. Suddenly Alwyn's father stood up beside him.

Alwyn trembled; he never knew what his emotion was—ignoble embarrassment, or terror of something present and invisible which was scarcely his friend, or the shock of intimacy with him who had, that which had, begotten him. . . .

He saw his father gaze at his mother, as if she were all that the universe contained. His mother had forgotten herself and his father; she was quite pale, and made somehow homely by her humility. Alwyn saw her gaze back at his father, and realized that she believed that with eyes accustomed to fields, horizons, and deep woods, more farsighted than hers—he was looking at God.

His father's voice shook. He said, "I know that my Redeemer liveth," and sat down.

WHEN Alwyn was seven years old a man came to visit his grandmother, a rancher from New Mexico whose name was John Craig. He ran his brown finger in and out of the small boy's hair and along his eyebrows, saying, "I had an uncle whose forehead was like that."

Alwyn's grandmother bent over him to see. "So it was," she said.

He came again just before the death of Alwyn's grandfather, and spent four or five afternoons at the farm, during which the old man stayed in the garden, not even coming to the house for his medicine or his usual nap on the sofa: apparently he did not like the stranger. Alwyn's father seemed to have known him a long time, but not well; and they both seemed embarrassed, as if, under circumstances unknown to the boy, they ought to have liked each other perhaps more, perhaps less.

The stranger brought the children expensive presents. He was well dressed, and wore two rings on his delicate but calloused hands—one silver Indian ring and one set with a piece of onyx on which was carved a cupid astride a fish. His face had an appearance of weariness and controlled excitement: lean and smiling, but smiling only around his mouth—the eyes, with brown upper lids drawn tight across them, never ceased moving about the room or over the countryside, watchfully but without anxiety. He walked with a loose-jointed motion, and Alwyn's grandmother said, "That is a regular horseback walk!"

Late in the afternoon she took her guest to the cemetery to see the new headstone on the grave of her two dead little girls. Alwyn stayed behind with his mother. "Who is Mr. Craig?" he asked.

His mother hesitated for a moment. "I don't know why you shouldn't be told. You are old enough now to keep the family secrets. You have heard us all speak of your father's younger brother Evan—he is Mr. Craig. He changed his name."

The small boy had never in his life been so astonished. He stared in the direction his grandmother and the stranger had gone, down the road toward the cemetery, staring over the head of the little old man in the garden who was the stranger's father, but would not speak to him. "Why did he change his name?" he cried.

His mother told him the little that she had been told; but he did not understand it very well, and years were to pass before he actually found out why. After his grandmother's death he went to New Mexico, and his uncle John Craig became a more intimate friend than his father had been able to be. This fact amused and touched the lonely, extraordinary man, for he himself had loved his uncle Leander more than his father.

During Evan's boyhood—before anyone had dreamed of such a man as John Craig, though his father often prophesied for him a disgraceful future— Leander Tower, in the "old bachelor's wing" of the

house, led an idle and, to everyone but his youngest
nephew, insignificant existence. Because he knew that
the family would have been suffering extreme poverty
but for his financial assistance, his brother's evident
scorn of his way of life did not embarrass him. His
sister-in-law was devoted to his comfort—it was a
long-established habit to love him; but the shadow
that was left of his character, if she had met him then
for the first time, would scarcely have attracted her
attention, as in the community it attracted no attention
at all. Only Evan took refuge in that shadow from
the pain of being misunderstood, the fatigue of adolescence which is more painful though less serious than
a man's fatigue, and from his other troubles as they
arose.

When Evan entered his room, interrupting his melancholy recollections, the old bachelor looked up with
tender interest but no more eagerness. Another unhappy boy coming into the room, a third youngster
coming into his life—he wanted neither to shut this
one out nor to keep him there. "Sit down, my boy.
What's the trouble now?"

"He called me a loafer because I came in from the
field half an hour before supper."

"He" always meant his father. The relations between these two were going from bad to worse. The
angrier Evan became the keener were his retorts, and
there was something insulting about his eyes. He
spoke in defense of things his father feared, criticized
things which were all but sacred, and never wanted
to go to church. The farm work always made him

unhappy, and sometimes made him sick; he had to run away to the woods, for example, at butchering time. Whenever he spoke of running away altogether, he was pleased and tempted by the fact that his father looked afraid, grew more gentle, and talked of the evil and hardship of great cities. Their anger sobered the whole family for days at a time, as if it were sickness in the house. His mother whipped him once or twice, but he would not cry out, and said, "Why don't you let him do his own whipping?"— which took away her courage.

"He called me a lazy rascal," the boy complained to his uncle with an air of resentful satisfaction, as if, detail by detail, he were giving evidence to convict his father of a crime—the usual crime of fathers. "I plowed all day and my head ached. Ma wouldn't listen when I told her."

"Yes, yes, I see. Your mother is the finest woman I ever knew. Your pa. . . You'll find out some day, whether you like it or not, that you're a chip off the old block. He always thought I was good for nothing. Maybe I was."

He did not reproach the boy nor tell him what, on a given occasion, he ought to have done; a boy's ignorance was a sort of wisdom, to which an unsuccessful old man could add nothing that would be useful. But little by little, as if his disappointment spoke with its own voice, against his will, he told Evan how he himself had lived and what he thought about life. He did not imagine that anyone could profit by that story, but it would distract the boy's attention for a few hours from his monotonous, half-imaginary, immature troubles.

In this way Evan came to know the young Rose Hamilton better than he knew his mother, Hilary and his cousin Timothy better than his own brothers. As an adolescent invariably does, he envied Leander his distress and disappointment—they were experience at least; and there was no place for them in present day Wisconsin so far as he could see. His lucky brother Jim had had a chance to get away, the only chance there was in that family. . . . And he felt himself drawn, as a lover to a series of rendezvous, toward the places where his own life must have been waiting for him, though he had no idea where they were and scarcely cared what it was to be.

Thus Leander shaped this boy's character as he had wanted to shape Timothy's, as he might have shaped Hilary's. But he had failed so often to exercise the power of his affection that he scarcely realized what was happening; in any case, he was now too old to take pleasure in it. He scarcely took notice of the breakdown in Evan's mind of certain moral principles— for example, superstitious respect of law and order, love of work for its own sake, and, in a measure, the fear of God; but the boy's father grew more and more suspicious of them both. Henry Tower had no power over his weak brother, but he had a right to determine that, while Evan was a minor living in his house, he should not have his own way about anything.

Then the newspapers brought to Wisconsin an account of the sinking of the *Maine*. Evan's mother flung out her arms with a curious gesture, and cried, "Now we'll have another war!"

She saw her son sitting round-shouldered over the papers every night and knew what he was making up his mind to do, but was afraid to speak of it, since he was a Tower—lest opposition give him the courage she hoped he would lack. War against Spain was declared.

Evan did not yet know what it was to be afraid. He came in to dinner one day after the others were seated, and stood behind his chair. "I'm going to enlist," he said.

His hands gripped the chair-back as if it were a weapon, as if he might have to fight his way out of the room. His brother Ralph sighed, thinking perhaps of the harder work that would be left for him to do. His mother covered her face with a corner of her apron.

His uncle muttered, "Don't you let him go, Henry."

His father answered, "You ought to be ashamed, Leander. A boy can't do a finer thing than serve his country. We need him on the farm, but we'll have to get along."

Evan did enlist. He enjoyed the months of novelty and excitement before they disembarked in a Cuban harbor. There the stale-smelling sea splashed over rocks and rotten wood. The large vegetation which was on top kept swelling while that which was underneath rotted. The sun was very yellow. He was lonely, but avoided the other men half involuntarily, and wanted to sleep more than ever before. At first he thought it was a fever about to begin, drank whisky, and took large doses of quinine, as he was advised to do; but he learned that he was sick only at heart.

One night he stood just above the level of the sea which glittered in front of the moon, at the corner of two roads full of ruts, between a high wall and a low wall, both crumbling away. He was thinking, it is time to get back to the barracks. . . . There was a lump in his throat as he remembered the leave-taking in Wisconsin.

Henry Tower had placed his hard hands on Evan's shoulders, which were well above his own. "Don't you forget," he had said, "that five of your folks fought in the last war. You're a strong boy; it won't hurt you. Never turn back, whatever happens." The light in his eyes had resembled, but had been too shining to be, that of affection.

Evan's mother had come out of the kitchen where she had been crying quietly, and embraced him with great dignity, as if sending a son away to war were a ceremonial part of her womanly destiny, like a wedding or a funeral. Her air of pride and resignation had made him feel the impersonality of maternal love —he was only one of her sons, doing what she had given him birth to do. That night in Cuba, in the weak moonlight, Evan smiled a little bitterly, as one who has scarcely known his own mother smiles at mothers in general. "Be a good soldier," she had said.

He wondered what his uncle was doing. Perhaps watching that same three-quarters moon, which looked full of milk like a breast; all alone in his room, perhaps, scribbling letters that he never mailed, or pretending to read. Evan's mother had written that he had been sick in bed after the boy's departure, and now planned to go to California; perhaps he was already on his way.

On that last morning in Wisconsin, Leander had preferred not to stand with the others around the horse and buggy; so Evan had gone to his room to say good-by. "Well, my boy," he had said, "now you're a soldier, as I was. It's a good thing that you're going alone, not with one of your brothers, the way I did. Write to your father sometimes as well as to your mother; it'll be hard on him while you're away, thinking maybe he hasn't been a good father to you. . . ."

A palm tree which leaned over one of the walls made a gesture of blessing Evan with its many-fingered hands. Over the other wall in regular breaths came the air of a garden, and up from the seashore, now loud and now faint, as it were a concertina in drunken hands, the singing of sailors. . . .

Leander had talked a long time, somewhat like an old schoolmaster. Before going back to the barracks, Evan wanted to remember all he had said. "Well, maybe it's good-by altogether for us. I'm getting old and my usefulness is over. You'll live to see great days, the twentieth century—maybe everything will be different then. Be friendly, but not too friendly, and keep strong. And don't get to doing things you don't really want to do. And when you've made a mistake, and things go against you, and you can't help it, don't

be ashamed to run away and leave them.   Don't be
ashamed to do whatever you've got to do. . . ."

Those were the words he had used, or very nearly
his words. "Start all over again. You can, as long
as you're alone in the world. That's my advice."

No more time to remember.   The barracks. . . .
For a moment Evan thought he was homesick; no, it
could not be that. He was not lonesome for Ralph
or his mother; he was glad to be far away from
his father. All his old uncle could give him was advice: how to live when he was away from his family,
how to live by himself. "Don't be ashamed to run
away and leave things. . . ." He wondered what he
ought to do, what he genuinely wanted to do, and
what he was going to be able to do.

For he had begun to hate the war, though he had
seen nothing of it but barracks, horse stables to be
cleaned, unemployed guns, and saloons—no horror,
no rage, and no death. Why did he hate it? He tried
desperately to think, but his mind, like a little mirror,
only reflected its own desperation, ridiculous desperation. . . . He smiled at himself, but bit his lips until
they bled.

The Americans, he thought, had no business to be
there: it was a foreign country; it was the South. He
had been told that they were there only to help in a war
for liberty, because they loved liberty. But even if
that were true, it meant interfering in a family quarrel, as if a stranger had come to his home in Wisconsin
to help him hurt and defy his father.

Then he had heard newspaper men say that America wanted Cuba for the sugar and tobacco, and that ammunition had been smuggled in to the rebels before our government had had any reason to take sides. One who had been drinking had declared that the *Maine* had been blown up from the inside, blown up by Americans to make America declare war. Evan did not know what to believe, but he was sick with suspicion.

Coming as a soldier to a foreign land, he learned, as soldiers often do, how little he loved his own. He imagined the profitable monotony of Wisconsin, where he had been so miserable as a boy, taking the place of Cuba's lattices, the shade of blossoming trees embossed on the dust, the pallid masonry, the gardens and flower markets, the scalloped water which became an ocean only at a certain distance from the island, beyond coral reefs which were like a fence—the work of the mysterious race they were there to wipe out, Spanish work. Out of the small churches came gusts of incense, mystery, and muttering—God was not worshiped like that in Wisconsin. He wanted to steal inside them and lose himself in the music which laughed and cried at the same time; but he could not overcome his timidity, and in fact was half ashamed of being a foreigner and a Protestant.

His imagination was aroused, not by the young, hot-headed American army, but by the natives; not by the natives who were rebels, but by their oppressors, the enemy. He had seen them as prisoners being pushed into the damp citadel—handsome, sallow men with the unabashed faces of eagles whose wings have been broken. The rebels were blacker, dirty fellows, weaklings with excited eyes like those of dogs, already jealous of the Americans. To fight a war of independence, they had had to become dependent on a new set of masters.

Then he began to believe that the Americans would lose the war. There were three spells against them—Spanish blood, the Church, and the heat. Sooner or later the rebels would prefer to be governed by their own kind rather than by foreigners; their mothers and sweethearts would have preferred it then. Handsome women who seemed to have been fasting came to look at the lists of dead and wounded; they shuddered in their fine veils without making a sound; and Evan believed that they wept not only because their sons were dead, but because they had died as rebels. Old mothers were behind the crumbling walls, praying to the God of Spain for the Spanish army, and kneeling beside them perhaps there were rows of black-eyed girls. All hating the Americans—hating him. In dilapidated carriages or in carts drawn by velvety burros he saw certain ones with brown, parrotlike faces who understood something of which men, above all young American men, were ignorant. He heard talk of spies and plots, of women dynamiting the town; men said, "They are tiger cats."

The Church was an enemy—innumerable priests in league with that Spanish God. Evan was afraid of the black-magic prayers whose precise meaning no one knew, going up among the organ pipes and bright images. The Americans did not pray. . . .

The heat was an enemy. Mimosa, magnolia, and

oleander—the sweetness of these Cuban lives was poison to Americans, at least to him. The country boy had never dreamed of such a host of doctors as there were, to keep them from falling sick—sick of the canned food, of the moist filth, of the women along the quays. In spite of them, the whole army would come down with a fever, and be driven out. Evan was astonished that no one saw what was going to happen; perhaps no one cared. He tried to tell another soldier, a dull giant named Hodge, who said that he was plain crazy—after which he was afraid to open his mouth.

Sooner or later, in any case, his company would be sent up in the hills to fight. Bushes and vines lay all over those hills to entangle them, bushes and vines like masses of green hair. He thought he would suffocate without the little coolness that puffed in to the seaport from the sea. War in tight, high, hot valleys in the heart of the island. Soldiers running back and forth, shooting in the sunlight. Somebody's blood, perhaps his own, soaking through a uniform like sweat, with sweat. . . . It was not the fear of death which overcame him when he thought of these things, but the fear of a loathsome disease—from time to time the fear of going mad. His mother had often said that the Towers were a nervous family. . . .

A month passed, in drill, in drinking, in caring for horses, and in other menial tasks such as he had had to do all his life. He had been unhappy before, almost always, in fact, but now his unhappiness was mixed with a wilder emotion. One afternoon he was told that his company would be moved the next day or the day after. Suddenly he realized that he was not going mad—it was much simpler than that. He was a traitor.

That night he sat by himself in a bar on the quay; he felt stupid and almost happy, and asked himself, not what a traitor ought to do when ordered to the front, but whether or not he had fallen in love with the girl who ran the bar. Her old father picked a guitar and tried to make her sing—she had sung at least once every evening. But she shook her head and walked back and forth with an air of preoccupation— three steps to the right, two to the left, and a turn upon her heels, as if walking were a difficult dance. At first two grizzled Cubans and a young rebel sergeant were there; they paid and went out, leaving the door open. The night scented the low room with leaves and the sea. The old man fell asleep and dropped his guitar, which murmured a little for a moment, on the floor.

The girl sat down beside Evan, and he tried to talk to her. She said the war would last many years. Unable to remember any more Spanish words, he touched (but no more than touched) her wrist with his mouth, and laid one hand on her knee, pretending to do so by accident. Parting her lips and lifting one eyebrow, she smiled—it was hardly a smile. Evan had no experience of love, and all the sensibility in his body gathered in his hand. The old man in the corner ground his teeth and sighed in his sleep.

Then someone came down the road, singing drearily, *There'll be a hot time in the old town to-night.*

It was Hodge, the soldier who had called Evan "plain crazy." He stumbled over the threshold, a great, swaying body which smelled of rum and the cavalry stables. He did not speak to Evan—he had not done so, in fact, since he had heard what Evan thought about the war. The girl rose to serve him.

He laid six one dollar bills on the table in a row, and counted them drunkenly with his forefinger. Evan saw the girl's eyes glitter at the sight of so much money; and when she brought Hodge's whisky she spread out her flowered shawl on one arm, swept four of the bills to the floor, and perched on the table. At once Hodge began to make love to her. Then she dropped her shawl, swung backward in his arms, adroitly gathered up the bills with it, and slipped them inside her dress as she folded it about her shoulders. Then she picked up the two bills which were left and tucked them in his pocket, saying: "Put away your money. You'll lose it."

Hodge did not seem to have seen what she had done. Evan asked for another drink. The girl served him indifferently, closed the door as if to discourage other customers, and went back to Hodge's knee. Evan could not look away from the drugged motions of the other soldier's head as he tried to kiss her—as mechanically, seductively, she avoided his mouth. An ignorant boy, he could not say to himself, This is not love. So he shut his eyes, confused at once by disgust and desire.

Suddenly the girl slapped Hodge and tried to get away. But he caught one of her ankles in his large right hand and continued to fondle her clumsily with the other. She gnashed her teeth, fluttered like a heavy bird in a trap, and cried out. Her father sat up jerkily, trotted behind the bar, came back waving a broomstick, and stumbled around the table—still half asleep and trying to wake up. The girl kept muttering to him, between hisses of anger, to let them alone. With fatuous patience, Hodge pushed her red skirt above her knee. She struck him again.

Evan did not dare to interfere; to all intents and purposes Hodge knew that he was a traitor. Furthermore, he saw that in the tussle a corner of one of the stolen dollar bills had appeared between the girl's breasts. He wanted to go, but if he did, it would be his turn to be chased by the old man with his broomstick, because he had not paid for his drinks.

Now the other soldier was furious; he shook the girl, and cursed at the top of his voice: "Damn dirty dogs! We'll fix you! Half nigger! Look out, I'll break every bone in your body."

He was weak because he was drunk; the girl was strong with anger, so the struggle was equal. She kicked him, and stood up on one leg; he still held the other in his fist like a trap. She screamed in Spanish: "You wait! you wait! Before this war is over . . ."

Hodge wrenched her ankle, and she sank to the floor.

Evan understood some of her words, and was glad that the other did not. She was chanting, chattering about the war, about relatives and friends in the Span-

ish army, about hideous revenges. "Stick you like pigs.
Pigs, all you foreigners!" she cried.

Terrified by what she was saying, her old father
dropped his broomstick, waved his arms, and tried to
make her keep still.

Then the door opened, and a lieutenant and a sergeant came in. There was a sudden silence. Hodge
relaxed his great fist. The girl stumbled away behind
the bar. The small, red-faced lieutenant glanced at
Evan, glared at Hodge, and said to the sergeant,
"Smith, take this drunken bastard away and lock him
up."

Smith saluted, with a look of disappointment at having work to do. Hodge was sober now. "Sir, that
bitch stole some of my money."

"Shut up!" snapped the officer. "Hell! Get out
of here!" They went. The officer settled into a
chair, sighed, grinned, and asked for whisky.

Tossing back her hair and looking ashamed, the girl
served him. He took her hand. She smiled, half closing her eyes, biting her lower lip—scarcely a smile.
It was beginning all over again.

The officer said in bad Spanish, "Now, you little
devil, give me that money." He lifted his index finger
and brought it down firmly on the paper money between her breasts. The girl began to cry, and behind
the bar the old man shook his head idiotically, and
called on the Virgin Mother under his breath.

The officer pulled out the dollar bills one after another. Then he whispered something to the girl, put-

ting the money in her small, red hand. She smiled, and sat on his knee.

Evan sulked on the bench at the other side of the room. He paid the old man what he owed, saw the tumbler of rum which he had not finished in front of him, and drank it at one gulp. Then he thought he was going to be sick.

The old man fell asleep again. The girl nestled in the officer's armpit. The officer kept looking at Evan as if to tell him to go.

Evan's arms lay very heavily on the dirty table; inside his stiff boots his heels were asleep, and tingled. He foresaw, with the extravagance of an innocent mind, the rest of the night on the narrow bed without sheets in the back room. Disgusted at the way another man succeeded in doing what he had wanted to do, he realized that his disgust was jealousy and his jealousy was mixed with shame. Shame of Americans—he was an American; this was war—he was a soldier; love— an hour ago he had been making love to the same girl. "Stuck like pigs, all you foreigners," she had said.

Time to get back to the barracks. . . . He loathed everything he could think of. To-morrow he was going up among the hills—the sweat, the flies, the pus running out of sores—to fight for what he loathed. "A boy can't do a finer thing than serve his country." To-morrow—he would not; better jump in the sea. To-morrow—he would if he could; he could not. So he stumbled out of the place and down the street.

A week later, about the time that his company went into action, Evan lay on the deck of a British freighter off the coast of Florida. He was still seasick. There had been a violent storm, and on the slopes of the waves nodded great masses of rust-colored seaweed in the shape of chrysanthemums. The ropes cried and were drawn in or loosened by barefoot men, working all around him. The full canvas, stiffly inflated, stood out over his head in a relief as hard as marble. The deserter lay on a pile of wet blankets, still dazed at what he had done.

A sailor named Marbury came with something to eat. It was he who had brought Evan away from Cuba, away from the war, away, indeed, from a whole life well begun, or badly begun. . . . Marbury called him John. He had said, back there in Cuba that night, whenever it was: "I don't want to know your name. I'll call you John—John . . . oh, let's say . . . Craig. You'll need a new name if you come with me."

Evan had stumbled out of the saloon on the waterfront. He had not known what to do with himself. He had stopped and stared into the dark space where the sea was making a loud noise. He had thought of running, jumping, and getting out of sight under the waves; that had been a gauge of his misery, not of his intentions—he had not had any intentions. He had stumbled down the road, and looked into another saloon, and seen another soldier; whereupon he had thought only of finding a place where there were no soldiers.

Then he had met a man who had touched his elbow and said: "See here, mate, what's happened? You come along with me."

Evan thought now that there must have been a dangerous look on his face, and when they had met under one of the lanterns the Americans had put up along the sea, the sailor must have seen it. He himself had seen a short young man wearing a jacket and no shirt, a sharp, ragged fellow; even his upstanding hair and his red face had looked ragged.

Very humbly, as if he had been arrested, Evan had followed the sailor. "Find a pub," he had muttered. "You need a stiff drink."

Evan could not remember drinking it. He had wondered why he had followed this man, and wished he would go away and let him alone so he could jump into the sea or whatever it was he had thought he had to do. He must have said something there in the saloon about jumping into the sea, since the Englishman had asked, "What ails you, damn it?"

Probably Evan had answered that he hated the war, that he was sick of the heat, and the Americans were going to lose the war, anyway—answered not very intellibly; for Marbury admitted now that he had not believed him. A man would be crazy to desert just because he wanted to; there must have been some trouble that he would not talk about.

Marbury had interrupted him. "Damn! You'd better come with me. Come to sea. Make an English sailor of you." He had continued to drink, wiping his mouth (which looked younger than the rest of his face) on the back of his hand, and watching Evan.

Evan had noticed that the back of his hand was

marked with a blue heart in a circle, and that he wore what seemed to be a pair of old bedroom slippers.

Then the sailor had murmured, looking round to be sure that he was not being heard, "You see, a man came on shore with me. Name's Pigeon. He got in a fight. Some bones broken. Lying upstairs in one of these houses. Some woman's taking care of him. He can't go back to the ship; she's the *Amber*, freight, for London. Can't even sit up. And we sail tonight. Hard luck. He's to blame. Drunk, he was. A man hadn't ought to fight with foreigners. That Eye-talian put his knee on his chest and hammered him. . . ."

Evan had laughed a little. A Cuban, scarcely human, kneeling on a man named Pigeon—a Cuban rather like an angel, Jacob's angel in the Bible. . . . Marbury had given a long, foolish account of the affair at least twice. Evan had listened with great interest, without realizing as yet that he was going to desert.

Then Marbury had said: "Damn it! Your soldiers there in the port will let you go with me in the boat because two of us came in. Not in that uniform. So I'll go back and see Pigeon and I'll steal his clothes. We'll put a stone in your uniform and pitch the blasted thing in the sea. Come along now."

Marbury had stood up; Evan had stood up; and to his amazement he had followed meekly. He had not been frightened; he had not been arrested. . . .

To Evan, on board the *Amber,* all this seemed to have taken place a long time ago. He staggered to his feet and began to be initiated into the mysteries of life on a ship. There were a number of them; that of Marbury's affection in particular, because of which he learned, he had been brought away from Cuba. "You're a crazy lubber," Marbury said, "but I like you. If I hadn't liked you, you could have jumped in the sea and be damned. I wouldn't have took the trouble with you I took."

In the beginning this affection seemed merely comic, like that of a dog which tries one's patience by leaping up, scratching with its paws, and breathing close to one's face. Later Evan had to take it seriously, and it warned him of the extreme limits of the outcast individualism in which he had taken the first step. He was a deserter, and Marbury was the only friend he had.

There was also a young sullen boy, miserably jealous of the attention the American was receiving. He said to Marbury: "You're always talking with that Yankee. You're not my mate any more." This reminded Evan of his uncle Leander's story of Hilary, who of course was his uncle, too, though even younger than he, being dead. . . .

And because he remembered how Hilary had disappeared in the Civil War, he wrote a letter to his mother, to be mailed as soon as the ship touched land:

DEAR MOTHER,

I have run away from the army. I can't explain it. I will be in a foreign country by the time you get this. I don't know when I can come back to America, if I ever can. I suppose you'll be ashamed of me. Try to think that I am still the same.

Your loving son.

And as the four-master staggered with infinite patience toward Europe, a sharp sadness took possession of him. Wisconsin with its crops of every color, its hickory-nut trees, its white sunrises and red sunsets— he would never see them again; no one would love him so faithfully, so intimately, as even his hard father had done. But it was something more than homesickness which hurt him; it was the keenest of regrets, that of a young man who has made his choice, for the infinite possibilities he has given up, when at last it is too late to change his mind.

So after dark, when he could steal away from Marbury and the rest, he crept into a corner of the boat, and clenched his teeth, and hid his face in a piece of wet canvas. They ran into a heavy mist one night; at regular intervals a bell was rung, and it had the tone of a dinner bell at home, deepened and made sadder by the sea. Over the taffrail, in the light of a number of lanterns which were hung up in case they should draw near another boat, each wave lifted its broad shoulders and its head covered with foam—lifted its head, and fell; but there was always another to take its place. And between one wave and another he put away the troubles of his youth: his family's broken hearts, and the shameful riddle of being a deserter, and indeed, his youth, which was a trouble in itself. They had served their purpose; he wondered what it was; soon he would not have time to wonder. He could not regret what he had done, any more than a dead man can regret having died. He said to himself, "It can't be helped; I'll have to make the best of it, and the best will be bad enough"; and by thinking that he had made peace with the past—in a measure, and in the manner of young, ignorant, unlucky men—he made his peace with the future.

The *Amber* went up the Thames to the city of London, and docked in the Pool. The sailors emptied the hold; the captain secured a cargo for Rio de Janeiro, and they put it on board.

Evan shared a bed with Marbury in a lodging house in Wapping. He had signed for the next voyage, not knowing what else to do. The night before they were to sail, Marbury went to bed at seven o'clock. Evan wanted to be alone, so he pretended to have lost his pipe, and said he was going out to buy another.

He thought he might never be there again, so he determined to set out on foot to see the whole of London. It was cold, and he walked briskly, as if he had a long way before him and a definite destination. The angry, dim autumn in the largest city in the world; a beast of a city, crouching in the smoke, never moving but seeming to move, because of the agitated swarms of its parasites. The vomit of chimneys and the backwash of the sea. . . . Striped above the shop windows, with holes burned in it here and there by the short street lamps, the fog was like a dirty woolen blanket, but it gave no warmth at all. Evan shivered and walked faster, thinking of the Cuban summer, that heat full of sleeping dogs, bottle-flies, and flowering bushes. Scarcely remembering the weeks at sea, he felt as if he had fallen out of Cuba through a trapdoor into a cellar containing millions of people.

He went into a pub to get warm, wondered what his father would say if he came through the swinging door and found him there drinking whisky, and was amused as if it were an idle fancy, as if in reality he had no father. When he went out again, his sense of direction told him that he was going away from the lodging house in Wapping; but he thought of Marbury as if he were a man he had known years ago, as if, that night, he had not a friend in the world.

He was in no hurry to return to the lodging house; indeed, he was curiously unwilling to. A few hours more, and the long voyage would begin. The sailors were a family, a large male family; in a few weeks on the intimate sea they would know him well; he was a deserter and should have no intimates. His place was there on the blackish pavement which extended for miles in every direction, or no direction at all; in the yellow fog where everyone, not only himself, had a secret, if only that of his identity; in the horde of men and women not keeping step, streaming through the darkness, stumbling, hurrying, limping. . . . A sore, sorry mob which no one would take the trouble to count—wearing secondhand clothes, bitten by fleas— in which he was safe. The light of the shops lit up only their ragged bodies, so that they seemed to have no feet; the light of the lamps poured upon their hats and folded shawls, so that they seemed to have no faces. There, when he met a slight, middle-aged man who lifted his elbows like his father, he could cross the road and never see him again; and when, under a street light, a man stared at him sympathetically as

Marbury had done on the Cuban waterfront, he could turn quickly down a side street. On the *Amber* bound for Rio he would not be able to escape from anything or anybody.

The great, squat city grew still. Only half-mad creatures without occupation, and a few others mysteriously, perhaps criminally busy, were left on the pavement. He crossed the river and came to the City. He knew that the powerful, the trustworthy, those who had parents, wives, children, and nothing to be ashamed of, lived and worked there. He would have had no business among them, but not one of them was to be seen. Footsteps and a shadow—a watchman; another —a policeman. Here and there a bit of paper revolved like a little skirt worn by an invisible body, and pairs of cats in areaways made music.

He came to the river again. There on the Embankment lay many men, wrapped in rags, in newspapers, in one another's arms; and a few women lean and shameless as men. Evan was comforted by the sight of that painful bed full of derelicts, equality and sleep their only comforts. They were his countrymen; his fatherland, like theirs, was disgrace, and this was its very capital. He could not cross the boundaries of that country however far he traveled—so why take passage on a ship for Rio? The Thames passed indifferently, and carried off a rowboat which winked its eye. He sat down beneath a coping and drew his knees up under his jacket. Near by, an enormous man rolled over and recited something in his sleep; to Evan's amazement, it was Spanish—a love song or a prayer, he could not determine which; for sounder sleep quickly laid its hand over the great mouth, which was apparently toothless.

Evan wondered if Marbury were asleep and what he thought of his absence. It was time to start back toward Wapping. Then he realized that he was not going back, not clambering aboard early next morning, not sailing to Rio. He smiled; yes, deserting again. . . . If he had not run away from an army and his family and a whole country, he might have been troubled by his bad faith toward Marbury, perhaps even toward the captain of the *Amber*. Now it was too late for scruples. He might as well sleep there, with the rest of his kind.

But the night grew colder and the pavement pressed through his flesh to the bone. He was not tired enough to sleep in spite of everything; besides, he was younger than anyone else there. So he rose and spent the rest of the night on foot.

He watched the city get up, trade by trade; the sun push through the smoke, a crooked, bloody thing; and parties of soiled pigeons revolve over the chimneys like flower pots, from which the smoke budded, and opened, and dropped large petals of soot. He ate breakfast in a coffee stand, and about nine o'clock wandered down an alley toward the Pool. The *Amber* had left the wharf; it was nowhere to be seen; and Evan was well pleased.

He found the charwoman mopping up the hall of the lodging house. "Your mate was wild," she said, in her strong, snarling voice. "Said you'd had your neck broke. Said if you'd given them the slip, you was out of your head." He slept all the rest of the day, glad to shut his eyes to his premonitions of what was going to happen to him that winter.

It was harder even than he had foreseen. He found work on the docks by the day or week, under abusive foremen, among lazy and suspicious men. There were days when he had little or nothing to eat. If he had foreseen this in Cuba, he would not have deserted; if he had not foreseen it in mid-Atlantic, he would have fallen ill or thrown himself in the Thames.

He grew gaunt, and smiled continually at all the reasons he saw never to smile again. He bought a Bible, read it from beginning to end, drew lines through many cruel chapters which he wanted to forget, and all but memorized the life of Jacob, the life of David, the death of Christ. But there was not a story of a deserter in the Bible.

One day in January he was hurrying through Soho in a fog inlaid with particles of snow. Just as he passed an antique shop a girl darted out of the door with a broom in her hand. Evan started back to avoid a collision, and slipped in the slush; his whole weight struck the windowpane, which cracked in a great star. The girl and he faced each other; he took off his hat. In his embarrassment he stared through the glass he had broken: there was a yellow satin chair, a fat gilt cupid with no nose, a tray of old rings. . . .

Then the girl said hastily, but without excitement, speaking with a pinched, rough accent: "You run away.

Fast. I'll tell my father I broke the window." She waved her broom as if she intended to break it again.

Evan hoped she would laugh at what had happened; she did not. This was a girl who was too proud to laugh when embarrassed. She was exceedingly brown of skin; extraordinary eyes, the lids equally heavy above and below; the whole face pointed downward to the willful mouth and the chin. Evan asked himself what her nationality was.

"But run away," she repeated, impatiently.

Evan remembered that he could come back again; so he went. He did not see the stamping crowds that night, nor the gas flares, nor the snow tossed here and there like dirty confetti. These things had lost their charm; even the convulsive movement in his empty stomach had lost its terrible novelty, and he did not mind having had no supper.

He was out of work on the three succeeding days, and suffered from hunger. He slept in a room below the level of the street, and had to cover his face with the bedclothes because of the rats which came hunting for crumbs and failed to find any—he was as hungry as they. He measured his misery by the dreams which ravished him in the damp, sagging bed—dreams of baking day in Wisconsin, of oranges and apples, of trumpets which sounded like small, southern roosters and woke him up.

As soon as he had money he returned to Soho and went bravely into the shop of G. Orfeo, Antiquary. But the girl was not there. An older woman came forward very quietly: the same heavily framed brown eyes, the same reddish-brown locks of hair; it must be her sister, Evan thought. But her eyes were gentle, too gentle, and her mouth drooped as if she had a habit of sacrifice. "What do you wish to see, sir?"

Evan swept the shop with his eyes, to discover what was there in the greatest number, so it would take him a long time to choose. "A ring, if you please," he said.

The woman watched his tar-stained fingers on the signets, intaglios, and semiprecious stones, with anxiety, even with suspicion. In great embarrassment Evan asked their prices, having only one pound in the world. There was one which he could have paid for, a silver band engraved with banal flowers. But just as he laid the pound note on the glass counter the other sister came down the staircase at the back of the shop.

"*Mais,* Gabrielle," she cried, "it is the one who broke the window! Good afternoon." She put out her pointed hand over the glass, over his money, the garnets, and the silver-gilt, and examined him steadily with her large eyes which seemed to be veiled, her eyes in mourning. . . .

"But what, this is your money?" she asked, lightly. "I think you are poor. I think it is all you have got. And the ring is nothing, very bad." She slipped it back into the showcase and handed him the pound note. Apparently the sister did not understand why; Evan was not sure that he did. "Now our father is gone to Paris, so you will take some tea with us, and tell us what you are, for example."

Her name was Susanne Orfeo. Their father was

Italian, their dead mother French; they had been born in Paris, where the father kept another shop on a quay of the Seine; they had lived in London for eight years.

For no particular reason Evan told them that his name was John Craig. The fact that he was an American pleased and excited them, even the timid Gabrielle, who sighed continually, as if all the good things of this world were denied her in advance; for as far as they knew, America was a land of nothing but preposterous wealth and liberty and pleasure. Susanne said she could not understand why he had ever left it. Evan explained that he had run away from home to see the world, and naturally said nothing about the war.

He returned again and again to the shop, at first rather surreptitiously because the father, having committed the shop and Susanne for several weeks to Gabrielle's care, had come back. Gabrielle was alarmed and manageable, like a mother who loves her children too much to say no to them. A devout Catholic, she insisted only that nothing should take place which would have to be confessed, and did not mind tricking her father because he never communicated.

Evan saw by her questions as to his present earnings, his prospects, and the attitude and position of his family in America, that she was hoping to arrange a marriage for Susanne. His answers were ridiculous, as he well knew; but she smiled approvingly, no matter what he said, her judgment distorted in his favor, as if, with pent-up yearning, she herself were to be the bride.

Ostensibly Susanne did not approve of this indirect

but repeated proposal of marriage, made in her name. Her indolent eyes would lose themselves in the grate fire, or be fascinated by a bit of brocade or the accidental spark of a well-cut stone, as if these things represented by a sort of code the face of another lover. Or she would seem to be tired of his presence, hiding her discontented face in a black-and-white feather boa which she wore. Or she would make fun of him with cruel good nature until her sister felt obliged to come to his defense. Gabrielle lent herself to this sincere and insincere play with tremulous intensity.

If the two sisters had seemed to have determined together that Evan should marry the younger, he would have been alarmed. It was a good thing, he thought, that he did not want to marry, for no girl in her right mind would accept a deserter, anyway. But the girl's seeming lack of interest promised him independence, gave him courage, and doubled his desire. He had lost his innocence since he had come to England, but was only sufficiently acquainted with love to feel its brute force; he did not know it well enough to recognize the profound, perhaps not wholly instinctive cunning of the sisters.

Then their father fell ill, and Susanne said: "If you please, come and work for us. We have told our father that we are afraid to keep here alone all this value," making a gesture of reference to the jewels, the carvings, the velvet, which included her lovely body in a circle of the damp, snowy light which came in from the street.

They took him upstairs to their father's bedroom.

Gabrielle said, *"Voilà, mon petit,* the American we have engaged to help in the shop. His name is John Craig."

Evan saw a man in a skullcap who ruffled the linen under his bearded chin with his weak hands, a withered man with a large, sharp nose. *"Comme tu veux.* . . . Good morning, sir. I do not keep the shop much longer. You see, I become old. We shall retire to Genoa. But for the time it is very well that you should work here."

His expert eyes estimated the young man's value, swung sideways in their sockets to glance at Gabrielle suspiciously, and rested upon his marriageable daughter's face with almost evil irony.

For a moment Evan, a deserter still, was afraid that he would pity him and smile—in other words, warn him that love was a trap.

But the old man was too sick to pity anybody or to attach any importance to the discoveries made by his aged penetration. He closed his eyes very slowly. "I do *not* care," he murmured, "what you do."

Susanne blushed, and they left the room.

Gabrielle nursed her father as she would have to do until the end of his life. Susanne kept the shop. There was nothing for Evan to do. The sudden well-being changed him overnight; a clean body and clean clothes, warmth, good food, friendliness. . . . Pride in having endured hardships all alone, and as it were by choice, made of the memory of his misery the rarest sort of pleasure. Then he told himself that he had been happier since he had come to London than hunger, cold, and fatigue had permitted him to realize; he was certainly happier than he had ever been in Wisconsin. He wanted never to have a home again, or to be surrounded by a family. People of his own kind provoked him to be unlike them—that is, unlike himself; but among those whom he might never understand, he understood himself and was his own best friend. He liked not having to give an account of himself to anyone; it was good luck to be so disgraced that little or nothing could be expected of him, that he need not expect much of himself. His only ambition was to escape the ambitions which others might have for him and oblige him to fulfill; and when he thought of his brothers at all, he pitied them. No one cared what he did nor what happened to him; he did not care himself, he believed, if only it were not what had always happened. He told himself that this must be the way his old uncle Leander had wanted him to live, when he had talked to him as a boy so incomprehensibly. Back there in Cuba, in despair and foolishness, by accident, he had chosen the life which suited him; he enjoyed being a deserter.

But he had fallen in love. Day after day the girl's beauty was half denied, half given to him. His enjoyment of what he had mingled with longing for what he could not have, and produced in his heart a childish irresponsibility and an intoxicating pain. At the end of two weeks of it, involuntarily—uttering the words at random in place of other words of love-making which her proud bearing forbade him to use—he asked Susanne to marry him.

But a mere proposal meant no more to her than love-making without a proposal means to many girls. She seemed to be waiting for a contract to be drawn up and signed by her lover, his parents, and her own, before giving her consent. In any case, she wanted plans to be made, a home chosen, and sums of money with which to begin life secured and counted. So she merely smiled, shook her head, and ran away.

Evan heaved a sigh of relief. What a confession he would have had to make if she had stayed to listen to it! And she less than any girl would want Evan Tower, an outlaw, for a husband. But she did not know that Evan Tower existed, and it had not occurred to him as yet that John Craig—a new man without a disgraceful past, without, indeed, any past—could exist. So he did not dare to say anything more about his confused desires. If he did, he might ask her again to be his wife, as it were against his will; she might refuse him, she might accept him—he would not know what to do in either case. His yearning gave him no rest; and it was not licensed, could never be licensed, by anything, perhaps not even by love on her part. Passion is lonely at best (hopeless or not, requited or not); he was lonelier in the pleasant shop than he had ever been sleeping in the cellar bedroom, working on the docks. He thought of going back to them.

Finally Susanne saw how humble and stupid passion may make a young man: he had not even realized that she loved him. . . . So she began to make plans herself, and the day came when she was able to make this announcement: "Father has sold the shop. He will

give us a thousand pounds now, and more when he sells
the Paris business."

Did that mean that she would marry him without
asking any questions? He hoped at least to see a somber warmth like his own kindle in her heavy eyes, but
was baffled by her self-possession, mystified by her air
of waiting; and she said nothing more. As time went
by, he learned something of the power of the Church,
the sources of the strength of women, and the character of the girl who, it seemed, was willing to marry
him, but unwilling to give him any proof of love.

One evening in June they came out of Hyde Park,
where the mist had rolled off the lagoons like ribbons
unwinding from great spools, and lamps had already
been lighted in the leaves not yet soiled by the summer.
Evan clung to Susanne's elbow, trying to substitute
the delicate muscles curving along the upper arm and
the forearm to the little pointed bone, for the un-
touched beauties which burdened his imagination like
a mania. They came to the dingy, stately, crowded
street.

Then Susanne swung her hand outward in a circle
(a familiar gesture) and said, "There is no future
here. I am not like the others, most other girls. I
have some ambitions."

Evan stared wistfully at the knots of self-possessed,
unscrupulous people so unlike Americans; the mysterious closed carriages; a square opening out at the
end of the long stem of a street like a large, old, gray
rose and pouring smoky perfume in their faces. He
compared London with the hard, poor farms which

were all that he had seen of the New World. Europe had given him maturity in exchange for his painful youth; it might give him Susanne as well; and he wanted to stay there and become a part of its old age.

"You know," the girl continued, "I made a vow long ago—never to marry a European. That is, not unless he would promise to take me to your country. We will go there. They will go to Genoa to grow old; we will be in your home. And we will get rich on the other side."

Evan stumbled at the end of every one of the short sentences. So that was what she had been waiting for. . . . It was America she wanted, America she loved in him. The deserter had become an ambassador, as deserters often do. Ambassador or not, he was still an outlaw—he could not go back. He would have to tell her. She would despise him—despise, blame, and scold him. He might as well desert again, go back to the docks and say nothing.

No. . . . A soldier's honor and promises to a friend had rested lightly on his impatience; love was heavy. So they returned through the hasty dusk, in silence, to the shop.

There Susanne struck a match under the paper and wood he had laid in the grate for the next morning, and pushed a sofa in front of it, and sank into the faded cushions. She was aware of his distress; she was waiting for an explanation. He himself waited for the purring and snapping of the fire to cease, unable to lift his voice above them.

At last he said, "You must know, Susanne, that I can't go back to America."

"Why can't you?"

"I deserted from the army. My real name is Evan Tower."

"That makes no difference—"

"If they caught me I'd be put in jail."

To his amazement, she did not reproach him; she did not seem to hold him responsible; she blamed the government of his country—which meant that she had already accepted him, accepted him in secret. Evan understood no more than this, and stared at her in stupid, passionate delight.

She had sprung out of the cushions and was pacing up and down the room. "No! No! They shall not! Fools! It is nonsense! We will show them!" She glared into the corners of the room as if they were occupied by uniformed enemies. "No! I hate your government!" Even in her anger she was thinking of what could be done, practically. "There must be an amnesty. You will have a beard. In the West . . . Mexico . . ."

Clearly she was saying: He is mine, he is mine; America is mine. His mind on fire because of her angry beauty, Evan rejoiced without thinking of the consequences.

Then she stood quietly in the center of the room and wrung her hands. "We *will* go back to America. We will hide. We, we alone, will not get caught. The army is nothing. No one will know. We dare to do it. You love me; you do not dare be afraid. Tell me.

Tell me if you are afraid. Tell me, if you . . ." She began to weep angrily, and clutched at his hands and shoulders.

Evan wondered why Gabrielle did not hear her weeping and come down; he did not know how to defend himself. So at last he heard his own voice saying that he would go, promising not to be afraid, promising to grow rich and respected in his own country— a land as unfriendly and as far away as if it had not yet been discovered.

Susanne lifted her head, drew back against the arm of the sofa, and smiled—a smile not of faith, but vigilance; not of contentment, but violent firmness and courage; not of an end, but a new, unwelcome beginning.

Her lover's heart beat heavily, heavy as never before with fear, simply because he had promised not to be afraid. He half regretted that he had comforted her, because he had reëstablished the wall of her ambition and willful virtue between them. But love went on speaking for him, saying what he did not believe: that America would be kind, that every law could be set at naught, that she should rule over the circumstances of their lives and over his heart, and that he would give her everything she wanted.

Then, by way of an appeal to her imagination and still more to his own, he took out of a showcase necklaces of garnets and slippery chains, thrust a comb like a studded shell into her hair, and folded about her an embroidered cope smelling of incense. The fire turned these hard ornaments into drops of water and disembodied sparks. But Susanne shook her head. These were old things; she wanted new. They were already hers; she wanted that which was his.

As he removed them, his cold fingers accidentally touched her cold throat and mechanically caressed her shoulders. So he gave her all he actually had to give—his kisses—brutally, softly, without asking leave, but not without seeing her face, upon which a girl's emotions could be seen in conflict with a woman's—terror with relief, distaste with satisfaction, the humility of the abdication of a girl's power with a woman's powerful vanity. But he covered her unwilling movements with his arms; they climbed the stairs together, and did not separate in the flickering hall.

When at last Evan came down into the shop alone, he found Gabrielle there. She was weeping. "Now you have committed the sin," she whispered. "Now you will leave me alone and go to America. I will never see you—" She fled to her room.

Evan settled his body, suddenly heavy, into the sofa cushions. The fire throbbed in an enviable exhaustion. He was not even tired enough to sleep, but felt instead that false weariness by virtue of which, in the midst of passion, one is able to consider the next step. The next step according to Gabrielle: "Now you will marry and go to America . . ." He had promised; and as a lover, like a fool, he had sealed his promise. Now that it was too late, he could think—of the short past and the long future ahead. It was as if he had been talking to himself for a long time, and had not been

able to hear because of his pounding lover's heart;
now its music had ceased for a few hours. . . .

He would marry Susanne, that was certain. He did
not want to marry,—he could not help it. Then they
would go back to America, venture across an incon-
spicuous border, and establish themselves in some half-
deserted place. Suddenly, surprisingly, his love of his
country caused him pain (he had not known that he
loved it). But he would have to be an Englishman
over there; he could be an American only in Europe.
And he would have to work, and seem to think what
others thought, and do what others did, and grow prosperous and worthy of respect—join the regiment and
march with the rest. . . .

He thought of the leave-taking in Wisconsin before
he had gone off to join that other, actual regiment; for
now he was taking leave of himself—he was going to
be married and return to America as John Craig, and
John Craig was saying good-by to Evan Tower.
"Don't make promises," his uncle Leander had said in
Wisconsin, "that'll be your trouble. Don't get started
doing what you don't like to do, because you're not
the kind of man who keeps at it. You needn't, as long
as you're alone in the world. You'd better keep alone.
. . ." Evan wondered if he were still in California
with Timothy Davis. What had he thought of his
having run away from the war? What would he
think of his marriage and the new promises? He
had such strange ideas. . . . He would probably be
frightened about what would happen—after they were
married.

Susanne and John Craig, man and wife. To all intents and purposes their marriage was over before it had begun; love had run its course. The rest of their lives would be a monument to it—a monument having on the outside an appearance of solidity, but hollow within, where, like the few breaths of air which are imprisoned inside a bronze, the bitter-sweet of youth, passion, and disgrace would be secreted. . . .

Outside in the fog London drew up its enormous knees and shifted its enormous shoulders.

Youth and passion—he saw more clearly than before what they were; he could see through them to the future, which would not be young and in which there would not be much passion; and he understood Susanne as if they had already been married for years. She would never cease to reproach him for having endangered her immortal soul by his love before marriage, nor forget why she had married him, nor overlook any of his failures. Others would excuse him for being a deserter—by never discovering the fact, or by forgetting it. She would go through the motions of forgiveness, and as long as he loved her keep him from forgiving himself. Perhaps she would not blame him, but instead think of him as a fool, not worldly-wise enough to deserve her respect. A man's madness, nipped in the bud; love itself was a man's madness. . . .

The small, naked flames in the hearth began to clothe themselves in ashes. He sought in his memory for a clear picture of her face, and found it—at once the face of a flower and a shopkeeper. How it had

had its way with him—and it was not done with him yet. At that moment there was more premonition than passion in his heart; there would not always be. Passion would be born again and again, but it would be weakened like this by each rebirth; and the day would surely come when he would wonder why he had given himself up. He was glad that it had begun only in fact, for it had been as if, bending over a rose, he had been prevented from taking a deep breath. Could one ever take a full breath, and have enough of love?

He was infinitely tired. Sitting in the antique shop where love had begun, he seemed to look back even upon its future, knowing what he would have to give in return for what Susanne had given or would give, the reparation that would be required of him for what he would take or had taken, as if it were by force: responsibility, secrecy, half-hearted hard work, fatigue. . . .

Hitherto apparently lazy, he had "worked harder to keep from working than anyone else ever worked," as his mother would say. Apparently a coward, he had run away from several kinds of tyranny; but now, it seemed, he had chosen to play the tyrant to himself. He went on enumerating the differences between the past and the future. He had evaded common responsibilities—little good it had done him; for now he would have to keep to the letter all these fantastic rules which life (or perhaps he himself) was making up as he went along. For example, he would have to learn never to hide his face, so that no one should discover that he had anything to hide. To obtain forgiveness for his youth, of which, like a fool, he had hoped to make others envious as he grew older. To give no one cause to be ashamed of him again, but to be ashamed of himself, in order to be able to be discreet mechanically. To make more friends than he wanted, and not to like any of the sort of people who resembled him, lest he should have to live down their disgraces as well as his own. To fulfill every expectation, to promise too much and keep his word. To condemn the man he would have liked to be to increasing obscurity, and make a self he did not like more and more prominent. To strip his genuine character little by little of its reality, and turn a disguise into an actual man. . . .

This meant the total disappearance of Evan Tower, that happy, unhappy boy who had done as he liked, and the rise of John Craig, an Englishman married to a French wife, neither happy nor unhappy, but growing rich in America. So with the passage of time, the soul of a man loses itself in his life.

His life in disguise; and when he died, only the disguise would lie quiet on the deathbed and be buried; he himself would have been dead a long time. No— not dead, merely condemned to death.

For he would always be a deserter. A boy hiding inside a man, an outlaw hiding inside a man who at last, at least, would abide by the law. If he liked, a homeless, lonely man in a foreign land might wear his disgrace as if it were nothing more than a shirt or a coat out of fashion. A lonely man surrounded by friends and family, a naturally homeless man at home, an expatriate resident in his own country, would have to wear it next the skin, like a tattooed rose, or star, or Marbury's blue heart in a circle. That was all. . . .

The fire sank. His excitement kept him warm, but his hopelessness was putting him to sleep.

More than ever a deserter, then. . . . The exile was returning home, which was inexcusable; the outlaw was going to avoid punishment—that is, break the law again. He was skeptical (his uncle had taught him that); but his own impulses were speaking to him as an angel speaks to a madman, a mother to a child; and when that angel spoke (with its limited vocabulary of passion, fatigue, homesickness, fear), he had no ears for his skepticism or for other men.

So he regarded himself with admiration and disdain, comparing the past with the present—for he seemed to have been young a moment ago—and comparing himself with other people and other things. The wooden saints in the shop, covered with flakes of gilt, sick with gold sores; the gaping showcases (for Gabrielle had not forgotten to lock up the jewels); the crystal ball in which he had never seen anything but a flaw shaped like Susanne's mouth; that dark-red, disastrous mouth itself—they had lost most of their charm. They were old things; he wanted new. Shining, unsatisfying, they belonged to his youth and were like it; and he was tired of being young. His uncle's warnings also belonged to it; all he would have to do with them from now on would be to prove that they had been mistaken; and it occurred to him that his uncle had come to be an old man without ever having grown up. He felt a great hunger for the evasions, the hypocrisies, the calculated movements, the disappointments, of middle age.

And there was the London dawn, strong and soiled as a man's middle age, crawling over the window sills, pushing between the plush curtains. He would not have time to go to bed. Before he crept upstairs he took off his shoes, unwilling that anyone should know that he had sat up all night, determined that no one should ever discover the madness of his thought.

The rest of his life was very much as he had expected it to be. He and Susanne were married at the end of the summer. Gabrielle took the invalid father to a small villa outside Genoa. The young couple went to Mexico City, and during the winter crossed into the United States without difficulty, and bought a ranch near Taos, New Mexico.

He wrote to his mother and received a long letter in reply, full of embarrassment and eagerness to be proud of him in one way or another, proud of his courage at least. In it, with later family news, she told how Leander had died on his way west. She added, "He did not live to hear of your trouble in the army"; evidently she was glad. . . . Leander might not have minded that particular disgrace, but now, if this new adventure ended still more shamefully, as it might, the old bachelor would not be alive to be embittered by it; and Evan said to himself, It is just as well. But the new adventure was not to end badly.

Susanne gave birth to a son who was christened Leander Orfeo Craig. The desert and the mountains

were little more than a place of exile for her—exile
less from Europe, which she did not love, than from
the brilliant life she had looked forward to; but she
recognized the danger of residence in a more law-
abiding part of the country. She grew strangely devout and wanted her son to become a priest; but Orfeo
adored his father, who grimly and patiently counter-
acted her influence. In 1906 the antiquarian G. Orfeo
died in Genoa, and Gabrielle came to live with her sister, bringing the rest of her father's fortune. Friends
of a bishop and a sinister old ex-governor, the two
women came to be powerful figures in the public life of
the State, and more and more independently, at one
end of the great adobe house, led the life of wealthy
Mexican devotees.

John Craig lived in the other wing, near the goats
and horses, among the cowboys, the firearms which
were less and less useful as time passed, the carved
saddles and faded saddle blankets, the star-shaped
spurs. He saw his wife only a few minutes a day,
but never loved another woman even for a night. His
life was that of the chief of a band of hard men—his
cowboys—all of whom, like himself, had secrets, vices,
great strength, and skill, whether with animals or enemies; and among whom he enjoyed the lonesome prestige of an officer or a criminal—like soldiers or accom-
plices, they did not believe him but believed in him.
Many of his neighbors as well were suspicious of his
past, but it seemed as natural in the Far West for a
man to be followed by an unpleasant story as by a
shadow. He kept out of politics, and made those who

did not wish him well fear him, stopping their mouths
at first by well-chosen threats, and then good-naturedly
letting them forget why they did not gossip about him
any more.　Gradually he became an influential citizen,
with whom even his wife's powerful friends had to
reckon.　The years went by, as much alike as cattle
marked with the same brand, his brand—a heart inside
a circle.　He did not make so much money as Susanne
wished nor even as he had expected, but was able to put
aside slowly a certain small fortune for Orfeo.

The boy looked somewhat like his mother, very little
like an American.　Thinking of him, his father thought
of his own boyhood: thus Orfeo seemed not merely
precious as a son, but of unique importance, as to a
weary regent, the sole heir to great wealth or a throne.
For he was the only living relative, John Craig thought,
of the boy who had died (at least seemed to die) within himself; and thus entitled to everything in manhood
which he imagined that boy might have enjoyed.　So
John Craig watched Orfeo with a certain fear—fear
of his evident mortality, of his lack of discontent which
was like indifference; a royally lovely child because of
whose gentleness an illusory kingdom (of irresponsibility, candor, and truancy) might get out of control
or, by someone, be taken away.

The child carried messages back and forth across
the patio between his parents; and because he resembled his mother as a girl, it seemed to his father that
he also bridged another distance—that between his
own heartbreaking youth and the rather heartbroken
satisfaction of the later years. His imagination followed

the tiny boy's solitary, symbolical footsteps back and forth in his life and across it, and wished that the years would bring him back where he had begun. Smiling mechanically, he wished that, as soon as he had saved enough money to insure his son's independence, John Craig, the rancher, might die, and his soul pass into Orfeo's life, and Evan Tower, the deserter, be disguised by nothing more than that fearless childhood, and begin all over again. . . .

And because he thought idly of beginning his life again, he thought how it actually had begun, and wanted to see Wisconsin, his parents, his brothers and sister, once more. They must have forgiven him by this time; one or another of them might understand him at last.

It would be a long journey—and then explanations, embarrassment, a certain amount of scandal, irreparable resentments that he had had the luck to have forgotten about. . . . A grown man had no business to seek to be understood. He was a fool, mysteriously a fool, he told himself—without caring in the least. He might as well set out; he always had, once he had thought of a place to go. In the court Orfeo was playing with a jet of water which balanced over a stone tub, balanced as it were in the very center of Taos Valley, that huge, hollow stone—balanced, lost its balance, straightened again, but could never be quite still, like a human life in the great hollow of a lifetime. . . . His life had lost its balance again, that was all.

So he went back to Hope's Corner. Wisconsin was less pretty than he had thought. His father, as he might have remembered, never forgave anything, and would not see him. His mother told him about all the relatives; he found little to tell her, for she was not even interested in his treason, his hardships, his marriage, his good and bad luck; it was as if she had brought him into the world to be a deserter—he had been one, and there was nothing more to be said. His presence seemed merely to remind Ralph of his resentment at having been deserted by both his brothers, left behind with their old father and the unprofitable farm and no opportunities. He did not have the courage to stop in Chicago to visit his luckier brother, the minister; and he told himself afterward that for lack of courage he had not stayed with his people long enough to accomplish what he had come for, whatever that was. . . .

So a few years later he went home again, and found himself no less a stranger than before. He could not share his mother's almost formal enthusiasm for the early days. He did not understand his brother's sensual, virtuous life. His sister-in-law Marianne, wistfully opinionated and brilliant like a saint, intimidated him. Flora, his little sister, laughed, wept, and liked everyone absent-mindedly, tremulously afraid to do wrong, but less like a saint than a nun. John Craig felt as if he had wandered backward (or forward) into an epoch peopled by wise children, troubled or at peace—even their trouble was a kind of peace—and he did not understand the games that, with touching solemnity, such children played.

But what had he expected? What could his family

have meant to him then? His uncle Leander, who more than anyone had encouraged him to be the stranger that he was, had been dead so many years, and was not even buried there. Was Evan Tower dead as well? Certainly he spoke of him to his mother as one speaks of a boy who has not lived to grow up; and if he was, his tomb was not in Wisconsin, except when and because he, John Craig, was there—in whose heart he was buried, dead or alive.

Leander and Evan, those two were his real family, and their souls had passed into his life—that is, John Craig's life. He had thought that he was tired of it; but he was a strong man, and had no other to live. So in Wisconsin he realized how precious it was— perhaps that was what he had come for. The spirits of his uncle and his boyhood having passed into it, he ought to be content with their dwelling place.

Having passed into his life; perhaps into Orfeo's after him. . . . There was also Ralph's eldest boy, Alwyn, a colorless youngster with raised eyebrows who was going to resemble Leander when he grew up. He seemed, childishly, to be trying to think his way into everything that came to his attention—John Craig imagined a key trying to fit every lock—and thus to hurt himself and keep himself in a slight but almost continual bad temper. It appeared, furthermore, that he and his father did not understand each other. So John Craig said to Alwyn, "You and my boy will be friends. You must come out and live with us for a while, before long. I'll raise up a colt or two for you to ride."

It was on the last day of that second visit that, intending to ask his aunt a question as an excuse, Alwyn slipped into his grandmother's sitting room in order to look at his uncle for the first time after his mother had told him who and what he was. They were looking out of the window, his grandmother with her large arms folded, his uncle, the stranger, resting one hand on his aunt Flora's shoulder. His grandfather had refused to come to the house while his son was there. Every night his grandmother reproached him, but he did not even trouble to answer; every afternoon they hoped he would change his mind. Alwyn tiptoed to the window, and no one spoke to him.

They could see his grandfather coming down the lane, coming toward the house at his usual stubborn pace. His head was thrown back; over his shoulder he carried a long thistle-hoe. He was coming toward the house; he had changed his mind at last. . . .

But just as he put out his hand to open the garden gate, he turned around and slowly, stubbornly, went back, out of sight.

The tears came to Flora's vague, affectionate eyes, and Alwyn's grandmother clapped her hands together. "I declare," she cried, "he does beat all! Evan, your father is a hard man."

"I guess, mother," John Craig said, "hardness runs in the family. At any rate, it ought to—we need it, the way we live." And as he spoke he smiled, but only about his mouth, rather lifelessly.

TWO locks of red hair falling upon her forehead like red shadows, Alwyn's aunt Flora, when she sang, bent her head timidly or looked straight up toward the ceiling as if it were a sky—and a sky full of beings which other people could not see. The sound of her voice rose and fell, often strained by emotions for which her thin throat was too slender a channel, often failing altogether when its sweetness made her sad.

Alwyn thought that she was beautiful like an idol, vaguely thinking of the bright-colored statues in Catholic churches as idols: her good-natured, dismayed face; her hair like rusted iron in a burdensome crown, broken into large curls at the nape of her neck; her hands blue-white, with perfectly twisted veins. To amuse him when he was a child, she drew sails upon little round lakes, rigid fountains, butterflies, and nosegays of forget-me-nots, coloring them from a watercolor box. When an adolescent, he always stood as near her as he dared, charmed by the perfume of attar-of-roses which drifted from her dress, the odor of orris root in her hair, and the atmosphere, like a delicate scent itself, of the life of a girl nearly thirty years old, gradually losing the freshness of girlhood without growing old, almost without growing older.

He knew that his company gave her pleasure as well; even with her brothers, his uncles, she was less at ease. Perhaps his love was the only love she had received which did not threaten to make itself felt with startling energy, threaten to possess and coerce her— and then fail to do so. They were of the same blood, which meant, she thought, that they shared moral principles and a religious faith; he was a mere child and her nephew. So their relationship afforded her a holiday from having to choose between one man and another, from the alarms and embarrassments of being an unmarried woman.

For two men had troubled five years of her life, less with emotions than with what she called "problems." The first had been Richard Wallace, the son of a wealthy farmer, a grown-up adolescent, wise in the policies and graces of his age; not clever, but with pride to take the place of vivacity. He had bright gray eyes, and drove the most violent and shining horses in the country. He had tired of many girls who loved him. Olive Templeton, a girl named Valentine, and Flora's cousin Edith, if they happened to be where he was, followed him with angry, intimate glances without ever speaking. Their grievances were only those of wounded vanity, for he had never profited by their self-abandonment. He had had a rendezvous almost every night for a number of years, and waited impatiently for nightfall as if it were a ceremony and a feast; but by day he had the look of a victim of his own love-making and his self-control.

Flora was pleased when her turn came to be the object of his fickle attentions. Her life as a woman would begin with an encouraging conquest, for, with perfect confidence in herself, she intended to be the first to enjoy his wooing and resist his charm. Dreaming vaguely of more serious love, she became his favorite, half conscious of her bravado and her disdain of him and of what he was doing; the disdain was ignorant as well as innocent.

She soon lost her ignorance; a great many serious new sensations made her humble. Each fought, against the other's magic, to keep his will power and above all his will to be good, intact; and a closer companionship developed in their common fear of companionship's magic. In solitude, in a buggy, behind excited mares which jerked the reins, there was his shoulder against her shoulder; his arm stealing behind her and patiently put away; the scent of his wiry hair and his tobacco; the hard pressure of his knees under the lap robe. Picnics and parties were only a truce; and after, once more, his breath on her cheek in the starlight.

His love whispering was meaningless but terribly comprehensible: never all of a sentence, often not all of a word. . . . He did not ask for privileges or favors, as if he neither wanted her to know his intentions nor wanted to know them himself; but continued to reach out his hand obstinately, dreamily: desire fast asleep, in a sleep of self-control. He rarely spoke of marriage. Flora could not believe that he loved her. Because of her vigilance to protect herself from seduction, she could not study her heart to learn whether or not she loved him.

She was frightened by the temptation of love, though she wanted to regard it as superficial. It never touched her so poignantly as in the Presbyterian church in Aaronsville where on Sunday mornings she sang of the Shepherd and his wild flock, of mansions with pillars, of being reborn, of death without a sting. She kept morality constantly in mind, as one carries an amulet; she came to love the amulet for itself, imagining dangers where there were none, in order to hold it in the palm of her hand. She prayed that Richard be preserved from evil and she herself from his charm. Kneeling by her bed, the linen and the indoor night spread out before her half-closed eyes, she realized without warning that her lips were parched and pressed on the air as if in a kiss, that Richard's kiss probably would not satisfy that yearning; and she wept. But she could not quite make up her mind to refuse him, if he should ask her to be his wife.

The neighbors watched them with a curiosity scarcely kind, scarcely Christian; her mother and sister-in-law observed that she had lost weight; no one discovered her trouble. When she happened to think of her original intention—to punish him for his frivolity and pride—she was contented for a few days. But the thought of Olive Templeton and the Valentine girl and Edith began to be intolerable; she feared to lose him as they had lost him, and determined never to surrender, less and less in order to triumph over him, but so that he would never tire of her. She clung to his love as those who are not unwilling to die cling to life—because it gives them an occupation in the meantime. She laughed as well as cried, but her laughter began to have a frightened sound.

Her only confidante was her sister-in-law Marianne,

in whose romance there had been obstacles and mis-understandings, but never any ignorance of her own wishes—or so it seemed by that time. The two epi-sodes had a certain similarity, at least in so far as all relations between young men and virgin girls, with the monotony of naturalness, are alike; and Marianne told her story because the emotions in it were unmis-takable, and the end encouraging. The two women, equally anxious to be perfect, also resembled each other up to a certain point. But Marianne had chosen her own ideals; they were at one with her wishes; and her renunciation had concerned only things which she would not have wanted in any case. Flora's desires, on the other hand, were so shadowy that she could not tell what was contrary to them, what to sacrifice to them. Able to be faultless in any way already deter-mined by another's imagination, by such an imagina-tion as her sister-in-law's, it was individual responsi-bility which weighed upon her. But Marianne, for reasons of conscience, was unwilling to relieve her of any part of that burden.

She tried instead to strengthen every germ of de-cision which seemed to begin to form in Flora's mind, praising Ralph, the girl's favorite brother, as her principal comment on Richard. "It is hard for a boy of Richard's disposition to be good," she would say. "Are you sure that he is a Christian?"

As far as she could see, there was little true love amid their emotions, their tumult of innumerable hesitations; but she would advise nothing but prayer, which brought Flora no nearer a solution—in fact, carried her thought, as if on the waves of a deep, invisible river, away from the problem itself. And afterward it had to be met with again; her bewilderment merely increased by having asked God to show her the way; so that the last time there was question of marriage, like the first, she was unprepared to give an answer.

That evening she and Richard were sitting on the lawn on a great rock shaped like the Ark of the Covenant. The moon shining in their faces as if it were a spotlight; night birds and sleepless birds in a radiance so bright that those whose eyes were made for the darkness could not hunt; and a splash of moonlight running down Richard's cheek, the tired cheek of a young man who has seemed to have been young for a long time. . . . "This can't go on," he whispered.

The moment had come: a promise or good-by.

"Will you marry me?" he asked, as if he were asking, not for delight—merely for relief from pain.

Flora felt that someone was watching them: not God perhaps, but a great Spirit less a stranger to the earth, which enjoyed her confusion—the moon was its hard eye. Through a thousand lilac leaves, the lamps of the house signaling to her: a vague audience of those who loved her, before whom she had to do the right thing. Through the maple leaves overhead, the stars, like lamps of another house.

"I think not, Richard," she said, wishing for a word as definite as yes or no, but meaning neither. She bent forward and clasped her hands.

He stood up. "You know I love you," he said. She had not known. "Tell me why you won't."

Her body drooped still more loosely on the great stone, but she threw back her head in order to see him, tall and silvered over by the rays of moonlight. What could she answer? That his morals did not satisfy her? That he would not make a good husband? She did not understand these things; she did not care; others cared—all their eyes were upon her from the windows full of lamps, from the sky full of stars; she would have to do as they thought best. Furthermore, she felt as if she had made other engagements long ago, when she was a little child, perhaps, and had forgotten for the moment what they were.

She did not know what she whispered in reply to Richard. "I can't hear you," he said. "I don't understand." He shivered in the light that was like that of day, clear and embarrassing.

The moment had passed—promise or good-by; it was good-by. Where were they? In the corner of the lawn of her own home; she wished they were far away, so he would have to go with her a certain distance (even the distance of the rest of her life, without yes or no) in which at last the moon's blinding, bright eye which confused her might close—for perhaps it was to blame. But the distance of the rest of a lifetime, like that from the corner of the lawn to the house door, seemed short; it was not worth while asking anyone to accompany her that far—she could go alone.

"Good-by, then," he said. A man moving over the damp lawn, moving quickly, so that the time she would have to call him back would be short, too short. . . . His feet, mechanically steady, made a sound of mowing down the well-illuminated grass.

Flora went first to the north wing where her brother and sister-in-law lived, and wept in Marianne's arms. "Be strong. I believe it is for the best," Marianne said.

She dried her eyes, and opened the door of her mother's part of the house. Her mother, who through the thin walls had heard her crying, was waiting in the center of the room under the hanging lamp. "What's happened?" She opened her large arms like those of a man. "Don't you cry," she said. "The one you want isn't always the best husband." She was ready to tell her own story.

"But I don't want him, mother," Flora whispered, moving toward her bedroom door.

A look of dismay on her broad, benevolent face, her mother stared after her, loving her more because she seemed too young to understand, trying to decide which member of the family she took after, and failing to do so. For in fact Flora resembled them all, beginning with her father (his fastidious, idealistic melancholy), and her mother (her lack of cunning, her willingness to wait and give in); preventing herself from doing things, just as they had prevented one another.

Sleepless, pacing barefoot on the rug of her room, night after night Flora watched the moon shrink. She began to believe that the unkind Spirit (not God, perhaps, but arrayed in moonbeams) had won—she had been fooled. Afraid to pray for the reverse of her other prayers, she closed her eyes and murmured softly, "Richard, come back, ask again," thinking she knew her answer now.

But nature took its course toward midsummer; he did come back. He was seen with a girl named Anne MacNeill, the pride of a poor Irish family. Everyone praised Flora's wisdom in having no more to do with him; but when she was alone she wrung her hands until the blood went out of them. Olive Templeton, Mary Valentine, her disappointed cousin. . . . She had not lost him as they had—she had found a way of her own; and she envied them the comfort of having been badly used.

She wandered down the lane with her apron full of green apples for the colt named Oboe. Over the meadow his cry of love and hunger as he trotted toward the gate. . . . A cloud of pleasure in his damp eyes, he took the apples one by one between his teeth, and broke them with a faint, crisp sound, their juice dripping from his mouth. Flora feared and adored him; and as she stared at his tough body, she saw in its place another creature, dark and dappled by the moon. Clinging to the gate, "Richard," she whispered, "I love you. Listen to me. I'll never love anybody else. I'm so lonely." It was like making love to a little dappled angel. Could she have said these things, she wondered, if she had been in Richard's all too human presence? The two apples which were left slipped out of her hand. Oboe rolled one out of the grass with his lips, and with his hoof, which looked like a gray porcelain cup, pawed the sod under the gate for the other, which had fallen out of reach.

Before autumn came, the family worried about her health and complained of her mournful retirement; so she accompanied her brother and Marianne to a large house-warming. She was ashamed of not having a sweetheart, and regretted the fact that she was young. From the corners of the new house came furtive glances of young couples holding hands, embarrassed by the presence of their mothers and the brightness of large oil lamps. Women with aprons over their best dresses bustled around tables of famous jellies and chicken pies, beaming at her supposedly broken but supposedly healed heart. Flora felt that her youth was mutilated, but men and women gazed at it mildly without seeing one scar.

A stranger was introduced: Herbert Ruhl, the new doctor, a brown, wiry man in his thirties. Someone played a blistered piano in which two or three bad strings tingled. Dr. Ruhl asked Flora to dance, but the girls of the Presbyterian church did not waltz. His eyes, under weatherbeaten eyelids, hardened when he looked at her. Someone whispered, "He's a Catholic." Then he asked if he might take her home; but she was drawn into a Virginia reel before she could say yes or no, which pleased her.

Marianne said, "Dr. Ruhl asked to take you home, didn't he? Then cousin Edith can come home with us—she is alone." Flora realized that a girl ought not to be alone; she would have to keep her fidelity to Richard a secret. She thanked the doctor.

From the beginning he seemed to have serious intentions. Flora found that she thought of him continually; but he was not young or handsome, so she felt safe from love. He became the family doctor, and they grew fond of him.

Only Flora's old father said, "I shan't be doctored by any man who takes orders from a priest." He seemed to divine the reason for Herbert Ruhl's frequent presence in the house, of which no one ever spoke to him; and three days before his death, when Flora was sitting beside him, holding one of his hands, smaller than her own, he said, "Don't ever marry a Catholic."

Marianne hoped, in the beginning, that contact with a good Protestant family would change the doctor's faith.

He would stop at the farm when he made his round of calls in the country, ask her to drive with him, and bring her home before dusk on his way back to Aaronsville. On these occasions he offered his love with patient candor. Meaning to marry her, he did not oblige her to give him an answer, but in spite of her requests asked again and again.

Flora would wait while he visited his patients, calling to mind pathetically the face of her other lover; but the day came when she realized that she did so by an effort of her will. She tried to want her hopelessness back, and envied Richard's other sweethearts their disconsolate ways of living. Her relation to him lost its romantic dignity—she had been so proud of her broken heart. But finally his troubled, light-gray eyes haunted her no more, and the years over which he had ruled so lightly, so uncertainly, shrank in her memory to a few unsatisfying moments.

Then, under Herbert's different appearance, she discovered a force which she had thought peculiar to Richard. The same breath on her cheek, the same fear of constrained movements in the dark, behind other less fiery horses; the misunderstandings, the paroxysms of timidity, the agreeable weakness, the slight nausea of disappointments. . . . But because Herbert was a man, not a boy, the pressure of his wooing had a definite and different purpose. He wanted to be repulsed, as if to test her fidelity as a wife, and was enjoying in advance a lifetime of peace. His confidence in her increased; she shrank from the liberties he took, by which it was revealed, but her resistance grew automatic; after years of having been loved, her senses could not have been taken by surprise.

She was profoundly tired. Her girlhood was lasting too long. She envied married women and old maids. She came into possession of the sort of knowledge one would like to be without. The key to her heart was so simple—the world might forge many; she averted her eyes from the young men she knew, lest they discover her weakness. The world itself was simple, and when she thought of her confusion in the face of it, she was ashamed and wanted another mind and another soul.

Herbert's hard glance opened her heart as if it were a key—more exactly, it turned in the lock as if made for it; but the lock seemed to have been set in a wall in which no doorway had been cut. There was a part of herself which would always be closed, until the very wall of life was destroyed. The faith of her family was a part of this wall.

Herbert was a devout Catholic. The time came when they talked of religion as it might concern their future lives; these discussions were in effect proposals of marriage, rejected proposals. If he had presented his religion theoretically, she might have ceased for a moment, in the pleasure of being able to understand, to be aware of her family's disapproval and her own lack of conviction. It was its human poetry which frightened her, each word with a vague, dangerous, earthly meaning—pope, purgatory, confession, absolution. . . . A sort of Italian king; veiled nuns (unveiled by a newspaper called *The Menace* to which her father subscribed); a pit full of souls covered with human transgressions, having lived on earth too long; whispering, whispering guilt through the barred windows of the confessional; all evil forgiven—and she did not even want to know what evil was.

The Church was so perfect in Herbert's eyes that she could not think of asking him to leave it. He talked of his boyhood by the hour: a priest who could forgive, without tolerating, any young sin; the same old man transfigured by embroideries and linen; his name carved on a wooden bench where he had knelt; the small bells of the parochial school. Flora realized that these were his dreams for their children, unable to imagine herself having children; and feared that if she began to yield, she might lose sight of herself and her obscure destiny, whatever it actually was, in the pleasure of yielding.

Then her brother John Craig came again, and she happened to hear him say to Marianne, "If Flora likes this young man, I don't see why religion should keep her from marrying him. She ought to be a Catholic, anyway. She is as pure as the snow, and hates having to decide things for herself. If she had to live with her other sister-in-law—I mean my wife, and I'm glad she doesn't—there'd be another story to tell. Indeed, I shouldn't be surprised if Susanne would make a nun out of her. She has the proper spirit for it."

"John," Marianne replied, "you are wicked to make fun of us all."

But after his departure, she was more severe about the unsuitability of the marriage, and seemed frightened. The community also had much that was well meant and a little that was malicious to say about a Tower turning Catholic.

Flora saw her love, what there was of it, sink into a quicksand of impossibility. If it had been greater, she might have been comforted by a sense of her sacrifice, though so little deliberate. As it was, she merely let herself be forced by the convictions of others into being afraid that it would escape from the quicksand. It did not.

One day at dusk she and Herbert were sitting on a

stone wall among strands of bitter-sweet, between trees thinly covered with brown foliage and dark brown fields. He said again, "Will you marry me?"

She felt her braids, like the silky hand of a spirit, slipping down the nape of her neck. She answered, "Dear, I believe that I love you. But I cannot marry a Catholic. We would not be happy."

He whispered, "You will love me more."

Flora understood bitterly that this was not an end, not a promise, not good-by—because Herbert was a strong man who could wait as long as she lived. She sighed, one sigh as small in proportion to her whole weariness as one prolonged breath to the breaths of a lifetime.

A sunset like a great, sumptuous couch. Flora imagined that she lay in it, safe from human intrusion as if it were a deathbed, and remembered her monotonous life, moment by moment—the moments of the past mingling with those of that very twilight, and resembling all those there would be in the future. She stared idly at the lights dying upon cloud after cloud, upon empty ether. Life no less could be transfigured but not transformed; life no less was a sky full of colors, whose future was to fade. . . .

She continued to sing bravely throughout the last years of her life. Alwyn listened, and envied all those who had taken part in her secret experience, not caring (because he was an adolescent boy) how much of it was misery, how much love, and how much the homesickness of a spirit which had not felt at home anywhere. He thought of a scarlet tanager he had seen fluttering in the fringe of a shower; for her voice was also a warning so sweet that one could not give heed. A bird's voice in a sugar-maple bough—both voice and transparent bough darkening slowly, and seeming most distinct in the moment before they cease altogether to be heard and seen. . . .

In her twenty-ninth year she fell ill. When Herbert first entered her room with his doctor's leather case, she cried: "I am not going to get well. I knew it all the time, I knew it. That was why I couldn't decide."

Thereafter she wept whenever he came, so pitifully at last that another doctor had to take his place. There was a week of hope, a week of losing it. Finally at midnight, in a shower which blew down with a mournful abundance on the garden, the tree tops, the mossy shingles of the house—in which for hour after hour no one exhaled a normal breath, and all their mouths were pressed into their hands, and tears ran down over their knuckles—the second doctor learned that he could not save her life.

Flora's mother left the room. They could hear her heavy tread up and down the porch. When she came in she stumbled over the threshold, and it was clear to everyone that she would never be strong again, that she would not thereafter be of much importance in life, and that, for her, life would have no importance at all.

Sunrise. Flora's face, tired and still confused, lay on the pillow between the two great ropes of red hair. The body of the sunlight floated through the window and lit on the flowered wool rug. Then she opened her eyes, and seemed to know that the light which stood like a curly-headed angel beside her bed was perfectly good, and it believed what she believed (though she may not have remembered clearly what that was), and it had come for her. She lifted her hands and placed them in one large, gilt hand of the sunshine.

14. His Maternal Grandparents, Ira and Ursula Duff

AFTER his aunt Flora's funeral, Alwyn went back to school in Aaronsville. He lived with his mother's parents, who had rented their farm and bought a little property in the town: a house, a fine lawn bounded by hedges, a vegetable garden, and a stable.

His grandmother Duff never lit the lamps until the shades were drawn, remarking that it was "indecent to be seen by Tom, Dick and Harry, as if you were an actor in plays." Stiff and delicate, she would stand in the bay window every evening as long as the dusk lasted. The large flowers of the lace curtains (as if roses and lilies had been burned and kept their shape in the ashes) stood out clearly against the partial darkness—through which bicycles swung, leaving prostrate columns of dust, and girls with strong arms interlaced loitered along the walks, and workmen went home. It was the normal small-town twilight which lay there, but the old woman stood before it momentously still, as if she were watching an enemy from a stronghold; and often, as if to pass the time of her vigilance, she sang, in an old, sweet voice:

> *"Dark is the night*
> *And cold the wind is—blow-ing!*
> *Hide me, my Saviour, till the storm is o'er. . . ."*

If her husband entered the room, she would shrug her round shoulders and continue:

"For the waves around me roll.
Hide me, hide me for my soul . . ."

Or she would sing other hymns, substituting for the verses she had forgotten the mystifying notes of the Italian scale.

She had been lovely in her girlhood, and still moved with a peculiar grace; her skirts and petticoats touching the floor, her small shoes going and coming among them. If she had ever been happy she would have been vain, and said, "My sisters were always in the fashion, whatever it was."

She betrayed a lifelong envy by wanting everyone to admire these sisters. One had married, for love, a man who was too easy-going and often drifted into financial straits, though they wanted for nothing. The other lived in St. Paul in circumstances of wealth and prominence, and rarely visited her poor sister. Both were haughty and beautiful women.

It was they who had induced her to marry Ira Duff. He had then been untidily handsome and a heavy drinker, keeping company with lazy, profane men and the women of bars and shanties. The Raeburn girls had been away to finishing school and were noted for style and vivacity, and he had been impartially in love with them, in spite of his other connections. But Anne and Arabella had had ambitious dreams and discouraged the unpromising lover, saying that it was not right for either of them to marry before their elder sister, and had accordingly brought pressure to bear upon Ursula. "Pa can't support three well-brought-up daughters." Their father had been losing his money in various ways. "One of us must marry," they had insisted.

So Ursula had accepted Ira Duff and set about to reform him. Her loveliness, the novelty of marriage, her superior birth and education, had undermined his former habits. He had signed the pledge against liquor and tobacco; the low ties had been broken, one by one; he had been converted and had begun to be influential in the church. It had been as if she exerted, to the glory of God and the foundation of a respectable life, all the influence she was ever to have over him. The reform had been accomplished in four years.

As an old woman she took her grandson's hand and pressed it against her tight collar, through which he could feel a round lump in her throat. "After four years of married life," she said, "I was standing by the garden gate, and I found that growth had begun. I knew that the cause was crying too much every day. So I made up my mind then and there never to cry again, whatever your grandpa did or said. And I haven't."

On another occasion she said, "Blessedly, there weren't many deaths in our family. My twins, Ferris and Forrest, died."

With his mother, Alwyn had often put flowers on their graves, under a mountain ash at Hope's Corner. There were two headstones of soft Middle Western marble, joined by a thin slab like the arm of one little boy laid on the other's shoulder: OUR TWINS . . .

BORN TO IRA DUFF AND HIS WIFE URSULA NÉE RAE-
BURN . . . DEPARTED THIS LIFE . . . HEAVEN WAS
THEIR DESTINATION.

"As a young woman I had a magnificent head of
hair. It was so heavy I could scarcely hold up my
head, proud as I was; and I could sit down on it like
a dress. Now when I gave birth to twins I looked at
myself in the looking-glass, and looked at the babies,
and I cut it off with a pair of shears. It was laugh-
able to see your grandpa's face when he came in—he
looked as if I had given away something that belonged
to him.

"They died of a sickness that they caught because
their father took them to a cattle market in a snow
storm; they were as pretty as pictures, and he wanted
to show them off among the men—he was always
one to make a great display." She made this accusation, and others like it, in a tone of perfect composure. "Well, they did not grow up to take sides
with their pa against me as the others did. But after
that, not one of our family died, and I thank the
Lord."

She took no account of the recent death of one of
her two other sons. He had had lung trouble; his
wife and daughters were Christian Scientists, for
whom it would have been dangerous and impious to
acknowledge his disease by taking him West; but for
some reason their transcendent faith had not availed.
At the church funeral his mother had sat in the family
pew in her ruffled black silk and veils, holding her
grandson Alwyn's hand, with a look of mystic satis-

faction. When the widow had cried out and flung herself on the coffin among the cut flowers, the aged woman had looked on without dismay, as if it were a natural occurrence; and when the mixed quartet had sung, "Beyond the smiling and the weeping, I shall be soon," the glance of her bright eyes amid their wrinkles had seemed to leap gayly up to heaven. Perhaps she had not realized that the dead man was her son; for her mind had begun to fail.

At first her sense of time grew morbid; she would forget the events of the previous day or the previous hour, and remember instead things which had been forgotten for fifty or sixty years.

Then she began to hide things. Having little to do now but conserve the souvenirs of what they had done in the past, both she and her husband took pride in orderly drawers, boxes, cupboards, and cubbyholes. Ugly ornaments and mementoes, which no longer reminded them of anything, were spread out about the house like the weapons and garments of savage tribes in a museum. Nothing was owned in common: her pin cushion stood beside his box of letters from their sons, on her cabinet organ; and each waited for the other to neglect or mislay one of these things.

Now the old woman began to permit herself to be put in the wrong; her strategy of many years broke down. As wanton as a magpie in her black bodice and white apron, she slipped his spectacle case into a closed umbrella, carried a paper-covered song book out to the privy, explaining that these were Unitarian hymns and she was a Presbyterian, and put an almanac on the organ in its place, opening it at a page on which the signs of the zodiac sat in a circle around a disemboweled man. She hid a valuable ring of fresh-water pearls so well that it was never found; and her husband expressed his disgust in pompous phrases, which she remembered.

Her modesty became a sort of madness. The human body exposed below the chin offended her as cobwebs had done when she had been a housewife, and like them aroused her industry. She made lacy curls with a pencil all over a nude photograph of one of her grand-daughters, two years of age. The man of the almanac wore a bathing suit of ink. There was a history of the conquest of America with innumerable illustrations, in which the savages offered their daughters to the discoverers in dresses which she drew, and even the slain lay beneath shrouds as fanciful as valentines—the work of many weeks. If Alwyn left his collar unbuttoned, she would steal up behind him and wrap a handkerchief about his neck, murmuring, "I can't abide nakedness."

Alwyn learned from his mother that she had always kept everything of an improper nature out of sight. She had had no roosters in her flock of hens, and bought eggs for hatching from her neighbors. She had persuaded her husband to plant a great hedge of cedars far from the house, behind which the cows and bulls together had been led. She had never allowed her babies to be seen until they were a month old.

Perhaps she wore, thus ostentatiously, the scar of

some amorous violence done by her husband in her youth. Perhaps she was trying to rid herself of memories of sweetness and abandon which made a discord in the pure concert of their hatred of each other.

The little house was full of symbols of malice, indeed seemed to have been equipped with the properties of some sort of malicious magic. Chenille balls dangling from table covers. Jagged leaves of variously colored kid forming a penwiper. A framed garland on an easel—fat callas and asters of dyed cotton under glass. Vases in the form of crucibles, one deeply crimped along the violet edge. A box of butterflies on pins. Each taboret wore a mock wedding veil. The cabinet organ stood by the window, a miniature temple, all niches and balustrades and pillars; and on the stops were printed in Gothic letters the row of enigmatic words: TREMOLO, DOLCE, VOX HUMANA. . . .

Many words were uttered in that house whose meaning was equally obscure. For Alwyn's grandfather, who was known as "the greatest talker in the country," used words which no one else understood, words which he did not understand, and words which do not exist, to swell a passionate theme, to confound his neighbors in an argument, and for their own sake. He would say, for example, "My farm was the very apocalypse of fertility, but the renter has rested on his oars till it is good for nothing," or "Manifest the bounty to pass the salt shaker in my direction." Something of the Bible, something of an Irish inheritance, something of a liar's anxiety, made of his most ordinary remark a strange and wearisome oratory.

For he was a liar. Diligently he turned the poor past into a golden age in which he had stridden, triumphed, above all persuaded; and still in his old age he labored to persuade man, woman, and child. On summer evenings Alwyn would see him in the pale-green garden like a stage setting, urging upon a neighbor his version of his life, and acting out its rôles. Between the beds of beets and onions he would stagger a little with the bearlike motion of a large man when he is old, and speak louder and gesticulate weirdly as the gathering dusk hid him from his audience.

His wife, standing with her grandson by the window, would say very softly, very sharply, "Your grandpa tells that riffraff he's so fond of up there in the garden a lot of lies."

And through the shadows closing down as if to shut him up and answer his arguments, he would catch a glimpse of the little woman who, in his youth, had made him a respectable man (a man whom she alone refused to respect); and a genuine sigh would make more impressive his complaints and his anecdotes.

Her honesty, even without a word, wounded and dishonored him. Therefore, perhaps, he hated the plain truth and looked down upon it, and strode away from it as quickly as possible into the remote past of his preposterous stories and ridiculous pretensions, where he could not be contradicted. But no—she had known him for sixty years and could always contradict him. When he was alone, melancholy actually distorted his old, loose face, as he brooded on what he had last said and wondered if in fact his arguments had been unanswerable.

There had been disgraces in his life which he was determined to change into heroisms. In particular, he had refused to fight in the Civil War, out of worldly interest, pride, and timidity, buying exemption from the draft three times and mortgaging his farm to do so. The family hoped the story would be forgotten. But he continued to lead casual guests into corners and, with his haggard body bent over like a question mark, amaze them with an account of what he called his "relations with government."

"Then by the great horned spoon who did I see?" one would hear. "None other but Ezra Winterbotham, the meanest man that ever walked up and down God's green earth, though well circumstanced, displayed in the height of fashion of an officer's uniform. Now he represented the authorities at Washington, the might of the law, the—" With his long thumb the old man drew in the air a word more impressive than any he could think of.

"Well, this here Winterbotham thundered and cursed God and swore that I'd be arrested simultaneously if I didn't go south with Company B. I saw it was fate coming at me and so I bowed my head."

He shook a twisted forefinger, now on one side of his listener, now on the other, to block the way of escape. "But no! No, said I to myself. So I rose in my wrath and denounced him. Gosh all firelocks! man, said I, you were intended by God to go to war, having made you so as you wasn't good for anything else. The good Lord meant such men as me, your humble servant, to sing his praises in other ways by becoming prominent citizens in times of peace."

Sitting by the window, his wife grew more and more stiff and courtly, as if all the world were looking at her.

"I'll buy a man, by cracky! said I. I'm not so poor in this world's goods that I've got to be ordered about by every cracker-box public speaker that gets delegated by hook or crook to Washington. I'll buy a man to do my fighting for me. There's aplenty as are waiting for such chances and that hain't any other future and wouldn't be man enough for it if they had. Men o' your ilk, Winterbotham!"

The strident voice mounted until everyone in the room was obliged to listen. One after another, his wife fixed their relatives or guests with a glance which made them uneasy, even frightened some, the very timid or young.

"And will you believe it, sir, that fellow, that authority, went off with his tail between his legs, uniform and all, and let me alone!"

His wife said serenely to a woman beside her, "It is a blessing Ira didn't go to the war. He'd have taken to drinking again, or worse. He wasn't so pious when we married as he is nowadays."

Or a new minister would make a pastoral call, and the old man would begin his history at once. The preacher, knowing that this was one of his most important parishioners, noted for severe sanctity, would try anxiously to understand. The old lady would look out of the window, and caress her full skirts, and pick dead leaves from the potted plants. But at last she would say, "Yes, it would be a very good story, if— it were true," and rise and go out of the room, leaving her husband to face the astonished clergyman.

He took his revenge. When they left the farm, for example, he insisted upon doing the cooking, and would not permit her to go into the kitchen except to wash dishes. He represented this as a great burden, though he liked keeping small, crowded places in order, and was vain of the indigestible meals he prepared. Everyone smiled at his recipe for pancakes, because it was a recipe for his stories as well: "One half of wheat flour, one third of rye, one third of buckwheat, and copious milk. . . ." Everyone smiled, but everyone pitied him—an old farmer with an able-bodied, sharp-tongued wife, so patiently doing the housework. . . .

His malice was exercised only under cover of pity and affection. Long before her mind began to fail, he would draw a relative or a neighbor into a corner and confide in a stage whisper, "Don't you forget it —my poor wife is doting in the decline of her powers." He appealed even to strangers to sympathize with her failings, describing them incidentally in full detail; and referred with marked unction to the trials which it was his lot to bear in a Christian spirit.

When they were alone together, he would say with

insulting simplicity, "I call it vicious, the way you behave," or, "You're a blamed fool, Ursula." Perhaps the fact that he did not trouble to scold her personally with his usual abundance of rhetoric hurt her more than his blame itself, to which, in sixty years, she may have grown accustomed.

Their grandson wondered if it had been his deliberate policy, from the beginning, to discredit her. Could he, in ignorance of his own heart, have done his work so well? Relatives and friends, one by one, coming to have a horror of her sharp tongue, her bitter disposition becoming a by-word. . . . The old man complacently watching loneliness widen around her, watching the manias of her old age increase, accumulating in his mind the pity of others for himself as a miser stores away secret treasure, sighing and pitying himself. . . . Alwyn decided at last that he sincerely thought himself a good man, a patient husband, a martyr. Especially after he began to suffer from a disease of the intestines, it was obvious that he lived in constant fear of incredulity, even as those do who are too naïvely honest to be understood. This manifest fear had an air of innocence; whoever might not have believed his stories, he himself in his old age seemed to believe every one.

But, though it was she who wore the look of victory, almost everyone did believe him. Despair is less expressive than mere melancholy; she would have been ashamed of seeming to deserve pity. His malice was like an instrument in his hands, silent or sounding loudly as it suited his purpose best. But when she said intolerable things, in her distant, melodious voice, it was not merely against her will; she had at those moments no will, and as if she had been hypnotized, felt neither fear nor sadness nor pleasure.

All the relatives and neighbors had watched the restlessness of her anger increase, quietly, rhythmically, like that of a whip; and heard what she had to say when she could endure it no longer. Everyone, on the other hand, had seen his tears. Only her daughter and her grandson loved her; only the Towers admired her. Even those who had experienced his perfidy held her responsible, and praised God that they did not have such a wife or mother.

Her sons had not even pretended to pity her. Now the one who had contracted malaria in the South when he had run away—as he thought, from her— was dead. The other, Andrew, a building contractor in Chicago, as melancholy and clever as his father, but with his mother's hardness, made life miserable for his wife and children, though he gave them everything that money could buy. He had no particular principles or faith, hating religion for its pretensions of peace on earth, its lack of power over hearts like his mother's—for that matter, like his own. She said frankly that his dissipated habits were a shame to her. Her husband blamed her less for driving their sons away from home than for acknowledging their weaknesses; and improved Andrew's character even as he had improved his own—by talking about it, hypocritically.

In the little house in Aaronsville a red-edged Bible

lay on a special shelf over the kitchen table. Every morning of their old age (just as when their wayward children had been at home) after the breakfast of fried potatoes and sweet rolls, he drew himself up to his full height, took down the book, and read a chapter. Then they knelt on the floor, each in front of a chair, and he raised his harsh voice:

"Guard us, dear adorable father, and guide us into one of thy mansions. Though roamers and strangers to thy charity, set us not aside with those who defile the highways and the byways. For liars, money changers, ungrateful relatives, and strange women triumph. Wither up their fig trees and put the seal of thy abundance on our undertakings. Bless my health, and keep our scattered children out of the dens of mischief. And hold in the hollow of thy hand the dear wife of my bosom. Without ceasing for half a century, we have labored and sung thy praises and kept faithful to each other and to thy true religion—though our steps totter, we are still the same. Forgive us our transgressions of word and deed, and lead us not into trouble, but bring our aged limbs into thy kingdom. Amen."

There followed a moment of silent prayer. When Alwyn knelt between them, more embarrassed by this posture of the love of God than the two sad ancient enemies whose knees bent with difficulty, he wondered if in that moment each prayed that the other might be punished, made sleepless by repentance, and have his heart divinely softened—that is, at their age, broken. . . . But when they rose, his grandfather's cunning face was transfigured and haughty. Wandering away to one of the windows, his grandmother seemed to regret that prayer had come to an end, her eyes, in spite of their cold color and weary eyelids, like a child's eyes blossoming with light. And when she glanced back at her husband, Alwyn realized that he was not only her enemy, but her priest.

She rarely spoke of religion, and had no reminiscences of its coming and going in men's hearts. Evidently it had nothing to do with love, of which she spoke with pride and regret, as Alwyn's other grandmother spoke of the old days—their glory, their poverty, their bravado. "My son," she would say, "there were broken hearts and romances. But young women in my day covered their nakedness, every one was modest and genteel. But the menfolks were inclined to be rough—they mingled with animals all day, and had many hardships to undergo. Don't ever be wild as your grandpa was."

Alwyn remembered their wedding picture: the young man's lips large and red, his eyes expressionless as eyes of crystal, his large hand closed on her arm as if it had often had its way with women; and beside him the little bride dressed in dark sacramental finery.

"Always behave like a gentleman," she continued. "In all my life, I knew only one gentleman. That was Leander Tower. He was accounted a little crazy in those days by many who were his neighbors. My life would have been different if I had married him. But I was already married, so I didn't love him. It was my duty to love your grandpa and I did it, hard and dishonest man that he was. As for Leander Tower, he loved nobody on earth but his relations."

Alwyn's mother said that she had never before referred to that secret.

Another day she said, to his amazement: "I don't regret a day of my life. Your grandpa is a virtuous man and God-fearing, though he was pretty unruly in his youth. Don't you forget that, just because he tells awful lies and is mean. He never drank. He never swore. He never ran after women. Not after we married. He never failed at churchgoing, or giving testimony, or praying before the public—and there wasn't a man in the township who could make such a fine prayer. There are few of whom I could say as much. Now I don't regret that he was hard on me, and maintains that my mind is failing. It has taught me to fear God and value the kingdom of heaven. Don't you ever think this world amounts to much."

But as they approached that kingdom of heaven their conflict did not abate. Their old bodies grew weaker, their minds confused; but they seemed to breathe a bracing air of eternity. Warned by the gnawing pain in his bowels, his fear of not being believed rose to a pitiful fury; but the days in which he might still bring about her wifely submission were numbered; so at last his malice was not even restrained by consideration of what people would say. Her sorrow took on the special clarity and peace of madness when her second childhood began. During the last years it was as if they lay on one deathbed—the dying hands interlaced by habit, by hatred of each other and love of God, the dying mouths murmuring truths without pity and complaining still.

(It was during this period that Alwyn lived with them—afraid of their old age, often shedding tears before he fell asleep, trying to ignore hate and understand love, and for the first time falling in love.)

The embrace of their two spirits was closer than love ever is. They had lived together half a century; now they could not be parted. Marianne Tower took her mother out to the farm, but could not induce her to stay more than one night. She could not sleep in the country; hate had become a physical habit, as passionate as the habits of the young. "I must go back this afternoon. I must look after my house. I must see what your father is up to."

When she returned to the little house, her husband's face lit up with pleasure, but before that expression had had time to change he would say, in her presence, "I know, daughter, you're inclined to see things your poor ma's way, but she is a great problem to me. She steals my medicine and spirits it away, and even carries it so far as to hide her own things. And I swear before the Almighty, I believe she does it a-purpose."

One afternoon during a school holiday, Alwyn and his mother drove to Aaronsville, intending to take her back with them. "No," she said, "I reckon I'd better not go. I have to see to my affairs. And your father is not contented if I'm not here."

Then she went upstairs, and came down presently, carrying in her hand the antlers of two stags, interlocked and covered with dust. She put them on the table. "I found these old things in the attic," she said mysteriously. "I don't understand what they're for, and I don't know where we got them. But I found them, anyway."

The old man came out of the pantry. "Ursula," he began, looking at his daughter as if this were a proof of all his contentions, "I pray to God that the day will come when you'll let my things alone. Tarnation! I don't blame you, but it's a crucifixion to me, the way you go rummaging in my belongings."

Marianne gazed beseechingly at her father. Her mother, ignoring him, gazed at the curio: the sharp horns harmless at last, spike wedged against spike, and a bit of the skull of each animal.

"I never saw that before," Alwyn said. "What is it? Where did it come from?"

The old man said: "I discovered this phenomenon at the foot of an old stump I was rooting up in my thirty-fourth year. It bears witness to the death struggle of two ferocious animals. Beside themselves, they struck one blow too many and got their horns tangled and lay there by that stump, as you might say snared, until they died. And here you have their rage to get at each other immortalized, and I say it ought to be in a museum."

His wife had not taken her eyes from the table. "Ira, Ira," she murmured, "you've told that story too many times. It's not yours, anyway. It's mine. You gave it to me."

He sighed and returned to the kitchen. She hunted

a little piece of black crêpe and painstakingly, lovingly, dusted the antlers. There was nothing to say. Alwyn's mother sat down and began to weep softly. The old woman took up the interlocked antlers and pressed them to her bosom, and started upstairs again. "No, Marianne, don't ever cry," she said, as if she were merely giving good advice.

Their son Andrew came from Chicago to see his father. Alwyn and his grandmother stood before the window, and in the garden the feeble old man gestured and talked to his son. "Who's that man up there in the garden talking to your father?" she asked. "You better go up and find out if he means to stay to dinner."

Her husband insisted that she recognized her son and pretended not to, out of spite. She often called Alwyn Andrew, even during her son's visit. At other times she treated him with exquisite formality, as if he were a man she loved, half a stranger. One day she gave him a begonia leaf, saying, "You're my sweetheart, you know."

The following winter Alwyn went to live with his uncle Jim; and while he was gone the old man passed away.

15. CONCLUSION: ANOTHER MOVING. HIS GRANDMOTHER TOWER'S DEATHBED.

MEANWHILE his grandmother Tower was looking forward to a short but momentous journey; making ready, not in secret, but before her children and grandchildren, telling them again and again where she was going and that she was willing to go. To the least known of the lands over which, like a lantern, the new moon hung. . . . She sorted and packed her few belongings, not to take with her, but to leave behind; and wrote on the backs of daguerreotypes, on the flyleaf of the hair album, and on slips of paper attached to the most precious keepsakes, the little scattered clauses of her last will and testament: "This is to be for Alwyn, Grandma," or, "To be sent to my son Evan, R. Tower. . . ." She also searched her memory to see if there were any stories of the early days which she had not told; and of those which the family knew by heart, repeated the ones which she thought it most important to have remembered, though it made her heart palpitate now to talk long at a time.

But she liked best to be alone under the sugar maples or before an open door, and to gaze at the lanes which still seemed new to her though fenced before her grandchildren were born, the tall trees which were younger than she, the stubble land covered with stones, the weedy summer hay. Apparently it was going to cost her more to leave the farm, its particular horizon, its portion of sky overhead, than to leave her surviving relatives or to part with life itself.

At the same time the Towers, her son and his family, were also preparing for a journey, another of the migrations which had scattered such families over America: less heroic and shorter than in former times, because the continent had been tamed, and there was no reason to go far now—it was more or less alike from coast to coast. John Craig and James Tower having, at the former's suggestion, given Ralph their shares of the farm, he and his mother had sold it to buy a smaller, more profitable one, without marsh or hills, about fifty miles away on the outskirts of the college town of Brighton.

The old woman had given her consent to this transaction because of her firm belief that the old should not be a burden to the young, above all when the latter were poor. And she had always maintained that people should be willing to leave the world after a certain age; now she would prove that she was willing, by going without a murmur away from the one valley which was all of it that she loved or knew. She would not be obliged nor even able to stay with them long, wherever they should go.

Ralph was glad to move. The four walls of the new home (in which no one of his blood had died, or been angry, frightened, or disappointed, or felt the pinch of poverty) seemed to promise to hold for him new prosperity, enthusiasm, rest. . . . The silver poplars standing all around it, like tall women dressed in leaves, seemed to beckon to him. His brothers' generosity had put an end to his resentment at not having had a chance as a boy; and now it seemed that by merely moving fifty miles away he was to come, first of his family, into a promised land of prolific livestock, abundant crops, and soft, level furrows without stones.

The farm which Henry Tower, with his farsighted eyes, his ax and divining rod, had picked out in the wilderness, had not kept many of the promises which on those early mornings it had made, or seemed to make. Royally vast and fertile in large part, the Northwest Territory had been spread out for the newcomers to take what they pleased. To Henry Tower, unwisely aristocratic, beauty and prosperity had looked alike. Misled, perhaps, by the spirits of ancestors homesick for European meadows and hunting highlands, he had chosen merely the loveliest piece of land he had ever seen, and upon it had built his hopes.

It would not have been unworthy of a pleasure pavilion or manor house. In one corner in a tiny forest wild roses, wild grapes and strawberries, mandrake and belladonna, were heaped on the sweet, moldy soil under the trees. In front of it low fields were flooded in spring with water full of frogs, where wild birds of every sort gathered to paddle and flutter, to stalk and doze, hunching their shoulders. Beyond those fields there lay a swamp over which the horizon was draped with melancholy tamaracks. In another direction there was a brighter vista: interwoven slopes, white roads, dwelling places, and far away a lake, glittering in the daytime as a lighthouse glitters at night. The house and barns were protected by small, high hills standing in a half circle. The tallest of those six hills arm in arm wore a hawthorn on whose wiry boughs every spring a few blossoms shone like bits of pink crystal and every summer a few lumpy thorn apples hung—a small tree shaped like a coronet. But it was the only emblem of wealth and power which that property could have enabled its owners to afford, except their intangible crowns in heaven.

For half of the farm lay on those hilltops, and there half of the earth was stone. The slopes were so steep that the wagons carrying home the poor harvest had to have their wheels chained and be brought down like sledges. The rains descended in torrents, rolling down bowlders, digging in the good fields gullies deeper than a man is tall, washing the top soil off into the swamp. The only valuable piece was twenty acres which Rose Hamilton had brought into the family as her dowry; even it was covered with deep-rooted, perennial weeds and thistles to choke the corn and corrupt the grain. Perhaps the very instincts which had impelled Henry Tower to settle there had prevented him and his sons from working the farm as effectively as might have been done, though to the end of time it would be an ungrateful tract of land.

The sale of it to a German farmer for his newly-married, middle-aged son took place in midsummer. After harvest an auction of farm machinery, some of the livestock, worn furniture, and household goods, was held. All afternoon the neighbors drifted about the place, bidding indifferently on this or that, and their wives handled and carried off bit by bit the intimate miscellany. Alwyn's grandmother wept at the abandonment of certain insignificant objects, the small children at the loss of others. Alwyn spent the night with his grandmother in the nearly empty rooms; she sat up in bed, her lips never at rest, and he could not be sure whether she was praying or whether people not actually there were keeping her company as well. The family slept in various neighboring houses.

The next day at dawn Alwyn and a hired man named Karl set out with two teams, the draft horses drawing a manure spreader loaded with crates, implements, tools, and small machinery, with a buggy and a corn planter hitched behind it; the driving horses a lumber wagon full of cages of poultry, cats and dogs in boxes, barrels of dishes and kitchen utensils, and trunks of clothes, behind which trailed the three-seated carriage that his grandmother cherished. Cattle and hogs had gone in a box car several days before. His father was to accompany the family and the old woman in an automobile. Thus, rather sadly, with less extravagant hopes, without canal boats or oxen or weapons, without cause for fear or singing—their modern migration was accomplished.

The east was covered with tiny clouds like the torn bits of paper which a newcomer finds in a dismantled house; the sun entered the sky like such a newcomer. Frost-bitten maples and ash covered the land with blotches of blood and rust; the débris of harvest lay in the fields. By the middle of the morning Alwyn and the hired man crossed the Iron Ridge and came to a new sort of countryside.

They ate dinner at the back of a dirty store in a town called Eden. Alwyn's companion, a huge man of thirty who was like an adolescent, had had to work so hard as a child that he was stoop-shouldered. When he was not using his hands, which he did with difficulty on account of their size, they hung slightly in front of him. Long after he had been spoken to, a scarcely perceptible movement of understanding would pass upward across his brick-red face, from the heavy mouth to the heavy blue eyes. Alwyn was fond of this Karl because, as a giant, he was mysterious, because he was warm-hearted and happier than other people.

It occurred to Alwyn then that his had been the last of the pioneer families in the community from which he and the hired man were driving their belongings away, and that Karl was like the men who were left. The early settlers had lived and done their work for others, not quite as they had meant to; because of their blood in his veins, Alwyn thought of them with pity and of the others with resentment. . . .

Most of the new people, Saxons and Bavarians, had come there without a penny. Then they had hired out to the settlers and put by more of their earnings than any Anglo-Saxons could. Steadily they had bought fields, farms, and at last groups of farms. These determined fathers made their women and children work like serfs—the healthy young ones hurried into the fields, the unhealthy allowed to die, and more begotten. Their sons were not permitted to marry until their late twenties, or later still; then, broken to harness, they were put upon adjoining farms. There was no talk among them of letting the young go their own way.

Meanwhile the original families seemed to be dying out; at any rate, they were being scattered. Delicate health, without any particular illness to cause it, began to be common among them; vague desires for an easier, less monotonous life arose. Money was spent on the education of children, thus lost to the family. Very few of the cleverer sons were willing to stay on the land; the daughters preferred not to marry farmers. Besides youngsters, certain fathers of families went further west; still more retired in middle life, discouraged and dependent on others, or content with just enough to live on.

The immigrants were glad to see them go. They believed that children should be envious of no one but their own elders; now there would be an end of the bad example of discontented Yankees going off to school or to town. And for their own comfort, no more interference with their primitive habits, such as beating their wives, animals and children, or their amusements, such as Sunday dancing and drinking. . . .

That morning before Alwyn had left the farm he had seen, standing in a row on the cellar door, about a dozen of the Duffy's whisky bottles which his grandfather had emptied while he was dying; during the auction someone must have gone into the cellar in search of just such traces of their private lives; and since all his family were eager prohibitionists, Alwyn supposed there had been complaints of their hypocrisy, and bad-tempered laughter. . . .

At nightfall the two young men and the string of vehicles were far from their destination. They turned off the highway to make a short cut by a number of diagonal roads. These led through a forest in which there were dogs howling (probably about a carcass or a pile of bones) across a sour-smelling marsh, past only very small, dark houses, through no villages. . . . They began to believe that they had lost their way. The hungry horses hung back, pushed each other out of the road, and tried to turn up every lane; they at least could not go on much longer. His father, used to finding his way in the North like an Indian, had described the turnings for him, with a schoolhouse, a tree, a hill, by which to recognize each one; and Alwyn looked forward miserably to his criticism, if they did not arrive when they were expected. But for a few hours not himself but what looked in the dark like an utter wilderness, was in control of him and of what he could do: he was willing and in awe of it; he was stubbornly hopeful, resentfully proud. . . . Then it occurred to him that such must have been the emotions with which the first journeys there had been accomplished, of which, probably, every heart in the early days had been full.

Those days were at an end; they were dead. For a few hours, for him (for other hours, perhaps, for others) they were imitated by accident, or in imagina-

tion roused from the dead. . . . Mornings encircled
with drab forest as if by a great hair wreath. Afternoons in which wild bouquets arranged according to
the language of flowers were passed from one innocent,
calloused hand to another—Alwyn, in that sense, did
not have innocent hands. Evenings whose hilltop sunsets faded as funeral wreaths fade, on the mounds in
which rest those who died in the heat of the day—of
the heat of the day. Nights like that night. . . .

"Hey!" Alwyn's companion called back from
the seat of the manure spreader, "my horses is
balkin' on me. What d'ya think?" The soft German voice. . . .

Day after day, in which there had been only the dry
voices of Americans continually expressing hope and
disappointment, praying, bargaining, bearing witness
to facts and to the Lord. Days linked at daybreak by
the sun rolling over the horizon like a great ball over
the boundary line of a game (that game had been
played, everyone had played and everyone had lost, or
perhaps everyone had won—in heaven at least).
Linked at noon by the things which happened every
day: the watering of badly fed horses (the younger
of Alwyn's team whinnied fiercely but was not answered); the feeding of cattle whose bags were black
with muck from the swamps (his grandmother had
told him how, during certain winters when the cattle
had nothing to eat but the strawstack and were sick,
his grandfather had slit open their tails and put in
pepper and salt); hurried meals of salt pork, bread,
and potatoes; horns of traveling venders of medicine

and fish, drawing up before the door; childbirth; the return of hunters from the woods. . . .

Suddenly, as if an instinct of his hunting ancestors had been waked in him, Alwyn thought he recognized a lightning-scarred tree of which his father had spoken, and shouted to Karl that there was a crossroads, and to turn to the right. He began to have hope and to dare to admit his fatigue.

Hope, hunting, quarrels with fathers, need, fatigue, and self-control—in those days there had been nothing but these emotions. He was determined that there should be other things for him at least. . . . Other things than mere body and soul kept together with determination, held together by hand, by inhuman-looking hands stained with sores. . . . No one had ever got enough sleep; night after night had been troubled by worry over the weather and the crops, by misunderstandings between husband and wife which there had not been time enough to settle, by the breakdown of women who had borne too much, some falling ill and welcoming death, some going mad and waking their distracted menfolk to talk nonsense. . . .

Then Alwyn realized that his instinct about the road had been mistaken; they had taken a wrong turning. His heart sank. What were they going to do? He put off telling the hired man.

Perhaps if he had paid more attention, instead of thinking about things which did not matter in the least that night. . . . Nevertheless, hypnotized by the jolting of the wagon, he could not stop. His thought was like the sort of nightmare in which terrors do not frighten, nor pains hurt—they were not his terrors and pains, except the one of having lost the way. Dreamy composite pictures which could serve no purpose. . . . Then his memory, working ingeniously against his will, suggested to him instead this or that about his relatives, details of which they were made up.

His grandmother Tower called his grandfather Duff "a snake in the grass"; there was a negro song which began, "The devil is a snake in the grass." . . .

He wondered if his father would go on doing taxidermy in the new home—killing, skinning, stuffing birds and animals.

His great-aunt Mary had driven like this all the way from Missouri to Wisconsin. A sort of migratory bird, with three husbands, beside her journeys which were like love affairs with various parts of the world.

Indeed, Alwyn thought, roads were to the Mississippi Valley what seas, wars, religions, had been to other places in history. Coming and going of men sick at their stomachs from the motion of their own feet, or saddle horses, or vehicles (as he was). In the beginning his hard boy-grandfather marking a trail on tree trunks with an ax—as if the thread through a labyrinth had slightly worn away its pillars here and there. Roads with no particular beginning or end had been the shifting foundations of life in the West—had been and still were. They gave a wretched monotony to one's thought about it, and one could not speak of its inhabitants without repeating the word. That night Alwyn thought of this common fact with wonder, with sickness of heart, with rather selfish pity for the pi-

oneers—race of religious, childish, energetic tramps
that they were—because he himself had gone astray
on a road that he did not know. He thought, It must
be midnight, but did not dare ask the hired man, who
had a watch.

Pathetically ambitious at that period of his life, he
wondered if he could make any use of the scanty
knowledge of such matters which he possessed. Did
modern men and women in cities have any curiosity
about old times, any interest in the way people lived
or had lived in the country? Probably little or none.
He knew that very soon he would be living in some city
or another—not where his relatives had passed their
uneasy lives and died, or got ready to die. He might
try to write something about them. . . .

It occurred to him discouragingly that he would then
be doing no more than his father did with birds and
animals: spreading out and cleaning the bones (the
drier, the better they would keep); choosing a single
attitude for each one and wiring it as firmly as possible; arranging them in groups as lifelike as groups of
lifeless bodies could be. His father also gave them
glass eyes, and painted their mouths and claws; the
paint faded. But then, so did living colors—on beak
and claw, and human face as well.

The biography which his grandfather Tower had
sat down to write had turned out to be nothing but an
account of the settlement of Wisconsin in his boyhood.
Had he not dared to lift the reticence, like a winding
sheet, which then hid or at any rate disguised the pity
of his life? Perhaps, though he had been eighty years

old at the time, to do so would have waked the pain of a man of twenty or thirty; probably it would have seemed to him a sacrilege beside. The name of Serena Cannon was not to be found on the pages which Alwyn had seen—she who had woven all the wreaths; "the whitest hands of anybody in those days," according to Alwyn's grandmother. He had heard his grandfather say, with a look of cruel exasperation, "She was too good for this world, and went straight to the Holy City." Alwyn determined that his life should not be tragic, so that he should be able to tell about it if he wanted to. . . .

Suddenly across the vacant fields he saw the lights of a town. Karl shouted. It was Brighton. That meant that his instinct about the crossroads had not been wrong; though of the third generation, a better pathfinder than he knew. . . . Lights, as in the Holy City to which all his people had wanted to go, soft and yellow. The tears came to his eyes and were gone at once. With a certain vanity, which meant that he was not so tired as he might have been, he told himself that he had never been so tired before. Miseries such as the jolting over the stony road, to which he had been trying not to pay attention for hours, took on a final intensity; the darkness, like a large animal, seeming to shake him, a small animal, between its teeth. He wondered if his long revery about the early days had not also been a sort of delirium. The last house before the entrance to the town was the new home.

He fell out of the high wagon as if asleep. There

was a great excitement of the dogs barking in crates, of lanterns and his little sisters. His mother gave him a kiss. It was only a little past ten o'clock. He scarcely woke up until the next morning.

He was pleased at their having a new though ugly house to live in, but as he passed his grandmother's bedroom door he realized that it was to have other uses than those of life. At breakfast he asked his mother if his grandmother had wept upon leaving the old home. She had not, and had been heard to say to herself with strange determination, "Not for long, I tell you." Just before the start she had put her head out of the automobile, but her eyes had not seemed to be focused on anything in particular. Until nearly noon she had not said a word, her mouth, hands, and great body trembling a little from time to time.

Alwyn went in to see her in her new bedroom. Two of his sisters were there working for her. Sitting in an armchair, wrapped up in a red-and-white bed-spread (quilted by her husband's first wife), she was supervising the arrangement of her photographs and keepsakes in a chest of drawers. Then she said: "Get my bed ready so I can lie down. Make it up with the head toward the window. For I declare, it makes me tired to look out at this flat country."

During the day she sent for her daughter-in-law. "Marianne," she said, "I'm not going to be able to do for myself from now on. I'll probably be sick 'most all the time until I die. You'll have to call in a doctor —or the relatives will complain. But I won't have a trained nurse. I want you to promise not to get one. It will make a lot of work for you and your children. Take it as easy as you can. I hope and pray it won't be for long. I am ready to go, and I want you to let nature take its course. That's all I have to say. Just let nature take its course."

A few days later Alwyn went away to school in Chicago. When he returned the following year in June she was evidently dying, and someone would have to sit up with her regularly. Alwyn had been ill; there was no question of his working on the farm; so he did the work of a night nurse all summer, until his grandmother died. She was glad that it was he, and glad that his father and mother could get their sleep, lest they be unfitted for the more important work in the busy season. "I can't tell any more stories," she said to Alwyn. "I'm not good for much these days, and it tires me to be talked to—you were always a great talker. So you'll just have to sit there."

During the winter she had grown emaciated; her pure white skin had relaxed; her cheeks had fallen; the large and regular bones made up a new face without much expression. She was dying of heart failure, with a variety of consequent sufferings: cold and fever, fitful nervous pain, partial starvation. During the worst attacks her heart began to stop beating as soon as she fell asleep; but though she had said months before that she was ready to die, she could not permit it to stop. She would shake herself, summon up her strength of character, gasp resolutely, begin again— before she knew what she was doing. Furthermore, she did not want to die in her sleep—apparently the only way she could—but upright in her bed, in full possession of her faculties, even, if she had dared to demand it, with her children and grandchildren about her, as she had lived.

Thus her illness was a bitter struggle between the oldest habit of her will, life, and the comparatively recent decision to die. She was a creature of habit, and had never been governed by her intellect; so it was not to be wondered at that the accomplishment of her purpose took the greater part of a year.

Alwyn sat in the doorway, the light of a lamp shaded in such a way as to shine directly on his book and softly over her bed—for she wanted to be able to see—and watched the struggle night after night. He had been ill enough himself to have thought, with genuine if somewhat theoretical fear, of death; here was an object lesson in reality. At first he was surprised that he did not suffer at the sight of her suffering, nor feel the simple emotions which such an event called for. His active mind was quicker to examine than to be impressed, and he habitually fancied that everything and everyone resembled himself in some respect; so, full of a childish eagerness to be in awe, he was fascinated instead. It was as if he were writing his own experience (speculations and confused, self-conscious emotions) on one side of a page, now helped, now hindered by the half-legible characters on the other side, the side of death. Too soon, in any case, the page would have to be turned.

Meanwhile his grandmother Duff was also dying,

her mind first. After her husband's funeral, Marianne and her brother had arranged with their cousin Clara to care for the aged widow. Clara Peters, otherwise Mrs. Rudolph, a rough, poor woman, also lived in Aaronsville. The people who rented the little house down the street had complained because the old woman had kept coming there and trying the door. She would call over the hedge, "I—ra! I—ra!" and in a matter-of-fact way tell passers-by that her husband had locked her out; this had given rise to gossip. She would go up to mocking girls in the street and offer to rearrange their low-necked dresses with pins. Then her excursions had begun to be dangerous as well as embarrassing, for she would stop in the middle of the street to think, giving no heed to automobiles. Clara Peters's husband was good for nothing, and she had to support the family by taking in boarders and doing washing; so at last, unable to keep watch over the old woman, who would not do as she was told, she had had to lock her in a room during the day. There, remembering and singing those Protestant hymns which most put the fear of God in one's heart, she had not been unhappy—at least she had never wept; but she had been as headstrong as ever. Indeed, on certain occasions Clara Peters—exasperated by her obstinacy, tried beyond endurance by her own affairs—had been unable to keep from striking her, as lightly as possible of course; no one could altogether blame her.

This situation had not been unendurable to Alwyn's mother only because there had been no help for it.

Her mother-in-law had required all her care that winter. They could not have afforded to hire help. There were also her younger children to think of; she had not dared to put before their wondering eyes the spectacle of two aged women dying—one of them, the dearest, out of her mind. Fortunately her mother was not suffering in any ordinary way: invulnerable in her second childhood, forgetting her punishments the moment after, singing like a child. . . . So with her usual fortitude and peace of mind, Marianne had done her duty among the Towers. But not a day passed on which she did not weep at the thought of abandoning her own mother for her mother-in-law's sake, and she had seemed to be growing older in honor of the former's old age.

Now in the summer the end was not far off for them both. Alwyn's mother waited most impatiently for her mother to be taken away. She went to see her nearly every afternoon; but the old woman called Clara Peters Marianne, taking pains, as courteously as ever, to hide her inability to remember who Marianne was.

Watching beside his grandmother Tower's deathbed, Alwyn thought how his grandmother Duff would sometimes call him by the name of her eldest son, Andrew, and the next moment call him her sweetheart. His mother told him that throughout the winter, never realizing whose son he was, she had asked with young, fitful tenderness: "How is my sweetheart? Now, tell me the news of my young man. Is he getting on well out in the world?"

No one else had ever said that; no one, alive or dead, had thus made a place for him in the story. The avowal of old woman's love was shameless because it was old. Her mind, wandering, darkened; and suddenly a few words, very clear and somehow in tune, though even less reasonable than the rest. Like the saying of an oracle, to be interpreted two ways; in a play on words, a menace or a promise. Alwyn felt that he ought to determine which it was, and take it into account in whatever he did. A sibyl on a tripod, though it was a far cry to Greece. Up had come once more a sort of intoxicating smoke of death, of the bitter hearths of its residence, and he himself, her grandson, spoken of as her only surviving son and sweetheart. . . . According to the habit of his mind, he began to read meanings into what she had said, hour after empty hour in the doorway of his other grandmother's bedroom.

A law in the hearts of the savagest men forbidding them to love passionately their mothers, grandmothers. (It seemed that now the law usually forbade civilized or over-civilized men to love them in any way at all. . . .) And Alwyn had heard at school of an obscure belief, indefinitely old and held by many races in common, that by the breaking of that particular law, heroes, men accorded divine honors, had been made of common men. A distorted, unacknowledged set of traditions, being by nature both sacrosanct and shameful. . . . The sea is our mother. The furrow, a womb for the harvest, and Adonis (the word Adonis means the Lord); the garden and the tomb in the garden; initiation nights; caves, fountainheads, and retreats, like what gives birth to men, giving birth to them anew. Baptism: "ye must be born again of water and the Spirit." Twice-born, and the second time with a certain invulnerability and radiance, with certain unearthly abilities, or abnormal knowledge of what was coming. . . . There were a great many facts to interpret in this way which, sitting there to watch one of his grandmothers die, Alwyn could not remember.

Had this actually been believed, or was it merely a theory of professors with nothing better to do? It did not seem to matter. As soon as Alwyn thought of it, this tradition which rites and legends were supposed to represent, became in its turn a symbol of something else.

The word mother meant that which had produced one; therefore, not only a woman—wilderness, squalor, ideals, manias, regrets, sensuality, what consolations there had been. . . . Curiosity was a child's love, a half-grown boy's, even his own, not long before —excited, needy, ignorant, and afraid of what was going to happen. The desire to understand was, after all, desire.

So some of these feverish, reactionary ones (he himself, for example) went back, in imagination, to what had produced them; their hope, anxiety, and interest went back. Against the law. The weak stayed; the strong returned—returned once more to the place from which they had gone back, from which then they would have to go forward. Backward and forward, two continual motions of the imagination making up that of their lives. Forward finally—but with as definite a purpose as could be added to what men have in common, habits of blundering. "Fumble and success," the rat in a cage of the psychology textbooks— the last and greatest success must be death. . . .

His grandmother began to reach for her handkerchief with a great hand which could not find its way. He gave it to her and smoothed the sheets under her chin.

At any rate, to proceed (if only toward death) on the basis of a little more experience than one had had time to acquire. Able to anticipate and control the next moment, perhaps infinitely little, by some understanding of what would make it what it would be— for was not each moment the child of those which had gone before? Able to build one's continual bridge from the past, across a sort of abyss in the dark, to the future, with a certain knowledge of at least one side of the abyss (the side from which one came) and a certain knowledge of other bridges: what they had been made of; how they had broken, with the hearts of their builders; why they had fallen again and again into the dark. Knowledge gained by breaking the law. . . . Alwyn thought with rather unreasonable pride that he had become a man in as nearly as possible the way that men had become heroes or gods.

His grandmother Tower was tossing very feebly, very slowly, from side to side of her pillow. He saw that the lock of gray hair on her forehead was like a dead star, ashes of a star. It was beginning to rain.

He had loved them indeed, and tried to see them clearly and at close hand, the old mothers who lay side by side in the past as she lay in the dim lamplight, as many as there were locks of hair in Serena Cannon's album—loved them with the fever of inquisitiveness of an adolescent about love. Now he was a man, he supposed. His heart was heavy and the innocence of his mind darkened with what he had found out, or fancied he had found out—with theories like this one about incest and knowledge of the past.

His grandmother was talking to herself, but she no longer had breath enough for those who overheard to be able to understand. Alwyn fancied that he could understand without being able to hear.

It had all been like that, his understanding. Of Wisconsin, for example, in the flower of its age, the wild flower of its age. His sweetheart among the parts of the world. . . . When he was born it was already a mother, even a grandmother. Actually he was innocent and ignorant of its love, its resistance, its abandon and spiteful changes of heart. He had not been in time to go out to meet it with oxen and teams of hungry, hurried horses. He had not handled a rifle, an ax, a hammer, or a plow, on its great and tedious body. Nor had he eaten in a sort of habitual starvation the turnips which according to his grandfather had tasted like "Paradise apples." He had not feared God, nor begotten children, nor lived by the sweat of his brow. And perhaps he never would. . . .

But it had been true love, and not altogether sterile, illusory as the relation had been. In imagination, as adolescent boys, night after night and one indoor afternoon after another, suffer the enjoyment of those whom they have never touched or never even seen —he also had exhausted his boyhood to master an abstraction, a wilderness in the abstract, and to wring from its hypocritically rich body—what? Just enough knowledge to live on. . . . And it was the mother of the weak, incalculable manhood which, within and protected by his immature arms, lay like a newborn child.

His grandmother had slipped down in her bed, which made it hard for her to breathe; so he lifted her up, with his arms under hers. Her shoulders, which slipped out of her nightgown, looked as if the skin had been polished. He remembered how she had used to bathe late in the afternoon, with water heated in a great copper kettle which the Towers had brought from York State, and how, when he was a small boy, she had sometimes asked him to wash her back with a red-flannel cloth. As he worked he had studied the twisted, bluish veins, and wondered dreamily why the heart took such devious paths; and she had said, "Rub hard. Get on with it, or I shall take cold! . . ." For the first time since she had been dying, the tears came to Alwyn's eyes.

He sat down again in his chair amid the books lying on the floor, under the lamp, and tried to stop his futile tears by forcing himself to go on thinking. Would he, having brooded feverishly upon the past, the particular long series of energies and passions which had in the end produced himself, himself to

be the part they would play together in the future—
would he then be a little more capable of a good life
than the others had been? The use of their common,
unlucky abilities blessed at last, for him? "Bless
unto our use this day our daily bread. . . ." And
his daily life well constructed like a bridge from one
day to another? Would he be able to see to it that
his heart did not break—not, at least, until he was
ready to die? He asked for no more supernatural
powers than these. . . .

Indeed his birthright, that of the son of one of the
poorest pioneer families, was wealth and power
enough, of a kind. A patrimony, an unearned inheritance, of knowledge of life, of skeletons in the closet,
of precepts which had led infallibly to resignation or
disappointment, handed down to him in his turn.
Everything that he knew about his family had been
told by someone to someone else, fact by fact, and
at last he had been told. So he resembled a young
man whose fortune, bequeathed by numerous relatives,
is so vast that he does not know what to do with it;
and he thought of the usual disorder of such a
life. . . .

A disorder like that of his grandmother Duff's un-
balanced mind: memories, inverted ideas, many-voiced
wandering symmetrical discords, the entire material
of three-quarters of a century's experience rewoven
more briefly in a deafening fugue—out of which at
last had come, like the phrase at the end of a fugue,
"You know, you are my only sweetheart." These
words sounded again and again in Alwyn's mind, the

bitter end of a tune broken off, and echoing after it a special sadness, unconsoled, but satisfied. Life then was like what was in the mind of a bitter woman in her second childhood, like a fugue. But apart from the sterile passion of an old woman for her grandson, the passion of the past and present for the time to come, of adolescents for what had gone before, various kinds of madness of the imagination for various reasons uncontrolled—apart from these things, was there any final phrase?

He ought to have known, if his passion of curiosity had done its work well. He had been so proud of being able to see a certain distance into the past. Was it a false perspective of his own invention? Seemingly he had increased his knowledge of life by adding to brief memories of his own, others' interminable recollections; but was it merely an adolescent's poor substitute for experience, before experience has had time to begin? He could not tell, but some day he would be able to.

For his life, scarcely begun, would repeat theirs; the materials more closely and differently combined, in closer harmony or perhaps with harsher discord— a restatement nevertheless. The materials determined in advance: certain human limitations, American characteristics, family traits. All the surprises there would be would result from the combinations (one interrupting another, one melting into another), the rhythm and order of the combinations. Otherwise, in so far as he was surprised by himself, he would know that he had made a mistake in his estimate of what he had to work with. Just as by the second generation he had revised his notions of the first, errors in his judgment of their lives in general would be corrected by the particular instance of his own. And his own, if he did his work well, ought to resemble a fugue, without a break (that is, without disaster) from beginning to end, without violent emphasis, each element in perfect relief, played without loss of memory or unsteadiness in either hand: counterpoint of their appetites, their frugality, cunning, vanity, idealism, and homesickness. . . . And the phrase at the end?

That night, between three and four o'clock, Alwyn thought that his grandmother was sinking rapidly. He had forgotten: death, of course, was the phrase at the end. But she got better before dawn.

What then was it going to be like, his life? (His mind, as if he were a maniac, went over and over the same ground; he could not stop it.) He knew that he would perpetuate in himself the immortal disagreement, the so-called warfare, between the sexes. At worst, for example, the struggle between his great-aunt Nancy and her husband Jesse Davis; at best the mysterious balance of his parents. That damage to his simplicity was done; he had thought too much of women with sympathy, of men with wonder.

Over the house (in which everyone but himself and his grandmother slept) the long, soft lightning and thunder interlaced with clouds and being drawn away in one direction or another, made a mass of voices in too close harmony.

He knew further that he would unite in himself

two races of men, the characteristics of two men: his grandfather Tower the aristocrat, painstakingly upright about a few unprofitable actions controlled by conscience, never changing his faithful and secretive mind; his grandfather Duff, a sort of Proteus, a hypocrite, a liar or rhetorician, profiting by everything. He would have to make some sort of peace between the fruitless pride of the one and the creative vanity of the other.

There would also have to be a compromise between his talent for poverty and his love of wealth; not, he hoped, the one his uncle Jim had made. He wondered at the fact that he was most deeply indebted to that one of his relatives who conformed to his standards, appealed to his imagination, the least. He felt for his uncle at once a vaguely disdainful pity and that admiration which, even against one's better judgment, often follows gratitude. Thanks to him, to his family by marriage, to a Chicago education and the leisure of going to school, there had been opened uncertainly to Alwyn a way of life which was neither his way nor that of their common blood relatives—less desperate than theirs, possibly less futile than his. Alwyn realized that he would not have had the courage to appreciate the comfortless glory which the pioneers and (his uncle excepted) the first generation of their children, deserved, but for this personal emancipation from their destiny, this more agreeable prospect. . . .

The morning came. His father woke, sent the dogs after the cattle, and came in to hear how the dying woman had passed the night. She was lying quietly, her head thrown back on the pillow; the breath of her nostrils alone seemed alive, like a small, rising and falling, colorless flame at one end of a burned-out log.

The next day his grandmother's condition seemed to improve, and his uncle Jim came. He brought the news that Mrs. Fielding as well was not expected to live more than a few months, and that after her death he and his sister-in-law, Miss Anne, were to be married. His mother told him that she wanted him to preach her funeral sermon, and he seemed exceedingly proud.

Alwyn had sometimes called Mrs. Fielding his third grandmother: the least loved, least pitiable, and perhaps most tragic of the three—representatively tragic. An old, pampered heroine of a great period in the nation's history, that of the birth and infancy of wealth; proud of herself as a proof that it had been a success. Alwyn believed that it had not been. She and her house had given him a history lesson.

Whenever he had come back from Chicago to the country he had looked about him with a half-willing, almost bitter enthusiasm. Neither Chicago nor Wisconsin had justified its existence. The city had surpassed all reasonable expectations, and no one who did not have something to gain by optimism was pleased with the result. It seemed able to do, more and more powerfully, only two things: grow rich, and complain. The country lives had been no more than self-supporting; in his mother's words, no worthy gifts to the world had been made. What then had the heroic efforts in the country come to? Shabby and gloomy farms, unserviceable virtues, broken hearts, large family reunions, grievances of those (like Alwyn himself) with ideas above their station, other grievances and old-time religion. . . . Where literal wilderness had been conquered, a wilderness still, overrun by peasant immigrants, but still ineffectually governed by the early settlers' wistful young, by their habits of poverty-stricken conquerors. There was this difference between Chicago and Wisconsin: in the country the avidity had never been assuaged. There were blank spaces between the badly cultivated fields; there were areas of craving and brute force which poverty had been too God-fearing, prosperity not eager enough, to lay hands upon. Across the Mississippi Valley the barbed-wire fences lay like the staves of music paper on which as yet there were scarcely any notes. . . . It had not kept its promise, so it was still the promised land.

Represented by Mrs. Fielding, in great towns like her town, the West had taken its first step toward a civilization; it had been a step in the wrong direction. Already moribund prosperity, abortive progress; men like Alwyn's uncle kept as close to the women as drones in a beehive, little or no posterity nevertheless. . . . Between them and the most brutish immigrants, the future, for its purposes, whatever they were, would find little to choose. Would it not have to fall back upon the past, upon the poor God of poverty and His remnant of pioneers, unchanged though dying out? Those who are best prepared for the second lap of a race are those who did not even get a start in the first.

Avid company of failures, out of date, behind the times, perhaps timeless. Ethically, socially, above all financially, they had made little progress; in modern methods of pretending to be happy, of pretending to have satisfied on earth their hearts' desire, they had made none at all. Pioneers because their unhappy dispositions unfitted them for everything else. . . . Imaginative but disillusioned; therefore talented for the sake of God, religious in hope of heaven. Amid the national opinionatedness, factitious gayety, cruelty by accident, grace and candor, ignorance, imagination, ugly opulence with or without wealth, a sense of poverty with or without actual need—theirs was the only glory, such as it was.

The Middle Ages of America (not middle age, but youth) were coming to an end, leaving behind countless denominations of Protestantism instead of cathedrals. Too soon, the holiness was going out of the land. There were modern inventions for warming the heart, and certain fires with too bitter smoke had been allowed to go out—except upon old-fashioned, unattractive hearths. And perhaps, if America was to justify its existence, to be justified for the massacre of redskins, the broken white hearts, the destruction of the city called Tenochtitlan or something of the sort —the children of those hearths, reared in, embittered and half-intoxicated by the smoke, would have to do the work. And they might well be ready for any outlawry; ready to betray, for the work's sake, those

whom they would continue to love even more than
they ought; to betray the West to the East in the warfare between the two in order to gain for the former
the advantages of defeat as well as victory; to betray
their native land as a whole for love of some char-
acteristically native land of their imagination. With
the recklessness, the scruples, the vainglory, which
characterize the sons of men who thought they had
failed. . . . Stronger than their fathers, because they
would have less fear of God; more desperate because,
lacking a God of resignation and forgiveness, failure
would be even more intolerable. The future of America, if it was to be worth troubling about, depended on
them.

Flattering and terrifying himself by his thought,
according to his family's habit of mind, Alwyn shrank
from this responsibility of being the hope of his native
land. And those original beginnings which, as he had
persuaded himself, were unchangeable among his relatives, perverted among his countrymen, unchanged in
him—just what had they been? He would probably
need to know. His thought ran superficially and not
impartially over the history of the country. . . .

Invariably at the end of these exercises of his imagination, another day beginning monotonously. . . .
His grandmother had rested well, as well as could be
expected. A little hue of life appeared in her face,
which seemed made of candle drippings and stone;
once more her fallen lips began to resemble, as they did
during the day, one dried rosebud laid on another
(the meager cinnamon roses of her youth). What

were like dim recollections of bright colors began to haunt the room and the flat country around Brighton, where they had brought her to die. Her illness seemed interminable.

The following day Alwyn could not sleep because of the heat. So he began to write a historical essay, summarizing in part what he had recently been thinking with so much assurance. Three or four days later, he read it to his mother, who said she was not quite sure she understood what it meant. He hoped that when he went back to school in the fall one or another of his teachers would praise it. He himself was uneasily proud of what he had done.

Then suddenly his grandmother Duff died. Alwyn had to stay with his other grandmother the day of the funeral, because his father had to go with his mother to drive the few mourners to and from the cemetery. But he went by train to Aaronsville the day before, in order to see the little woman again. She was scarcely recognizable: in a coffin which was too large, amid the glued ruffles and pleats of tulle, lay a bit of natural elegance—that was all. Her face had lost its vigilant look, its aged vanity, indeed all resemblance to herself; it was like that of a young girl in a fairy tale who had withered overnight. Alwyn went back to Brighton. Only the spectacle of his grandmother Tower's anguish saved him from the extreme sorrow of wishing, for a few days, to follow his grandmother Duff through that transformation, whatever it led to. Upon her return, his mother said bitterly that beside the grave the Aaronsville preacher had spoken with a sort of cold embarrassment, apparently under the impression that she had not been a good woman.

Meanwhile Alwyn's satisfaction at having written an essay led him to try to keep a diary in the daytime of what he thought when his responsibility and his grandmother's suffering, like a mixture of stimulating drugs, kept him wide awake all night. But the choking sound of her breathing and ceasing to breathe—which, from the room above, he could not hear but imagined he heard—made it impossible. So he slept or waited unhappily for the sleepless vigils in which duty took the place of ineffectual ambition. A watchdog's duty, though death was a housebreaker, a robber, who would be welcomed by everyone.

The nights came and went. Now there was less theorizing with which to pass the time. He had lost his courage, the courage of his convictions, and could no longer pretend to be clever and more farsighted than others, than the rest of his family. Too long, like a sort of detective, he had spied upon them, studied to convict them—of their everlasting glory, he thought resolutely but without much enthusiasm. Futile unweaving and reweaving of the evidence, vain praise, generalizations of what was passing away before his eyes (he himself was such a generalization). . . . He was glad that the rapidly approaching end put a stop to it. He had a sense of having gone too far, and felt the peculiar shame of an outlaw who has not even done a dangerous thing.

Indeed, it was an instinctive law for Americans, the one he had broken. Never be infatuated with nor try to interpret as an omen the poverty, the desperation, of the past; whoever remembers it will be punished, or punish himself; never remember. Upon pain of loneliness, upon pain of a sort of expatriation though at home. At home in a land of the future where all wish to be young; a land of duties well done, irresponsibly, of evil done without immorality, and good without virtue. Maturity, responsibility, immorality, virtue are offspring of memory; try not to remember. America had as yet nothing worth remembering—no palaces, no enchanting antiquity, even the plunder of Tenochtitlan or whatever the city was called, had been taken away. The past was by nature tragic. No tragic arts ought to flourish; tragedy was treason, the betrayal of state secrets to the enemy, even the enemy in one's self. Memory was incest. . . .

The fact that Alwyn had thought so fanatically about the past of others during those summer months, always and only in relation to his own future, meant, he supposed, that he had lost interest in it, temporarily at least. There was a tide in such matters; now it ran the other way. And in that direction waited an insufferable event, at least one—one more death.

He felt also a sickly anxiety about his own—life or death, he scarcely knew which; and was ashamed of it. For he understood that fear is the most impious of the emotions: disdain and suspicion of God, or the gods, no matter which. He remembered that in the most frightened period of his childhood, his sixth or seventh year, there had been a pen like a cave inside the strawstack where the old sows crawled away to have their litters, with a hole through the straw a little higher than his head, to pour in their corn and swill. One day he had happened to be standing near it when he heard from somewhere inside, a soft, sickening sound. Beat by beat, deep in the pitch-black hole, like those of a fatal drum. When he held his breath, it had grown louder. Stiff with fright, half-hypnotized, he had got away; and when far enough away, had cried. Thereafter, the thought having been almost as painful as the experience, he had returned from time to time, hoping the sound would have ceased; it had never ceased. More than a year had passed before he had learned what it was: his own heart beating. . . .

Then the days in the new home near Brighton began to resemble the night watches—both strained as one's throat is strained by thirst, sorrow, or fright. A sort of poor, concrete poetry took the place of Alwyn's prosaic analysis and judgments; at last even it failed. He had no longer anything to think about, and wondered why. Suddenly, sitting as usual in the doorway of his grandmother's room, he realized that death had come. Scarcely invisible, it entered the room, and apparently in haste, approached his grandmother's bed.

Her sickness rose off and on in a crisis lasting half an hour or an hour, so violent that it could not have been endured longer at a time, and now increasingly frequent. The doctor had prescribed certain drugs for these attacks. Speaking severely, she had asked what their effect would be; she was willing to have her sufferings lessened, but wanted no attempt made to lengthen her life. The doctor had been obliged to admit that her condition could not be improved and these medicines might even hasten the end, with which answer she had been content.

Now she never lay flat in her bed and scarcely ever slept. The heat was intense, and on her cheeks and forehead a cold sweat mingled with that of the breathless chamber and the season. Her head would fall, her heart stop, and be started again with an effort of her whole body, throughout which this rhythm of convulsion was constantly accompanied by a heavy trembling. Sometimes she could not keep her mouth closed; then Alwyn would tie a cloth under her chin and over her head, which she disliked, as if that particular weakness were moral. She seemed to suffer pain but never made a sound, except that, loud and hideous, of continuing to breathe by sheer will power, though against her will.

At other times she was at peace. She never lost consciousness in the slightest degree; and Alwyn was certain that whenever she could sit quietly with her eyes closed, her mind was clear and patiently occupied with what had gone before, or what according to her simple faith was still to come. Sometimes, usually during the day, she was able to speak with a certain ease, in her rough, still beautiful voice; then she would ask, "What are the men doing in the fields now?" or ask one of her grandchildren if he remembered something she had told him long before.

During the periods of respite, death seemed to keep

watch with Alwyn, and covered him with its abstraction and ignorance, and obliterated his pretentiousness, his good memory, his hopeless ambitions. Suddenly it would turn its attention from him to the old woman on whose account it was there. Then like one of those spectators who, because of love or some other preöccupation, go to the same theater night after night, heartsick and tired, Alwyn watched the struggle, on the pillows and among the folds of bedclothes, with the invisible actor angel; the print of its rough touch pitting her cheeks and throat here and there, hollowing out her temples, twisting her great·hands which lay loosely open; and he imagined he could hear its breath as well as hers, blowing back and forth upon her mouth and nostrils.

Then Alwyn's impassibility came to an end; he suffered an agony of excitement. One night he burst into tears in front of the gasping, uncomplaining old woman. It was not heartbreak because she was soon to die—he hoped it would be soon—he was crying for futilities, futilities of affection, pleasure, talk, no matter what. Anything to relieve the useless pain, his pain, to relax his useless ardor, his miserable concentration. Useless—because she was going to die, anyway. His grandmother's eyes were wide open, and she gazed at him attentively without a sign of disapproval or compassion.

The following afternoon his uncle John Craig arrived, a few days earlier than he had been expected. Alwyn went to the station. "Hello. If you're not a grown man!" he said by way of greeting. "But I

might have known it.   My young Orfeo will soon be
as old as his father."

He himself looked worn and was turning gray, but
had a younger expression than before, that of a man
with plans to carry out, or perhaps only risks to run.
"My boy will be here day after to-morrow.   He's
coming on from that school he goes to in the East.
You'll probably get on well together.   It's a family
tradition that cousins and so on should be friendly.
That is, if they get a chance.   I was sort of left out
of it."

He seemed to dread going into his mother's room,
following his brother's and sister-in-law's eyes to her
door from the threshold of the house, and finally
stepping forward alone with a strange, formal humility, as if he feared that his presence would remind
her of tragic things and imagined, mistakenly, that
she was now not strong enough to bear them all with
composure.

The very news of his coming, as if it were a medicine (the last which would take effect), had given her
new strength.   Lying back against the mass of pillows,
she had breathed easily, and looked able to wait another lifetime, though her great bones now wore a mere
veil of flesh.   It was as if the struggle had been altogether within herself, rather than between herself and
death; her desire to live a few days more to see her
son was stronger than for almost a year her desire to
die had been.

That night John Craig wished to take his nephew's
place; but Alwyn stayed up with them a few hours,

pretending to be uncertain whether she would need the emergency drugs before morning, and offering to give his uncle the necessary instructions.

John Craig sat closer to her bed than she had ever permitted Alwyn to sit, and she asked him to talk to her: "You know, mother," he said, "the last time I was in Oklahoma, I looked up the place where uncle Leander was buried. I suppose I was his favorite, of your children. I sometimes think I loved him too much—I mean, on account of father." He glanced up at her face, as if to see whether he should be embarrassed by what he had said.

But she replied, "I loved him best."

"They buried him in a very pleasant place, not too crowded. I finally got hold of the little old fellow who took care of him, a Catholic priest. I don't know if you ever heard. . . . The cemetery is Catholic. The priest seemed to think that made him die one, more or less. I don't suppose uncle Leander paid much attention to what he said. I thought it was funny. You see, I got to be a Catholic too, when I married. He kept asking for a lot of us, uncle Hilary and Tim Davis and you. The little priest had it all written down; kind of him, I thought. Well, I put up a big monument, granite. I couldn't remember when he was born, so I left that blank, and they promised to put it in afterward. And I thought if there was anything else you wanted written on it, a verse or something . . ."

Alwyn heard his grandmother say with some difficulty, "You always were a good boy, Evan."

John Craig's voice broke slightly. "You never said that before, mother."

"Well, I meant to. . . . I guess the war and all that—was harder on you than it was on us. Your pa minded. But you might have got killed or died. That would have been hard on me. That was what I said to myself about Leander, after the Civil War." There was a long pause while she took breath. "Your children'll have a better chance," she went on. "Yours and Ralph's. I try to think of them when it seems hard. I wasn't able to do much for mine, I guess. Try not ever to blame me for anything, when I'm gone."

John Craig, when not at his mother's bedside, seemed to prefer to talk to his nephew than to his brother or sister-in-law, and to have, in doing so, a mysterious purpose which amused him. "See here," he asked, "haven't you had about enough of Wisconsin? Does Chicago and Jim's house suit you? I thought it was a woman's town, when I was there. You'd better come along with us, West. Or come soon, anyway. I spoke to your mother, and she's willing to try to spare you for a while," he added with a suggestion of affectionate mockery. "Mothers usually have to, whether they're willing or not, more's the pity."

Alwyn's grandmother lost ground during the day; the periodical failing of her heart began again, but much less extremely. Her body had no longer the force either to produce or to endure the former suf-

ferings. The doctor thought that most of her suffering and nearly all of her life were over.

The following morning Orfeo Craig arrived. Alwyn was astonished and pleased. He was not like a
member of the family nor even like an American; he
had no appearance either of the country or the sort of
city Alwyn knew. He was exceedingly dark, with
strange variations of the same dark, burned rose without pinkness in his mouth and skin. His eyes were
heavy-lidded, dark, and bright. He seemed never to
have a sharp or clever look under any circumstances.
Alwyn was glad, feeling a greater humility than he had
previously known, the measure of which was his pride
in his own mere intelligence, for example. If his
cousin compared him with himself in that respect
alone, he might find that he merited affection. . . .
Such ideas revealed even to himself his desire for
their friendship. John Craig looked as happy as if
for him, who had known in his day too little either
of friendship or family affection, something more important than good relations between the sons of the
family were at stake.

Alwyn had never seen his grandmother's face so
radiant, even in the days of her strength, as when
her unknown grandson was taken into her room. Even
Alwyn's youngest sisters had realized that something
ceremonial and happy was about to take place, and
slipped inside the doorway. She lifted her trembling,
open hands to the level of her breast in the gesture
of reverence or good tidings, and gazed a long time
at the strange boy.

At last she remembered herself. She called him by his first name, Leander, and said, "You do not see me as I once was. Children, get out the photographs."

The little girls, enchanted to have a part in the formalities, fluttered across the room to the chest of drawers and took them out—three daguerreotypes in cases, some tintypes in an album, two yellow photographs mounted on worn pieces of cardboard: a girl, a young wife, a woman aging but not less strong. . . . She told the girls to spread them out on her bed where she could see them as well. They looked at them together.

Then with her greatest dignity, as if a duty had been done, she said: "Now you'd better go out. I can't have you here any longer. I am an old sick woman now."

A few more days passed. She said that she was glad that her son and grandson who lived so far away were staying until the end. John Craig watched with her during the night. The boys sat by the door during the afternoon, often talking to each other in whispers, beckoning to the children, as they came and went, to hush.

Late one afternoon Orfeo thought that Alwyn looked pale, and sent him out in the fresh air. Alwyn wished that it were the Hope's Corner countryside which lay about the new house, in which, however, the lives of those he loved throbbed and failed as much like a single hollow heart of joy and sorrow, as ever in the old home. And over the distant marshes, amid the harvest, under the loaded fruit trees, the dusk beginning to mingle with the sunshine was the same: that dusk peculiar to Wisconsin, tossed by hunting night-hawks, rocked by the motion of flocks coming home. . . . And there were ghosts there as much as any-where, worthy of being loved, the same, in fact, as everywhere else: spirits so great, vain, and tender as to resemble gods. Ghosts of the little local history, of misunderstood friends and lovers, of members of the family; a legion of them in straggling procession. For years, Alwyn remembered, he had not been able to take his eyes off their shadowy ceremony, their dis-order like that of the strong farm hands and their sweethearts under the trees on summer nights such as this which was falling. For years his mind had been troubled by their faint instruments in concert, just as in his childhood by those to which ghostly soldiers (his grandfather and his brothers and friends) had marched on the warm, blood-spattered rock in the South during the war. Distracting flutes; and little drums in the air about his birthplace, even about the new, unsympathetic house where his grandmother had been brought to die, beating a dead march; and beat-ing like his own heart as he grew to manhood and got ready to leave these things—glad to go and leave them behind. But he felt that he would have need of them all, gods or pioneers or whatever they were, to lead an entire life; and if there were any he had not called upon, those would probably take him by surprise; cer-tain of them, those of the passions and disasters, would spring on him when he was lonely, have their way with him, and leave him hurt for a while by the side of the road—the last one would leave him dead. Out of pride he wanted to be able to love and praise them all, even the last one. . . .

His daydream was interrupted by Orfeo calling from the porch, calling him to come in at once, because their grandmother seemed to have stopped breathing, and perhaps it was an ordinary occurrence, and he might be mistaken, but he was not sure what it meant.

She was dead. They called their two fathers, who suddenly grew unfamiliar and pale. They were pre-occupied with many things of which Alwyn had not thought in connection with the long-anticipated event, and it seemed that the young who had had an important part to play while she had been dying, had nothing to do with the burial of the dead. Alwyn and Orfeo were told merely to go to the town and send a message to their uncle Jim; but they were glad to be free.

So they set out through the garden and the melon patch, over a fence, and up a hill. Orfeo thought they should buy as many flowers as possible. Alwyn looked back at the small house, seeing another in its place, indeed several others, one of which, the earliest, had stood in a melon patch. And as they went on in the dusk, he whispered to himself good-by to them, those who were dead: his great, gaunt grandmother, and the other little one as well, who had called him her sweetheart in the madness of her old age.

Paris, February 1925—
Villefranche-sur-Mer, November 1926.